The Illustrious House of Ramires

This book is part of a series ASPECTS OF PORTUGAL

So far published: *In the Wake of the Portuguese Navigators* by Michael Teague • *Camões* translated by Keith Bosley; illustrated by Lima de Freitas • *The Grand Peregrination* by Maurice Collis • *They Went to Portugal Too* by Rose Macaulay • *Trade, Inquisition and the English Nation in Portugal 1650–1690* by L. M. E. Shaw • *The Portuguese Seaborne Empire 1415–1825* by C. R. Boxer • *The Book of Disquietude* by Fernando Pessoa; translated by Paul Zenith • *The Peregrination* by Fernão Mendes Pinto; translated by Michael Lowery • *Cousin Bazilio* by Eça de Queirós; translated by Roy Campbell • *The Illustrious House of Ramires* by Eça de Queirós; translated by Anne Stevens.

Now we come to the best of all Portuguese novelists, Eça de Queirós, of whom Zola said, 'he is far greater than my own dear master, Flaubert'. Roy Campbell

EÇA DE QUEIRÓS was born in 1843 at Póvoa de Varzim in north Portugal. His father was a magistrate; he duly studied law at Coimbra. After travelling widely he entered the diplomatic service. Married, he became a devoted family man, a good host, a wit, raconteur, dandy, aesthete, bon viveur. He served as a consul in Havana, Newcastle, Bristol and Paris, where he died in 1900.

Beneath this calm surface ran strong currents of sensitivity and imagination. His first writings – travel articles, essays, short stories – were favourably noticed by Portuguese critics: his early novels *The Sin of Father Amaro* (1876), and *Cousin Bazilio* (1878), cast in the Naturalism of Flaubert, Balzac and Zola, won him recognition as a writer of European standing. *The Maias* (1886) confirmed his growing reputation. The voice in these novels is urbane, exact, amused, ironic; but the comedy is tempered by warm sympathy for human frailty and a poignant sense of the fragility of human happiness. In his later novels, notably in *The Illustrious House of Ramires* (1900) and *The City and the Mountain* (1901), he changed the setting from the city to the countryside. Whereas, before, he had mocked the greed, pretentions, and hypocrisies of fashionable society, he now turned his ironic gaze on less familiar targets: the liberal reformers and the idea of progress itself. Yet none of his novels was written *à thèse*: his enjoyment of everyday life, his insights into character, his sense of the unpredictability of individual destiny make his novels vibrant and keep them contemporary.

His excellent prose glides through real experience and private dream in a manner that is leading on toward the achievements of Proust. V. S. Pritchett

The portrait of Eça de Queirós above is by Rafael
Bordalo Pinheiro. Courtesy of the British Library

EÇA DE QUEIRÓS

The Illustrious House of Ramires

Translated by Anne Stevens

CARCANET

in association with

THE CALOUSTE GULBENKIAN FOUNDATION

Published in 1992 by Carcanet Press Limited 208–212 Corn
Exchange Buildings, Manchester M4 3BQ

Cover design by Kim Taylor, based on a print by Furitani Korin
in *Oriental Flowers* edited by Wolfgang Hageney. Edition
Belvedere, Rome 1981.

This book belongs to the series *Aspects of Portugal*, published in
Great Britain by Carcanet Press in association with the Calouste
Gulbenkian Foundation and with the collaboration of the
Anglo-Portuguese Foundation.

Series editors: Eugenio Lisboa, Michael Schmidt, L. C. Taylor.

A CIP catalogue record for this title is available from the
British Library

ISBN 0 85635 968 8

The publisher acknowledges financial assistance from the
Arts Council of Great Britain.

Printed digitally since 2001.
Carcanet Press Limited, *now at* Conavon Court, Blackfriar Street
Manchester M3 5BQ UK   www.carcanet.co.uk

INTRODUCTION
V. S. Pritchett

ECA DE QUEIRÓS (1845–1900) is the Portuguese classic of the nineteenth century – not an Iberian Balzac, like Galdos but, rather, a moistened Stendhal, altogether more tender, and, despite his reformist opinions, without theories. He was a diplomat, something of a dandy and gourmet, whose career took him abroad in France, Britain, the Near East, Cuba and the United States, and he was responsive to the intellectual forces that were bringing the European novel to the height of its powers. The temptations of a light and elegant cosmopolitanism must have been strong, for he is above all a novelist of wit and style, and he was amused by the banalities of diplomatic conversation.

But the foreign experience usually serves to strengthen his roots in the Portuguese idiosyncrasy: under the lazy grace, there is the native bluntness and stoicism. A novel like *The Illustrious House of Ramires* is very rich, but it also contrives to be a positive and subtle unraveling of the Portuguese strand in the Iberian temperament. The soft, sensual yet violently alluring Atlantic light glides over his country and his writing, a light more variable and unpredictable than the Castillian; no one could be less 'Spanish' and more western European, yet strong in his native character.

The fear that one is going to be stuck in the quaint, exhaustive pieties of the *folklorico* and regional novel with its tedious local colour, its customs and costumes, soon goes at the sound of his misleadingly simple and sceptical voice. The Portuguese love to pretend to be diminutive in order to surprise by their toughness. Portuguese modesty and nostalgia are national—and devastating. In an introduction to an early short story, 'The Mandarin', he wrote a typically deceptive apology to its French publishers, in which he puts his case. 'Reality, analysis, experimentation or objective certainty,' he said, plague and baffle the Portuguese, who are either lyricists or satirists:

We dearly love to paint everything blue; a fine sentence will always please me more than an exact notion; the fabled Melusine, who devours human hearts, will always charm our

vii

incorrigible imagination more than the very human Marneffe, and we will always consider fantasy and eloquence the only true signs of a superior man. Were we to read Stendhal in Portuguese, we should never be able to enjoy him; what is considered exactitude with him, we should consider sterility. Exact ideas, expressed soberly and in proper form, hardly interest us at all; what charms us is excessive emotion expressed with unabashed plasticity of language.

Eça de Queiroz, we can be certain, did not commit the folly of reading Stendhal in Portuguese. The most exact of novelists, he read him in French, and the comedy is that he was very much a romantic Stendhalian—he was even a Consul-General—and in exactitude a Naturalist. Under the irony and the grace, there are precision and sudden outbursts of ecstasy and of flamboyant pride in a prose that coils along and then suddenly vibrates furiously when emotion breaks through, or breaks into unashamed burlesque.

He was an incessant polisher of his style. The following passage, from *The City and the Mountains,* shows his extraordinary power of letting rip and yet keeping his militant sense of comedy in command. His hero has just been thrown over by a cocotte in Paris. His first reaction is to go and eat an expensive meal of lobster and duck washed down by champagne and Burgundy; the second is to rush back to the girl's house, punching the cushions of the cab as he goes, for in the cushion he sees, in his fury, 'the huge bush of yellow hair in which my soul was lost one evening, fluttered and struggled for two months, and soiled itself for ever'. He fights the driver and the servants at the house, and then he goes off home, drunk and maddened:

Stretched out on the ancestral bed of Dom 'Galleon', with my boots at my pillow and my hat over my eyes, I laughed a sad laugh at this burlesque world. . . . Suddenly I felt a horrible anguish. It was She. It was Madame Colombe who appeared out of the flame of the candle, jumped on my bed, undid my waistcoat, sunk herself onto my breast, put her mouth to my heart, and began to suck my blood from it in long slow gulps. Certain of death now, I began to scream for my Aunt Vicencia; I hung from the bed to try to sink into my sepulchre which I dimly discerned beneath me on the carpet, through the final fog of death—a little round sepulchre, glazed and made of porcelain, with a handle. And over my own sepulchre, which so irreverently chose to resemble a chamberpot, I vomited the lobster, the duck, the pimientos and the Burgundy. Then after a super-human effort, with the roar of a lion, feeling that not only my innards but my very soul were emptying themselves in the process, I vomited up Madame Colombe herself. . . . I put my hat back over my eyes so as not to feel the rays of the sun. It was a new Sun, a spiritual Sun which was rising over my life. I slept like a child softly rocked in a cradle of wicker by my Guardian Angel.

This particular novel savages Paris as the height of city civilization, a wealthy Utopia; it argues for the return to nature in the Portuguese valleys. Eça de Queirós can still astonish us in this satire with his catalogue of mechanical conveniences. They are remarkably topical. (His theatre-telephone, for example, is our television or radio.) The idea of a machine civilization that has drained off the value of human life recalls Forster's *The Machine Stops*. Maliciously Queirós describes our childish delight in being ravished by a culture of affluence or surfeit. He was in at the birth of boredom and conspicuous waste. One brilliant fantasy of the hero is that he is living in a city where the men and women are simply made of newspaper, where the houses are made of books and pamphlets and the streets paved with them. Change printed-matter to the McLuhanite Muzak culture of today, and the satire is contemporary. The hero returns to the droll, bucolic kindness of life in Portugal, in chapters that have the absurd beauty of, say, Oblomov's dream.

The prose carries this novel along, but one has to admit there is a slightly faded *fin de siècle* air about it. *The Illustrious House of Ramires* is a much better rooted and more ambitious work. Obviously his suggestion that the Portuguese are not experimentalists is a Portuguese joke, for the book is a novel within a novel, a comedy of the relation of the unconscious with quotidian experience. One is tricked at first into thinking one is caught up in a rhetorical tale of chivalry *à la* Walter Scott; then one changes one's mind and treats its high-flown historical side as one of those Romances that addled the mind of Don Quixote; finally one recognizes this element as an important part of psychological insight. What looks like old hat reveals its originality.

Ramires is an ineffectual and almost ruined aristocrat who is rewriting the history of his Visigothic ancestors in order to raise his own morale. It is an act of personal and political therapy. He is all for liberal reform, but joins the party of Regenerators or traditionalists whose idea is to bring back the days of Portugal's greatness. Ramires revels in the battles, sieges and slaughterings of his famous family and—while he is writing this vivid and bloody stuff—he is taking his mind off the humiliations of his own life. The heir of the Ramires is a dreamer. He is a muddler and his word is never to be relied on. He shuffles until finally he gets himself in the wrong. This is because he is timid and without self-confidence: he deceives a decent peasant over a contract and then, losing his self-control when the peasant protests, has him sent to prison on the pretext that the man tried to assault him. Then rage abates and he hurriedly gets the man out of prison.

Ramires has a long feud with a local philandering politician of the opposite party, because this man has jilted his sister; yet, he makes it up with the politician in order to get elected as a deputy— only to see that the politician does this only to be sure of seducing the sister. The price of political triumph is his sister's honour and happiness. How can he live with himself after that? Trapped continually by his pusillanimity, he tries to recover by writing one more chapter of his novel of chivalry, fleeing to an ideal picture of himself. What saves him—and this is typical of the irony of Queirós—is his liability to insensate physical rage, always misplaced. He half kills a couple of ruffians on the road by horsewhipping them and, incidentally, gives a fantastically exaggerated account of the incident; but the event and the lie give him self-confidence. He is a hero at last! He begins to behave with a comic mixture of cunning and dignity. He saves his sister, becomes famous as a novelist, long-headedly makes a rich marriage, and tells the King of Portugal that he is an upstart. Total triumph of luck, accident, pride, impulse in a helplessly devious but erratically generous character loved by everyone. Tortured by uncertainty, carried away by idealism and feeling, a curious mixture of the heroic and the shady, he has become welded into a man.

And who is this man? He is not simply Ramires, the aristocrat. He is—Portugal itself: practical, stoical, shifty, its pride in its

x

great past, its pride in pride itself raging inside like an unquenchable sadness. There is iron in the cosiness of Queirós. He has the disguised militancy of the important comedians. His comic scenes are very fine, for there is always a serious or symbolic body to them. His sensuality is frank. His immense detail in the evocation of Portuguese life is always on the move; and the mixture of disingenuousness and genuine feeling in all his characters makes every incident piquant.

A match-making scene takes place in the boring yet macabre crypt where the ancestors of Ramires are buried. Ramires knows his ancestors would have killed his sister's lover; all *he* can do is to pray feverishly that her silly, jolly, cuckolded husband will never find out. Prudence and self-interest suggest caution; not mere caution but an anxious mixture of politeness, kindness, worldly-wisdom and a stern belief in dignity, if you can manage it, plus the reflection that even the most inexcusable adulteries may have a sad, precious core of feeling. Ramires is not a cynic; nor is Eça de Queirós. He is saved from that by his lyrical love of life, his abandonment—for the moment—to the unpredictable sides of his nature; in other words, by his candour and innocence. His people live by their imagination from minute to minute. They are constantly impressionable; yet they never lose their grasp of the practical demands of their lives—the interests of land, money, illness, politics.

In the historical pages of Ramires's historical novel, there is a double note, romantic yet sardonic. The scenes are barbarous and bloody—they express the unconscious of Ramires, the dreams that obsess him and his nation—but the incidental commentary is as dry as anything in Stendhal. During a siege:

The bailiff waddled down the blackened, spiral stairway to the steps outside the keep. Two liegeman, their lances at their shoulders, returning from a round, were talking to the armourer who was painting the handles of new javelins yellow and scarlet and lining them up against the wall to dry.

Yet a few lines farther down, we shall see a father choose to see his son murdered, rather than surrender his honour. The violence of history bursts out in Ramires's own life in the horse-whipping scene I have mentioned earlier. The sensation—he finds—is sublime. But when Ramires gets home his surprise at the sight of real blood on his whip and clothes shatters him. he does not want to be as murderous as the knights of old. He is all for humanity and charity. He was simply trying to solve his psychological difficulty: that he had never, in anything until then, imposed his will, but had yielded to the will of others who were simply corrupting him and leaving him to wake up to one more humiliation. It is a very contemporary theme.

The making of this novel and indeed all the others, is the restless mingling of poetry, sharp realism and wit. Queirós is untouched by the drastic hatred of life that underlies Naturalism: he is sad rather than indignant that every human being is compromised; indeed this enables him to present his characters from several points of view and to explore the unexpectedness of human nature. The elements of self-surprise and self-imagination are strong; and his excellent prose glides through real experience and private dream in a manner that is leading on toward the achievements of Proust.

From *The Myth-Makers* by V. S. Pritchett. (Chatto and Windus, London 1979)

1

IN THE HEAT and silence of a Sunday in June, the Nobleman of
the Tower had been sitting working since four o'clock in the afternoon, with his slippers on and a light linen jacket over his pink cotton
shirt. Gonçalo Mendes Ramires (who was known as the 'Nobleman
of the Tower' by everyone in his ancient village of Santa Ireneia
and in nearby Vila Clara, a neat and charming town, and even in the
larger town of Oliveira) was working on an Historical Novel, *The
Tower of Don Ramires*, destined for publication in the first number
of the *Literary and Historical Annals*, a new review founded by José
Lúcio Castanheiro, an old friend of his from Coimbra dating back
to the Patriotic Circle, when they were together in the Severinas'
House.

The library, a light and spacious room, with blue-washed walls
and heavy blackwood bookshelves, where, amid the dust and grave
leather bindings, lay thick volumes from convents and legal parchments, overlooked the orchard through two of its windows, one with
a small balcony and stone seats with velvet-cushioned tops, the other
a broader one, with a verandah deliciously perfumed by the honeysuckle which entwined the railing. It was in front of the brightness of
this window that the table stood, an immense table with twisted legs,
covered by a faded red damask cloth, and burdened this afternoon
by the stiff volumes of *The Genealogical History*, the whole of
Bluteau's *Vocabulary*, and various volumes of *Panorama*, and in the
corner a pile of Walter Scotts on which stood a glass full of yellow
carnations. From here, from his leather chair, Gonçalo Mendes
Ramires, pensive before the sheets of foolscap paper and scratching
his head with the duck-quill pen, could see the inspiration of his
novel—the Tower, the ancient Tower, square and black against the
lemon-trees of the orchard which grew around it, with a little ivy
dressing the cleft corner, its deep loopholes barred with iron, its
battlements and turret clearly silhouetted in the blue of the June sky
—a sturdy survival of the fortified manor, the famous Manor of Santa
Ireneia, country seat of the Mendes Ramires since the middle of the
tenth century.

Gonçalo Mendes Ramires (as the Squire of Cidadelhe, a most

5

severe genealogist, admitted) was without doubt the most genuine and ancient nobleman in Portugal. Very few families, even centuries-old ones, could trace their descent by so pure a line, and a male line at that, back to those distant Lords that maintained castle and walled lands between the River Douro and Minho, when the French barons descended with banner and cooking-pot and Burgundian troops. The Ramires family went on, always with a male and legitimate descendant to carry on the line, from the son of Count Nuno Mendes, the gigantic Ordonho Mendes, lord of Treixedo and of Santa Ireneia, who in 967 married Dona Eduarda, Countess of Carrion, daughter of Bermudo the Gouty, King of Leon.

Older in the Peninsula than the Portuguese Earldom, but like it, Santa Ireneia grew inflexibly, acquiring a reputation and resisting fortune and time. Soon, at every important step in the History of Portugal, there was always a Mendes Ramires outstanding for his heroism, his loyalty, his noble actions. One of the most valiant of the line, Lourenço, nicknamed the Butcher, foster-brother of Afonso Henriques (with whom, the same night in Zamora Cathedral, he kept vigil over his arms before receiving his knighthood) appears at once in the Battle of Ourique where Jesus Christ also appeared, on fine clouds of gold, nailed to a cross ten ells high. At the siege of Tavira, Martim Ramires, Friar of Santiago, broke through a fortification with blows of his axe, and bursting through the scimitars which sliced off his two hands, emerged on the walls of the barbican with blood spurting from his wrists and crying jubilantly to the Mestre, 'Don Paio Peres, Tavira is ours! Portugal for the King!' The old Egas Ramires, shut up in his Tower, the drawbridge raised and the barbican bristling with archers, refused to receive King Fernando and Leonor Teles who were travelling through the north of the country, hunting and merry-making,—so that the presence of that *adulteress* should not taint the immaculate purity of his home! In Aljubarrota, Diogo Ramires, the Minstrel, scattered a body of crossbows, killed the Governor of Galicia, and by his hand, and none other, the royal banner of Castile fell to the ground, which his brother-in-arms, Don Antão de Almada, used to swathe himself in as he took it, accompanied by singing and dancing, to the Mestre of Avis. Beneath the walls of Arcila, two Ramires fought gloriously side by side, the ancient Soeiro and his grandson Fernão, and in front of the old man's body, pierced by four arrows and stretched out beside

6

the Count of Marialva's body, Afonso V knighted, at one and the same time, the Prince his son and Fernão Ramires, murmuring with tears in his eyes, 'May God make you as good as these that lie here.' But then Portugal took to the sea! Then rare indeed were the fleets and battles in which a Ramires did not feature—while the noble captain in the Persian Gulf has become a tragic sea legend—the captain who, when the *Santa Barbara* sank, put on his heavy armour and standing upright on the forecastle, went down in silence with his sinking ship, leaning upon his great sword. In Alcacer Quibir, where two Ramires met a magnificent death at the side of their king, the younger, Paulo Ramires, a standard-bearer, neither wounded nor hurt in the least but not wishing to live after the death of his King, seized a jennet and a battle-axe, rushed into the Moorish throng shouting, 'Begone, tardy soul, and serve that of your King!' and disappeared for ever. Under the Philips, the Ramires kept sulkily to their lands, drinking and hunting. They reappeared with the Braganzas, and a Ramires, Vicente, Governor of Arms of Entre Douro and Minho for Don João IV, invades Castile, defeats the Spaniards under the Count of Venavente, and takes Fuente Guinal, over whose violent sacking he presides from the verandah of a Franciscan Convent as he stands in his shirt-sleeves eating slices of water-melon. But as the nation degenerated, so did the noble race . . . Álvaro Ramires, a favourite of Don Pedro II, and a ruffian, used to alarm Lisbon with the trouble he caused, and stole the wife of an inspector in the Royal Treasury whom he had beaten to death by Negroes. Then he set fire to a gambling-house in Seville after losing a hundred doubloons there, and finished by commanding a pirate hooker in the fleet of Murad the Ragamuffin. During the reign of Don João V, Nuno Ramires shone in court, had his mules shod with silver and ruined the family by celebrating sumptuous Church ceremonies where he sang in the choir dressed in the habit of a monk of the Third Order of St Francis. Another Ramires, Cristovão, President of the Table of Conscience and Order, acted as go-between in the affair between King José I and the daughter of the Prior of Sacavém. Pedro Ramires, Purveyor and Administrator of the Customs, was renowned in all the Kingdom for his obesity, his wit and his feats of gluttony with the Archbishop of Tessalonica in the Palace of Bemposta. Inácio Ramires accompanied Don João VI to Brazil as his Chamberlain, began to trade in Negroes, returned with a chest full of pieces of gold which an administrator of his, a former Capuchin friar, managed to steal from him, and finally died at his country seat after being gored by an ox. Gonçalo's grandfather, Damião, a liberal doctor of letters devoted to the Muses, disembarked with Don Pedro in Mindelo, composed the rhetorical proclamation of the Party, founded a newspaper, *The Antifriar*, and after the Civil Wars, dragged out a rheumatic existence in Santa Ireneia, swathed in a thick woollen cape, translating into the vernacular, with the aid of a dictionary and a packet of snuff, the works of Valerius Flaccus. Gonçalo's father, sometimes adhering to the Regenerators, sometimes to the Historicals, lived in Lisbon in the Universal Hotel, wearing out the soles of his shoes up and down the steps of the Mortgage Bank and along the Arcade, until a Minister of Home Affairs, whose concubine—a singer in São Carlos—had become infatuated with him, appointed him (to get him away from the Capital) Civil Governor of Oliveira. Gonçalo was a graduate who had failed his third year examinations at university.

It was in this same year that Gonçalo Mendes Ramires was initiated into the world of letters. A colleague of his, resident in the same house, José Lúcio Castanheiro, a very lean, very emaciated Algarvian who wore enormous dark glasses, had founded a magazine called *The Fatherland*, 'with the lofty intention' (the prospectus sonorously affirmed) 'of reawakening, not only among the academic youth but throughout the country, from Cape Sileiro to Cape Santa Maria, the dying love of the beauty and grandeur and glories of Portugal!' Devoured by this idea, 'his Idea', and feeling that here lay his career, almost his mission, Castanheiro incessantly and with the stubborn ardour of an apostle, proclaimed throughout the taverns in Sofia Street, through the cloisters of the University, in his friends' rooms amid cigarette smoke, 'the necessity, *caramba*! of reviving tradition! of clearing Portugal, *caramba*! of the deluge of foreign matter inundating it!' As the magazine appeared regularly three Sundays running and actually published studies full of italics and quotations on The Chapels of Batalha, The Taking of Ormuz and The Embassy at Tristão da Cunha, it immediately began to be considered as a dawning, as yet pale but sure, of a National Renaissance. Some of the finer spirits of the University, especially the friends of Castanheiro, who shared the same house, the three who were interested in matters of learning and intelligence (because of the other three, one was a brawler, one a guitarist, and the third a scholar), were warmed by this patriotic flame and began to delve into the great tomes in the library, never before consulted, of Fernão Lopes, of Rui de Pina, Azurara, for feats and legends—'only Portuguese ones, only ours [as Castanheiro implored] that will re-awaken a consciousness of our heroism in this disheartened nation'. Thus was created the Patriotic Circle of the Severinas' house. It was then that Gonçalo Mendes Ramires, a very charming youth, fair and slim, his skin the healthy white of porcelain, with fine, smiling eyes easily moved by pity, always elegant, with his neat gown and polished shoes—presented to Castanheiro one Sunday after lunch eleven sheets of paper entitled 'Dona Guiomar'. In this he recounted the ancient story of the chatelaine who, whilst her bearded sire was far away at the Crusades, girded in iron and flinging a battle-axe at the gates of Jerusalem, welcomed in her chamber with naked arms, one moonlit night in May, her curly-locked page . . . Then winter roars and the castellan returns, with a beard longer than before and a pilgrim's staff. From the lips of the castle bailiff, a spying fellow.with a sour smile, he learns of the treachery, the stain on his pure name, honoured throughout the Peninsula! Alas for the page! Alas for the lady! The bells toll for the dead. At the entrance to the keep, the hangman waits in a scarlet hood, leaning on his axe between two blocks covered with black draperies. And at the tearful end of *Dona Guiomar*, as in all such stories from the Collections of Love Poems, two white rose-bushes spring forth beside the two graves dug far out in the wilds, and the roses and their fragrance mingle with the wind. Thus (as José Lúcio Castanheiro observed, pensively scratching his chin), nothing shone forth from this *Dona Guiomar* that was 'Portu-guese alone, ours alone, blossoming from our soil and race!' But this mournful tale of love took place in a castle in the Riba Coa: the names of the knights, Remarigues, Ordonho, Froylas, Gutierres, had a delicious Gothic flavour about them, and on every page resounded cries of 'I' faith! . . . Thou liest, rogue! . . . Fetch me my black stallion, page! . . .' And through all this vernacular emerged a sufficient number of stable-boys in light mantles, mendicant friars concealed in the shadows of their cowls, tax-collectors laden with leather pouches, stewards slicing fat loins of pork . . . The novel, therefore, marked a salutary return to national sentiment.

'And then,' added Castanheiro, 'our Gonçalinho comes up with

9

such a terse, energetic style, with such a fine archaic flavour . . . An excellent archaic flavour! Reminds one of *Bobo, the Monk of Cister*! . . .[1] Guiomar is no more than an indistinguishable chatelaine who could be from Brittany or Aquitania. But in the bailiff, and even the castellan, we see real men, and Portuguese in body and soul, from Entre Douro and Cavado . . . Yes, sir! When our Gonçalinho becomes acquainted with our past and our chronicles, we shall at last have in our literature a man who really feels our fatherland, who feels our race!'

Dona Guiomar filled three pages of *The Fatherland*. That Sunday, to celebrate his entry into the literary world, Gonçalo Mendes Ramires invited his comrades from the Circle and other friends to supper, where he was acclaimed, after chicken and peas, while the panting waiters of the *Camolino* were replenishing the bottles of Colares, as 'our Walter Scott!' He, on his part, had already modestly announced a book in two volumes founded on the annals of his own family, on a fierce event illustrating the sublime pride of Tructesindo Mendes Ramires, the friend and standard-bearer of Don Sancho I. Because of his temperament and the detailed knowledge of costume and decoration that he had revealed in *Dona Guiomar*, and also because of the antiquity of his lineage, Gonçalinho seemed gloriously destined to restore the historical novel in Portugal. He had a mission —and he began there and then to walk round Coimbra with his cap pulled over his eyes, like one reconstructing a world. That was the year when he failed his exams.

When he returned from vacation to his fourth year, the ardent group of patriots no longer seethed in Mathematics Street. Castan-heiro, a graduate now, was vegetating in Vila Real de Santo António: with him disappeared *The Fatherland;* and the zealous youths that used to delve into the Chronicles of Fernão Lopes and Azurara, abandoned by the apostle who had spurred them on, fell back on the novels of Georges Ohnet and returned to their cues in the billiard-rooms of Sofia Street. Gonçalo also returned a different man, wearing mourning for his father who had died in August, and with his beard longer; though still always charming and affable, he was now graver and no longer inclined to late suppers and nights on the town. He

[1] Written by the major Portuguese historian, poet and novelist, Alexandre Herculano (1810–1877).

took a room in the Hotel Mondego, where he was waited upon by Bento, an old, white-tied servant from Santa Ireneia; and his best friends now were three or four boys who were thinking of going into politics, carefully studied the Parliamentary Journal, were acquainted with a few intrigues at Court, proclaimed the necessity for a 'positive Orientation', and 'extensive rural development', considered the University's lack of respect for Dogma a contemptible, Jacobin frivolity, and even when they sauntered in the moonlight through the poplar grove or over Nostalgia Rock, ardently discussed the two Party leaders—Bras Vitorino, the young leader of the Regenerators, and the aged Baron of S Fulgencio, the old leader of the Historical Party. Inclined towards the Regenerators, because Regeneration traditionally represented ideas of conservatism, cultured elegance and generosity, Gonçalo then frequented the Regenerator Centre of Couraça, where at night he would advocate, as he sat drinking black tea, 'strengthening the power of the Crown' and 'a broad colonial expansion'. Then, when spring arrived, he cheerfully relinquished his political gravity and stayed up till all hours indulging in feasts of salt cod to the sound of guitars in Camolino's tavern. But he never again referred to his great two-volume novel; and he either gave up or forgot his former mission of Historical Art. It was not until Easter of the fifth year that he took up his pen again—to publish in the *Porto Gazette*, against a neighbour of his, Dr André Cavaleiro, whom the S Fulgencio Ministry had appointed Civil Governor of Oliveira, two very bitter letters of an intense and most personal rancour (to the point of poking fun at 'His Excellency's fierce black moustache'). He signed himself Juvenal, as his father had once done when he published political articles from Oliveira in the same *Porto Gazette*, a paper on which he had friends, and Vilar Mendes, a distant relative of his, editing the Foreign Section. But he had read his friends in the Centre 'the two decisive blows which had knocked Sr Cavaleiro[1] off his horse!' One of these serious youths, nephew of the Bishop of Oliveira, did not conceal his amazement.

'Oh, Gonçalo, I always thought you and Cavaleiro were close friends! When you were in your first year here at Coimbra, if I remember rightly, you lived in Cavaleiro's house in St John's Road ... And isn't there a long-standing friendship between the Ramires and the Cavaleiros? I don't know much about Oliveira, I've never

[1] *Cavaleiro:* literally 'horseman'.

11

set foot there, but I've got an idea Corinde, Cavaleiro's estate, borders Santa Ireneia!'

Gonçalo's face, his smooth, smiling face, frowned with displeasure, and he drily remarked that Corinde did not border Santa Ireneia: that between the two properties flowed, most appropriately, Horse-Kick Stream; and furthermore, Sr André Cavaleiro, who was more of a horse than a horseman, was a detestable animal that grazed on the other side! The Bishop's nephew applauded and laughed,

'A good joke that, yes, sir!'

A year after he graduated. Gonçalo went to Lisbon to deal with the mortgage on his Praga estate near Lamego, on which certain ancient dues of ten *mil-reis* and half a chicken payable to the Abbot of Praga were interminably delaying the decision of the board of the Mortgage Bank. He also went to get to know his party leader, Bras Vitorino, more intimately, to show his loyalty and submission to the party, and to collect some subtle advice on political conduct. Now, one night, as he was coming home from dinner in the house of the old Marchioness of Louredo, 'Aunt Louredo', who lived in Santa Clara, he bumped into José Lúcio Castanheiro in the Rossio, who was now employed in the Treasury, in the National Estate Department. Leaner and more emaciated than ever, with even bigger and darker glasses, Castanheiro still burned, as at Coimbra, with the flame of his Idea—'the resurrection of Portuguese sentiment'. Now, expanding his plans for The Fatherland to proportions worthy of the Capital, he laboured assiduously to create a fortnightly magazine of seventy pages, with a blue cover, entitled *Annals of History and Literature*. It was a night in May, warm and soft. As they strolled round the dry fountains of the Rossio, Castanheiro, with a roll of paper and a thick, calf-bound volume under his arm, after recalling the long, delightful discussions they had had in the Rua da Misericordia, and cursing the lack of intellectuality in Vila Real de Santo António—returned avidly to his Idea, and begged Gonçalo Mendes Ramires to let the *Annals* have the novel that he had announced in Coimbra, on his ancestor Tructesindo Ramires, standard-bearer of Sancho I.

Gonçalo laughed and confessed that he had not yet begun the great work!

'Ah,' murmured Castanheiro, stopping short, his dark glasses fixed on him, cold and diconsolate. 'So you didn't persist, then? You didn't remain loyal to the Idea?...'

He shrugged his shoulders in resignation, now accustomed, in the course of his mission, to such neglect of patriotism. Nor would he allow Gonçalo, ashamed before that faith which had remained so pure and devoted, to refer, by way of excuse, to the laborious task of making an inventory after Papa's death...

'Well, well! That's that! *Procrastinare lusitanum est.* Work now during the summer... For the Portuguese, my boy, the summer is the time of happy events and great deeds. It was in the summer that Nuno Álvares was born in Bonjardim! In the summer that Aljubarrota was fought and won! In the summer Gama reached India! ... And in the summer our Gonçalo is going to write a superb little novel!... Anyway the *Annals* don't appear till December, characteristically on the 1st December. You, in three months, can resurrect a whole world. I'm serious, Gonçalo Mendes! It's a duty, a sacred duty, especially for the young generation, to collaborate in the *Annals*. Portugal, my boy, is dying for lack of national sentiment! We are dying wretchedly of the evil of not being Portuguese!'

He stopped—and waved his lean arm, like the thong of a whip, in a gesture that lashed the Rossio, the City, the whole Nation. Did his friend Gonçalinho know the reason for this rot? The fact is that the worst Portuguese despised their fatherland—and the best did not know it. The remedy? Make Portugal known, make it popular. Yes, dear friend! Organize, with great clamour, propaganda for Portugal, so that everyone should know it—at least as well as James's Chest Syrup is known, eh? Everyone must adopt it—at least as much as they'd adopted Congo soap. Known and adopted, everyone should love it, love its heroes and praiseworthy deeds, and its blameworthy ones, too, in all its aspects, even its very paving-stones. It was to this end, the greatest to be attempted in this murky century of our History, that he had founded the *Annals*! To shout aloud! To thunder throughout Portugal, proclaiming on the rooftops the wholly unexpected news of its greatness! It was the descendants of those who had once created the Kingdom, more than anyone else, who should take upon themselves the sacred task of remaking it! How? By reviving tradition, *caramba*!

'Look at yourselves! Throughout the history of Portugal, one beautiful Ramires after another. Even the High Judge, the one that

13

got through two whole sucking-pigs at a Christmas supper. Just one gigantic belly, really. But what a belly! There's a heroic vigour here evoking race—a race stronger than could be expected from human strength, as Camões said. Two sucking-pigs, by Jove! Makes him quite endearing! And the other Ramires, the Silves one, the one at Aljubarrota, those at Arcila, those that went to India! And those five courageous ones, of whom perhaps you have never even heard, who died in the Battle of Salado. Now, to resuscitate these valiant men, and reveal their heroic souls and inflexible wills, would be a superb lesson to the young generation. Really envigorating, by Jove! A revival of the consciousness of having been so great should shake them out of this flabby consent in remaining small! That's what I call reviving tradition! And for this to be done by yourself, a Ramires, how *chic*! By Jove, how *chic* it really would be! A nobleman, the most noble nobleman of Portugal, to reveal the heroic spirit of our Fatherland, without having to set foot outside his country residence but simply by opening up the family archives, a family over a thousand years old. It's stupendous! You don't have to make it a long novel . . . A complicated novel would not be in keeping with the militant spirit of the magazine. A short story would do, twenty or thirty pages . . . Of course *The Annals* can't pay you anything at the moment. But you're not in need of money, either. What the deuce! Our object is not money but a great social revolution . . . And then, my boy, literature leads to everything in Portugal. I know our Gonçalo's been frequenting the Regenerator Centre in Coimbra lately. Our little stories could lead us to S Bento![1] Nowadays it is the pen, where once it was the sword, that builds kingdoms. Think on these things! And now goodbye, because today I must copy out Henriques' Study of Ceylon into legible script . . . Don't you know Henriques? You don't. Nobody does. Whenever there's some doubt, in one of the big European academies, on Singhalese history or literature, they cry out over here for Henriques!'

He hurried off clasping his roll and volume—and Gonçalo could still discern him, in the light of a doorway in Nunes' Tobacconist's, waving his lean apostle's arm in front of an obese character with an enormous white waistcoat who recoiled in alarm at being thus disturbed as he was quietly enjoying his fat cigar and the soft May night.

[1] S Bento: the Portuguese 'Parliament' situated in Lisbon.

The Nobleman of the Tower returned to the Braganza Hotel meditating on the Patriot's idea. Everything about it was inviting—and would be advantageous to him: his collaboration with a reputable magazine of some seventy pages, alongside writers, University professors, former Ministers, even Counsellors of State; the antiquity of his family, older even than the Kingdom, made popular by a story of beauty and heroism, from which the bravery and eminence of the Ramires' soul shone out with splendour; and finally the academic seriousness of his character, his fine taste for erudite research, revealed at the very moment when he was endeavouring to enter on a Parliamentary and political career! . . . The work itself, the moral composition of the ancient Ramires, the archeological resurrection of the Afonsine atmosphere, a hundred pages of foolscap to fill with solid prose—none of this alarmed him. No, because he already had his *oeuvre*—and well planned and told, too. His Uncle Duarte, a brother of his mother's (a lady from Guimarães, of the Balsas family) during his years of idleness and imagination, from 1845 to 1850, between taking his degree and his appointment as an Attorney, had been a poet, and had published in *The Bard*, a weekly paper appearing in Guimarães, a poem in blank verse called *The Castle of Santa Ireneia*, which he had signed with the two initials, DB. This castle was his own, the ancient manor, of which only the black tower remained, amid the lemon-trees in the orchard. The poem sang, in romantic strains, of an incident of feudal arrogance, which glorified the name of Tructesindo Ramires, standard-bearer to Sancho I in the battles between Afonso II and the Princesses. This volume of *The Bard*, bound in morocco, with the Ramires arms on it—a black goshawk on a scarlet background, stood in the family archives like a chapter in the heroic chronicle of the Ramires. Many a time, Gonçalo, taught by his mama, had recited the first lines of the poem, of most harmonious melancholy:

'In the pallor of evening, amid the foliage
Gilded by the autumn sun . . .'

It was this sombre achievement by his distant ancestor which Gonçalo Mendes Ramires had decided to use when, in Coimbra, his friends from *The Fatherland* and companions of suppers had acclaimed him 'our Walter Scott'—to compose a modern novel, but with epic realism, in two volumes, forming a richly coloured study

15

of the Portuguese Middle Ages . . . Now it would serve him, with delicious facility, for the short sober story of thirty pages which was required by the *Annals*.

In his room at the Braganza Hotel, he opened the verandah window. Leaning over, finishing his cigar, in the dormant mildness of the May night, before the silent majesty of the river and the moon, he considered with relish that he would not even have the tiresome task of scrutinizing chronicles and boring old manuscripts. No, indeed! All the historical reconstruction had been carried out, most capably, with deftness and skill, by Uncle Duarte. The fortified Manor of Santa Ireneia with its deep, defensive moats, the barbican tower, the keep, the dungeon, the beacon and the banner; old Tructesindo, enormous, with his white flock of hair and ancestral beard spread over his coat-of-mail; the Moorish serfs with leather pouches, digging irrigation-ditches in the vegetable-gardens; priests by the fireside mumbling scraps from *The Lives of Saints;* young pages on the jousting-fields—everything took fresh life, with startling relief, in Uncle Duarte's poem! He could still remember certain incidents—the jester being whipped, the banquet with the stewards opening barrels of beer; Violante Ramires' journey to the Monastery of Lorvão . . .

> 'Beside the Moorish fountain, beside the elms,
> The procession stops . . .'

The whole plot, with its passion of barbaric grandeur, the savage battles in which family feuds were settled by the dagger, heroic words uttered by steely lips—there it all was in dear Uncle's verses, sonorous and nicely balanced:

> 'Hear me, monk! The manor of Don Ramires
> Would fall apart stone by stone
> If ever a bastard, vilely shod,
> Should tread its undefiled floors!'

Really, all that was needed was to superimpose the mellifluous tones of 1846 Romanticism upon its terse, virile prose (as Castanheiro agreed) of an excellent archaic colour, reminiscent of *O Bobo*. Would this be plagiarism? No! To whom, more than to him, a Ramires, belonged the memory of these historic Ramires? The resurrection of old Portugal, so beautifully described in *The Castle of Santa Ireneia*, was not the work of Uncle Duarte alone, but of all the Herculanos and Rebelos and Academies and scattered erudition. Anyway, who nowadays knew of this poem, or even of *The Bard*, a slim weekly magazine which had been produced for five months in a provincial town?... He hesitated no longer, the temptation was too strong. As he undressed, after drinking down a cup of water with bicarbonate of soda in it, he was already forging the first line of the story in the lapidary style of *Salammbô*: 'In the Manor of Santa Ireneia, one winter's night, in the lofty hall of the Keep . . .'

Next day, he went to speak to José Lúcio Castanheiro in the National Estate Department, in a hurry, because he had promised, after a meeting in the Mortgage Bank, to accompany his cousins, the Chelas, to an Exhibition of Embroidery in Gomes' Bookshop. He informed our Patriot that he could count on him to be ready for the first number of *The Annals* with his story whose title he had already decided: '*The Tower of Don Ramires*'.

'What d'you think?'

Delighted, José Castanheiro threw up his bony arms, covered to the elbow with alpaca sleeves, to the vaulted roof of the narrow corridor in which he had received him.

'Wonderful! "*The Tower of Don Ramires*"! The sublime deed of Tructesindo Mendes Ramires, told by Gonçalo Mendes Ramires! . . . And all in the same Tower! In the Tower, old Tructesindo does the deed, and seven hundred years afterwards, in the same Tower, our Gonçalo recounts it! By Jove, my boy, by Jove! This is really renewing tradition!'

*   *   *

Two weeks later, back in Santa Ireneia, Gonçalo sent a servant with a cart to Oliveira, to the house of his brother-in-law, Barrolo, married to Gracinda Ramires, to bring back from the well-stocked classical library which Barrolo had inherited from his Uncle, Dean of the Cathedral, all the volumes, of the *Historical Genealogy*— 'and [he added in a letter] all the old volumes which could be found there under the title *Chronicles of King So-and-So* . . .' Then, from under the dust of the bookshelves he disinterred the works of Walter Scott, odd volumes of *Panorama*, Herculano's *History*, *O Bobo*, and *The Monk of Cister*. Then furbished with an entire ream of foolscap ready on his desk, he began to copy out Uncle

Duarte's poem, still inclined to transfer to a bitter December morning, as more in keeping with the feudal roughness of his ancestors, that whole sumptuous procession of ladies and monks and men-at-arms which Uncle Duarte had disposed against a backcloth of soft autumnal melancholy in the plains of Mondego . . .

> 'In the pallor of evening, amid the foliage
> Gilded by the autumn sun . . .'

But as it was then June and the moon was waxing, Gonçalo finally decided to take advantage of the sensations produced by the heat, moonlight and groves of trees which the village provided, and to erect, at the very beginning of his story, the immense black Manor of Santa Ireneia in the silence of an August night, beneath a resplendent full moon.

He had already filled two pages effortlessly, aided by *The Bard*, when trouble with his tenant, Manuel Relho, who tilled his land for a rent of 800 *mil-reis*, came and disturbed the Nobleman of the Tower as he sat immersed in the fresh and novel inspiration of his work. Relho, who for many orderly and composed years had deliberately and merrily got drunk every Sunday, had, ever since Christmas, begun to indulge in violent, scandalous fits of drunkenness three or four times a week, when he beat his wife, filled the farm with deafening roars and leapt out on to the road to stand there dishevelled and to defy, stick in hand, the quiet village. Finally, one night, as Gonçalo sat at his desk after drinking his tea, laboriously digging into the foundations of the Manor of Santa Ireneia, he suddenly heard Rosa, the cook, cry out: 'Help, help us against Relho!' As she shouted and as the dogs barked, first one stone and then another crashed against the aged verandah of the library! Nervous, Gonçalo Mendes Ramires thought of his revolver . . . But that very afternoon his servant Bento had taken his sole and ancient weapon down to the kitchen to clean off the rust and polish it! So he ran, disconcerted, to his room, locked the door and pushed a cupboard against it in such desperation that some crystal jars, a tortoise-shell box and even a crucifix, fell and broke. Afterwards, the shouts and barking died away in the yard but that night Gonçalo did not budge from his well-fortified refuge; he sat and smoked, piqued and hurt that Relho, whom he had forgiven so many times and whom he had always treated so pleasantly, had stoned the windows of the Tower! Early in the morning he spoke to the village authorities; Rosa, still trembling, showed the bruises made by Relho's fingers on her arms; and the man, whose lease expired in October, was dismissed from the farm, with his wife, his chest and his bed. Immediately, a farmer from Bravais, José Casco, respected throughout the neighbourhood for his seriousness and exceptional diligence, presented himself and offered to rent the Tower. Gonçalo Mendes Ramires, ever since the death of his father, had decided to increase the rent to 950 *mil-reis*. Casco went down the steps with head bowed. He returned the next day, went over the fields very carefully, crumbled the soil between his fingers, scrutinized the stable and the cellar, counted the olive-trees and grape-vines; and with a great effort and a heavy sigh, offered 910 *mil-reis*! Gonçalo would not yield, certain of his right. Then José Casco returned again with his wife; then, one Sunday, with his wife and a *compadre*,[1] and there was a slow scratching of the shaven chin, a few more suspicious turns round the threshing-place and the orchard, lengthy disappearances into the granary—all of which made that June morning intolerably long to the Nobleman, seated in the garden under a mimosa tree on a stone bench with the *Porto Gazette* in his hands. When a pale-faced Casco came to offer him 930 *mil-reis*, Gonçalo Mendes Ramires flung down the paper and declared that he would cultivate the ground himself, to show them what a rich piece of land it was, treated with modern methods, with phosphates and machines! The man from Bravais then gave a deep sigh and accepted the 950 *mil-reis*. The Nobleman, in accordance with ancient custom, shook the farmer's hand—who went into the kitchen to down a large glass of wine, wiping from his forehead and from the protruding veins of his neck the nervous perspiration which was drenching him.

But, as if hindered by all these cares, Gonçalo's over-flowing vein of inspiration dried up—it was no more than a miserable little cloudy stream. When he sat down at his desk that afternoon to describe the armoury of the Manor of Santa Ireneia one moonlight night—all he could manage was a slavish conversion of Uncle Duarte's smooth verses into a watery prose, without that little something to modernize them, to provide a majestic grandeur, nostalgic beauty for those massive walls where the moonlight, sweeping over the plains, made

[1] *Compadre:* close friend of the family through his relationship as god-father or sponsor at baptism or marriage.

the heads of the tall lances and the tops of the helms sparkle. From four o'clock in the afternoon, in the silence and heat of that June Sunday, he laboured, forcing along his pen like a slow plough carving through stony ground, striking out resentfully and peremptorily any line he felt inelegant and dull, sometimes in a frenzy, withdrawing and reinserting his morocco-slippered feet beneath the table; sometimes motionless and abandoned to the sterility which restrained him, eyes fixed distractedly upon the Tower, that so difficult Tower, black between the lemon trees and the blue, surrounded by the twittering and swooping of swallows.

Finally, thoroughly discouraged, he flung down the pen which refused to work for him. He put away the precious volume of *The Bard*, slamming the drawer shut.

'Damn! I'm absolutely stuck! It's this heat! And then that wretch Casco, all morning!'

He read again, gloomily scratching the back of his neck, the last untidy, crossed-out line.

'In the broad, lofty room where the broad, pallid rays of moonlight . . .' Broad, broad! And the pallid rays, the eternal 'pallid rays'! And this cursed castle was so complicated, too! And Don Tructesindo, whom I just can't see clearly, and so ancient! Horrible, the whole lot!

He knocked aside his leather chair, bit into his cigar angrily and marched out of the library, slamming the door behind him, thoroughly bored with his work, with that complicated and confused Manor of Santa Ireneia, and with his ancestors—huge ironclad men with ringing voices who remained as elusive as wisps of smoke.

2

YAWNING AND TIGHTENING the cords of the wide silk trousers which were slipping down round his waist, Gonçalo, who had been lazing around all day, stretched on the blue damask divan with a slight pain in the region of the kidneys, languidly crossed the room to glance at the time on the ancient Chinese-lacquered clock in the corridor. Half-past five! To rouse himself he contemplated a walk along the cool road leading to Bravais. Or of a visit (owed since Easter) to old Sanches Lucena, once again elected deputy at the April general elections by the Vila Clara constituency. But the journey to *Feitosa*, Sanches Lucena's estate, meant an hour's ride on horseback, most unpleasant with that nagging pain in the kidneys which had attacked him last night after tea in the Club in Vila Clara. And as he drifted hesitantly along the corridor to call to Bento or Rosa to bring him up a lemonade, there came through the open verandah doors a thick metallic voice which grew coarser as it joked, and rolled across the yard with a hollow-sounding cadence like a mallet hammering:

'Oh, Sô[1] Gonçalo! Oh, Sô Gonçalo! Oh, Sô Gonçalíssimo Mendes Ramires! . . .'

He immediately recognized Titó, António Vilalobos, a distant relative, companion from Vila Clara, where this stout and excellent man, of old Alentejan stock, had settled for no apparent reason other than his bucolic love of the town. For eleven years he had filled it with his powerful limbs and slow rumble of his powerful voice and his idleness which he exhibited on benches, in corners, in shop doorways, at the bars of taverns and in sacristies where he chatted and argued with the priests, and even in the cemetery philosophizing with the grave-digger. He was a brother of the old squire of Cidadelhe (the genealogist) who had given him a monthly allowance of eight *moedas* to keep him far away from Cidadelhe—and from his wretched harem of country-girls, and from the forbidding task he was now diligently working on—*The True Inquiry*, an examination into the bastards, crimes and illegitimate titles of the Portuguese aristocracy.

[1] Sô—abbreviation for Senhor.

21

Gonçalo, ever since he had been a student, had always loved this kind-hearted Hercules, who had won him over by his prodigious strength, his matchless ability to drink a whole cask and eat a whole lamb, and above all by his independence, a supreme independence that, supported by his great cane and the eight *moedas* jingling in his pocket, feared nothing and wanted nothing from Heaven or Earth. Leaning over the verandah, Gonçalo shouted,

'Oh, Titó, come up! Come up while I dress. Have a glass of Hollands . . . Then we'll walk as far as Bravais . . .'

Seated on the edge of the round dry pool which decorated the patio, and raising his large, frank, tanned face with its thick red beard to the manor, Titó slowly fanned his face with his old straw hat.

'I can't . . . Listen, do you want to have supper tonight with me and João Gouveia in Gago's? Videirinha and his violin are coming, too. We're having baked mullet, a magnificent one. It's enormous— I got it this morning from a woman from the coast for five *tostões*! Baked by Gago himself! How's that? Gago's going to open a new cask of wine, one of the Abbot of Chandim's. I know that wine. It's some of the best there is.'

Titó, with two fingers, delicately shook the soft lobe of his ear to emphasize the point. But Gonçalo, jerking up his trousers, hesitated.

'My dear chap, I've had such a wretched stomach since yesterday . . . And ever since last night such an ache in the kidneys, or the liver or the spleen; I don't know which, somewhere in the innards here! . . . All I was going to have for supper today was chicken broth and boiled chicken. Still, let's go! But let's be careful; tell Gago to get a nice roast chicken for me. Where are we meeting? At the Club?'

Titó got up off the edge of the pool, pushing his straw hat to the back of his neck.

'I'm not wasting my time at the Club today. I've a lady waiting for me. See you between 10 and 10.30 at the Fountain. Videirinha's coming too with his guitar. Cheerio! See you between 10 and 10.30! Right? And a nice roast chicken for His Excellency with the pain in the kidneys!'

He crossed the yard with bovine torpor stopping near the gate to pluck from a rose-bush a rose with which he adorned his olive-green velvet jacket.

Immediately Gonçalo decided not to dine, confident of the advantages of a fast till ten o'clock, after a walk to Bravais and through the Riosa valley. Before going to his room to dress, he pushed open the glass door at the top of the dark stairway leading to the kitchen and called for the cook, Rosa. But neither that good elderly woman nor Bento, for whom he shouted furiously, too, answered, in the heavy silence amid which lay, as if abandoned, those sombre foundations of large flag-stones and the great vault which remained from the ancient manor, burnt in the time of King Don José I, and restored by Vicente Ramires after his campaign in Castile. Then Gonçalo descended two steps of the worn stairs and let out another of those loud yells with which he deafened the Tower ever since the bells had stopped working. He was going down still further to invade the kitchen when Rosa came to his aid. She had gone out into the back-yard with Crispola's daughter and hadn't heard the Doctor!

'I've been yelling here for an hour! And neither you nor Bento answers! . . . It was to say I'm not having any dinner. I'm having a late supper in Vila Clara with some friends.'

Rosa, from the sonorous depths of the corridor, protested in despair. Surely the Doctor wasn't going to go without anything to eat till late at night? She was the daughter of a former gardener of the Tower, brought up at the Tower, cook at the Tower when Gonçalo was born, and had always addressed him as 'master' and even as 'darling little master', until he went to Coimbra and became, for her and Bento, 'the Doctor'. Now the Doctor should at least have a bowl of chicken broth which had been simmering since midday and which smelt like Heaven on earth!

Gonçalo, who never disagreed with anything suggested by Rosa or Bento, consented—and he was already on his way up again when he called back Rosa to ask after Crispola, a poor widow with a hungry brood of children, who had fallen sick at Easter-time with a malignant bout of fever.

'Crispola's getting better, Doctor. She's up again. The girl says she's up . . . But she's very weak.'

Gonçalo went back down a step, leaning forward to participate more confidentially in this tale of sorrow.

'Listen, Rosa, if the child's still around, poor little soul, give her the chicken I was going to have for supper, to take home. And the broth . . . Give her the lot! I'll have a cup of tea and biscuits. And look here, send ten *tostões* to Crispola, too. Send two *mil-reis*! And

23

don't send the chicken and the money just like that without a word
... Tell her I hope she soon gets better and I'll be round one day
to see how she is. And tell that animal Bento to send me up some hot
water!'

Back in his room he stood in his shirt-sleeves in front of his mirror,
an immense cheval-glass hung between two gilt columns, and studied
his tongue which looked rather furred, and then the whites of his
eyes, which he feared might have the yellowish tinge of a bilious
attack. He finished by contemplating his new appearance, since he
had had his beard shaved off in Lisbon, keeping only the thin-
curled chestnut moustache and a wisp of beard below the lip which
accentuated the length of the fine aquiline face which was always
creamy-white in colour. What saddened him was his hair, nicely
waved but fine and thin, and in spite of all the lotions and creams he
put on it, already needing a parting higher than before, nearly at the
top of his head.

'What an infernal nuisance! Thirty years old and already going
bald!'

Still he did not leave the mirror, in satisfied contemplation,
remembering Aunt Louredo's recommendation in Lisbon: 'Oh,
nephew dear, such an intelligent and elegant young man should not
bury himself in the country! Lisbon has no young men. We need a
good Ramires here!' No, he wouldn't bury himself in the provinces,
motionless beneath the ivy and melancholy dust of lifeless things like
the Tower! ... But how could he lead an elegant life in Lisbon,
among his noble relations, with the 1,800 *mil-reis* of rent which was
all he had left after his father's debts had been paid? Really he would
only want to live in Lisbon if he secured a good political position—a
seat in São Bento, an intellectual influence in his Party, slow and
secure steps towards Power. But this ambition, so sweetly dreamed
of in Coimbra during the hours of facile talk in the Hotel Mondego,
was very remote in reality. Almost unachievable, far away behind a
tall, jagged wall with neither door nor gap in it! A Deputy! How
could he be? With that awful S Fulgencio and his Historicals in
power for three long years, General Elections were a thing of the
past. Even supposing there were some by-election, what chance had
he of achieving anything, he who, ever since Coimbra, spurred by
the elegance of traditions, had always so frivolously proclaimed himself a Regenerator, in the Centre at Couraça, in his letters in the

Porto Gazette, and in the bitter public criticism of the Governor of the District, the detestable Cavalheiro? . . . All he could do now was wait. Wait, and work as he waited, improving his social contacts, carefully building on the foundation of his exceptional historical name, a small political reputation, weaving and spreading a precious net of political friendships from Santa Ireneia to Black Horse Square . . . That was it! There was the splendid theory—but how were contacts and reputation and political friends to be achieved? 'Work as a lawyer, write for the papers!' had been the smiling, distraught advice of his leader, Bras Vitorino. Established as a lawyer in Oliveira, or even in Lisbon? He couldn't, with the innate, almost physiological horror he had of official records and judicial documents. Start a paper in Lisbon like Ernesto Rangel, his friend from Coimbra at the Hotel Mondego? It was a simple task for the adored grandson of Sra Dona Joaquina Rangel who had 10,000 casks of wine stored away in warehouses in Gaia. Fight his way through a Lisbon newspaper? These last weeks in the capital, always in the Mortgage Bank or with his cousins, he had not formed any solid and useful relations with the two big Regenerator Papers, *The Morning* and *The Truth.* So really in this wall which divided him from fortune he could discover only one little hole, difficult to get through but possible— *The Annals of History and Literature,* with its collaboration by Professors, Politicians, even a Minister, and even an Admiral, Guerreiro Araujo, that thundering bore. He would therefore make his debut in *The Annals* with his *Tower,* revealing his imagination and his wealth of learning. Then moving from Fiction to the more respectable field of Erudition, he would produce a study (which he had thought of in the train, returning to Lisbon) on *The Visigothic Origins of Public Right in Portugal . . .*' It's true he knew nothing about such origins and such Visigoths. But with the magnificent *History of Public Administration in Portugal* which Castanheiro had lent him, he should be able to compose an elegant summary quite effortlessly . . . Then, jumping from Erudition to Social and Pedagogic Sciences, why not cook up a good *Reform of Juridical Education in Portugal* in two tedious articles, from a Statesman? Thus would he advance, keeping close to the Regenerators, constructing and perfecting his literary pedestal until the Regenerators were back in power, and the desired triumphal door in the wall stood wide open. As he stood in the middle of the room, in his pants, his arms akimbo,

Gonçalo Mendes Ramires concluded that he had to get a move on with his novel.

'But whenever am I going to get this *Tower* finished? Stuck like this, dried up, with my liver upset? . . .'

Bento, an old man with a dark, clean-shaven face and handsome white curly hair, very clean and neat in his cotton jacket, came leisurely in carrying a jug of hot water.

'Oh, Bento, look here! Did you find in a case which I brought from Lisbon, or in a box, a glass bottle with a white powder in it? It's an English medicine which Dr Matos gave me. It has an English label on it with an English name, I can't remember exactly—some fruit salts.'

Bento stared at the ground and closed his eyes in thought. Yes, in the bathroom, on top of the red trunk, there was a bottle with powder in it, wrapped in a parchment like those in the Archives.

'That's it!' shouted Gonçalo. 'I needed some documents while I was in Lisbon because of those confounded Praga dues. And I made a mistake in the confusion and took a totally worthless document from the Archives. Go and get it. But be careful with the bottle!'

Bento, careful and consistently slow, was still fixing agate cuff-links into the Doctor's shirt, and unfolding on the bed, for him to put on, his light cheviot jacket and well-pressed trousers. Gonçalo, once again fascinated by the idea of writing articles for *The Annals*, was going through *The History of Public Administration in Portugal* when Bento returned with a roll of parchment from which hung, at the end of a tattered ribbon, a lead seal.

'That's it!' cried the Nobleman, flinging down the volume on to the window-seat. 'I rolled it in the parchment so it shouldn't break. Unwrap it and put it on the chest-of-drawers . . . Dr Matos advised me to take it with warm water, between meals. It fizzes, I believe. And it cleans the blood and clears the head . . . I certainly need my head cleared! You take some too, Bento. And tell Rosa to take some. Everyone takes it these days, even the Pope!'

Bento carefully unwrapped the bottle, spreading on the marble top of the chest-of-drawers the stiff parchment whose sixteenth-century writing appeared wrinkled and yellow and dead. Gonçalo, buttoning his collar, remarked,

'This is what I brought so carefully to unravel the mysteries of the Praga dues. A parchment from the time of Don Sebastian . . . All I can understand is the date, fourteen hundred . . . No. Fifteen hundred and seventy-seven. Just before the journey to Africa. Ah, well, it was useful to wrap the bottle in.'

Bento, who had selected a white waistcoat from the large drawer, cast a furtive glance at the venerable parchment.

'It was a letter that King Don Sebastian sent to some ancestor of yours, no doubt, Doctor.'

'Of course,' murmured the Nobelman, standing before the mirror. 'And asking for something worth having, some nice fat sum. In the old days, being king meant having plenty of income. Nowadays . . . Don't tighten the buckle so much, man! My stomach's been swollen these last few days . . . Nowadays the institution of royalty is wearing somewhat thin, Bento!'

'So it seems,' replied Bento gravely. 'The *Século* claims the days of Royalty will soon be over. They were saying so only yesterday. And the *Século* is a very well-informed paper . . . In today's, I don't know if you've read it, Doctor, they've got Sanches Lucena's big birthday party and the firework display, and the feast they had in *Feitosa*.'

Ensconced in the damask divan, Gonçalo stuck out his feet to Bento, who was lacing up his white boots.

'That Sanches Lucena is an idiot! Now what good will it do this man, sixty years old, to be a Deputy, spend months in the Francfort Hotel in Lisbon, forsake his lands, and leave that beautiful estate? . . . What for? Just to say "Hear, hear" every now and again! He'd do better to let me have his seat, I, who am more intelligent, have no great estate to look after and like the Hotel Braganza. And speaking of Sanches Lucena, tell Joaquim to have the mare ready tomorrow, at this time in the afternoon, so I can go to *Feitosa* and see the brute . . . I'll wear that new riding-outfit I brought from Lisbon with the high gaiters . . . I haven't seen Dona Ana Lucena for more than two years. She's a beautiful woman!'

'When you were in Lisbon, Doctor, they passed here in their calash. They even stopped, and Sr Sanches Lucena pointed out the Tower to the lady . . . A really perfect woman, she is! She had a large pair of lorgnettes with a long handle and a long chain, all in gold . . .'

'Bravo! Soak this handkerchief in eau-de-Cologne, I've such a heavy head today! . . . Dona Ana was a farm-labourer, wasn't she? A country-girl, from Corinde?'

27

Bento protested, the bottle held in mid-air, looking in consternation at the Nobleman.

'No, sir! Sra Dona Ana Lucena is of very low birth! She's the daughter of a butcher from Ovar. And her brother fled from justice because he killed the blacksmith from Ílhavo.'

'So here we are,' resumed Gonçalo, 'butcher's daughter, brother fleeing from justice, a beautiful woman with gold lorgnettes . . . She deserves my new suit!'

*   *   *

At ten o'clock, Tító was waiting in Vila Clara, seated on one of the stone benches of the Fountain, under the Judas trees, with his friend João Gouveia, who was Administrator of the town. Both fanned themselves with their hats silently, enjoying the coolness and the murmur of the slow water in the shade. The half-hour was striking on the clock of the Town Hall when Gonçalo, who had been delayed at the Club by a game of ombre, appeared announcing that he was suffering from a dreadful hunger—'the historical hunger of the Ramires family'—and hurrying them off to Gago's, would not even allow Tító to go down to Brito's shop to get a bottle of sugar-cane brandy from Madeira, 'very old and most excellent'.

'No time! To Gago's, to Gago's, quick! Otherwise I'll be devouring one of you two instead, Ramirically hungry as I am!'

But as they were going up the road, it was he who stopped, arms crossed, jocularly questioning the Local Administrator on the latest stupefying action by *his* government. So *his* government, *his* Historical friends, *his* honourable S Fulgêncio—had appointed António Moreno Civil Governor of Monforte! António Moreno, in Coimbra so aptly called Miss Antoninha Morena! No, really, it was the lowest form of degradation to which a country could stoop! After this, the only way to achieve a perfect balance in the Administration was another appointment, and an urgent one at that—Joana Salgadeira as Lady Attorney-General of the Crown!

João Gouveia, a little man, very dark and very dry, with a moustache more bristly than piassava fibre, stiff in a short overcoat and a bowler-hat tilted over one ear, could not disagree. An impartial servant of Historicals or Regenerators, he had always accepted with impartial irony the appointment of young graduates, whether they were Historicals or Regenerators, to high administrative posts. But in this case it had nearly made him sick, lads! Civil Governor, and of Monforte, António Moreno, whom he had found many a time in his room at Coimbra dressed up like a woman with his dressing-gown undone and his pretty face covered in face-powder! . . . Clasping the Nobleman's arm, he reminded him of the night when José Gorjão, very drunk, with a top-hat and revolver, had furiously demanded Father Justino, also drunk, to marry him and Antoninha before a niche of Our Lady of the Happy Death! But Titó, who was waiting for them, brandished his cane and declared to these gentlemen that if they had time to crawl along the road like that, discussing politics and indecency, he would go back to Brito's and get his brandy . . . Immediately, the Nobleman of the Tower, always ready for a joke, shook off the Administrator's arm and galloped up the road, hands clasped as if gripping the reins of a frisky horse.

In the tall dining-room of Gago's, at the top of the steep, narrow stairs which led up from the tavern, the supper, laid at a corner of the long table lit by two paraffin lamps, was tasty and cheerful. Gonçalo, who claimed he had been miraculously cured after the walk to Bravais and the excitement of the card-game, at which he had won nineteen *tostões* from Manuel Duarte—began with a dish of eggs and smoked sausage, devoured half the mullet, consumed his 'invalid's chicken', cleared the dish of cucumber salad and finished off with a pile of quince jelly cubes; and as he accomplished this noble work, he emptied (without any flushing of that pure white skin) a glazed mug of Alvaralhão wine, because after the first sip of the Abbot's new wine, he had cursed it, to Titó's annoyance. At dessert, Videirinha appeared, 'Videirinha of the guitar', renowned player in Vila Clara, chemist's assistant, and poet with verses on love and patriotism already published in *The Independent Paper of Oliveira*. He had dined that night, together with his guitar, in the house of the honoured Barros, who was celebrating the anniversary of his decoration; and Videirinha would accept only a glass of Alvaralhão in which he crushed a cube of quince jelly 'to sweeten his throat'. Then at midnight, Gonçalo told Gago to make up the fire and brew some coffee, 'really strong, terrible coffee, Gago, old man! A coffee capable even of drawing talent from the honoured Barros!' This was the divine hour of guitars and fados. Videirinha had already moved into the shadows, clearing his throat and tuning the strings, posing with a melancholy air against a high bench.

'Let's have *Soledad*, Videirinha,' begged good old Titó, in pensive mood, rolling a fat cigarette.

Videirinha sobbed out *Soledad* with delicious feeling:

'When you go the cemetery,
Ai Soledad, ai Soledad . . .'

Then, as he finished to applause, and as he adjusted the tuning-pegs, the Nobleman of the Tower and João Gouveia talked, with their elbows on the table, and their cigars smoking, of the sale of Lourenço Marques to the English, a sale furtively arranged (according to the papers of the Opposition who were horrified by the affair) by S Fulgêncio's Government. Gonçalo was horrified too! Not with the alienation of the colony—but with S Fulgêncio's cheek! That this obese, bald-headed man, sacrilegious son of a friar who later became a grocer in Cabecelhos, should sell for a few pounds, just to keep himself in power for another couple of years, a piece of Portugal, venerable territory heroically trodden by the Gamas and the Ataides, the Castros and his own ancestors—was for him an abomination which justified any violence, even a revolution—and that the Braganza house should be buried in the mud of the Tagus! Chewing roasted almonds non-stop, João Gouveia observed:

'Let's be fair, Gonçalo Mendes! You must admit the Regenerators . . .'

The Nobleman smiled with a superior air. Ah! If the Regenerators had brought off this fantastic deal—all very well! First, the Regenerators would never have committed the indecency of selling Portuguese land to Englishmen! They would have negotiated with French, or Italians, with the Latin races, their brothers . . . And then this fine, sonorous metal would have been used to develop the country honestly and wisely, with experience. But this awful, bald-headed S Fulgêncio! . . . Furious, choking, he called for Hollands, because that brandy of Gago's was a foul poison!

Titó shrugged his shoulders in resignation.

'You wouldn't let me get the brandy I wanted to, so you can put up with it now . . . And the Hollands is even fouler. Not fit for those Negroes in Lourenço Marques that you want to sell . . . The indecency of these Portuguese—to sell Portugal! You sir, as Administrator, should forbid such talk.'

But the Town Administrator admitted that he allowed it and

without reservations . . . Because he, as a member of the Government, would sell Lourenço Marques and Mozambique and the whole Eastern Coast! In great chunks, by auction! The whole of Africa put up for sale, under the hammer, in Black Horse Square! And did his friends know why? On the healthy principle of strong administration —(he stretched out his arm, almost rising from the stool, as if in parliament); for the healthy reason that all property in distant lands which cannot be developed through lack of money or people should be sold so that we could see to repairing our own roofs, fertilizing our fields, filling our stables, developing the fine land beneath our feet . . . Because Portugal still had a magnificent province to cultivate, to irrigate, to till, to sow—the Alentejo!

Titó's voice roared out, disdaining the Alentejo as a thin skin of land of poor quality which, apart from a few leagues of fields around Beja and Serpa, would never repay the effort put into it, and whose granite showed through at the slightest scratching of its surface.

'My brother João has an enormous estate there, absolutely huge, and all it yields is 300 *mil-reis*!'

The Administrator, who had formerly been a lawyer in Mértola, protested in annoyance. 'The Alentejo! It was a province that had been abandoned, it's true. Abandoned disgracefully for centuries, through the imbecility of governments . . . But rich, nevertheless, rich, fertile land!'

'Look at the Arabs . . . But why go back to the Arabs! Only the other day Freitas Galvão was telling me . . .'

But Gonçalo Mendes, who had also spat out his Hollands with a grimace, came to his aid, summarizing the matter with a sweeping statement, condemning the whole Alentejo as a wretched illusion!

Stretching across the table, the Administrator shouted,

'Have you ever been in the Alentejo?'

'I've never been to China, either, but . . .'

'Then don't talk about things you don't know about! The magnificent vines alone that João Maria planted . . .'

'So what? A hundred casks of cheap wine! And in other places leagues and leagues without . . .'

'It's a granary!'

'A wilderness!'

Amid the tumult, Videirinha, warbling away in lonely ardour,

31

carried away by a torrent of 'ais' from the Fado of Areaso, lamented mournfully about a pair of black eyes, captors of his heart:

> 'Ai, it's from those black eyes of yours
> That all my misfortune comes . . .'

The paraffin in the lamps came to an end, and Gago, requested to bring candles, appeared in shirt-sleeves from behind a cotton curtain, his calculated humility illuminated by smiles, to remind the good gentlemen that it was past one o'clock in the morning. The Administrator, who loathed late nights, which were harmful to his throat (horribly susceptible as he was to tonsillitis), pulled out his watch aghast. Hastily buttoned into his overcoat, his bowler-hat more askew than ever, he bade the slow Titó hurry, since they both lived up at the far end of the village—he in front of the Post Office and his friend in Teresas Lane in a house formerly inhabited by the public executioner of Porto who was found stabbed there.

Titó, however, would not hurry. With his cane under his arm he still insisted on calling Gago from the dark far end of the narrow room to have a whispered discussion about the complicated sale of a rifle, a superb Winchester rifle pawned to Gago by the son of the notary, Guedes, from Oliveira. When he got to the bottom of the stairs, he found the Nobleman of the Tower and João Gouveia at the door of the tavern, bathed in the moonlight which framed the sleeping street, at grips in the usual argument about the Civil Governor of Oliveira—André Cavaleiro!

It was always the same squabble, personal, furious and vague. Gonçalo was imploring him not to mention in his presence, for our dear Lord's sake, the name of that bandit, that Sr Cavaleiro, ludicrous despot who was disorganizing the whole District! João Gouveia, very tense, very dry, with his hat tilted still further over his ear, assuring him of the superior intelligence of his friend Cavaleiro who had established cleanliness and order, like Hercules, in the stables of Oliveira! The Nobleman was roaring and Videirinha, his guitar carefully slung on his back, was begging his friends to go back into the tavern so as not to alarm everyone in the street.

'Especially since Dr Venâncio's mother-in-law, poor soul, has been ill in bed since yesterday with pains in her side.'

'Well then,' shouted Gonçalo, 'don't give me this sickening nonsense! For you, Gouveia, to say that Oliveira never had such a

Civil Governor as Cavaleiro! I don't complain for my father's sake. He's been gone these three years, unfortunately. And I agree he was not a good Governor. He was weak, he was sick . . . But after him we had the Viscount of Freixomil. And then Bernadino. You worked with them. They were real men! But this animal Cavaleiro! The first quality required of the highest official of a District is not to be ludicrous. And Cavaleiro is a complete farce! His ministrel's locks, his terrible black moustache, his languid come-hither eye, his protruding stomach and his blah-blah-blah! It's farcical! And stupid, an elemental stupidity of the sort that begins in the hoofs and works upwards, increasing as it rises. Oh, my dear sirs, what an animal he is! Not to mention the fact that he's a scoundrel.'

Standing stiffly in Tító's enormous shadow, like a post beside a tower, the Administrator bit his cigar. Then, finger raised, he asked with mordant calm:

'Have you finished? Then listen, my Gonçalo, listen! In the entire district of Oliveira, note, the entire district, there is no one, absolutely no one, who can compare, not by a long chalk, with Cavaleiro, in intelligence, character, manners, knowledge and political subtlety!'

The Nobleman of the Tower was shocked into silence. At length, flinging up his arm in harsh, arrogant contempt, he said flatly,

'This is a subordinate's opinion!'

'And those are the words of an unmannerly fellow!' howled the other, swelling up, his bulging little eyes flashing.

Suddenly there appeared between them, sturdier than a beam, Tító's arm, casting a shadow on the pavement.

'Now, now, boys! What foolishness is this? Are you drunk? You now, Gonçalo . . .'

But Gonçalo, with one of those generous, winning gestures of his that charmed everyone, humbled himself and admitted with an air of apology, that he had been brutal.

'Forgive me, João Gouveia! I know perfectly well that you defend Cavaleiro for friendship's sake and not because you are dependent on him. But what do you expect? When anyone talks to me about this "horse", I don't know, it must be contagion, but I start braying and kicking!'

Gouveia, without feeling resentful, was immediately reconciled (he had admiration and affection for the Nobleman of the Tower), gave a sharp tug to his overcoat and merely observed 'that Gonçalinho was a nice boy but said some harsh things . . .' Then, taking advantage of Gonçalo's aplolgetic mood, he began to sing the praises of Cavaleiro again, but this time more moderately. He recognized certain weaknesses. Yes, that arrogant air of his . . . But what a heart the man had! And Gonçalinho ought to consider . . .

The Nobleman, once again repelled by such praise, took a step back, raising his hands.

'Listen, João Gouveia! Why didn't you eat any of that cucumber salad upstairs just now? It was divine—even Videirinha fancied some! I had a second helping, I finished the dish . . . Why was this? Because you have physiological horror, a profound horror, of cucumbers. You and cucumbers are incompatible. There is no sort of logic, no subtle persuasion that will allow the cucumber entrance. You don't doubt that it is excellent, since so many people adore it, but you cannot eat it . . . Well, I feel towards Cavaleiro how you feel towards cucumbers. I cannot accept him! There are no sauces, no amount of reasoning that will make him digestible. I find him nauseating. He just won't go down! He makes me vomit! Now listen . . .'

But Titó, fed up with all this, intervened with a yawn,

'Right! I reckon we have had our fill of Cavaleiro, and more than enough! We are all very nice people and now all we should do is disperse. I've had a woman, I've had mullet . . . I'm worn out. And dawn's not far off. What a disgrace!'

The Administrator gave a start. The devil take it, it was late! And he with a Registration Committee at nine o'clock in the morning! To dispel any remaining ill-feeling, he gave Gonçalo a good hug. As the Nobleman was going down towards the Fountain with Videirinha (who on these nights of merrymaking in Vila Clara always accompanied him along the road as far as the gate of the Tower), João Gouveia turned round yet again, hanging on to Titó's arm in the middle of the road, to remind him of a precept of 'Some philosopher or other':

' "It's not worth spoiling a good supper for the sake of bad politics . . ." I believe it was Aristotle.'

Even Videirinha, who was tuning up his guitar again, preparing for a trill to the moon, murmured respectfully as he softly plucked the strings:

'It's not worth it, Doctor . . . It's really not worth it, because,

34

with Politics, a thing's white one day, black the next, and then in a twinkling it's vanished altogether!'

★   ★   ★

The Nobleman shrugged his shoulders. Politics! As if he had been thinking of the official, of the Civil Governor of Oliveira, when he had insulted André Cavaleiro of Corinde! No! What he detested was the man—the false man with the languid eyes! Because between the two of them existed one of those bitter feuds that, in former times, in the time of Tructesindo, would have driven them one against the other with the cold thrust of lances, and their bands of vassals behind them! As they strolled along the road, the moon reposing on the tops of the Valverde Hills, and while the slow lament of the Fado of Vimioso trembled from Videirinha's guitar, Gonçalo Mendes Ramires remembered bit by bit the story that had so filled his idle hours. The Ramires and the Cavaleiros were neighbouring families, the former with the old Tower in Santa Ireneia, older than the kingdom itself, and the other with a well-tended and profitable estate in Corinde. When he, a boy of eighteen, was immersed in boring work prior to university, André Cavaleiro, then an undergraduate in his third year, treated him as a serious friend. During the holidays, since his mother had given him a horse, he appeared every afternoon at the Tower; and very often, under the groves of trees in the grounds, or walking through the outskirts of Bravais and Valverde, he had confided to him, as to a mature mind, his political ambitions and his ideas of life, which he intended to be serious and completely devoted to the State. Gracinha Ramires was then blossoming into the flower of her sixteen years; even in Oliveira they called her 'the flower of the Tower'. The good Miss Rhodes, Gracinha's English governess, was still alive at the time, and she, like everyone in the Tower, admired André Cavaleiro fervently for his affability, his long, romantic, wavy hair, the gentle languor of his large eyes, and the ardour of his recitations of Victor Hugo and João de Deus. And she, with that weakness which invades the soul and modifies principles in the face of the sovereignty of Love, had smiled on lengthy conversations between André and Maria da Graça under the Judas trees, and even letters exchanged at nightfall over the low wall by the spring. Every Sunday, Cavaleiro dined at the Tower: and the old steward, Rebelo, had already got together, with

35

a lot of effort and muttering, 1,000 *mil-reis* for Senhorina Graça's wedding present. Gonçalo's father, the Civil Governor of Oliveira, always busy and caught up in political intrigue and debts, spending only Sunday mornings in the Tower, approved of the match— Graça being a gentle and romantic girl who, without a mother to watch over her, was already something of a problem and a worry in his life. Although André Cavaleiro did not represent, as he did, a family with a vast history, older than the kingdom, of the bluest blood of the Gothic kings, he nevertheless came from a good family, son of a general, grandson of a High Court Judge, with a legitimate coat-of-arms in his palatial house at Corinde, and rich lands all round, well sown and mortgage-free. Also, as he was the nephew of Reis Gomes, one of the Leaders of the Historicals, and already a member of the Historical Party (since his second year at University), a brilliant career in politics and administration was assured. Finally Maria da Graça was ecstatically in love with that gleaming moustache, the strong shoulders of a courteous Hercules, and the gallant demeanour which swelled his breast and gave him such an impressive appearance. She, in contrast, was petite and fragile, with shy, greenish eyes which turned moist and languid when she smiled. Her skin was of the transparency of fine porcelain, and her magnificent hair, shinier and blacker than the tail of a battle charger, came down to her feet, and she could completely cover herself in it, she was so sweet and small. When the two of them walked along the paths in the grounds, Miss Rhodes (whose father, Professor of Greek Literature in Manchester, had filled her with mythology) always thought of 'Mars full of strength and Psyche full of grace'. Even the servants of the Tower were enraptured by 'the handsome pair'. Only Sra Dona Joaquina Cavaleiro, André's mother, a fat, bad-tempered lady, disliked the tender assiduity of her son at the Tower, for no special reason except that she 'distrusted the girl's looks and would have liked a plainer-looking daughter-in-law'. Fortunately, when André Cavaleiro entered his fifth year, the disagreeable matron died of dropsy. Gonçalo's father received the key to the coffin and Gracinha went into mourning; Gonçalo, living in the same house as Cavaleiro in S João Street in Coimbra, wore a black band on the sleeve of his gown. Everyone in Santa Ireneia thought that now the splendid André, freed of his mama's importunate opposition, would ask for the hand of the 'flower of the Tower' after his graduation. But after this desired event, Cavaleiro set out for Lisbon, because elections were being prepared for October, and he had received a promise from his uncle, Reis Gomes, then Minister of Justice, of 'becoming deputy' for Braganza.

All this summer he spent in the Capital, then he went to Sintra, where his dark, languid eyes softened various hearts; then in an almost triumphal journey to Braganza, with fireworks and shouts of 'Long live the nephew of Counsellor Reis Gomes!' In October, Braganza 'confided to Dr André Cavaleiro (as it said in the *Tras-os-Montes Echo*) the right to represent them in Parliament, with his profound literary knowledge and his outstanding powers of oratory . . .' He then returned to Corinde; but during his visits to the Tower, where Gracinha's father was convalescing from gastric fever, which aggravated his old diabetes, André no longer avidly drew Gracinha, as in former days, towards the silent shadows of the garden, but preferred to stay in the blue room, talking politics with Vicente Ramires, who, wrapped in a rug, did not move from his armchair. And Gracinha, in her letters to Gonçalo at Coimbra, was already lamenting that André's visits were no longer so sweet nor so intimate as before, 'as he was always so busy these days, getting ready for his post as Deputy . . .' After Christmas, Cavaleiro returned to Lisbon for the opening of the session, well equipped, with his servant Mateus, a handsome mare he had bought in Vila Clara from Manuel Duarte, and two boxes of books. The good Miss Rhodes maintained that Mars, as befitted a hero, would only reclaim Psyche after accomplishing a noble deed, a debut in the House 'with a magnificent speech, full of eloquence'. When Gonçalo appeared at the Tower during the Easter vacation, he found Gracinha wan and restless. The letters she had received from André, who had made his debut 'with a magnificent speech, full of eloquence', were shorter and cooler every week. The last (which she showed him in secret), written in the House, told her in three hastily scrawled lines 'that he had had a lot of committee work to do, that the weather had turned fine, that the Count and Countess of Vilaverde were holding their ball that night and that he was missing his faithful Gonçalo . . .' Gonçalo Mendes Ramires, at once, that same afternoon, spoke freely to his father, who lay thin and weak in his armchair.

'I consider André is behaving very badly towards Gracinha . . . Don't you think so, Father?'

Vicente Ramires merely agitated, in a gesture of defeat and sorrow, his bony hand, his signet ring slipping from his finger at every movement.

Finally, in May, the session in the House ended—the session which was of such interest to Gracinha, anxious as she was 'that they should hurry up and finish their discussions and start their holidays'. Almost immediately, she in Santa Ireneia, and Gonçalo in Coimbra, learnt from the papers that 'the talented young deputy, André Cavaleiro, had left for Italy and France, on a long voyage of study and recreation'. Not a word to his chosen one, almost his fiancée! . . . It was an insult, a brutal insult, of the kind that, in former times, in the twelfth century, would have sent all the Ramires, with horsemen and foot-soldiers, surging over to the Cavaleiro home, to leave everything blackened by fire and every serf hanging from a hempen rope. Now Vicente Ramires, wasted and mortally ill, simply murmured, 'Disgraceful fellow!' Gonçalo in Coimbra, roaring with anger, threatened to box the scoundrel's ears one day! The good Miss Rhodes unpacked her ancient harp to console herself and filled Santa Ireneia with woeful notes. Everything ended in the tears that Gracinha, so heart-broken that she did not even bother to comb her hair, shed for weeks in the secrecy of the Judas trees in the belvedere.

Even now, after all these years, when he remembered his sister's tears, so keen a fury filled Gonçalo, that he swished his cane over the hedges bordering the road, as if aiming at Cavaleiro.

They were walking now near Portela bridge, from which the fields stretched in the distance, and from where the whole of Vila Clara could be seen bathed in moonlight from end to end, from the Convent of St Teresa, near the Fountain, to the new wall of the cemetery on the hill with its fine cypresses. Down in the valley, also bright in the moonlight, stood the little church of Craquede, Santa Maria de Craquede, the remains of the ancient monastery where lay, in their rough granite tombs, the great skeletons of the Afonsine Ramires. Under the arch, the slow stream, trickling between the pebbles, rippled softly in the shade. Videirinha, carried away by the silence and nostalgia and tranquillity, sang, to the accompaniment of a throbbing bass-string:

'In vain are your complaints,
Useless your sighs,

For I am as if dead,
And you will see me nevermore! . . .'

Gonçalo returned to his memories, reviewing the sorrows that had
later befallen the Tower. Vicente Ramires had died one afternoon
in August, painlessly, stretched out in his chair on the verandah,
his eyes fixed on the ancient Tower, murmuring to Father Soeiro:
'How many Ramires will it yet see, in this house and in its
shadows ? . . .' Gonçalo had spent the whole of his vacation in the
dark archives, unaided (because their steward, the good Rebelo,
had also been called to God), turning over papers on papers, finding
out the state of the house—reduced to the 2,300 *mil-reis* that was the
income from rent on Craquede, the Praga estate and the two historic
ones—Treixedo and Santa Ireneia. When he returned to Coimbra,
he left Gracinha in Oliveira, in the house of a cousin, Dona Arminda
Nunes Viegas, a well-off and very kind-hearted lady, who inhabited
a mansion in the Terreiro da Louça, full of portraits of ancestors and
genealogical trees, where, dressed in black velvet, and seated on a
damask sofa, amid attendants who sat spinning, she read over and
over again the chivalric novels—*Amadis, Leandro the Handsome,
Tristam and Brancaflor*, the *Chronicles of the Emperor Clarimundo* . . .
It was here that José Barrolo (owner of one of the richest houses in
Amarante) met Gracinha Ramires, and loved her with a profound,
almost religious passion—strange in such an indolent, fat boy with
rosy cheeks like an apple, who was so lacking in spirit that his friends
called him José 'Bacoco'—the simpleton. The good Barrolo had
always resided in Amarante with his mother and had not heard of the
betrayed romance of the 'flower of the Tower'—which indeed had
never gone beyond the thick groves in the grounds of Santa Ireneia.
Under the compassionate, romantic patronage of Dona Arminda,
engagement and marriage were shortly and sweetly sealed in three
months, after a letter from Barrolo to Gonçalo Mendes Ramires,
swearing 'that the pure affection he felt for cousin Graça, for her
virtues and other estimable qualities, was so great that he could find
no terms in the Dictionary to describe it . . .' There was a luxurious
wedding and the bridal couple (at Gracinha's request, so as not to go
too far from her beloved Tower), after a filial visit to Amarante, set
up their nest in Oliveira, at the corner of King's Square and Weaver's
Street, in a palatial house which the 'Bacoco' had inherited, together

with some extensive grounds, from his Uncle Melchior, Dean of the Cathedral. Two years passed quietly and uneventfully. Gonçalo Mendes Ramires had spent his last Easter vacation at Oliveira when André Cavaleiro, appointed Civil Governor of the District, took up office with great pomp, fireworks and bands playing, the Civil Government building and the Bishop's Palace illuminated, and Cavaleiro's arms cut out in transparent, coloured paper in the Arcade Café and the Treasury. Barrolo knew Cavaleiro almost intimately, admired his talent, his elegance and his political verve. But Gonçalo Mendes Ramires, who dominated the good 'Bacoco' absolutely, immediately warned him not to visit the new Civil Governor, nor even acknowledge him in the street, and to acquire, as a result of his marriage, the hatred that existed between the Cavaleiros and the Ramires! José Barrolo gave in submissively, though amazed and uncomprehending. One night, in their room, putting on his slippers, he told Gracinha about Gonçalo's odd behaviour.

'For no reason at all, for no offence given, merely because of politics! Just imagine! A fine fellow like Cavaleiro! We could have had such a nice little group!'

Another tranquil year passed. That spring, in Oliveira, where he had stayed on for Barrolo's birthday party, Gonçalo began to suspect, began to scent, began to discover a most monstrous infamy! The proud gentleman with the black moustache, Sr André Cavaleiro, had once again begun, with supreme impudence, to court Gracinha Ramires, from afar now and silently, with penetrating glances full of longing and languor—now trying to procure as a mistress that fine aristocrat, that Ramires whom he had spurned as a wife!

*   *   *

Gonçalo was so immersed in these bitter thoughts as he walked along the white road that he did not notice the gate of the Tower, nor the little green door at the corner of the house, at the top of three steps. On he went, keeping close to the garden wall, when Videirinha, who had stopped still with his fingers silent on the strings of his guitar, called to him, laughing,

'Oh, Doctor, are you going on to Bravais at this hour of night?'

Gonçalo stopped, brought back abruptly to the present, searching in his pocket for his key in the loose change there.

'I didn't notice . . . How beautifully you have played, Videirinha! With the moon shining, after supper, there's no more poetic companion imaginable . . . You must really be the last of the Portuguese minstrels!'

To the chemist's assistant, son of a baker in Oliveira, this familiarity with the great Nobleman, who shook his hand in the chemist's in front of Pires the chemist himself, and in Oliveira in front of the authorities, was indeed a glory, almost a crowning glory, and ever new, ever delicious. Immediately moved by Gonçalo's words, he plucked the strings with new vigour.

'Then to finish, Doctor, we'll have the greatest ballad of all!'

This was his famous song, the *Fado of the Ramires*—a series of heroic pictures celebrating the legends of the historic family—which for months he had been perfecting and completing, aided in his delightful task by the elderly Father Soeiro, chaplain and archivist of the Tower.

Gonçalo pushed open the green door. In the corridor, a dying night-light spluttered, now dry of oil, beside the silver candlestick. Videirinha, taking up his stance in the middle of the road, with an ardent twanging of strings, fixed his eyes upon the Tower, whose battlements and black turret, above the roofs of the great house, merged with the luminous silence of the summer's night. Then, to the Tower and to the Moon, he flung his praises and laments: to the doleful melody of a Coimbra fado, full of sighs, he sang:

> 'Whosoever would see you and not tremble,
> Tower of Santa Ireneia,
> On nights when the moon is full . . .
> So black and silent as you are,
>> Ai, so black and silent as you are,
>> Tower of Santa Ireneia!'

He stopped to thank the Nobleman who had invited him up to drink a reviving glass of Hollands, but immediately went back to his song, delighted to be serenading, and as ever carried away by the flavour of his verses, by the fascination of the legends, while Gonçalo disappeared—with playful apologies to the Minstrel 'for shutting the castle door'.

'Ai! Here you stand, strong and sublime,
With a story in each of your battlements here,
Tower older than the Kingdom itself,
Tower of Santa Ireneia! . . .'

He began the stanza of Muncio Ramires, Lion's Tooth, when
from above, in a room opened to the cool night, a light went on—
and the Nobleman of the Tower, with lit cigar, leant over the
verandah to receive the serenade. More fervent now, almost sobbing,
Videirinha's song throbbed into the night. Now it was the stanza of
Gutierres Ramires, in Palestine, on the Mount of Olives, at the doorway of his tent before the barons who acclaimed him with naked
swords; but he refused the Duchy of Galilee and dominion of the
Transjordan. He could not, in truth, accept land, even holy land,
in Galilee . . .

'For he had already in Portugal
His lands of Santa Ireneia!'

'That's good!' muttered Gonçalo.
Videirinha, more and more enthusiastic, began another new verse,
composed that week, recounting the funeral procession of Aldonça
Ramires, Santa Aldonça, brought from the Convent of Arouca to the
family home at Treixedo, on the pallet on which she had died, borne
by four Kings!
'Bravo!' shouted the Nobleman, hanging over the verandah.
'That's wonderful, Videirinha! But you've got too many kings . . .
Four kings!'
Ecstatically raising his guitar aloft, the chemist's assistant de-
livered yet another verse, this time one composed much earlier—
the story of the terrible Lopo Ramires who, when dead, had arisen
from his tomb in the Monastery of Craquede, mounted a dead jennet,
and all night long galloped through Spain to fight in the Navas de
Tolosa Battle. He cleared his throat—and still more mournfully
attacked 'The Headless One':

'The silent black figure passes by . . .'

But Gonçalo, who loathed that legend and the silent, decapitated
figure wandering along the battlements of the Tower on winter

nights with his head in his hands—moved away from the verandah to stop the endless chronicle.

'That's enough now, don't you think, Videirinha? It's after three o'clock—dreadful! Listen—Tító and Gouveia are dining here at the Tower on Sunday. You come along, too, with your guitar and some new song; but something less sinister . . . *Bona sera*! What a beautiful night!'

He flung down his cigar and shut the French windows of the drawing-room—'the old drawing-room'—covered with those sombre, sorry-looking portraits of the Ramires, whom he had always called, ever since he was young, 'his ancestral scarecrows'. And as he walked along the corridor, he could still hear, echoing in the distance, through the silence of the moonlit fields, rhymed lines describing great deeds done by his forefathers: .

> 'Ai! There in that great battle . . .
> King Don Sebastian . . .
> The youngest of the Ramires . . .
> The standard-bearer's page . . .

When he had undressed, blown out the candle and hastily crossed himself, the Nobleman of the Tower went to sleep. But his room filled with shadowy shapes and there began a dreadful, frightening night. André Cavaleiro and João Gouveia burst through the wall, clothed in coats of mail, mounted upon horrible baked mullet! And slowly, winking the evil eye, they attacked his poor stomach with jabs of their lances, which made him groan and twist upon the mahogany bed. After that it was the awesome dead Ramires from Vila Clara, his bones creaking within his armour, and King Don Afonso II, gnashing sharply-pointed wolf's teeth, dragging him off to the Battle of Navas. He resisted, his heels wedged in the paving-stones, shouting aloud for Rosa, for Gracinha, for Tító! But Don Afonso gave him such a blow in the kidneys with his iron glove that it sent him from Gago's tavern to the battlefield in the Serra Morena, full of brilliance and excitement with pennants and arms. And immediately his Spanish cousin, Gomes Ramires, Master of Calatrava, bending over his black jennet, tore out the last of his hair to the resounding roars of laughter of all the Saracen host and the wailing of Aunt Louredo, borne there on a pallet on the shoulders of four kings! Finally, worn out, all hope of rest gone, dawn appearing at the chinks in the windows and swallows cheeping in the eaves, the Nobleman of the Tower thrust back the sheets for the last time, jumped out of bed and opened the window—and breathed in the delicious silence and freshness and green of the quiet garden. But how thirsty he was! So thirsty that his lips were parched! Then he remembered the famous fruit salts which Dr Matos had recommended and he picked up the bottle and ran in his night-shirt to the dining-room. There, panting, he dropped two heaped spoonfuls into a glass of Bica Velha which he drank down in one gulp of its pungent effervescence.

'Ah, how refreshing, how magnificently refreshing!'

He returned in exhaustion to his bed and went straight off to sleep again, far away on the lush green of a meadow in Africa, under the murmuring coconut-palms amid the spicy perfume of radiant flowers, which sprang out from between golden rocks. It was Bento who dragged him out of this perfect bliss at midday, worried about 'the Doctor lying in so late'.

'The fact is I had an awful night, Bento! Nightmares and all manner of horrors and confusion and skeletons ... It was those wretched eggs and smoked sausage; and the cucumber, too ... Especially the cucumber! That was that animal Tító's idea! Then at dawn I drank those fruit salts and now I feel fine! Really excellent! I even feel capable of working. Send me a cup of strong green tea along to the library. And some toast.'

*   *   *

A few moments later, in the library, a flannel dressing-gown on over his night-shirt, sipping slow draughts of tea, Gonçalo sat beside the verandah and again read the last line of his novel, so dull and scrawled, with the 'wide rays of moonlight bathing the wide armoury ...' Suddenly, with a brilliant flash of clarity, he could see expressive details of that summer's night in the Castle—the heads of the sentinels' lances flashing silently along the battlement of the wall and the melancholy croaking of the frogs on the muddy banks of the ditches ...

'Excellent touches!'

He drew his chair closer thoughtfully, and once again consulted his Uncle Duarte's poem in the volume of *The Bard*. With his mind clear, feeling the images and sentences surge up like bubbles in

44

water that has been confined and is suddenly released, he attacked that section in Chapter One where the old Tructesindo Ramires, in the armoury at Santa Ireneia, is talking with his son Lourenço and his cousin Don Garcia Viegas, 'the Wise One', about weapons for the war . . . War! But why? Perhaps, swift-footed among the trees on the hills by the border, a Moorish vanguard was on the move? No. But soon, unhappily, 'in that land already liberated and Christian, noble Portuguese lances would be crossed against each other . . .'

Thank heavens! His pen was moving again. Paying close attention to the pages marked in a tome of Herculano's *History*, he sketched in confidently the period in which his novel took place—which began with the quarrel between Afonso II and his brothers and sisters because of the will of his father, Don Sancho I. At the beginning of this chapter, the Princes Don Pedro and Don Fernando were already despoiled of their lands and wandering through France and Lyons. Accompanying them was the powerful cousin of the Ramires, Gonçalo Mendes de Sousa, proud head of the Sousa family, who had also left the Kingdom. And now, enclosed in their castles of Montemor and Esgueira, the Princesses Dona Teresa and Dona Sancha denied Don Afonso his royal prerogative to the towns and fortresses, lands and monasteries which their father the King had so generously given them. Now, before he died in the Castle of Coimbra, Don Sancho had beseeched Tructesindo Mendes Ramires, his foster-brother and standard-bearer, knighted by himself in Lorvão, ever to serve and defend the most beloved of all his daughters, the Princess Dona Sancha, Lady of Aveiras. Thus did the Grandee swear beside the bed where, in the arms of the Bishop of Coimbra and with the Prior of the Order of the Hospital holding the candle, the dying conqueror of Silves lay, dressed in sackcloth like a penitent. But lo! a bitter quarrel arose between Afonso II, fiercely jealous of his authority as a King, and the Princesses, proud and spurred to resist by the monks of the Temple and by the prelates to whom Don Sancho had left vast slices of his kingdom. Immediately Alenquer and the surrounding areas of other castles are laid waste by the royal hosts who have returned from Navas de Tolosa. Then Dona Sancha and Dona Teresa beseech the aid of the King of Lyons who comes with his son Don Fernando into the lands of Portugal to succour the 'oppressed ladies'. At this point Uncle Duarte, in his Castle of

Santa Ireneia, asked Sancho I's standard-bearer with supreme dignity:

> 'What will you do, eldest of the Ramires?
> For if with the Leonese band you join forces,
> You betray the reigning monarch!
> But if the Princesses you leave undefended,
> You betray the oath you made the late king! . . .'

But such a doubt did not trouble the spirit of the loyal, forthright Tructesindo, whom the Nobleman of the Tower was painting in such detail. No sooner did he receive, from the brother of the alcaide of Aveiras, disguised as a mendicant friar, a message of distress that night from the Lady Dona Sancha, than he ordered his son Lourenço to reach Montemor at the first glimmer of dawn, with fifteen lances, fifty foot-soldiers from his lands and forty cross-bows. He, in the meantime, would give the alarm—and in two days would be on the march with all his kith and kin, and a stronger body of liegemen and archers, to join his cousin *Sousão* who was in the vanguard of the Leonese coming down from Alva do Douro.

So, at the first rays of dawn, the Ramires standard, the black goshawk on a scarlet background, was planted before the bristling stockade, and beside it, on the ground, tied to the post by a leather strap, shone the ancient seignorial emblem—the deep, sonorous, polished cook-pot. Throughout the castle, servants hastened back and forth, taking down helmets, and dragging heavy coats-of-mail clattering over the stones. In the yards the armourers sharpened the javelins, and lessened the discomfort of cuisses and greaves by padding them with layers of oakum. The officer-in-charge was already checking on supplies of victuals for the two hot days' march. And in all the neighbouring hamlets of Santa Ireneia, in the quiet of the afternoon, Moorish tambours sounded, muffled in the woods, rat-a-boom, rat-a-boom, or louder on the hill-tops—rat-a-tat, rat-a-tat,—summoning the mercenary horsemen and foot-soldiers drawn from the ranks of the Ramires' own men.

Meanwhile, the alcaide's brother, still disguised as a friar, returning to the castle of Aveiras with the good news of swift aid, silently crossed the drawbridge across the moat . . . Here, to relieve the sombre picture of events on the eve of war, Uncle Duarte had introduced a gallant note to his poem:

46

'And from the maiden filling the pitcher at the fountain
The friar stole a kiss and breathed "Amen"!'

But Gonçalo hesitated to mar the grandeur of that beautiful armed sortie with a friar's kiss . . . And he was pensively chewing his penholder when the door of the library creaked open.

'The post, sir.'

It was Bento with the papers and letters. The Nobleman opened only one, sealed with the enormous seal of the Barrolo arms, and pushed aside the other which he recognized as a detested letter from his Lisbon tailor. Immediately he slapped the table with the palm of his hand:

'Oh, confound it! What day is it today? The fourteenth, isn't it?'
Bento waited with his hand on the door-handle.

'It'll be sister Graça's birthday soon. I forgot completely; I always forget. And I haven't a nice present for her . . . What a nuisance!'

But the evening before, at the card-table in the Club, Manuel Duarte had announced he was paying a quick visit to Lisbon, for just three days, to see about his nephew's job in the Public Works Department. So Gonçalo hurried to Vila Clara to ask Sr Manuel Duarte to buy a pretty sunshade for her in Lisbon, a white lace one . . .

'Sr Manuel Duarte has taste, excellent taste! And tell Joaquim not to saddle the mare, as I won't be going to see Sanches Lucena. Oh, Lord, when will I get this wretched visit over? It's over three months now . . . Still, the beautiful Dona Ana won't age much in another two days, and old Lucena won't die.'

The Nobleman of the Tower, who had decided to risk the frivolous kiss, picked up his pen again and rounded off his conclusion with elegance and harmony:

'The maiden cried in fury, "Fie, fie, villain!" And the friar, whistling to himself, trotted swiftly in his sandalled feet along the stream beneath the shade of the tall beeches, while throughout the fresh valley as far as Santa Maria de Craquede, the Moorish tambours beat, rat-a-boom, rat-a-boom, summoning the Ramires' vassals in the softness of the afternoon . . .'

47

3

THROUGHOUT THAT LONG WEEK, in the quiet hours of the afternoon, the Nobleman of the Tower worked assiduously and with good results. That morning, after ringing the lunch-bell in the corridor, Bento had twice pushed open the library door and informed the Doctor that if lunch was left much longer it would certainly spoil. But bent over his sheet of foolscap, Gonçalo had grunted 'I'm coming', without putting down his pen, which swept across the paper like the keel of a boat cutting through calm water, in his haste to finish the first chapter before lunch.

Ah! what an effort this lengthy chapter had cost him all these days, with the immense tower of Santa Ireneia rising up, and the whole of a bygone age of Portuguese history to condense with a few broad strokes of the pen; and the Ramires troop to supply with provisions, and not the least ration in the saddle-bags to be forgotten, or the bolt of a cross-bow in the boxes on the mules' backs! But fortunately, he had already, the day before, moved out of the castle the body of men under Lourenço Ramires who were going to bring aid to Montemor, with a colourful glitter of helmets and lances round the unfurled standard.

Now he had reached the point where it was again night, the tattoo had sounded and the signal fire on the barbican tower burned bright, and Tructesindo Ramires had descended to the ground-floor hall of the keep to sup—when outside, in front of the moat, three loud blasts on a trumpet announced a nobleman's approach. Without the bailiff waiting to ask the lord's permission, the drawbridge rose creaking on its iron chains and clattered to rest in the stone supports. The visitor arriving in haste was Mendo Pais, friend of Afonso II and head of his Privy Council, married to the eldest daughter of Tructesindo, Dona Teresa—whose white neck and gracious walk, lighter than the flight of a bird, had earned her the nickname among the Ramires of Royal Heron. The lord of Santa Ireneia ran to the entrance to welcome his beloved son-in-law with an embrace—'a strong-limbed knight with golden locks, the fair white skin of the Gothic race . . .' And hand in hand the two entered the vaulted hall lit by torches held in rough iron holders attached to the walls.

In the middle stood the solid oaken table with stools all the way

48

round to the top where, in front of a rough linen cloth covered with tin plates and gleaming pewter tankards, the seignorial chair rose with its goshawk worked solidly in the tall back from which hung, on its silver damascened belt, Tructesindo's sword. Behind loomed the black depths of the hearth, its fire extinguished, and the space now filled with branches of pine and its mantelshelf decorated with shells between leech jars, beneath two bunches of palms brought back from Palestine by Gutierres Ramires, 'the Overseas Ramires'. Near one chimney-support, a falcon, still feathered, dozed on its perch. To one side, on a bed of rushes on the stone floor, lay two enormous hounds, also asleep, their noses on their paws and their ears trailing on the ground. Bulls made of chestnut wood supported a cask of wine in one corner. Between two iron-barred loopholes a monk, his face hidden by his hood, sat on the edge of a chest, reading an unrolled parchment in the light of a smoking candle . . . Thus did Gonçalo adorn the sombre Afonsine hall, with details taken from Uncle Duarte and Walter Scott, from narratives in *Panorama*. But what an effort it was! . . . Then, after placing on the monk's knees a folio printed in Mayence by Ulrick Zell, he had to cross out the whole erudite line when he remembered, pounding his fist on the table, that printing had not yet been invented at the time of his ancestor Tructesindo, and all he could give his monk was 'a parchment with yellowed letters'.

Pacing the echoing tiles from the fireplace to the arched doorway sealed off by a length of leather drawn to, Tructesindo, his white beard spread over his folded arms, listened to Mendes Pais who had come as relative and friend, travelling without vassals and wearing over his grey woollen tunic only a short sword and Saracen dagger. In haste and covered with dust, Mendo Pais had galloped from Coimbra to beg Tructesindo, in the name of the King and his sworn oath, not to join the forces of the Leonese and the Princesses. Already he had listed all the reasons invoked against the ladies by the learned notaries of the Council—the resolutions of the Council of Toledo, the Bull of the Apostle of Rome, Alexander, the ancient law of the Visigoths! . . . Apart from anything else, what wrong had their royal brother done the Princesses for them to call Leonese forces into Portuguese lands? None at all! Don Afonso did not deny them either authority over, or income from, the towns and castles that Don Sancho had granted them. The King of Portugal merely wanted not an inch of Portuguese soil, neither waste nor cultivated land, to lie outside his sovereignty. Mean and grasping, Don Afonso? . . . But had he not given the Lady Dona Sancha 8,000 *maravedis*?[1] And his sister's gratitude was the Leonese crossing the frontier and the fall of the beautiful castles of Ulgoso and Contrasta, of Urros and Lanhoselo! The oldest member of the House of Sousa, Gonçalo Mendes, was not with the Knights of the Cross fighting at Navas, but was serving the Princesses, behaving like a Moor, despoiling Portuguese land from Aguiar to Miranda! And already on the hills of Alem-Douro was the traitorous banner with the thirteen torteaux —and behind, sniffing the air, the Castro wolves. A threat indeed, with Christian arms menacing the Kingdoms—while Muslims and Ismaelites still roamed at large in the south of the country! The worthy lord of Santa Ireneia who had done so much to help found the Kingdom, was surely not going to destroy it, carving off some of the choicest portions for monks and rebel ladies! Thus did Mendo Pais, with nervous steps, exclaim, and so hot was he from his efforts and his emotion that he twice filled a wooden bowl with wine and swallowed it in a single draught. Then, wiping his mouth on the back of a trembling hand, he cried,

'Go to Montemor by all means, Sr Tructesindo Ramires! But go as a messenger of peace and good will, persuade your Lady Dona Sancha and the Princesses to return to him whom they must acknowledge today as their father and their King!'

The huge Lord of Santa Ireneia stopped and fixed on his son-in-law severe eyes beneath the arcs of eyebrows as shaggy and white as bramble bushes on a frosty morn.

'I will go to Montemor, Mendo Pais, but to offer my blood and the blood of my own so that those to whom justice is due should obtain justice.'

Then Mendo Pais lamented, distressed at such heroic obstinacy.

'Greater the pity! Greater the shame! It will be the good blood of noblemen spilt for evil revenge . . . Senhor Tructesindo Ramires, know that, in Canta Pedra, Lopo de Baião, the Bastard, awaits you, to impede your passage with a hundred lances!'

Tructesindo lifted his great face with such a great proud laugh that the hounds growled grimly and the falcon stretched its wings slowly as it awoke.

[1]*Maravedi:* old Gothic coin formerly used on the Peninsula.

'Good news and high hopes for me then! Now tell me, my lord head of the Privy Council, do you come with such excellent and confident news to intimidate me?'

'To intimidate you, sire? Not even the Archangel St Michael could intimidate you, were he to descend from Heaven with all his hosts and his fiery sword! Well do I know it, Sr Tructesindo Ramires. But I married in your house. And as in this battle you will not be aided by me, I want you, at least, to be well advised.'

Old Tructesindo clapped his hands to call his servants,

'Come, come, let's to supper! To supper, Friar Munio! And you, Mendo Pais, forget your worries.'

'I have no worries! What harm could I fear might come to you from a hundred or two hundred lances barring your way?'

And as the monk rolled up his parchment and approached the table, Mendo Pais added sorrowfully, slowly unbuckling his sword-belt,

'One thing only continues to worry me. And that is that this battle, my father-in-law, will put you on bad terms with your king and country.'

'Son and friend! I shall be on bad terms with king and country but on the right side of honour and conscience!'

This lofty cry of loyalty was not born in Uncle Duarte's poem. And when he discovered it, with unhoped-for inspiration, the Nobleman of the Tower flung down his pen, rubbed his hands and exclaimed in delight,

'By Jove! There's talent here!'

He concluded the chapter there and then. He was exhausted, at his work-desk since nine o'clock, reviving with intensity, and with nothing in his stomach, the mighty vigour of his forebears! He numbered the sheets, and locked *The Bard* carefully in the drawer. Then standing at the window, his waistcoat unbuttoned, he boomed forth, in the deep, grave tone that Tructesindo would have used, the fine phrase: 'I shall be on bad terms with king and country, but on the right side of honour and conscience!' And he felt these words contained the very essence of the Ramires soul, as the Ramires were in the twelfth century—sublimely loyal, bound to their word more than a saint to his vow, and, to keep their promise, ready and willing to sacrifice all their goods and peace of mind and even their lives!

Bento, who had desperately tinkled the bell once again, pushed open the library door.

'It's Pereira . . . He's downstairs in the yard and wants to speak to you, Doctor.'

Gonçalo Mendes frowned with impatience, thus dragged away from those lofty realms where he breathed the noble spirits of his race:

'Confounded nuisance! Pereira? What Pereira?'

'Pereira—Manuel Pereira da Riosa. Pereira the Brazilian.'

He was a farmer with a farm in Riosa, called the Brazilian because he had inherited twenty *contos* from an uncle, an adventurer from Pará. He had bought some land, taken the lease of the *Cortiga*, the much spoken-of lands of the Count of Monte Agra, wore a fine woollen overcoat on Sundays, and commanded sixty votes in the Parish.

'Ah, tell Pereira to come up and we'll talk over lunch . . . Have another place laid.'

✱   ✱   ✱

The dining-room of the Tower, opening through three French windows on to a wide, covered verandah, still contained, from the time of his grandfather Damião (the translator of Valerius Flaccus), two beautiful Arras tapestries representing the Expedition of the Argonauts. Porcelain from India and Japan, odd pieces of great value, filled an immense mahogany cabinet. On the marble tops of the sideboards shone the remains, still richly beautiful, of the famous Ramires plates which Bento was constantly dusting and polishing with care and affection. But Gonçalo, especially in the summer, always lunched and dined on the fresh light verandah, covered with matting and with the walls half-tiled in eighteenth century tiles, and offering in one corner, for the leisurely enjoyment of a cigar, a deep straw settee with damask cushions.

When he entered with the morning's newspapers that he had not yet opened, Pereira sat waiting for him, leaning on a huge scarlet sunshade, pensively considering the garden that stretched from there to the poplars on the banks of Horse-Kick Stream and to the gently rolling hills of Valverde. He was a thin, wiry man, all bones, with a large dark-skinned face, small blue eyes and a scruffy little beard hanging between an enormous collar secured by gold buttons. A man of property, accustomed to the City and dealing with the authorities, he held out his hand to the Nobleman of the Tower without embarrassment and accepted the chair he pushed towards the table—which was dominated by two antique crystal jugs, one full of lilies, the other holding sparkling wine.

'Well now, what good wind has blown you to the Tower, Pereira, my friend? I haven't seen you since April!'

'That's right, your Lordship, not since that Saturday when we had that heavy thunderstorm, on the eve of the elections,' agreed Pereira, stroking the handle of the sunshade which he still held between his knees.

Gonçalo, in famished haste for his lunch, rang the silver bell. Then smiling,

'And your votes, Pereira, my friend, went as usual straight to the eternal Sanches Lucena, as rivers go to the sea!'

Pereira laughed, too, with a pleased laugh that showed his bad teeth. The constituency belonged to Sanches Lucena! A well-off gentleman, good-natured, intelligent and willing to please . . .

When he got the Government's support, as had happened in April, not even Jesus Christ, if he had come down to earth and put himself up as candidate for Vila Clara, would have ousted the big man of *Feitosa*!

Bento entered leisurely, in a black lustrine jacket over a gleaming white apron, with a plate of fried eggs. The Nobleman, unfolding his napkin, screwed it up and pushed it aside distastefully.

'This napkin has been used! I'm sick of complaining. I don't mind a torn napkin, a mended one or a patched one, but I want it white and fresh every morning and smelling of lavender!'

Then noticing Pereira, who was discreetly moving back his chair:

'What? Aren't you lunching, Pereira?'

No. He thanked the Nobleman but that afternoon he was eating with his son-in-law in Bravais, as it was his grandson's birthday.

'Bravo! Congratulations, Pereira, my friend! Give him a kiss from me . . . But at least have a glass of wine.'

'I never touch either wine or water between meals, your Lordship.'

Gonçalo smelled the food, pushed aside the eggs and demanded the 'family supper', always a heavy and tasty meal at the Tower, beginning with the thick soup of bread and ham and vegetables which he had adored ever since a boy and which he called 'my big platter'. Then buttering a biscuit,

'But frankly, Pereira, this Sanches Lucena does no credit to the Constituency! He's an excellent man, of course, respectable, obsequious . . . But he's stupid, Pereira, quite stupid!'

The farmer slowly wiped his hairy nostrils with his red handkerchief, screwed up in a ball.

'He knows about things, thinks carefully . . .'

'Yes! But thought and carefulness don't stem from the brain! And then he's very old, Pereira. How old is he? Sixty?'

'Sixty-five. But from a very hardy family, your Lordship. The grandfather lasted till he was a hundred. I can remember him, in the shop.'

'How do you mean, in the shop?'

Pereira, screwing up his handkerchief even more tightly, was surprised that the Nobleman did not know the story of Sanches Lucena. The grandfather, Manuel Sanches, was a haberdasher in Porto, in Rua das Hortas. And also married to a very striking girl, very flashy . . .

'Right!' interrupted the Nobleman. 'This is all to the credit of Sanches Lucena. People who have got on, moved up . . . And I agree, Pereira, that the Constituency ought to send to Lisbon a man like Sanches Lucena, who had land and roots and interests, a name . . . But he must be a talented man, too, and a man with daring. A deputy who, in matters of great importance, in crises, will get up and move the House! And you know, Pereira, in politics, he who shouts most gets the most done. Look at the road to Riosa! It's still only down on paper, in red pencil . . . And if Sanches Lucena were the sort of man to shout in the House, Pereira would already have his carts creaking along that road.'

Pereira shook his head sadly.

'Perhaps you are right. There has never been anyone to shout loud enough about that road to Riosa. Perhaps you are right there!'

But the Nobleman was silent now, absorbed in the delicious-smelling soup served in a new tureen with sprigs of mint. Then Pereira drew his chair nearer the table, with hands that half-a-century's toil on the land had turned black and hard like roots. He stated that he had dared to intrude upon the Nobleman at lunch-time because they were going to start cutting timber the following week over near Sandim, and he wanted, before other decisions were made, to discuss with his Lordship the matter of renting the Tower.

Gonçalo stopped eating with a smile of astonishment.

'Did you want to rent the Tower, Pereira?'

'I wanted to discuss the matter with you, sir. Since Relho has been dismissed . . .'

'But I've already talked to Casco—José Casco of Bravais! We came to a sort of unofficial agreement some days ago . . . A week ago.'

Pereira slowly scratched his thin beard. What a shame, then, what a shame . . . He had heard only on Saturday about the disagreement with Relho. If the Nobleman did not take exception to the inquiry, how much had he rented it for?

'No exception at all, man! 950 *mil-reis*.'

Pereira took from his waistcoat-pocket a tortoise-shell box and slowly inhaled a pinch of snuff, his long face inclined to the ground. A great pity that, for the Nobleman's sake, too. Still, since he'd given his word . . . But it was a shame, because he liked that land; he'd been thinking of approaching the Nobleman as far back as St John's Day; and though times were somewhat difficult he had been thinking of offering 1,050—or even 1,150!

Gonçalo forgot his soup, filled by an emotion that flushed his delicate features at the suggestion of such an increase in his rent— and the excellence of such a tenant, a man distinctly well-off, with plenty of money in the bank, and the finest farmer for miles around!

'Are you serious, Pereira?'

Pereira put down his snuff-box on the table-cloth decisively.

'Your Lordship, I'm not a man to come to the Tower to make a mock of you! A serious proposal and a contract as soon as you please. But if a deal had already been made . . .'

He picked up the box and was pressing a large hand on the table to help himself up, when Gonçalo stopped him, pushing aside his plate.

'Listen, Pereira! I haven't gone into details with Casco. You know what I mean, you know how these things are . . . Casco came, we talked a bit; I asked 950 *mil-reis* and a pig at Christmas. First he agreed, yes, that was all right. Then later he changed his mind, no . . . He came back with a compadre, then later with his wife and the compadre's son, and his dog! Then again alone. He walked all over the grounds, measuring, smelling the earth; I believe he even tasted it. You know how Casco behaves! . . . Until finally, one after-

55

.

noon, he gave a groan and accepted the 950 *mil-reis*, without the pig.
I gave in about the pig. A handshake and a glass of wine. It was
arranged that he would come back to settle the matter of the papers.
I haven't seen him since, not for nearly a fortnight! I suppose he's
changed his mind, gone back on his word . . . To sum it up, I have
no firm agreement with Casco. It was a conversation in which we
merely established, as a basis to work on, the rent at 950 *mil-reis*.
And as I detest vagueness, I had already been thinking of finding a
better man!'

But Pereira scratched his chin, somewhat suspicious. He liked
things straight in business matters. He had always got on well with
Casco. Not for anything would he interfere in Casco's affairs, an
irascible, violent man. He wanted things clear-cut, he didn't want
to start a load of trouble. Nothing had been put in writing, true. But
had the Nobleman and Casco given their word or not?

Gonçalo Mendes Ramires hastily finished his soup, filled a glass
with wine to calm himself, and then looked straight, almost severely,
at the farmer.

'What a question, man! If I had given Gonçalo Ramires' word
decisively to Casco, would I be doing business with you now,
Pereira, or even merely talking to you about renting the Tower?'

Pereira lowered his head. That was true! Well, then, in that case,
he would state his offer clearly. As he knew the land and had already
made evaluation, he would offer the Nobleman 1,150 *mil-reis* and no
pig. But he would not supply the family with milk, vegetables or
fruit. The Nobleman, living alone as he did, had little use of all this.
But the Tower, being an ancient house, swarmed with dependants.
They all took whatever they could, abused their privilege . . . Anyway, that was his principle. Moreover the orchard and vegetable-
garden would supply more than enough for the Nobleman's table
and the servants. The orchard and vegetable-garden wanted looking
after better, but he, for his love of the Nobleman, would be pleased
to go over it and soon it would be splendid. As for any other conditions, he would accept those in the former lease. The papers to be
signed the following week, on Saturday . . . Was that a deal?

Gonçalo, after a moment's hesitation and nervous blinking,
offered Pereira his hand.

'Shake hands! Now we know where we are! That's giving our
word!'

'And may Our Lord bless it,' concluded Pereira, leaning on the enormous sunshade to even himself up. 'So it's Oliveira then, on Saturday, to sign the papers . . . Will you be signing, sir, or Father Soeiro?'

But the Nobleman was thinking.

'No, Pereira, that's no good. On Saturday I'll be in Oliveira, it's true, but it's my sister Maria da Graça's birthday . . .'

Pereira bared his bad teeth again in a smile of respectful affection.

'Ah, and how is Dona Maria da Graça? It's ages since I've seen her! Not since last year, at the Passiontide Procession in Oliveira . . . A lovely lady! And so friendly! And Sr José Barrolo? A really excellent person, too, Sr José Barrolo . . . And what fine land he has, the *Ribeirinha*! The best estate for twenty leagues around! Beautiful land! André Cavalheiro's place, *Biscaia*, which adjoins it, bears no comparison—it's like a thistle to a cabbage.'

The Nobleman of the Tower, peeling a peach, smiled,

'Nothing of André Cavalheiro's is any good, Pereira! Neither land nor soul!'

The farmer seemed surprised. He had imagined the Nobleman and Cavalheiro were still close friends. Not in politics, no! But privately, as two gentlemen.

'What? Myself and Cavalheiro? Neither as gentlemen nor as politicians. Because he is neither gentleman nor politician. He's nothing but a *cavalo*—a horse—and a resentful one at that.'

Pereira remained silent, eyes on the table. Then repeating the arrangements,

'So that's understood, then, on Saturday in the city. And if it's no trouble to your Lordship, we'll go to Guedes, the notary, and have the matter settled. Your Lordship will be going to your sister's house, of course . . .'

'As usual. Come at three o'clock. We'll talk to Father Soeiro while we're there.'

'It's ages since I've seen Father Soeiro, too.'

'Oh, the ungrateful creature rarely puts in an appearance at the Tower these days. He's always in Oliveira, with sister Graça, the apple of his eye . . . Won't you even have a glass of port, Pereira? . . . Right, then, till Saturday. Don't forget my kiss to your grandson.'

'That I couldn't forget, your Lordship . . . No, really! You mustn't get up! I know my way down the steps perfectly well, and I

57

must drop into the kitchen, anyway, for a word with Aunt Rosa. I've known the Tower since the time of your papa, God rest his soul! And I had always hoped to have the grounds under my cultivation and see them grow into something to be proud of!'

Over coffee, his newspapers forgotten, Gonçalo enjoyed the excellent deal he had made. Two hundred extra *mil-reis*. And the Tower in the hands of Pereira, with his love of the soil and his knowledge of farming which had transformed the barren land of Monte Agra into a marvellous stretch of cornfields and vineyards and vegetable-gardens! Apart from which he was well-off, capable of paying in advance. This was yet another piece of evidence of the value of the Tower, this eagerness of Pereira's—so careful and stingy—to rent it. He almost regretted not getting 1,200 out of him. There was no doubt the morning had been fruitful. And really there had been no hard and fast agreement with Casco. They had merely had a talk on the possible leasing of the Tower, to be discussed in more detail later, at a proposed rent of 950 *mil-reis*. And how foolish he would have been, through over-scrupulous attention to that conversation, if he had refused Pereira and retained Casco—a mediocre farmer—the sort that scratches everything out of the land to get enough to eat and leaves it poorer every year, exhausted, sucked dry!

'Bento, bring me some cigars! And tell Joaquim to have the mare saddled for five to five-thirty. I'm at last going to *Feitosa*. Today's the day!'

He lit a cigar and returned to the library. Once again he read the magnificent final line: 'I shall be on bad terms with king and country but on the right side of honour and conscience!' Ah, how the very soul of the ancient Portuguese burst forth in that cry, with his devout love and respect for his word and honour! And standing beside the verandah, with his sheet of foolscap between his fingers, he considered the Tower for a moment, the dusty, iron-barred loopholes, the solid battlements which remained intact, and over which now swept a flock of pigeons . . . How many mornings, in the fresh hours of dawn, had Tructesindo leaned against those battlements, then new and white! All the land around, cultivated or untilled, had undoubtedly belonged to the Grandee. And Pereira, at that time serf or farm-hand, would have approached his lord only on his knees and trembling. But he would not have paid 1,150 *mil-reis* in legal tender. But neither would Grandpa Tructesindo have needed it, by Jove!

When the bags of money were growing scarce in the chests, and his people beginning to mutter about the delay in receiving their wages, the loyal Grandee had the ill-defended granaries and cellars of the small towns round about supply him—or else at a bend in the road the tax-collector returning from collecting the royal dues, or the Genoese pedlar, his mules laden with packages. Beneath the Tower (as Papa used to relate), the feudal dungeons remained heaped with litter now but with the remains of iron chains still visible, attached to pillars, and in the vaulted roof the ring from which had hung the strappado, and on the stone floor the holes where the rack had stood. And in this deaf, damp hole, tax-collector and pedlar, priests and even bourgeois from free towns had screamed beneath the whip or on the rack, until they surrendered, in agony, their last *maravedi*. Ah, the romantic Tower, praised so lovingly by Videirinha's songs on moonlit nights, how much torture it had seen and concealed!

Suddenly, with a yell, Gonçalo seized a volume of Walter Scott from the table and flung it mercilessly, like a stone, against the trunk of a beech-tree. He had caught a glimpse of Rosa the cook's cat, creeping up the tree, claws dug into a branch, arching its back ready to spring on a nest of blackbirds.

*   *   *

When Gonçalo, elegant in his new riding-suit, black polished gaiters and white chamois gloves, brought his mare to a halt that afternoon in front of the gate of *Feitosa*, a tattered old man with long white hair falling over his shoulders and an abundant beard covering his chest immediately got up from the stone bench where he had been sitting eating slices of smoked sausage and drinking from a gourd. He informed Gonçalo that Sr Sanches Lucena and Dona Ana had gone out in their carriage. Gonçalo asked the old man to ring the bell, and handed a card to the boy who half-opened the richly-worked gilt gate with an S and an L interwoven beneath the coronet of a count.

'Is Sr Sanches Lucena well?'

'The Counsellor is a little better now.'

'What? Has he been ill?'

'The Counsellor was seriously ill three or four weeks ago.'

'Oh, I'm terribly sorry! Tell the Counsellor I'm extremely sorry!'

He called the old man who had pulled the bell and gave him a *tostão* for his trouble. Curious about his long beard and flowing locks, like those of a beggar in a melodrama, he asked:

'Do you beg around these parts?'

The man raised his dirty, bloodshot eyes, red from dust and sun but nevertheless smiling—almost happy.

'I go to the Tower, too, your Lordship. And thanks be to God, they treat me very well there.'

'Then when you go again, tell Bento . . . You know Bento?'

'Do I know him? And Senhora Rosa . . .'

'Then tell Bento to give you some trousers, man! You're not decent with the trousers you've got on!'

The old man laughed, a slow, toothless smile, looking with fondness at the sordid rags that flapped around his shins, blacker and more fleshless than winter branches.

'They're torn and tattered, it's true . . . But Sr Dr Julio says they suit me that way. Dr Julio, when I call, always takes my photograph. I went by there last week . . . He took one with chains hanging from my wrist and a sword raised high . . . I believe it was to show the Government.'

Gonçalo laughed and clapped the spurs to his mare. He considered prolonging his journey to Valverde; then he would come back via Vila Clara and tempt Gouveia to share the roast goat on the cherrywood spit in the Tower, to which he had invited Manuel Duarte and Tító the previous evening at the Club. But as he was crossing the 'Cross of Souls', where the road from Corinde, so pretty with its lines of poplars, crossed the hill from Valverde, he stopped. He had noticed in the distance, towards Corinde, an indistinct mass which could be a cartload of firewood and a butcher's gig, a woman with a red scarf waving her arms from the saddle of a donkey, and two farm-hands with spades on their shoulders. Then suddenly the whole scene broke up—the woman trotting off on her little donkey, out of sight behind some trees; the gig bouncing away in a light cloud of dust; the cart advancing with a slow creaking noise towards the 'Cross of Souls' and the labourers walking down towards a stretch of land between the ridges of a hay-field. The only creature remaining in the road, as if abandoned, was a man with his jacket over his shoulders, limping along painfully. Gonçalo, curious, trotted over.

'What happened? What's the matter with you?'

The man, with one leg drawn up, raised a pained, wincing face, almost unconscious, shining with beads of sweat.

'May God give you a good afternoon, your Lordship! What do you suppose is the matter with me? The trials of life!'

And groaning incessantly, he told his story. For months now he had suffered from a sore on his ankle, which had not dried up, with either plasters, the powder of myrtle-berries or charms . . . And now he was on his way up to see to one of the terraces on Dr Julio's land, to help a friend who was ill with malaria, and whoosh! a rock falls down straight on to the sore leg, scrapes off some skin, splinters the bone and leaves him in that sorry state! He'd even ripped the tail from his shirt to mop up the blood and tie on top of his handkerchief.

'But you can't walk like that, man! Where are you from?'

'From Corinde, your Lordship. Manuel Soalha, from the little village of Finta. I'll get myself there somehow.'

'How about all these people here a few minutes ago? Wasn't there one of them who could help you? A gig, two strong men . . .'

A sudden, extra-sharp pain, from attempting to put down his foot, wrenched a cry from Solha. But he smiled as he panted . . . What did his Lordship expect? Everyone is in a hurry, has his own business to attend to . . . And the girl on the donkey had promised to pass by Finta and inform them. Perhaps one of his boys would turn up with the mare he had bought at Easter—and which, unfortunately, also limped!

The Nobleman leapt lightly to the ground.

'Here: one mare's as good as another. Take mine!'

Solha gazed at Gonçalo in amazement.

'What an idea! Holy Father! . . . So am I supposed to ride on horseback while your Lordship goes on foot?'

Gonçalo laughed.

'Listen, man, with all this talk of "you on horseback," and "I on foot", and "please do" and "no, thank you," we're losing precious time. Get up there, keep quiet and trot on to Finta.'

The man withdrew to the edge of the road, shaking his head and staring in alarm as if witnessing a sacrilege.

'Definitely not, your Lordship, definitely not! I'd rather die here of starvation, with the sore all rotten!'

Gonçalo stamped his foot imperiously.

'Get up, there, I'm the one who gives the orders here! You're a farm-labourer and I am a doctor graduated from Coimbra: I am the one who knows and I am the one who gives the orders!'

Solha, immediately surrendering in face of the dazzling power of superior wisdom, silently caught hold of the mare's mane, respectfully put his foot in the stirrup, helped by the Nobleman who, without removing his white gloves, lifted the foot bandaged in rags and stained with blood.

Then, when he was in the saddle with a relieved 'Ah', Gonçalo asked,

'How's that?'

All the man could do was mutter the name of Our Lord, in gratitude and wonder at such charity.

'But this is all topsy-turvy . . . Me, here, on the Nobleman's mare, and the Nobleman, Sr Gonçalo Ramires of the Tower, on foot in the road!'

Gonçalo joked, and to shorten the journey, asked about Dr Julio's estate where improvements were going on and vines being planted. Then, as Manuel Solha knew Pereira the Brazilian (who was thinking of leasing Dr Julio's lands), they discussed this wily man and the excellence of *Cortiga*. Unembarrassed now, sitting erect in the saddle and enjoying this intimacy with the Nobleman of the Tower, Solha had forgotten his sore, the tormenting pain. And walking alongside the stirrups, attentive and smiling, the Nobleman hurried along in the dust.

Thus they approached the Holy Fountain, one of the spots best celebrated in song of all the beautiful countryside. There, the road, cut out of the side of a hill, widened, forming an open space, from which one could see the whole valley of Corinde with its numerous farm-houses and groves of trees, cornfields and streams. Out of the slope of the hill, covered with oak-trees and mossy crags, gushed the famous spring which even in the time of King João V, had been known to cure abdominal troubles—and a devout lady of Corinde, Dona Rosa Miranda Carneiro, had had it piped down from the top to a marble tank, from which it now flowed to the benefit of all through a bronze spout, beneath the image and auspices of Santa Rosa de Lima. On each side of the tank curved two long stone benches, shaded and cooled by the spreading branches of the oaks. It is a quiet spot where one can pick violets, have picnics, and where ladies of the nieghbourhood can sit and chat on Sunday afternoons, listening to the blackbirds and enjoying the bright, well-populated and verdurous expanse of valley.

Before, however, opening on to the Holy Fountain, near the small village of Serdal, there is a sharp bend in the road from Corinde, and there, suddenly, the mare stopped with a jerk, ears pricked, which obliged the Nobleman of the Tower, distrusting Solha's horsemanship, to lay a hand on the reins. It was the unexpected sight of a carriage—a calash lined in blue, with a pair of horses covered with white nets against flies, and on the cushions, very erect, a coachman with a moustache, uniform with a scarlet collar and a hat with a yellow cockade. Gonçalo was still holding the mare by the rein like a loyal muleteer on a dangerous path, when he saw, sitting on one of the stone-benches, beside the fountain, with a rug over his knees, the elderly Sanches Lucena. At his side crouched a footman, cleaning with a handful of grass the boot that Dona Ana held out to him, catching up her unbleached linen gown with one hand and laying the other, gloveless, on her slim, inclined waist.

The extraordinary appearance of the Nobleman of the Tower, tugging at the reins of his mare, astride which calmly sat a labourer in shirt-sleeves, disturbed the calm of that peaceful, sleepy corner. Sanches Lucena stared, his glasses stared, in a burst of curiosity which brought him to his feet, his neck stuck out and his rug fallen onto the grass. Dona Ana swiftly withdrew her foot, adopted an air of haughtiness and gravity befitting the lady of *Feitosa*, picking up, like a badge of office, her gold-handled gold lorgnette hanging by its golden chain. Even the footman grinned in astonishment at Solha.

But Gonçalo, with his usual ease and elegance, had already greeted Dona Ana and warmly clasped the astonished hand of Sanches Lucena and was now rejoicing in this happy meeting, because he had just come from *Feitosa*! There he had learnt from a servant, an exaggeration no doubt, that the Counsellor had been ill these last weeks. How was he? Was he well? He looked excellent!

'Don't you agree, Dona Ana? He looks admirably well!'

With a soft movement of her head and a gentle wave of the cluster of white feathers on her red straw hat, she replied in a slow, thick, cooing voice which made Gonçalo shudder,

'Sanches is enjoying better health now, thanks be to God.'

'A little better, yes, thank you, Sr Gonçalo Ramires!' murmured the bent, lean old man, pulling back the rug over his knees.

With his glasses glittering and fixed on Gonçalo, and a burning curiosity that almost set his sharp, waxen face aglow, he went on,

'But excuse me, sir! What are you doing walking along the Corinde road in this state, on foot, holding the reins while a labourer goes mounted?'

Laughing, especially in the direction of Dona Ana, whose beautiful black eyes with their deep, liquid radiance were also waiting, serious and reserved, Gonçalo recounted the accident suffered by the good man whom he had met on the road, dragging a wounded leg . . .

'So I offered him my mare . . . And if you'll permit me, sir, and you, madam, I must see about the rest of his journey . . .'

He turned to Solha who, intimidated once again by the presence of the lady and gentleman from *Feitosa*, sat crouched in the saddle, hat in hand, as if trying to reduce his stature, and removed his feet from the stirrups, ready to dismount. But Gonçalo told him to trot on to Finta and send the mare back with one of his boys to the Holy Fountain, where he would stay a while with the Counsellor. When Solha set off, profusely acknowledging his gratitude, contorted in the saddle as if impelled, in spite of himself, by the smiles and waves with which the Nobleman bade him farewell, Sanches Lucena's astonishment burst out once more.

'Really, a thing like that! I could have imagined anything except Sr Gonçalo Mendes Ramires holding a labourer's reins on the road from Corinde! It's a repetition of the Good Samaritan . . . But even better!'

Gonçalo joked with him, sitting beside him on the stone bench. Oh, the Good Samaritan had not deserved such a complimentary passage of the Gospels merely for offering his donkey to a sick Levite: he must have had far greater virtues . . . And smiling to Dona Ana, who was sitting on the other side of Sanches Lucena, casting her lorgnette with majestic languor over the trees and spring she knew so well, he said,

'It's two years, madam, since I had the honour . . .'

But Sanches Lucena gave a shout,

'Oh, Sr Gonçalo Ramires! You've got blood on your hand, sir!'

The Nobleman looked, startled. On the white chamois glove were two purplish stains.

'It's not my blood! It must have been when Solha mounted and I held his wounded foot.'

He tore off the glove and threw it into the weeds behind the stone bench. And continuing to smile,

'No, madam, I haven't had the pleasure of seeing you since the Baron of Marges' ball in Oliveira, that famous Carnival Ball. It's over two years, when I was still a student. I remember that you were magnificently dressed as Catherine of Russia . . .'

As he smiled upon her with his beautiful, tender eyes, he thought, 'Splendid creature! But common! And what a voice!' Dona Ana also remembered the Marges' Ball.

'You are mistaken, sir. I didn't go as a Russian, I went as an Empress . . .'

'That's right, the Empress of Russia, the Great Catherine. And such taste! Such opulence!'

Sanches Lucena turned his gold spectacles slowly towards Gonçalo and pointed a long, pale finger at him.

'And I remember your sister, too, Senhora Dona Graça. She was dressed as a Viana peasant . . . It was a sumptuous reception, which is to be expected—our Marges is always a magnificent host . . . And I haven't seen your sister to talk to since that evening. Only at a distance, in church . . .'

He did not often live in his house in Oliveira these days, however, although he kept it ready for use with servants and horses; whether it was the air or the water, he did not know, but living in the city did not agree with him.

Gonçalo's interest quickened.

'But actually, sir, what is it you have had?'

Sanches Lucena gave a bitter smile. The doctors in Lisbon had not known exactly. Some attributed it to the stomach, others to the heart. Whatever it was, some essential part was impaired. And he had attacks—severe attacks. Still, with God's help and a strict diet and plenty of milk and rest he hoped to last a few years longer.

'Oh, of course, of course!' exclaimed Gonçalo cheerfully. 'And don't you find that your visits to Lisbon and the House and politics —the terrible politics—excite you and exhaust you?'

No, on the contrary, Sanches Lucena got on quite well in Lisbon. Better than in *Feitosa*! He enjoyed the distraction of the House. And as he had friends in the Capital, a small, select circle . . .

'One of our most excellent friends you must know, sir. He is a relative of yours—Don João da Pedrosa.'

65

Gonçalo, not knowing the man, or even the name, murmured politely,

'Yes, yes, Don João, of course . . .'

Sanches Lucena continued, passing a skeletal hand over his white whiskers, an almost transparent hand displaying an enormous sapphire signet ring,

'And not only Don João . . . Another of our friends is a relation of yours, sir, too, a close one. We have often spoken of you and your family. Because he, too, belongs to the highest nobility—Arronches Manrique.'

'Such a friendly gentleman, such an amusing gentleman!' added Dona Ana, with a conviction that made her bosom rise—a bosom whose perfection and fresh exuberance was accentuated by her well-fitted jacket.

Gonçalo had never heard of this sonorous name either, but he did not hesitate.

'Oh, Manrique, of course . . . But really, I have so many relations in Lisbon and I go there so seldom! . . . And you, madam, Senhora Dona Ana . . .'

But Sanches Lucena insisted, delighted with this conversation about aristocratic parentage,

'You naturally have all your noble relations in Lisbon, sir. I believe you are the cousin of the Duke of Lourençal, are you not? Duarte Lourençal! He does not use his title through Miguelism,[1] or rather through habit, but nevertheless he is the legitimate Duke of Lourençal. He is the representative of the House of Lourençal.'

Gonçalo, smiling attentively, unbuttoned his coat to get out his old leather cigar-case.

'Yes, that's right, Duarte . . . We are cousins. He says we are cousins, so I suppose we must be. I understand so little of genealogical trees! There is indeed so much interbreeding in Portuguese families; we are all related to each other, not only through Adam, but also through the Goths . . . And you, Dona Ana, madam, do you prefer living in Lisbon?'

But noticing that he had taken out a cigar and had distractedly bitten off its end, he exclaimed,

---

[1] Miguelism: Political party of Don Miguel of Braganza, King of Portugal (1828–1834).

'Oh, forgive me, madam . . . I was going to smoke without asking if you . . .'

She acknowledged his apology, lowering her long lashes.

'You may smoke, dear sir. Sanches does not smoke, but I like the smell.'

Gonçalo thanked her, privately nauseated by that thick, sugary voice, that awful 'dear sir' and 'this gentleman' and 'the other gentleman' . . . But he also thought, 'What magnificent skin! What a beautiful creature!' And Sanches Lucena inexorably continued, extending a bony finger,

'The person I don't know very well is Don Duarte Lourençal, I haven't that consummate honour as yet, but his brother, Sr Don Filipe. A most excellent, excellent gentleman, as you yourself must know, sir. And what talent, too! What talent on the cornet!'

'Ah!'

'What, do you mean, sir, you have never heard your cousin, Don Filipe Lourençal play the cornet?'

Even the beautiful Dona Ana was aroused, and a soft smile appeared on her full lips, redder than ripe cherries, over the fresh gleam of her small teeth.

'Oh, he plays divinely! Sanches is very fond of music; and so am I . . . But you understand, here in the country, with no resources . . .'

Gonçalo, flinging aside the match, at once exclaimed, with sincere interest,

'Then you ought to hear a friend of mine, Videirinha, who's really marvellous on the guitar!'

Sanches Lucena was surprised at the name and its commonness. The Nobleman added simply,

'The boy is a dear friend of mine. He comes from Vila Clara—José Videira, the chemist's assistant . . .'

Sanches Lucena's glasses glittered in sheer amazement.

'The chemist's assistant and a friend of Sr Gonçalo Mendes Ramires!'

Yes, from their student days, when they had taken exams together at the Liceu. Videirinha had even spent his holidays at the Tower, with his mother who used to work there as a seamstress. Such a fine boy, so simple and friendly . . . And really, on the guitar he was a genius!'

'He's got a marvellous ballad at the moment called *The Fado of the Ramires.* The music is actually a Coimbra fado, a well-known one. But the verses are his, amusing little quatrains on incidents in our family history—legends and fictitious tales . . . He's made a superb fado out of it. Only the other day he was in the Tower with myself and Titó . . .'

At this familiar, boyish name, Sanches Lucena gave another start: 'Titó?'

The Nobleman laughed.

'It's an old nickname of ours for António Vilalobos.'

Sanches Lucena then flung his arms in the air as if someone very dear to him had appeared down the road.

'António Vilalobos! But he's one of our very closest and most faithful friends! A most excellent, excellent gentleman! Almost every week he's kind enough to visit us at *Feitosa* . . .'

Now it was the Nobleman's turn to be amazed at such an intimacy to which Titó had never once alluded when in Gago's, or in the Tower, or at the Club when the name of Sanches Lucena was bandied about in political discussion.

'Ah, you know him, sir . . .'

But Dona Ana, who had got up abruptly from the bench and stooped to pick up her glove and sunshade, reminded her husband that it was growing cooler and there was always a mist at that hour of the day from the warm valley.

'You know it never does you any good . . . And it doesn't do the horses any good either, standing still like that for so long.'

At once Sanches Lucena apprehensively pulled a thick white silk scarf from his pocket to wrap round his neck. And apprehensive, too, for the horses, he at once got up laboriously from the stone bench with a weary sign to the footman to pick up the rug and tell the coachman. However, stooped and leaning on his stick, he crossed over to the parapet which bordered the road above the sharp drop to the valley below. And he confessed to Gonçalo that that was his favourite spot in the neighbourhood of *Feitosa*. Not only because of the place, the praises of which had been sung by 'our melodious Cunha Torres', but because from the terrace of the Fountain, effortlessly, seated on the bench, he could see his extensive lands.

'Look there, sir, beyond those chestnut trees as far as the plain, and that hillock where that little yellow house is, with the pinewood behind, that's all mine . . . The pinewood's mine, too. Over there, from that row of poplars, this side of the pasture, that's mine, too. That bit over by the chapel belongs to Monte Agra. But beyond that, beyond that grove of holm-oaks, it's my land again, all up that hill!'

The livid finger, the skinny arm within the black cashmere sleeve, rose above the valley. Beyond those pastures, past the cornfields . . . Then that wild land—all his! And behind the thin bent figure with his hat stuck on the back of his head, the scarf pulled up to the pallid ears which seemed barely attached, stood Dona Ana, white and healthy like a marble statue, an oblivious smile on her greedy lips, her beautiful bosom swelling, accompanying the lengthy enumeration as she cast her lorgnette over the pastures and the pinewoods and the cornfields, already thinking—'All mine!'

'Now, over there, behind the olive grove,' concluded Sanches Lucena respectfully, 'belongs to you, Sr Gonçalo Mendes Ramires.'

'To me?'

'To you, sir, or rather it's connected with your family. Don't you recognize it? Over there beyond the windmill goes the road to Santa Maria de Craquede. The tombs of your ancestors lie there. That's another ride I like occasionally. Only about a month ago we visited the ruins thoroughly. And you can imagine how impressed I was! The most ancient part of the monastery, those great stone coffins, the sword fixed to the vaulted roof above the tomb in the middle . . . It's really moving! And I consider it very fine of you, very filial, sir, to keep that bronze lamp alight night and day . . .'

Gonçalo mumbled a reply with a smile, because he could not remember the sword and had never ordered the lamp to be kept alight. But Sanches Lucena was now asking a very special favour of Sr Gonçalo Mendes Ramires. Would he allow them to drive him to the Tower in their carriage? Gonçalo refused in some alarm. He could not! He had arranged with the man with the sore leg to wait there at the Fountain for his mare.

'But my footman can wait here and take it to the Tower for you.'

'No, no, sir. If you don't mind, I'll wait. Then I'll cut along the path by Crassa because I have to be at the Tower by eight o'clock, because I have Titó coming to dinner.'

Dona Ana, from the middle of the road, immediately hurried her husband along with renewed warnings of the cold, of the damp night air. But beside the calash, Sanches Lucena stopped once more to assure Gonçalo, his bony hands on his chest, that he would never forget that afternoon.

'Because I saw a thing that has seldom before been seen: the greatest nobleman in Portugal, walking along the Corinde road, leading by the reins, on his own horse, a common labourer!'

Aided by Gonçalo, he climbed laboriously up the steps. Dona Ana was already ensconced in the cushions, clasping aloft in her hands, like an insignia, the shining handle of the golden lorgnette. The footman stiffened and crossed his arms, and the sumptuous calash, with the white splashes of the horses' nets, merged into the silence and semi-darkness of the road, beneath the spreading branches of the beeches.

'What a bore!' exclaimed Gonçalo, annoyed at wasting such a lovely afternoon. An intolerable person, that Sanches Lucena, with his Don This, and Don That, and his vain talk of his 'select circle', and 'all mine' over hill and dale! His wife was a splendid piece of meat, as befitted a butcher's daughter, but without the slightest scrap of charm or soul. And what a voice, good Lord, what a voice! Fawning, pretentious creature! All he now wanted was to get his mare back and gallop off home to the Tower and give vent to his nausea for the Sanches couple, to Titó, friend of the *Feitosa* household!

The mare was not long arriving, at a canter, mounted by Solha's son who, immediately he caught sight of the Nobleman, leapt to the ground, and hat in hand, blushing and bowing, stammered that his father had reached home safely and prayed God to repay the Nobleman's kindness.

'All right, all right! Regards to your father and tell him I hope he's soon better. I'll send someone along to see how he's getting on.'

He leapt into the saddle and galloped via the easy short-cut through Crassa. But at the gate of the Tower he found a boy from Gago's with a note from Titó telling him that he was unable to come to the Tower as he was leaving that week for Oliveira.

'How ridiculous! I'm going to Oliveira, too, but I'm still dining today! He could even have come with me in the carriage . . . What was Don António doing when you left?'

The boy thoughtfully scratched his head.

'Senhor Don António came to the house for me to bring the message . . . But I believe there's some party on, because he went to

Uncle Cosmo's, the firework-seller, and bought some fire-crackers . . .'

Those unexpected fire-crackers made the Nobleman exceedingly envious.

'Where's the party, do you know?'

'I don't know, your Lordship . . . But it seems like a big do because Sr João Gouveia ordered two big plates of cod pasties from the boss.'

Cod pasties! Gonçalo felt as if he had been cruelly betrayed.

'The beasts!'

Suddenly he thought of a good revenge:

'If you see Sr Don António or Sr João Gouveia again today, don't forget to tell them that I'm very sorry . . . That I was having a party here at the Tower tonight, too. And there were ladies coming. Sra Dona Ana was coming. Don't forget, will you?'

Gonçalo leapt up the steps laughing at his joke. But later that evening, at nine o'clock, after a vast, lengthy dinner with Manuel Duarte, he went into the portrait-room, lit only by the gilt lantern in the corridor, to fetch a box of cigars. He glanced casually out of the open window and saw a man below, beneath the shade of the poplars, prowling round and watching . . . Looking more attentively, he thought he recognized the powerful shoulders and bovine walk of Tító. But no, it couldn't be—the man was wearing a woollen jacket and hood. Curious now, treading stealthily, he moved over to the verandah. The shape, however, had left the road and disappeared into the trees of a lane that went round by Miranda's farm and led on to the road in Portela, near the first houses in Vila Clara.

4

THE MANSION BELONGING to the Barrolos in Oliveira (known since the beginning of the century as the *Cunhais*) had its aristocratic façade with its twelve verandahs overlooking King's Square, between the deserted little lane that led to the barracks and Weaver's Street, an old, badly cobbled street, steep and narrowed by the long terrace of the garden and by the front wall of the ancient yard of the Monica nuns. This morning, just as Gonçalo, in the calash from the Tower driven by Torto and his pair, entered King's Square, who should be coming up Weaver's Street round the corner of *Cunhais*, on a black horse with a magnificent mane, its hooves striking the cobbles with elegance and nobility, but the Civil Governor, André Cavaleiro, in a white waistcoat and straw hat. With a quick glance from the depths of the calash, the Nobleman caught him lifting his long-lashed, black eyes to the iron-barred verandahs of the mansion. He started, slapping his knee and growling 'scoundrel' under his breath. When he dismounted at the door (a low door which seemed crushed by the weight of the immense coat-of-arms of the Sas above it), he was seized by such overwhelming indignation that he did not notice the effusive welcome of the old door-keeper Joaquim, and left the presents which he had brought for Gracinha—the sunshade and a basket of flowers from the Tower, wrapped in tissue paper—behind him in the carriage. Upstairs, in the waiting-room, where he was met by José Barrolo who had hurried there when he heard the rattle of the old carriage in the silent square, he at once gave vent to his anger, in a fit of rage, flinging down his dust-coat on to a leather chair.

'Heavens above! Can't I come to this city without immediately coming face to face with that animal Cavaleiro! Always here in the Square, in front of the house! What confounded luck! Can't he find some other place, he and his bushy moustache, to cavort with his jade?'

José Barrolo, a plump young man with curly red hair and a narrow, fair moustache on his face which was rounder and redder than a ripe apple, replied ingenuously,

'Jade? Oh, my dear fellow, he has a beautiful horse at the moment! A beautiful horse, that he bought from Marges!'

'All right, then. So he's an ugly donkey on the back of a beautiful horse. Let the pair of them keep to their stable. Or let them go and graze over Devesas!'

Barrolo's large mouth, showing his superb teeth, sagged in awe. Then suddenly, doubled up and stamping his feet on the floor, he burst into a roar of laughter which nearly choked him, his veins swelling with blood:

'Oh, that's wonderful! The Club ought to hear that . . . An ugly donkey on the back of a beautiful horse! And both of them grazing! You're on top form today, dear fellow! What a joke! Both of them grazing—the Civil Governor and his horse . . . Oh, that's wonderful!'

He rolled round the room, clapping radiant hands on fat thighs. Gonçalo, somewhat appeased by the ovation applauding his facetiousness, added,

'Here, let me give you a hug—if I can get round you! How's the family? Gracinha? Ah, here's the flower herself!'

It was her, running delightedly with her light, childish step towards her brother, her magnificent hair flying loose over a lace peignoir. He clasped her in his arms and gave her two noisy kisses. Immediately, taking a step back, he declared that she looked prettier, plumper . . .

'You're definitely plumper—taller even! What is it? A nephew for me? No, nothing yet?'

Gracinha blushed, with that slow, gentle smile of hers which made her green-hued eyes still tenderer.

'If she doesn't want an heir, she doesn't!' cried José Barrolo, swaying about, his hands deep in the pocket of his jacket which accentuated his fat hips. 'It's not her old man's fault . . . She just doesn't want one!'

The Nobleman of the Tower chided his sister.

'We need a boy, you know. I won't marry. I'm not the sort: and if you don't co-operate it will be the end of both Barrolos and Ramires! The extinction of the Barrolos would be a good thing. But if the Ramires die out, it will be the end of Portugal. So, therefore, Dona Graça Ramires, hurry up, in the name of the Nation, a son and heir! A nice big fat heir whom I propose should be called Tructesindo!'

Barrolo protested in horror.

'What? Tructesindo? Not likely! If that's to be his fate, I'm not having anything to do with it!'

But Gracinha put a stop to these spicy jokes, asking after the Tower and Bento and Rosa the cook and the garden and the peacocks. As they talked, they made their way into the adjoining room which had three verandahs overlooking the Square and was adorned with Indian cabinets and heavy gilt and blue damask chairs. Barrolo rolled a cigarette and demanded the story of Relho and the row. He had also fallen out with the leaseholder of *Ribeirinha* because of some pines that had been cut. But this row with Relho was really something tremendous.

Gonçalo, sunk in the corner of the deep, blue sofa, lazily unbuttoning his light cheviot jacket, answered,

'No, it was all very simple. For months now Relho had been in a permanently drunken state ... One night he let out a shout, threatened Rosa and seized a gun. I went downstairs and in a flash the Tower was rid of Relho and rows.'

'Didn't the local officer come, with his men?'

Gonçalo shrugged his shoulders impatiently.

'The officer came, but only afterwards, to keep things legal! The man had already taken himself off, and at the run! As a result I have leased the Tower to Pereira, Pereira da *Riosa* ...'

He told them about this excellent piece of business, settled on the verandah at lunch, between two glasses of sparkling wine. Barrolo admired the rent and complimented him on the leaseholder. Couldn't Gonçalo discover another Pereira for the Treixedo land?—such rich soil and so badly cultivated.

Sitting on the edge of the sofa, her beautiful hair, which she had washed that morning and which smelt of lavender, falling over her shoulders, Gracinha gazed at her brother tenderly.

'How's your stomach now? Are you better? Do you still indulge in suppers with Titó?'

'Oh, that brute!' cried Gonçalo. 'A couple of days ago he promised to dine with me at the Tower, and Rosa even roast a young goat on the spit, magnificent ... Then he didn't come: I believe he had some infamous orgy with fire-crackers even. He's coming to Oliveira this week ... Oh, that's another thing—did you know Titó was on close terms with Sanches Lucena?'

He recounted then, with happy exaggeration, their meeting at the

74

Holy Fountain, the horror the beautiful Dona Ana had inspired in him, the unexpected discovery of Titö's familiarity with *Feitosa*.

Barrolo recalled that one afternoon, some time before St John's Day, he had seen Tító parading up and down in front of *Feitosa*'s front gate with a little white lap-dog on a lead.

'But what I don't understand, my boy, is this "horror" of yours for Dona Ana! By Jove, she's a superb woman! The movement of the hips when she walks, those enormous eyes, those breasts . . .'

'Enough of this foul talk, you libertine!' cried Gonçalo. 'How can you, beside your wife here, flower of all the Graces, dare to praise such a lump of meat!'

Gracinha, laughing and without feelings of jealousy, declared that she could understand José's admiration. Really, Ana Lucena was so beautiful, so striking!

'Yes,' agreed Gonçalo, 'beautiful like a beautiful mare . . . But that voice of hers, thick and haughty . . . And her lorgnette and her manners . . . And her "this gentleman", and "the other gentleman" . . . Oh God, she's awful!'

Barrolo swayed about in front of the sofa, his hands plunged in the pockets of his short jacket.

'Sour grapes, Senhor Don Gonçalo, sour grapes!'

The Nobleman turned in fury to his brother-in-law.

'Not even if she offered herself to me on her knees, in her chemise, with Sanches' two hundred *contos* on a gold platter!'

Smiling, as red as a peony, and with a scandalized 'Oh', Gracinha smacked her brother's arm as he pulled her playfully towards him.

'Give me your cheek again, and another kiss, to purify us! Really, merely thinking about Dona Ana is enough to encourage people to violent fancies . . . You were asking about my stomach. Yes, dear, it's a bit upset. And heavier, too, the last few days, ever since the goat on the spit and the company of that tippler Manuel Duarte. Have you got any Vidago water here? . . . Barrolinho, be an angel and have a bottle, a nice, cold one, sent up. Oh and ask if they have sent up a basket and a cardboard-box I left in the calash. Have them put in my room. And don't unwrap them, it's a surprise . . . Listen! And have some hot water sent in to me. I need a complete change of clothes. There were clouds of dust all the way!'

When Barrolo waddled out whistling, Gonçalo rubbed his hands and exclaimed,

75

'You're looking splendid, the pair of you! Beginning to complement each other perfectly. You are definitely looking fitter, plumper. I really thought it was a nephew. And Barrolo's slimmer, lighter-looking . . .'

'Oh, José goes for walks now and rides and does not sleep so often immediately after supper.'

'And what about the rest of the family? Aunt Arminda, the Mendonça crowd? All well? . . . And Father Soeiro, what's become of our saint?'

'He had a slight attack of rheumatism, very slight, though. He's better now, always in the Bishop's Palace, in the library . . . It seems he's amusing himself by writing a book on Bishops.'

'Yes, I know, the History of Oliveira Cathedral . . . I've been working hard, too, you know, Gracinha. I'm writing a novel.'

'Ah!'

'Just a short one, a novelette, for the *Annals of History and Literature*, a magazine founded by a friend of mine, Castanheiro. It's about a historical fact to do with our family. About an ancestor, a very ancient ancestor of ours, Tructesindo.'

'Interesting. What did he do?'

'All sorts of horrors! But it's very picturesque. It shows the Palace of Santa Ireneia in the twelfth century in all its splendour! A beautiful reconstruction of ancient Portugal, in fact, and especially of old Ramires. You'll like it. There are no love affairs, it's all wars. There's only a Dona Menda in the background, one of our ancestors, whom I am not even sure really existed. Rather good, don't you think? And you see, as I am interested in getting into politics, first of all I have to get known, make a name for myself . . .'

Gracinha smiled sweetly at her brother, with her usual adoration.

'Have you any ideas now? Aunt Arminda persists in her opinion that you ought to go into the Diplomatic Corps. Only a few days ago she was saying, "Ah, the only place for our Gonçalinho now, with that name and elegance of his, is a great Embassy!" '

Gonçalo inched his way out of the vast sofa, buttoning up his light jacket.

'To tell you the truth, I have had an idea for some days . . . Possibly it came to me from an English novel, an exceedingly interesting one, incidentally, which I recommend, on the ancient mines in Ofir, *King Solomon's Mines* . . . I've got ideas of going to Africa.'

'Oh, no, Gonçalo! Africa?'

The servant entered with two uncorked bottles of Vidago water on a salver. Hastily, in order to enjoy the effervescence, Gonçalo filled an enormous cut crystal glass. Ah, what delicious water! Now that Barrolo had returned, announcing that he had carried out the gentleman's orders, he finished,

'Right! Then we'll talk at lunch, Gracinha! Now I must wash and change my clothes because I can't stop itching . . .'

Barrolo accompanied his brother-in-law to his room, one of the most spacious and attractive in the mansion, lined with canary-coloured cretonne, and with a verandah opening on to the garden and two balcony windows looking on to Weaver's Street and the old trees of the Convent of the Monica nuns. Gonçalo impatiently snatched off his coat and flung aside his waistcoat.

'You're looking splendid, Barrolo! You must have lost seven or eight pounds! They are obviously the pounds Gracinha has put on . . . If you start complementing each other like that, you'll be perfect.'

Standing before the mirror, Barrolo stroked his waist, smiling delightedly.

'I really do think I have got slimmer . . . My trousers even feel looser.'

Gonçalo opened the deep drawer of the handsome chest-of-drawers with its gilt fittings, where he always kept some spare clothes, (even two dress-coats) to avoid having to carry suit-cases back and forth between Cunhais and the Tower. He was smiling and advising the good Barrolo to continue to slim without flagging, for the sake of future Barrolos—when below, in the silence of Weaver's Street, rang out the hooves of a magnificent horse, slowly and rhythmically striking the cobbles.

Immediately suspicious, Gonçalo ran to the window still holding the shirt he was unfolding. It was him! It was André Cavaleiro going down the hill, clutching the reins while the horse gracefully and noisily picked its way sideways down the ill-cobbled street. Gonçalo turned to Barrolo, his eyes flashing with anger.

'This is an affront! If this brazen-faced fellow comes by here again on his damned jade, right under our windows, I'll pour a bucket of dirty water over him!'

Barrolo peered out uneasily.

77

'He's on his way to the Lousadas, I suppose . . . He's very friendly with the Lousadas at the moment. I'm always seeing him round here . . . He must be going to the Lousadas.'

'Let him go to the devil! Isn't there any other way in the whole town to get to the Lousadas? Twice in half an hour! Insolent wretch! I'll have his mop-head and moustache doused with soapy water, as sure as I am a Ramires, son of my father Ramires!'

Barrolo nervously pinched the skin on his chest, uneasy at such noisy outbursts of hatred disturbing his calm. Already, at Gonçalo's insistence, he had sorrowfully broken off his friendship with Cavaleiro. Now he foresaw a quarrel, a scandal which would put him on bad terms with Cavaleiro's friends, bar him from the Club and the sweet pleasures of the Arcade, and make Oliveira more tedious than his *Ribeirinha* or *Murtosa* estates, abhorred places of solitude. He could not contain himself, but ventured the usual comment:

'Oh, Gonçalinho, all this fuss because of politics!'

Gonçalo nearly broke the jug, so furiously did he replace it on the marble-topped wash-stand.

'Politics! Here you go with politics again! You don't pour dirty water over Civil Governors because of politics. He's no politician anyway; he's merely a scoundrel! Moreover . . .'

But he finished by merely shrugging his shoulders and saying no more to the poor innocent with the fatuous face, who saw in Cavaleiro's prowling around the *Cunhais* only 'his lovely horse' and 'the shortest way to the Lousadas!'

'All right!' he concluded. 'Now leave me alone and let me dress . . . I'll look after moustachio!'

'See you later, then . . . But no foolishness, remember, if he passes by again. Agree?'

'No foolishness, only justice—in bucketfuls!'

He slapped the resigned back of the good Barrolo who made his way down the corridor sighing and lamenting the rashness of Gonçalinho's nature and the disproportionate anger 'politics' provoked.

While he vehemently soaped and washed himself, and then dressed with irritable haste, Gonçalo ruminated on such an intolerable scandal. Invariably, as soon as he set foot in Oliveira, he met the man with the long locks, trotting up and down beneath the windows of the mansion, on the jade with the flowing mane! What

78

distressed him was to perceive in Gracinha's heart—poor tender, unprotected heart, a stubborn vestige of love for Cavaleiro, deeply suppressed yet still alive, still capable of blossoming forth again . . . And there was no other deep sentiment to defend her in her life of idleness in Oliveira—neither the sense of her husband's superiority, nor the delight of a child in the cradle. All that could help her was her pride, a certain religious respect for the name of Ramires, the fear of a small, prying and gossiping community. Her salvation lay in abandoning the town and retiring to the seclusion of one of Barrolo's estates, the *Ribeirinha*, or better still, *Murtosa*, with its beautiful wood, the mossy walls of the convent, and the surrounding village to occupy her in her role of grand chatelaine. But that was out of the question. Barrolo would not consent to losing his game of ombre at the Club the few moments' chat in the 'Elegant Tobacconists' and the banter with Major Ribas!

On fire with the heat and emotion, Gonçalo opened the verandah. Below, on the short tiled terrace, bordered by china pots, which led on to the garden, stood Gracinha, her hair still loose over the peignoir, talking to another lady, a tall, very thin lady in a sailor-hat decorated with poppies, who held in her arms a big bunch of roses.

It was 'cousin' Maria Mendonça, wife of José Mendonça, a school-friend of Barrolo's from Amarante, and now captain of the Cavalry Regiment stationed in Oliveira. The daughter of a certain Don António, (now Viscount) of the Manor of Severim, she was devoured by the idea of aristocratic family connections and aristocratic lineage, and was always cunningly linking the vague nobility of Severim with all the noble houses of Portugal, above all and with most delectation, with the great Ramires family. When the regiment settled in Oliveira, she had immediately addressed Gracinha by the familiar 'tu' and Gonçalo as 'cousin', with that special familiarity which typifies persons of superior blood. She also, however, maintained close relations with rich Brazilians in Oliveira—even with the widow Pinho, owner of the draper's who (according to gossip) kept her sons, when young, supplied with jackets and trousers. She was also on very friendly terms with Dona Ana Lucena, visiting her both in the town and in *Feitosa*. Gonçalo liked her charm, her keenness, the malicious vivacity which enlivened her so that she crackled delightfully like a branch in the fire, burning gaily. And when she raised her shining lively eyes at the sound of the window squeaking open, she wore a simultaneous look of affection and surprise.

'Oh, Cousin Maria! What a pleasant surprise, as soon as I arrive and open the window . . .'

'And for me, too, Gonçalo! I haven't seen you since your return from Lisbon! . . . And you're distinctly handsomer, too, with that moustache . . .'

'They tell me I'm absolutely gorgeous, irresistible! I'd even advise you not to come too close, Cousin Maria, in case you catch fire!'

She let her heavy bunch of roses hang disconsolately.

'Oh, heavens, then I'm lost, because I promised Cousin Graça I'd dine here this evening! Oh, Gracinha, for the love you bear me, put a screen between the two of us, I beg you!'

Gonçalo leant over the verandah and delighted by Cousin Maria's wit, shouted in reply,

'No, I'll put a lampshade on to reduce my brilliance! . . . How's your fine husband? And the little ones? How's the fair flock?'

'Surviving—with a little bread and the grace of God . . . See you later, then, Cousin Gonçalo! And be merciful!'

He continued to laugh, delighted, as Cousin Maria, after a little whispering and two hasty kisses on Gracinha's face, disappeared, leanly elegant, through the glass doors of the drawing-room. Gracinha went slowly up the three marble steps into the garden. From the verandah Gonçalo could still see, through the sparse foliage and between the box hedges, the white peignoir and thick loose hair shining in the sunlight like a cascade of jet. Then the gleaming black and bright lace disappeared beneath the laurel bushes of the path which led to the gazebo.

But Gonçalo did not move from the window, absent-mindedly filing his nails and suspiciously peering through the curtains as if afraid that Cavaleiro would appear again on his jade, now that Gracinha had disappeared in the direction of the pleasant gazebo—constructed in the eighteenth century in imitation of a little temple of love—which was at the end of the long garden terrace and dominated Weaver's Street. But the cobbles remained silent beneath the spreading shadows of the trees of the mansion and the convent. Finally he decided to go down, ashamed of his spying and certain that his sister would not expose herself like that to Cavaleiro on the narrow verandah of the gazebo, her hair dishevelled above the peignoir.

He was closing the door when he found himself in the arms of Father Soeiro who caught him round the waist with affection and respect.

'Oh, most ungrateful Father Soeiro!' exclaimed Gonçalo, slapping the chaplain fondly on his fat back. 'So what sort of behaviour's this? Over a month without putting in an appearance at the Tower! Gonçalinho doesn't seem to exist for Father Soeiro any longer; there's only Gracinha nowadays . . .'

Father Soeiro was so moved that a tear almost glinted in the meek little eyes which seemed even darker between the freshness of his plump rosy face and his snow-white head, and he smiled, clasping his hands together over the alpaca cassock from which peeped the corner of a red check handkerchief. It wasn't that he did not wish to pay a visit to the Tower, but there was his work in the library of the Bishop's Palace . . . And then there was his rheumatism . . . And Senhora Dona Gracinha was always expecting her brother one day or other . . .

'All right, all right, then!' Gonçalo stopped him cheerfully, 'as long as he has not forgotten the Tower . . .'

'As if I could!' murmured Father Soeiro with deep feeling.

Along the blue-walled corridor, decorated with coloured engravings of Napoleon's battles, Gonçalo recounted the latest news of the Tower.

'As Father Soeiro knows, we had that scandal with Relho . . . Just as well, because I've made an excellent deal. Just imagine! I leased the grounds a few days ago to Pereira the Brazilian, Pereira da Riosa, for 1,150 *mil-reis* . . .

The chaplain, about to take a pinch of snuff from a gold-plated silver box, stopped and stared at the Nobleman in amazement.

'Now would you believe how people invent things! I heard that you had made a deal with José Casco, José Casco of Bravais. I even mentioned it to Senhora Dona Graça at lunch on Sunday . . .'

'Yes, well,' interrupted the Nobleman with a slight flush colouring his fine features. 'It's true Casco came to the Tower and we talked. First he wanted it, then he didn't. You know how Casco is. A real nuisance . . . I couldn't get him to decide. So when Pereira turned up one fine morning and made me a proposal, I, feeling entirely free, accepted, and gladly! Just imagine! An excellent increase in rent and Pereira as leaseholder . . . You know Pereira well, don't you, Father?'

'A capable fellow,' agreed the chaplain, scratching his chin with some embarrassment. 'There's no doubt about that. And a good one. So as there was no definite arrangement with Cas . . .'

'Pereira's coming to town next week,' Gonçalo went on hurriedly. 'Perhaps you wouldn't mind letting Guedes, the notary, know, Father Soeiro, and we can get this fine contract signed. The conditions are the usual ones. I believe there is some reservation about vegetables and the pig . . . Anyway, you'll be receiving a letter from Pereira.'

As they went downstairs Gonçalo, dabbing his moustache with his perfumed handkerchief, went straight on to comment jokingly on the famous Ramires Fado which Father Soeiro had collaborated on with Videirinha. Oh! Father Soeiro had supplied him with some really excellent legends! But that one about Santa Aldonça was adorned with exaggerations . . . Four kings carrying our saint on their shoulders!

'Too many kings, Father Soeiro!'

The good chaplain protested, at once interested and serious in his love for that work that glorified the family.

'Really now! If you'll excuse me, sir! It is perfectly true. Father Guedes of Amaral tells the story in his *Ladies of the Court of Heaven*, a wonderful book, an extremely rare work, which Senhor José Barrolo has in his library. He does not say which kings they were but he does say there were four . . . "On the shoulders of four kings and accompanied by numerous counts." But José Videirinha objected that he could not put in the counts because of the rhyme.'

The Nobleman laughed, hanging the straw hat which he had been wearing on a hook at the bottom of the stairs.

'Because of the rhyme, poor old counts . . . But the Fado's delightful. I have brought a copy with me for Gracinha to sing at the piano. But to go on to another matter, Father Soeiro. What do they say round here about our Civil Governor, Senhor André Cavaleiro?'

The chaplain shrugged his shoulders, cautiously unfolding his enormous red check handkerchief.

'As you know, sir, I don't understand anything about politics.

And moreover, I don't frequent cafés where politics are discussed
. . . But it seems he is liked.'

In the corridor, a fat footman with opulent red whiskers, whom
Gonçalo did not know, was ringing the lunch bell. Gonçalo told him
Senhora Dona Maria da Graça was down the garden.

'She's just come in, Senhor Don Gonçalo!' replied the footman.
'And she sent me to ask if you would like Amarante green wine from
Vidainhos for lunch, sir.'

Yes, definitely, Vidainhos wine. Then smiling, he added,

'Oh, Father Soeiro, tell this footman that I am not "Don". I'm
simply Gonçalo, thanks be to God!'

The chaplain murmured that nevertheless, in documents of the
First Dynasty, there were some Ramires entitled 'Don'. As Gonçalo
had stopped before the drawn curtains of the drawing-room, the
good man made a bow and scrupulously, ceremoniously reverent,
begged the Nobleman to go ahead.

'Really, Father Soeiro, for the love of God!'

But the chaplain, with affectionate respect, insisted,

'After you, dear sir.'

Gonçalo pulled aside the curtain and gently pushed the chaplain
ahead of him.

'Father Soeiro, in the documents of the First Dynasty it is already
established that saints don't walk behind sinners!'

'It's you who give the orders, sir, and always so charmingly.'

*　　*　　*

After Gracinha's birthday, Gonçalo was returning one afternoon,
about three o'clock, with Father Soeiro from the Library in the
Bishop's Palace, when he heard in the antechamber the roar of Tito's
voice, which filled the blue room like a slow roll of thunder. He
snatched back the curtain and shook his fist at the huge man filling
one of the large gilt armchairs, his new, shiny-studded boots
stretched out on the flowered carpet.

'You infamous wretch! So you cast me aside the other day, did
you, without a thought, after I'd prepared you a superb goat, roast
on a cherrywood spit! And what for? For some low orgy, with cod
pasties and fire-crackers!'

Tito did not move from his blissfully comfortable seat.

'Absolutely impossible. I met João Gouveia in the afternoon at

83

the Fountain and it was only then we realized it was Dona Casimira's birthday. A sacred day!'

Those late suppers in Vila Clara, those nights on the town, complete with guitar, always impressed Barrolo, who fancied taking part. Now he asked, looking at them with a keen eye, from the edge of the table where he was carefully crumbling packets of tobacco into a Japanese tureen,

'Who's Dona Casimira? You people in Vila Clara discover some types . . . Tell me all about it!'

'A monster!' declared Gonçalo. 'She's a great heap of a woman, round as a barrel, with revolting whiskers on her chin. She lives near the cemetery, in a little dark hole that reeks of oil where this gentleman and others in positions of authority go to play tombola and flirt with coquettes in short red coats and dishevelled hair. It's too indecent even to relate in front of Father Soeiro here!'

The chaplain, who had moved noiselessly into a discreet shadow, between the fringed satin of a curtain and a heavy Indian chiffonier, shrugged his shoulders in laughing consent, as if accustomed to every ugly form of Sin. Tító patiently corrected the exaggerated picture which the Nobleman had drawn.

'Dona Casimira is fat but very clean. She even asked me to buy her a new bidet today in town. The house does not smell of oil and is situated behind the Convent of Santa Teresa. The coquettes are merely her nieces, two lively girls who enjoy laughing and joking . . . Father Soeiro could, without fear . . .'

'All right! All right!' Gonçalo interrupted. 'Charming people! Let's leave Dona Casimira who now has a new bidet for her bath! Let's go on to another piece of infamy by Senhor António Vilalobos!'

But Barrolo, curious insisted,

'No, no, go on, Tító . . . Her birthday, was it? A good old time, I bet?'

'A quiet supper,' replied Tító with all the seriousness befitting this party of friends. 'Dona Casimira had a delicious meal of chicken and peas for us. João Gouveia brought a dish of Gago's cod pasties which went down very well. Then we had some fireworks in the garden. Videirinha played and the girls sang . . . Quite a nice time.'

Gonçalo waited, irresistibly fascinated by the Casimira supper-party.

'Right. Finished? Now to the other piece of infamy, but a grave one this time! So our friend Senhor António Vilalobos is on intimate terms with Sanches Lucena, visits *Feitosa* every week, has tea and toast with the beautiful Dona Ana, and hides these glorious privileges furtively from his friends?'

'Not to mention,' burst in Barrolo, highly amused, 'that he takes her little lap-dogs for a walk, too!'

'Not to mention,' echoed Gonçalo in deep tones, 'that he takes her little lap-dogs for a walk, too! Now answer that, my fine friend!'

Tító's vast body stirred in the depths of the armchair, he drew in his shiny-studded boots and slowly stroked his bearded face which was flushing a slight pink. After staring at Gonçalo intensely, with an effort at cunning which made the reddish hue deepen, he answered,

'Have you by any chance ever asked me whether I knew Sanches Lucena? You never inquired . . .'

The Nobleman protested. No! But constantly in the Club, in Gago's, in the Tower, they had shouted aloud the name of Sanches Lucena in political discussions! Nothing more natural, or even more prudent, than Sr Tító's alluding to his famous friendship! If only to avoid him, or his friends, in the presence of Sr Tító who ate toast at *Feitosa*, treating the Sanches Lucenas like so much rubbish!

Tító raised himself from his armchair. Plunging his hands deep into the pockets of his alpaca jacket and shaking his shoulders indifferently, he rejoined,

'Everyone has their own opinion of Sanches . . . I've only known him for four or five months, but I feel he is serious, knows what he's about . . . As for his ability in the House . . .'

Gonçalo indignantly bellowed that they were not discussing the merits of Sr Sanches Lucena, but the secrets of Sr Tító Vilalobos! The new footman, poking his red whiskers through a gap in the curtain, announced that the Administrator of Vila Clara was looking for the gentleman . . .

Barrolo immediately left his bowl of tobacco.

'Senhor João Gouveia! Show him in! Bravo! We've got all the lads from Vila Clara here today!'

Tító, from the window where he had taken refuge, bellowed out in a voice like thunder which smothered the importunate remarks about Sanches and *Feitosa*,

'We came together! And by chance, in a wretched old carriage

... One of the jades lost a horseshoe and we had to stop in Vendinha. It wasn't a waste of time though, because they've got a white wine there now that's first class!'

He tweaked the lobe of his ear to show his appreciation. He noisily advised Barrolo and Gonçalo to go to Vendinha to try this celestial refreshment.

'Even Father Soeiro would be tempted to a good mugful there, in spite of the sin!'

But João Gouveia entered, sweltering with the heat and covered with dust, a red mark on his forehead from his hat and the excessive temperature, buttoned up in his black frock-coat, black trousers and black gloves. Out of breath, he silently clasped the hands of his friends who welcomed him. He collapsed on to the sofa, imploring his friend Barrolo, for the love of God, to bring him something cool to drink!

'I nearly went into the Café Monaco. But then I reflected that in the magnificent house of the Barrolos the drinks would be safer.'

'Just as well! What would you like? Orgeat? *Sangria*?[1] Lemonade?'

'Sangria.'

Wiping his neck and forehead, he cursed the obscene heat in Oliveira.

'And there are some people who like it! The top man here, the Civil Governor, always chooses the hottest hour to go for a ride. Even today ... He was in the office till midday, then he had his horse brought to the door and off he trots on to the Ramilde Road which is like the depths of Africa ... I don't know how his brains don't sizzle in the heat!'

'Oh, that's simple,' answered Gonçalo. 'He hasn't any!'

The Administrator bowed gravely,

'All we needed was Senhor Gonçalo Mendes Ramires here with his little barbed comments. Don't let's start now, don't let's start. This brother-in-law of yours, Barrolo, is a ferocious beast! And always has a sharp rejoinder!'

The good Barrolo stammered uneasily that Gonçalinho did not spare his humour where politics were concerned ...

'Well, look here!' declared the Administrator, wagging his finger at Gonçalo. 'This Senhor André Cavaleiro who has no brains, was

---

[1] *Sangria:* a refreshing drink made of red wine, lemonade, fruit and ice.

86

only this morning, in the office, showering praises upon the brains of Senhor Gonçalo Mendes Ramires! . . .'

Gonçalo, very serious, replied,

'That's all that's needed, of course. For the Civil Governor to be completely absurd, all he has to do is to consider me an ass!'

'Excuse me!' cried the Administrator, who had got up and was buttoning up his coat in preparation for battle.

Barrolo, alarmed, hastily stepped in and put a hand on Gouveia's shoulders to calm him and settle him down again on the sofa.

'No, my dear fellows, no! Politics, no! And we're not having quarrels about Cavaleiro again . . . Let's get on to what's most important. Are you having dinner with us, João Gouveia?'

'No, thank you, I've already promised to dine with Cavaleiro. Inácio Vilhena's going. He's going to read an article he wrote for the *Guimarães Bulletin*, on some moulds used for making martyrs' bones, discovered during the repairs going on in the Convent of S Bento. I'm curious . . . And how's Senhora Dona Graça? Well? Father Soeiro I haven't seen for months. You never come to the Tower now! But always looking in excellent health, always flourishing. Oh, Father Soeiro, what's your secret for eternal youth?'

The chaplain smiled timidly from his corner. The secret? Live sparingly—not consuming it with ambition or disappointment. As far as he was concerned, life was very simple and very calm. And apart from his rheumatism . . .

Then, blushing with awkwardness, through the evangelical precepts issuing from his lips,

'But even my rheumatism is an evil that has its advantages. God, who ordains these things, knows why he ordains them . . . Suffering is edifying. Because when we suffer, we are led to consider the suffering of others . . .'

'Well, do you know,' replied the Administrator with cheerful incredulity, 'when I have my sore throat attacks, I don't think about other people's throats! I only think of mine, which causes me trouble enough. And now I'm going to treat it to that delicious sangria . . .'

The footman offered him the shining silver tray laden with glasses of sangria in which floated slices of lemon. Everyone sampled it, everyone drank it, even Father Soeiro to show Sr António Vilalobos that he did not disdain wine, gracious gift from God—for as Tibulus teaches, with good reason, in spite of his being a pagan, *vinus facit dites animos, mollia corda dat*, it strengthens the soul and softens the heart.

João Gouveia, with a sigh of content, replaced the glass which he had emptied at one gulp on the tray, and asked Gonçalo,

'Tell me now, what's this fantastic story about a party at the Tower the other evening with some ladies, with Dona Ana Lucena ? I didn't believe it when Gago's boy found me and gave me the message. Then afterwards . . .'

But from between the curtains at the window, where he was finishing his sangria, Tító's voice once again burst forth, also to question the Nobleman,

'Oh, Sô Gonçalo! What's this Barrolo was telling me a little while ago ? That you have ideas of leaving for Africa ?'

There was almost terror mingled with João Gouveia's amazement. To Africa ? . . . What ? Take a job in Africa ?

'No! Go and plant coconuts! Plant cocoa! Plant coffee!' exclaimed Barrolo, slapping his thighs delightedly.

Tító approved of the idea! He, too, if he could get a little capital together, ten or fifteen *contos*, would try his luck in Africa, trading with the black men . . . And also if he were smaller and drier. Men of his vast build, needing lots of food and lots of wine, don't survive in Africa—they burst!

'Gonçalo's all right. He's lean and tough. He doesn't drink too much brandy; he's just what is needed for an Africanist. And I'll tell you another thing—it's a far more decent career than the other one you're mad about—being a deputy! What for ? So you can amble up and down the Arcade and flatter Counsellors ?'

Barrolo shouted agreement. He could not understand, either, Gonçalo's stubbornness in wanting to become a deputy. What a nuisance it would be! At once there would be plots, and insults in the newspapers, all the filth. Worst of all one had to put up with the electors.

'I wouldn't do it, not even if they nominated me Civil Governor afterwards, with a title to boot, and a Grand Cross on a ribbon, like Freixomil!'

Gonçalo listened with a silent, superior smile, laboriously rolling a cigarette with Barrolo's tobacco.

'You don't understand . . . You don't understand how Portugal is organized. Ask Gouveia here . . . Portugal is an estate, a beautiful estate run by a partnership. As you know there are commercial partnerships and rural ones. The one in Lisbon is a political partnership which rules the estate called Portugal . . . We Portuguese belong to two classes: five or six million that work on the land or that live on it and simply sit and watch, like Barrolo, and pay; and some thirty odd individuals on top, in Lisbon, who form a partnership—those who receive and rule. Now I, as a matter of inclination, a matter of necessity, as a matter of family habit, wish to govern my estate. But to enter this political partnership the Portuguese citizen needs a qualification—to be a deputy. Just as one needs a qualification when entering the magistrature—a degree in law. That is why I wish to begin as a deputy so that later I can become a member of the partnership and rule . . . Isn't that so, João Gouveia?'

The Administrator had returned to the tray of drinks to enjoy another glass, sipping it slowly this time: 'This is indeed the career: candidate, deputy, politician, counsellor, minister, mandarin. This is the career . . . And it is better than going to Africa. They grow cocoa in the Arcade in Lisbon, too, and there's more shade there!'

Barrolo, in the meantime, had his arm on Titó's mighty shoulder and was huddled with him in the bay window, exchanging ideas and joking.

'Actually, although I do not belong to the partnership, I also rule in those parts of Portugal which are of most interest to me, because they belong to me! I'd like to see this S Fulgêncio or Bras Vitorino, or any of the politicians in Black Horse Square, start meddling with my property in *Ribeirinha* or *Murtosa* . . . They'd be welcomed with a shot-gun if they did!'

Leaning against the window, Titó looked impressed and scratched his beard.

'Yes, Barrolo! But in *Ribeirinha* and *Murtosa* you have to pay the taxes that they decide. In those districts you have to put up with the people they put in authority. You get roads there if they choose to have them built. You sell your wheat and your casks of wine at a greater or lesser profit according to the laws they make . . . And the same with everything. Gonçalo's right. It's the devil! Those who make the laws are those who make the profit . . . D'you know, my landlord in Vila Clara, after Michaelmas Day, is going to put up the rent of the house I live in, a tiny place that nobody else wants because the public hangman was killed there and still puts in an appearance now and again . . . And Cavaleiro, who's a member of the Partnership, lives rent-free in the beautiful palace of São Domingos, complete with coach-house, and garden and orchard . . .'

Barrolo put his hand with a horrified 'Sssssh!' to Titó's mouth, to restrain his loud voice, afraid that Cavaleiro's privileges, noised abroad like this, would once again awaken Gonçalo's fury. But the Nobleman did not hear, attentive to the words of João Gouveia who, sinking into the sofa after his sangria, was once more exclaiming how amazed he was to find, at the Fountain in Vila Clara, the boy from Gago's, with the message about the party at the Tower.

'I began to suspect you were really giving a party when it struck nine, and then half-past nine, and Titó had not arrived for Dona Casimira's supper! . . . Well, I thought, he got the message, too, and has slipped off to the Tower! Finally, when he arrived in his hooded jacket I realized it was just one of Sr Gonçalo's jokes . . .'

The Nobleman leaned forward with a sudden odd suspicion.

'In his hooded jacket? Titó wore a hooded jacket that night?'

But at that moment Barrolo recoiled in haste from the window into the room with a cry of horror.

'Oh, my dear boys! Lord help us! Here come the Lousadas!'

João Gouveia leapt up from the sofa as if danger were threatening, hurriedly buttoning his frock-coat; Gonçalo, in his confusion, collided with Titó and Barrolo who were drawing back for fear of having been seen through the large windows; even Father Soeiro prudently left his corner where he had been looking at the *Porto Gazette*. All of them, like soldiers peering through a loophole in a fortress, studied the Square, gilded by the four o'clock sun, visible below the mossy roofs of the rope-factory. From the direction of Pegas Street, the Lousada sisters, very stiff and slender, both wearing short black silk capes with beads, advanced, two well-defined shadows stretching out behind them on the cobbled square.

The Lousada sisters! Dry, dark and as noisy as two cicadas, for years they had pried into everyone's lives in Oliveira, spread spiteful gossip, plotted and schemed. In the whole of that unfortunate city there existed no stain, no blemish, no cracked teapot, no aching heart, no empty pocket, no half-open window, no dust in any corner, no vaguely discerned shape, no new hat introduced in church, no cake ordered from Matildes, that their four beady jet-black eyes missed—and that their wagging tongues, between irregular teeth, did not comment upon with strident malice! From them stemmed all the anonymous letters that infested the District; devout folk regarded their visits, at which the two sisters prattled away for hours and agitated their skinny arms, as a sort of penance; and always, wherever they passed, suspicion and apprehension were rife. But who dared resist the two Lousada sisters? They were daughters of the decrepit, venerable General Lousada; they were related to the Bishop; they had influence in the powerful religious association of Our Lord of Penha. And their chastity was so inflexible, so ancient and withered and so widely blazoned abroad by them that Marcolino of the *Independent* had nicknamed them the Two Thousand Virgins.

'They're not coming here,' shouted Titó with immense relief.

In the middle of the Square, beside the railings that surrounded the ancient sundial, the two sisters had stopped, and raising their dark noses, were sniffing the air and peering towards the little church of St Matthew, where the bell was ringing for a baptism.

'Oh, the devil take it, they *are* coming here!'

The Lousadas, minds now made up, were attacking the gate of *Cunhais*! Then there was panic! As Barrolo fled, his fat legs trembled and nearly knocked over the chiffoniers, the tubby Indian pitchers. Gonçalo shouted that they should hide in the orchard. Gouveia searched for his bowler in confusion. Only Titó, who loathed them and whom they called Polyphemus, retired calmly, sheltering Father Soeiro beneath his strong arm. The terror-stricken band was bursting through the curtains when Gracinha appeared in a cool, strawberry-coloured silk dress, smiling in astonishment at the fleeing men.

'What is it? What is it?'

Suppressed cries enveloped the sweet, threatened lady: 'The Lousadas!'

'Oh!'

Titó and João Gouveia hurriedly clasped the hand she held out to them in dismay. The door-bell tinkled awesomely. The file of men fled, on each other's heels, with Father Soeiro being dragged along in the rear, and disappeared into the library which Barrolo bolted, shouting to Gracinha a last-minute inspiration:

'Hide the sangria!'

Poor Gracinha! At a loss, with no time to call the footman, she carried the heavy salver, with a desperate effort, to a bench in the corridor—because the Lousadas, if they had discovered it, would have spread throughout the city and higher than the Tower of St Matthew, a horrific story of orgies and drunkenness. Then she glanced breathlessly into the mirror to make sure her hair was tidy. As firm as if she was in an arena, with the simple, smiling temerity of the ancient Ramires, she awaited the assault of the terrible sisters.

★   ★   ★

The following Sunday, after lunch, Gonçalo accompanied his sister to the house of their Aunt Arminda Vilegas, who, the evening before, when taking her footbath (as was her habit every Saturday) had scalded her foot and taken to her bed in alarm, demanding a reunion of the five surgeons in Oliveira. Afterwards Gonçalo finished his cigar under the acacias of the Terreiro da Louça, thinking of his novel neglected in the Tower the last few weeks, and of the famous event in Chapter Two which tempted him and awed him—the meeting of Lourenço Ramires with Lopo de Baião, the Bastard, in the fatal valley of Canta Pedra. He was returning to *Cunhais* (since he had promised Barrolo to go for a trot as far as the Estevinha Pinewoods to enjoy the cool of the Sunday afternoon) when, in Candle Lane, he met Notary Guedes, who was coming out of *Matildes* Cake Shop with a large parcel of cakes. The Nobleman swiftly crossed the road, while Guedes, heavy and large-bellied, stood on the edge of the pavement on the tips of his small, varnished, shoes and uncovered, with a sweeping bow, his bald head crested in the middle with the famous tuft of grey hair which had earned him the nickname of Tufted Guedes.

'Really, my dear Guedes, do put your hat on. How are you? As vigorous and youthful as ever! Good for you! Have you spoken with Father Soeiro? Pereira da Riosa is coming to town only on Wednesday, after all . . .'

Yes, yes! Father Soeiro had dropped into the office to let him know—and he must congratulate the Nobleman on his new lessee.

'A very competent man, Pereira! I've known him for twenty years. Look at the Count of Monte Agra's property, sir! I can still remember it from before—a barren piece of land if ever there was. What a model of an estate it is now! The vines he has planted alone! A very competent man! And you, sir, are you here for long?'

'Two or three days . . . The heat in Oliveira is unbearable. It's a bit cooler today, fortunately. What's the news? How's the political situation? Is our friend Guedes still the good Regenerator, loyal and ardent, eh?'

Suddenly, the notary, his parcel of cakes clutched to his black silk waistcoat, waved his short fat arm with a slow indignation that reddened his face and the whole of his forehead up to the brim of his white hat with the black band.

'Who wouldn't be, Senhor Gonçalo Mendes? Who wouldn't be? Look at this latest scandal!'

Gonçalo's smiling eyes immediately became wide and serious.

'What scandal?'

The notary took a step back. Didn't the Nobleman know about the latest authoritarian action by the Civil Governor, by Sr André Cavaleiro?'

'What was that, my friend?'

Guedes raised himself on to the tips of his small ankle-boots, puffed his chest up and out and exclaimed,

'Transferring Noronha! . . . Transferring poor Noronha!'

But a lady, also obese, with a thick growth of hair on her upper lip, almost bursting out of her rich, rustling Sunday silk, was dragging a little whimpering boy by the hand, and now she stopped and stared at Guedes, because the worthy gentleman with his corporation, his parcel of cakes and his indignation was barring the doorway of *Matildes*. Hastily the Nobleman lifted the latch of the glass door to let her enter. Then he went on eagerly,

'You're off home, Guedes, my friend, aren't you? That's in my direction. Let's walk and talk . . . Well, now, imagine this! But now Noronha? Which Noronha's this?'

'Ricardo Noronha . . . You know him. The paymaster in the Public Works Office.'

'Ah, yes, yes . . . So he's been transferred? Transferred arbitrarily?'

They were walking down Drill Street, and amid the silence and solitude of the closed shops, Guedes' anger burst out again, wilder this time.

'Wickedly, Senhor Gonçalo Mendes Ramires, most wickedly! And to Almodôvar, to the borders of Alentejo! To a land with no resources, no form of entertainment, no families!'

He stopped, his cakes pressed to his heart, his protruding eyes gleaming at the Nobleman. Noronha! A diligent, most honest worker. And with no political tendencies, none whatsoever. He was neither Historian nor Regenerator. His party was his family; he kept three sisters, three flowers. A man greatly esteemed in the city, full of talent! He had an extraordinary gift for music! Ah! Didn't Sr Gonçalo Ramires know? He composed some beautiful pieces for the piano! A wonderful person for parties, for birthdays. It was he who always organized the amateur dramatic presentations in Oliveira ...

'There was no one to match him for rehearsals, even in the Capital! No one! And then, whoosh, he is suddenly sent to Almodôvar, to Hell, with his sisters and few sticks of furniture! The piano alone! ... Just imagine, sir, the cost of transport for the piano alone!'

Gonçalo shone.

'It's a fine scandal all right. How fortunate I met you, my dear Guedes! Doesn't anyone know the reason?'

Once again they began to walk along the narrow pavement. The notary shrugged bitterly. The reason? Officially, as in all such cases of authoritarianism, it was a transfer in the public interest ...

'But all Noronha's friends throughout the city know the real reason ... The real, secret, hideous truth!'

'And what's that?'

Guedes glanced discreetly up the road. An old woman was crossing it, limping, carrying a pitcher. And the notary whispered in a low voice close to the Nobleman's startled ears, 'The fact is, Sr André Cavaleiro, the base fellow, was taken with the eldest Noronha sister, Dona Adelina, an excessively beautiful creature, tall, dark and statuesque! Repelled (for the girl is intelligent, a pearl, and perceived his vile intentions), who does the Civil Governor take his revenge on? On the paymaster! To Almodôvar with the girls and their sticks of furniture! It was the paymaster who paid!'

'A nasty piece of knavery!' murmured Gonçalo, bathed in smiles and pleasure.

'And note, sir,' exclaimed Guedes, his fat hand shaking above his hat. 'Note, sir, that poor Noronha, in his innocence, being such a good man and always ready to please his superiors, only a few weeks ago dedicated a delightful waltz to Cavaleiro! *The Butterfly*—a lovely waltz!'

Gonçalo could not contain himself, but rubbed his hands together triumphantly.

94

'A really dirty piece of work!... Hasn't anyone said anything? This opposition paper, *The Oliveira Clarion*—hasn't it denounced him, alluded to the incident?'

Guedes hung his head dejectedly. Sr Gonçalo Ramires knew the people on the *Clarion*. Style—and a flowery, profuse style it was. But as for divulging, in a grave case like Noronha's, for instance, the naked truth—they had very little courage, no nerve. And then Biscainho, the chief editor, was slyly moving over to the Historicals. Ah, hadn't Sr Gonçalo Mendes Ramires been informed about this? Well, this scurrilous Biscainho was changing sides. Obviously Cavaleiro had offered him some job. Apart from all that, how could the matter be proved? These were personal things, family matters. You could not publicize the statement by Dona Adelina, a virtuous maiden—and what eyes!... Ah, if it had been in the time of Manuel Justino and the *Oliveira Dawn*!... That was a man who would have printed on the first page in a big headline: 'Attention! Because the highest authority in our District attempted to bring dishonour onto our Noronha family...!'

'He was the man all right! Poor devil, and he's lying in St Michael's Cemetery... Now, Senhor Gonçalo Ramires, despotism reigns unchecked!'

He panted and snorted, exhausted by his passionate outburst. They silently turned the corner of Drill Street into the beautiful, newly paved Princess Dona Amélia Street. At the second doorway Guedes, still panting, stopped, and taking his door-key from his pocket, invited the Nobleman in to rest a while.

'No, no, thank you, my kind friend. I have had great pleasure, immense pleasure, in meeting you... This story of Noronha is fantastic! But nothing surprises me where the Civil Governor is concerned. I'm only surprised they didn't run him out of Oliveira, as he deserved, with kicks and boos! Still, not all good folk lie in St Michael's Cemetery... See you tomorrow, Guedes. And thank you!'

From Princess Dona Amélia Street to King's Square, Gonçalo ran with the joy of someone who has discovered a treasure and carries it hidden beneath his cape! And it was here indeed that he carried 'the scandal, this delightful scandal' that he had been searching for so ardently because he desired it so ardently, in order to bring about the ruin of the Civil Governor in his loyal city of Oliveira, which had greeted him with such acclamations! And by the grace of God, this 'delightful scandal' would also ruin the man who had captured Gracinha's heart, where, in spite of the bygone insult, he remained like a maggot in a fruit gnawing a hole and causing harm . . . He had no doubts of the efficacy of the scandal! The whole city would turn against this womanizer of a leading authority who had oppressed and exiled an admirable civil servant—because the poor man's sister refused his kisses. And Gracinha? . . . How could Gracinha resist such a disillusion—her dear André impassioned by the Noronha girl and rejected by her with distaste and derision? Oh, the scandal was superb! All that was needed now was for it to explode really noisily over the roof-tops of Oliveira and over Gracinha's heart, like a benignant thunderstorm that clears the air. He would take control of this thunderstorm which would sweep over the entire north. He would free the city of a detestable Governor, and Gracinha of a false dream. Thus, with a few skilful strokes of the pen, he would be working *pro patria et pro domo*!

In *Cunhais* he ran to Barrolo's room, who was dressing and humming the *Fado of the Ramires*, and shouted through the door with a thrill of resolve,

'I can't go to Estevinha with you. I must do some writing urgently. Don't come up, don't disturb me. I need peace!'

He paid no attention to the forlorn protests of Barrolo, who came running out into the corridor in his pants. He leapt up the stairs. In his room, after swiftly removing his coat and sprinkling his forehead with eau-de-Cologne, he sat down at the table—where Gracinha always placed, between vases of flowers, for his work, the monumental silver ink-stand that had belonged to Uncle Melchior. Without hesitation, without even a draft, in one of those easy flows of words that stem from passion, he composed a bitter letter to the *Porto Gazette* against the Civil Governor. At once the title blazed forth—*A Monstrous Assault!* Without disclosing the name of the Noronha family, he recounted in detail, as an event that was vouched and even witnessed by him, 'the foul, villainous attempt by the leading authority of the District on the modesty, the peace of mind and the honour of a sweet child of sixteen summers!' Then came the scornful rejection—'with which the noble child had opposed the administrative Don Juan, whose beautiful moustache is the wonder of our people!' Finally came 'the base, unspeakable revenge taken by the gentleman on the zealous employee (who is also a talented artist), arranging that this disgraceful Government should transfer him, or rather cast him, cruelly exile him, with his family of three delicate ladies, to the limits of the Kingdom, to the most arid and barren of our provinces, since it was impossible to bundle them off to Africa in the sordid hold of a frigate!' Before ending, he let out a growl or two against 'the political agony of Portugal'. With sorrow and consternation, he recalled the worst times of Absolutism, innocence buried in dungeons, the inordinate will of the Prince, as the only expression of the Law! He ended by asking the Government if it would cover up for this agent of theirs—'this grotesque Nero who, like the other, in former times, the great one in Rome, tried to introduce seduction into the hearts of the best families, and committed those abuses of power, motivated by lust, which has always been, throughout the centuries and civilizations, the curse of the just!' And he signed the letter *Juvenal*.

It was nearly six o'clock when he went down to the drawing-room, light-footed and resplendent. Gracinha was hammering away at the piano, studying the *Fado of the Ramires*. Barrolo (who had not dared to take a walk alone) was lying on the sofa, leafing through a famous *History of the Crimes of the Inquisition*, which he had begun when still a bachelor.

'I've been working for two hours!' exclaimed Gonçalo at once, opening wide the window. 'I'm worn out. But, thanks to God, justice has been done . . . This time André Cavaleiro will really fall off his horse!'

Barrolo immediately closed his book, his elbow on the cushion, and asked uneasily,

'Something happened?'

Gonçalo, planted in front of him, with a sweet, fierce smile on his face, rattled his keys and money in his pocket and answered,

'Oh, nothing much. A trifle. Just a small piece of infamy . . . But for our Civil Governor, infamous actions are trifles.'

Under Gracinha's fingers, the *Fado of the Ramires* grew faint, an indistinct murmur of the keys.

Barrolo waited, wide-eyed.

'Out with it!'

Gonçalo poured out his story with relish.

'An outrage, man! Noronha, poor Noronha, persecuted, humiliated, outcast! Together with his family . . . To the inferno, to the Algarve!'

'Noronha the paymaster?'

'Noronha the paymaster. It was the unfortunate paymaster who paid!'

With great delight he related the lamentable story: Sr André Cavaleiro passionately in love, aflame for the eldest of the Noronha sisters. Every day assaulting the girl with bouquets and letters and verses and the clatter of his jade's hoofs outside her window. He even went so far as to send her an old hag to tempt her . . . The girl, an angel full of dignity, remained unmoved. She did not show disgust, she merely laughed. It was a joke in the Noronha family to read over tea the ardent verses in which he called her 'Nymph, evening star . . .' Really, the whole business was grossly sordid and ridiculous!

The wretched *Fado of the Ramires* faded away into a tumult of unharmonious and disordered notes.

'And I didn't hear a thing about it!' murmured Barrolo in amazement. 'Either in the Club or in the Arcade!'

'Well, my dear friend, the person who *did* hear, and a great explosion at that, was poor Noronha. Cast away to the lowest regions of Alentejo, to a diseased land, full of swamps. It's death . . . It's the death penalty!'

At this apparition of Death stalking through the swamps, Barrolo clapped a hand on his knee suspiciously.

'But who the devil told you all this?'

The Nobleman of the Tower looked at his brother-in-law in disdain, with pity.

'Who told me? Who told me Don Sebastian died at Alcacer Quibir? . . . They are facts. It's History. All Oliveira knows. Actually, only this morning, I was talking about it with Guedes. But I already knew about it! . . . And I felt sorry. What the devil! There's no crime in being as passionately in love as poor André was. He was madly, wildly in love. He even burst into tears once in the office, in front of the Secretary-General. And the girl laughing her head off!
. . But what is a crime, and a vile one, is this persecution of the brother, the paymaster, an excellent employee, extraordinarily talented . . . And it is the duty of every man of good will, who values the dignity of the Administration and the dignity of customs,

to denounce such infamy . . . I, for my part, have fulfilled my duty, and with some brilliance, praise be to God!'

'What have you done?'

'I have buried my trusty Toledo pen in the flank of the Civil Governor, right to the top!'

Barrolo, impressed, pinched the skin on his neck. The piano had fallen silent: but Gracinha did not move from the stool, her fingers still upon the keys, as if her thoughts were far away from the large sheet where the triumphant verses on the Ramires family were set out in Videirinha's neat hand. Suddenly Gonçalo was aware, in that suffocating stillness, of the disdain filling her. Touched by her emotions and anxious to come to her aid, to prevent a sob which might unavoidably escape, he ran to the piano and patted the poor stooped, trembling shoulders affectionately.

'You can't cope with this beautiful fado, my girl! Leave it, and I'll trill a verse in Videirinha's celebrated style. But first be an angel and call down the corridor for a glass of cold water from the Old Well.'

He set about the keys, and began a verse at random in an unmelodious endeavour:

'Now in that great battle,
Four valiant Ramires . . .'

Gracinha had disappeared without a sound through a gap in the curtains. Then the good Barrolo, who had been standing in front of his Indian bowl, thoughtfully and carefully rolling a cigarette, ran and leant over Gonçalo announcing, with slow certainty,

'Well, my dear fellow, it's as I say . . . This Noronha girl is a superb woman! But what I can't believe is that she would disdain the man's advance. With Cavaleiro such a handsome fellow, and Civil Governor into the bargain? I don't believe it. Cavaleiro tasted the fruit, I bet!'

And his cheeks glowing with admiration, he exclaimed,

'The scoundrel! There's no one in Oliveira to beat him where women and horses are concerned!'

5

THE *Porto Gazette* with its avenging letter was due to burst on
Oliveira on Wednesday morning, Cousin Maria Mendonça's birthday. But although Gonçalo did not fear (safe-guarded as he was by
his pseudonym *Juvenal*) a vulgar quarrel with Cavaleiro in the streets
of the city; nor even with one of his tough, subservient political
friends, like Marcolino of the *Independent*—he withdrew discreetly
to Santa Ireneia on the Tuesday, on horseback and accompanied by
Barrolo as far as Vendinha, where they both tried the white wine
praised by Titó. Then, to recall the memorable spot where, in his
novel, Lourenço Ramires met the Bastard of Baião in a disastrous
clash of arms—he took the path through the orchards of the small,
dispersed village of Canta Pedra, which led to the Bravais Road.

At a slow trot, he passed the Glass Factory and the Cross, always
covered in pigeons which fluttered down from the pigeon-loft of the
factory. He was entering the hamlet of Nacejas when, at the window
of a clean little house surrounded by vines, appeared a pretty girl,
dark-skinned and fine-featured, in a jacket of blue material and with
an embroidered lawn scarf over her abundant locks. Gonçalo, pulling
up his mare, greeted her with a tender smile:

'Excuse me, gentle maid . . . Am I on the right road for Canta
Pedra?'

'Yes, sir, you're on the right road. Down there, at the bridge,
turn right towards the poplars. Then it's straight ahead . . .'

Gonçalo sighed and mischievously replied,

'I'd prefer to stay . . .'

The girl blushed. The Nobleman turned in his saddle to enjoy
her fine olive features between the pots of carnations in the window
of the brightly whitewashed house.

At that moment, from a leafy path beside the road, emerged a
hunter in a jacket and red cap with a rifle slung across his shoulders
and two pointers following him behind. He was a fine big fellow and
there was an air of arrogance and presumption to everything about
him, from the tread of his undyed shoes to the swagger of his silk-
swathed waist and his light-complexioned face with its golden
side-whiskers. At a glance he took in the Nobleman's smile and

gallant attentions. He stopped short, fixing his beautiful long-lashed eyes upon him with slow arrogance. Then he passed disdainfully, without moving aside to let the mare pass down the hill, and almost caught the Nobleman's leg with the barrel of his gun. Further on, he gave a sharp derisive little cough—with a still more insolent click of his heels.

Gonçalo spurred on his mare, immediately overcome by that humiliating fear, that slight creeping of the flesh, that always, in the face of any risk, any threat, irresistibly drove him to withdraw, to retreat, to run away. At the bottom of the hill by the bridge, furious at his timidity, he stopped his horse and looked back again at the flower-adorned white house. The strapping young fellow had stopped and supported himself on his rifle under the window where the dark-haired girl was hanging out between the carnations. Leaning back arrogantly, after laughing to the girl, he pointed to the Nobleman with a sweeping gesture of challenge, his head held high, the tassel of his cap stuck in the air like a fiery cockscomb.

Gonçalo Mendes Ramires set off at a gallop down the leafy lane between the poplars which follows the Donas Stream. In Canta Pedra he did not remain to study (as he had intended in order to improve his novel) the valley and the winding stream, the ruins of the monastery of Recadães on the hill, and on the crest in front the windmill which is situated on the blackened stones of the ancient and famous Manor of Avelãs. Moreover, the sky, which had been grey and cloudy since morning, had darkened over by Craquede and Vila Clara. A warm breeze rustled the parched foliage. Drops were already splashing into the dust when he turned, still galloping, on to the Bravais Road.

At the Tower he found a letter from Castanheiro. The Patriot was anxious to know 'if this *Tower of Don Ramires* was indeed rising to honour the arts as the former one, the original, had risen in ancient times, in a happier age, to the glory of arms'. And he added in a postscript, 'I am planning to have enormous posters stuck on every corner of every city in Portugal with letters a yard high announcing the appearance of the redeeming *Annals*! And as I intend to promise your precious little novel in them to the public, I should like friend Gonçalo to inform me whether it has, in the manner of 1830, an inviting sub-title, like *Episodes from the Twelfth Century*, or *Chronicle of the Reign of Afonso II*, or *Scenes from the Portuguese Middle Ages*.

I should recommend a sub-title. Like the basement of a building, the sub-title increases the value of a book and gives it solidity. To work, then, Gonçalo, with that brilliant imagination of yours! . . .'

This idea of enormous posters with his name on them, and the title of his novel in brightly coloured letters covering every corner of Portugal, delighted the Nobleman. At once, that night, to the sound of the heavy rain which was falling noisily into the foliage of the lemon-trees, he picked up his manuscript again, interrupted in the full sonorous opening lines of the second chapter . . .

Here, in the freshness of dawn, Lourenço Mendes Ramires, with his body of horsemen and infantry, was making his way to succour the Princesses. But as he was entering the valley of Canta Pedra, behold! the valiant son of Tructesindo discerned the host of the Bastard of Baião, waiting since daybreak (as Mendes Pais had warned them) to bar their passage. Now, in this gloomy tale of blood and slaughter, there suddenly burst forth, like a rose in the crack of a fortress, a note of love, which Uncle Duarte had sung in the *Bard* with elegant melancholy.

Lopo de Baião, whose fair, aristocratic, Gothic beauty was famous throughout the land of Entre Minho and Douro, which called him the Bright Sun, was passionately in love with Dona Violante, the youngest daughter of Tructesindo Ramires. On St John's Day, at Lanhoso Castle, where there were celebrations including bull-fights and jousting, he had met the lovely maiden, whom Uncle Duarte in his poem had praised with blinding delight:

> 'What liquid brilliance in those black eyes!
> What heavy locks of lustrous ebony!'

She had also surely given her heart to that boy, as fair as gold who, on that festive afternoon, flourishing banderillas at the bulls, had won two sashes embroidered by the noble Lady of Lanhoso—and at night, in the merry-making, had moved with such superb elegance in the Marchatins Dance. But Lopo was a bastard, and of the Baião family, enemies of the Ramires through ancient disputes over land and hierarchy since the time of the Count Don Henrique—disputes later aggravated during the quarrels between Dona Teresa and Alfonso Henriques, when at the Barons' Council in Guimarães, Mendo de Baião, supporting the Count of Trava, and Ramires the Slaughterer, foster-brother of the young Prince, flung their steel gloves in each other's faces. Faithful to their age-old hatred, Tructe-sindo Ramires had refused, with harsh arrogance, the hand of Violante to the eldest Baião, one of the heroes of Silves, who had gone one Christmas to the Castle of Santa Ireneia to beg her in marriage to Lopo, his nephew, the Bright Sun, offering an almost meek settlement for the marriage and the subsequent peace. This insult shocked the house of Baião—who were proud of Lopo, in spite of his being a bastard, for his prowess and chivalrous charm. Then Lopo, his heart sorely, and his pride cruelly wounded, tried, to satiate his aching desire and to sully the fair name of the Ramires —to kidnap Dona Violante. It was in spring, when all the plains of the Mondego were green. The gracious lady, accompanied by squires from the Manor and relatives, was travelling from Treixedo to the Convent of Lorvão where her aunt Dona Branca was abbess. Tenderly, Uncle Duarte introduced the romantic note in the *Bard:*

'Beside the Moorish fountain, among the elms,
The mount drew to a halt . . .'

From beside the elms near the fountain emerged the Bright Sun who, with his men, had been watching from a hill-top! But at the very beginning of the short battle, a cousin of Dona Violante, the gigantic lord of the Manor of Avelim, unarmed him and held him for a moment on his knees beneath the flashing point of his dagger. With his life pardoned, growling with blind rage, the Bastard hastened away with the few knights from his castle who had accompanied him on his daring attack. From thenceforward the rancour between Baião and Ramires families blazed fiercer. And behold now, at the beginning of this War of the Princesses, the two enemies face to face in the narrow valley of Canta Pedra! Lopo had a band of thirty lances and a hundred cross-bowmen of the Royal host. Lourenço Mendes Ramires had fifteen horsemen and ninety infantrymen of his own.

August was coming to an end: and the long months of excessive heat had turned all the grass yellow, all the famous pastures of the valley, even the leaves of the alders and the ashes along the edge of the Donas Stream which meandered along between gleaming stones, thin trickles of water which babbled softly. On a hillside over by Ramilde, stood out, from among the imposing, bramble-covered ruins, the blackened Round Tower, the remains of the old Manor of Avelãs, burnt during the barbarous fights between the Salzedas and the Landins, and now inhabited by the groaning soul of Guiomar de Landim, the Ill-Married. On the opposite, highest hilltop, dominating the valley, the Convent of Recadães extended its new stone walls, with its strong turret and battlements like a fortress, from which the monks leaned, peering out uneasily at the glint of arms that had filled the valley since daybreak. And the same fear tormented the neighbouring villages—because, over the hilltops, people hurried with bundles, covered wagons and narrow processions of cattle to the holy and walled refuge of the convent.

At the sight of such a strong body of horsemen and foot-soldiers, spread out as far as the edge of the river beneath the shadows of the ash-trees, Lourenço Ramires drew in his reins and halted his men beside a pile of stones where a rough cross stood rotting. And his scout, who had given his horse the bridle and lay protected beneath his leather shield, in order to reconnoitre the host, immediately returned without being hit by arrow or stone, and shouted:

'They are the troops of the Baiãos and the royal host!'

Their passage was barred! And their numbers so unequal! But the dauntless Ramires did not hesitate to advance and join battle. Had he arrived at the valley alone, with only a hunter's javelin, he would have flung himself against the Bastard's entire host . . . Meanwhile, the Baião's officer-in-command had advanced, his emaciated sorrel curvetting, and his sword held high above his morion adorned with heron's feathers. He cried out in a loud voice, and his proclamation thundered throughout the valley:

'No further! No further! Your way is barred! The noble Lord of Baião is bade by order of the king and through his mercy to spare your lives if you retire quietly and speedily!'

Lourenço Ramires shouted,

'At him, cross-bowmen!'

The arrows whistled. The entire short flank of horsemen from Santa Ireneia trooped into the valley, their lances at the ready. Tructesindo's son, standing up in his heavy iron stirrups, beneath the flapping standard which the standard-bearer had hastily drawn from its cover, opened the visor of his helmet so that they should see his intrepid face clearly, and spat insults of furious pride at the Bastard:

'Call to your aid as many villains again as follow you here, and I shall trample over you and them all and reach Montemor tonight!'

The Bastard, on his bay, which was covered by a net of mail, laced in gold, brandished his iron-clad hand and called out,

'Back! Back to where you came from shall you go, treacherous knave, but only if I mercifully send your father your body on a litter!'

These violent challenges were contained in tranquilly measured lines in Uncle Duarte's poem. After strengthening them, Gonçalo Mendes Ramires (feeling his soul swelling with the heroism of his race, as if by a wind blowing across a vast plain) flung the two valiant bands against each other. A fearful battle, fearful cries . . .

'Forward! Forward!'

'At them!'

'Hold fast for Baião!'   .

'Strike for the Ramires!'

Amid the clouds of dust and tumult, whistle the bolts and the rough clay balls hurled from slings. Horsemen from Santa Ireneia, horsemen from the royal host, in small bands, charge, collide, in a confusion of hurled javelins that shatter, of arrows that penetrate; and both groups flee and return—while beneath them, on the churned-up earth, some badly injured man kicks convulsively and screams, while others stagger dazedly beneath the shelter of the trees in search of a cool stream. In the midst of the fray, in the noblest field of conflict, aloft on the rearing chargers, gasping under the weight of their coats-of-mail, the smooth flat blades of the two-handled swords flashed and shone, biting into the metal covers of the shields: and already, from his high red leather saddle-bow, some stiff, steel-clad gentleman tumbles to the ground with a thud as his armour hits the soft earth. Knights and noblemen, however, as if in a joust, merely had to cross lances to knock down their adversary, their harness crumpling under them, letting out shouts of excitement and arrogance; and it was on the enemy band below, on whom the worst of the slaughter fell, that they crashed their weighty swords, that they swung their battle-axes, shattering the iron helmets like so many clay-pots.

Through the crowd of foot-soldiers of the Baião force and those of the royal host, Lourenço Ramires advanced more swiftly than a sharp-edged scythe through tender shoots. Each leap forward of his trusty stallion, bathed in sweat, furiously shaking his tapering muzzle, brought forth curses or cries of 'Jesus!' and a pierced body would arch and fall, arms twisting in agony. His ardent desire was to strike a blow at Lopo. But this morning, the Bastard, generally so valiant and daring in battle, would not leave his position on the hillside, where a row of lances guarded him like a stockade; with shouts, not blows, he spurred on his men! In his desperate attempt to break through the living barrier, Lourenço spent all his energy, harshly defying the Bastard with violent insults: 'Villain!' he cried. 'Varlet!' Already through the broken texture of his camail, through his cuirass at the shoulder, there came slow trickles of blood. A heavy arrow had split asunder the straps of the left greaves and pierced the leg from which more blood streamed, soaking the oakum lining. Then struck by an arrow in its haunch, his great charger tumbled, rolled on the ground, snapping its plaited girth as it kicked. Swiftly, freeing himself from his stirrups with a leap, Lourenço Ramires came face to face with a spiked wall of spears and swords which closed round him—while from the hill top, leaning over in his saddle, the Bastard shouted,

'Wait! Stop! Tie his hands!'

Climbing over corpses, the brave youth flung himself, with breathless energy, against the shining, flashing weapons that retreated and tried to escape. And the cries of Lopo de Baião re-echoed triumphantly:

'Alive! I want him taken alive!'

'Not while any soul remains within me, villain!' roared Lourenço.

Still more furiously was he rushing upon his foes when a sharp, heavy stone struck him on the arm—which fell inert, his sword dangling, still fixed to his wrist by its chain, but as useless as a frill on a cuff. In an instant he was secured by foot-soldiers who seized his throat while others with blows of their javelins struck at his braced legs. Eventually he fell stiff as a log—and in the cords with which they at once bound him, he lay rigid, without bascinet or helm, his eyes painfully closed, his hair matted with dust and blood.

Lourenço Ramires has been captured! Facing the litter of beech branches on which they laid him, after hastily sprinkling him with cool water from the stream—the Bastard, wiping off, with the back of his hand, the sweat which poured down his beautiful face and golden beard, murmured with feeling,

'Ah, Lourenço, Lourenço, how grievous, when we might well have been brothers and friends!'

Thus, aided by Uncle Duarte and Walter Scott, and by articles in *Panorama*, Gonçalo reconstructed the ill-fated battle of Canta Pedra. And with this outburst of Lopo's, with its sorrowful theme of forbidden love, Chapter Two came to an end, at which he had laboured three days—so immersed in his work that all around him the world seemed reduced to silence and shadows.

★   ★   ★

A series of fireworks exploded in the distance, over by Bravais, where on Sunday the famous pilgrimage of Our Lady of the Lights was to take place. After the rain of the last three days, a coolness had descended upon the earth, softer and clearer above the greener fields. As there was still a good half-hour till dinner, the Nobleman picked up his cane, and just as he was, in his old working-jacket, went down to the road and took the path that runs between the wall of the Tower and the fields of rye where, in the twelfth century, stood the barbicans of the Manor of Santa Ireneia.

Along the silent path, still damp from the rains, Gonçalo thought about his brilliant forefathers. How they sprang to life in his novel, concrete, vivid figures! Really, so sure an understanding of those Afonsine souls showed that his soul was of the same carat and came from the same rich block of gold. Because a puny heart, or a degenerate one, would not know how to tell such virile tales of such virile eras: and neither the good Manuel Duarte nor the excellent Barrolo would understand enough to reconstruct such lofty characters as Martim de Freitas or Afonso de Albuquerque . . . He hoped the critics would stress this point when later they studied the *Tower of Don Ramires*—because Castanheiro had assured him of considerable reviews in *News* and *The Morning Post*. Yes! It was this that should be brought out clearly (and he would point this out to Castanheiro!)—that the Noblemen of Santa Ireneia reappeared in their descendant, if not by continuity of the same daring deeds, at least by the same lofty understanding of heroism . . . What the deuce! He could not, in the reign of the awful Sao Fulgêncio, destroy the house of Baião, destroyed some six hundred years before by his ancestor, Leonel Ramires—nor win back from the Moors the well-fortified Monforte, with its languid Civil Governor, Antoninho Moreno! But he felt the grandeur and the historic value of the intrepidity which in earlier times had led his family to lay waste rival houses and storm Moorish towns; and he resuscitated these fearless men by knowledge and art, and brought them into contemporary life, they and their hearts and souls, their costumes their powerful sword-blows and their sublime bravura. He was, then, within the spirit and expression of his century, a good Ramires—a Ramires of noble spirit, not in heroic actions but in intellectual ones, as befitted an age of intellectual activity and peace. The newspapers, which so mercilessly censured the decadence of the Portuguese aristocracy, should in all justice affirm (and he would make a point of telling Castanheiro!): 'Here is one, the greatest of all, who, within the manners and customs of his age, maintains and honours the spirit of his race!'

As he thought these thoughts, which made him tread still firmer on the ground trod by so many members of his family—the Nobleman of the Tower arrived at a corner of the wall of the grounds, where a steep and narrow path divided them from the pinewoods and scrub. Of the noble gate that formerly existed in this spot, with engravings and coats-of-arms, only the two granite gate-posts remained, yellowish-green with moss, and boarded up now against the cattle by a series of roughly-nailed boards, eaten away by the years and by rain. At this moment, from the far end of the path, barely visible in the shadows, a creaking ox-cart drew up, loaded with wood, and led by a pretty little ox-driver.

'May the Lord give you a good evening, sir!'

'Good evening, my beauty!'

The slow cart drew to a halt. From behind appeared a man, tall, thin and dark, with a staff on his shoulder, and dangling from the staff a bunch of cords.

The Nobleman of the Tower recognized José Casco of Bravais. So he continued on his way, as if in thought, along the edge of the pinewood, whistling and touching the flowers in the hedgerow with his cane. The man, however, walked quicker and pronounced the Nobleman's name sharply in the silence of the wood and the evening. Gonçalo Mendes Ramires' heart gave a leap, he stopped, and with an effort his lips curved in an amiable smile:

'Hello, there! It's you, Casco! What can I do for you?'

Casco choked and his ribs heaved under his grimy working jersey. Then, unwinding the cords from his quince-wood crook, and sticking its pointed end into the ground, he said,

'The fact is I have always been honest with the Nobleman and I don't deserve that he should break his word to me.'

Gonçalo Ramires raised his head with slow, laboursome dignity, as if he were lifting an iron mace,

'What are you saying, Casco? Break my word? How have I broken my word? . . . By renting the Tower? That's good! Had we signed anything? You never came back, never turned up again . . .'

Casco was silent, amazed. Then, with a burst of anger that made his white lips tremble, shook his dry, hairy hands which were clasped round the handle of his staff,

'If there was anything signed, the Nobleman couldn't back out of it! . . . But it was as if there were, as far as honest people are concerned! . . . Even you yourself said when I accepted, "Good! It's a deal!" And you gave your word!'

Gonçalo, uneasy, assumed the patient air of a benevolent lord.

'Listen, José Casco. This is not the place, here in the road. If you want to talk to me, come to the Tower. I am always there, as you know, in the mornings . . . Come along tomorrow, it's no trouble.'

He headed off towards the pine wood, his legs feeling weak and his spine a-tremble, when Casco intercepted him with a light jump and planted himself defiantly before him, barring his way with his crook.

'Your Lordship's going to speak here and now! Your Lordship gave his word! . . . You're not making a fool of me like this . . . Your Lordship gave his word!'

Gonçalo glanced warily round, in anxious hope of aid. But only solitude and thick woods surrounded him. Along the road, barely visible in the fast disappearing daylight, only the vague outline of a wood cart could be seen, creaking in the distance. The high branches of the pine-trees murmured with a sleepy, remote sigh. In between the trunks of the trees shadows and mist were growing denser. Then Gonçalo, terrified, attempted to make an escape by means of the concept of Justice and Law, which always puts fear into country labourers. So like a friend advising a friend, very gently, with his lips dry and trembling, he suggested,

'Listen, Casco, listen, man! You can't settle things like this, shouting! Something unpleasant might happen, the local officer might appear. Then there'd be a court-case and prison. And you've got a wife and young children . . . Listen! If you find you have any cause for complaint, come to the Tower and we'll talk the matter over! We'll settle things peacefully, man . . . Not shouting like this! The officer might come along, and then it'd be a prison cell . . .'

At this, Casco suddenly grew in stature on the lonely road, tall and black like a pine-tree, in a fury that made his flashing, almost bloodshot eyes protrude.

'So now your Lordship's threatening me with Justice! Not content with treachery you threaten me with prison! Then heaven help me, I'll smash these bones of yours before I go to prison!'

He raised his crook . . . But then, with a flash of reason and respect, he cried out between clenched teeth, his trembling head thrown back:

'Run, your Lordship, run, before I lose control! Run or I'll kill you and that'll be the end of me!'

Gonçalo Mendes Ramires ran to the boarded-up gate between the old granite posts, leapt over the roughly-nailed boards, ran along by the vine-covered wall in a mad chase like a hunted hare! At the edge of the vineyards, near the maize-field, a wild fig-tree spread its branches covered with dense foliage inside an old, disused and roofless granary. In this refuge of stone and branches the Nobleman of the Tower crouched, gasping for breath. Dusk was enshrouding the fields—and with dusk, a serenity that enveloped leaves and grass. Encouraged by the silence and calm, Gonçalo abandoned his well-protected shelter. He began to run, tip-toeing softly in his white boots over the ground still moist after the rain, until he reached the wall of the Mãe-d'Agua. Again he stopped, exhausted. And believing he saw in the distance, at the edge of the wood, a white patch—a labourer in shirt-sleeves, he let out a frantic yell: 'Oh Ricardo! Oh, Manuel! Hello, there! Is there anybody there?' A vague light dissolved into the vague foliage. A frog croaked in a ditch. Shivering, Gonçalo continued along the path till he came to the corner of the orchard, where he found a closed gate, an old gate offering little protection, swinging on its rusty hinges. Gonçalo hurled his shoulder furiously against it, a shoulder that terror had hardened like iron. Two of the boards gave and he crept through, tearing his jacket on a nail. At last he could breathe freely in the safety of the walled orchard, in front of the verandahs of the house open to the coolness of the evening, beside the Tower, his Tower, black, a thousand years old, blacker and seemingly more burdened by the years in contrast to the soft clarity of the new moon which was rising.

Hat in hand, wiping away his perspiration, he entered the garden and went round the edge of the bean-field. Now, suddenly, he was invaded by bitter anger at the helplessness which he had experienced, in such a well-populated farm, thick with people and dependants! Not a tenant, not a labourer, when he had called out in such desperation at the edge of Mãe d'Agua! Of his five servants, not one had run to his aid—and him lost there, a stone's throw from his barns and stables! If a couple of men now ran up with sticks or spades they could still probably catch Casco along the road, and thrash him like an ear of corn.

By the chicken-houses, he heard a girl's high-pitched laughter and crossed the yard to the lighted doorway of the kitchen. Two boys from the farm, Crispola's daughter and Rosa, were chatting together, comfortably seated on a stone bench under the cool dark vines. Inside the fire spluttered—and the pot of broth simmered, filling the kitchen with its smell. The Nobleman's fury broke loose.

'What's this? A party? Didn't you hear me shouting? I met a drunk by the pinewood who didn't recognize me and came at me with a scythe! Luckily I had my cane with me! I shouted and yelled . . . What for? Everyone's sitting here gossiping, with supper being got ready! What impudence! Next time it happens I'll put the lot of you in the street . . . And if anyone protests he'll feel my stick round him!'

His face flushed, bold and arrogant. Crispola's daughter immediately slipped away, slunk into the recess behind the kneading-trough. The two young men had risen and were now bent like two stems of corn in a strong wind. While Rosa crossed herself in terror, and dissolved into laments about 'the awful things that will happen!' Gonçalo, delighted by the two men's submissiveness, both so strong, with such thick staffs leaning against the wall, quietened down a little.

'Really! You must all be deaf in this wretched house! Apart from which the orchard gate's closed! I had to knock it down. It's in pieces now.'

Then one of the young men, the braver of the two, a fair-haired fellow, with a horse-like chin, thinking that the Nobleman was complaining about the fragility of the neglected gate, scratched his head and apologized,

'Well, I'm very sorry, your Lordship! But since Relho left, there's been another board nailed on and a new lock fixed—and a strong one, too!'

'Strong!' scoffed the Nobleman. 'I smashed the lock and I smashed the new board . . . It's all in pieces!'

The other fellow, more at ease and sharper-witted, smiled to please the Nobleman.

'In heaven's name! . . . You must have some strength, your Lordship!'

His companion, convinced of the fact, stuck out his enormous chin and agreed:

'What strength! That gate was really strong . . . And a new lock, too, since Relho left!'

This assurance of his mighty strength, praised by these tough young men, wholly comforted the Nobleman of the Tower who now became gentle, almost paternal.

'Thank God I have strength enough to knock down a gate, even a new one. What I couldn't reasonably do was drag a drunk with a scythe along the road to the village authority. That's why I called and shouted. So that you could get hold of him and take him to the officer. Still, it's over now. Oh, Rosa, give these boys an extra mug of wine with their supper. We'll see if next time it gives them a bit more courage, makes them appear . . .'

He was now like a lord of former times, a Ramires of past centuries, just and wise, who had reproved his vassals for some weakness—and then immediately forgave them, trusting to their future prowess. Then, with his cane at his shoulder like a lance, he made his way up the gloomy kitchen stairway. Upstairs, in his room, no sooner did Bento appear to dress him than he began his epic tale again, more detailed this time, more terrifying—dismaying the sensitive man who stood transfixed beside the chest-of-drawers, without even putting down the jug of hot water, the varnished boots and the heavy armful of towels . . . Casco! José Casco of Bravais, drunk, going for him, without recognizing him, with an enormous scythe, shouting out, 'Die, you scoundrel! . . .' And him in the road, in front of the brute, with only a cane to defend him! But he leapt aside, the scythe went into the trunk of a pine-tree . . . Then he rushed at him, brandishing his cane, shouting for Ricardo and Manuel, since they were accompanying him. Casco stood confused, then backed away and disappeared up the path, staggering and grunting . . .

'What do you think of that? If it hadn't been for my courage the man would have shot me with his rifle!'

Bento, who stood there gaping, almost dribbling, the water-jug forgotten and dripping on to the carpet, blinked in confusion, more amazed than ever.

'But you said he had a scythe, sir!'

Gonçalo stamped his foot impatiently.

'He ran at me with a scythe. But he was walking behind his cart and in the cart he had his rifle. Casco's a hunter, he always carries his rifle with him . . . Anyway, here I am, at the Tower thanks to God's mercy. And also because, in these cases, I don't lack nerve!'

He hurried Bento—because what with all the commotion and the effort, his legs were positively trembling with exhaustion and hunger . . . And as for being thirsty! . . .'

'Thirsty more than anything else! Make sure the wine's nice and cold. The green wine and the alvarelhão so I can mix them.'

Bento, with a deep, shuddering sigh of emotion, filled the basin and laid out the towels. Then he remarked gravely,

'It seems to be a disease in these parts. The same happened to Sr Sanches Lucena in *Feitosa*.'

'What do you mean, to Sr Sanches Lucena?'

Bento then came out with a terrifying tale brought to the Tower, during the Nobleman's stay in Oliveira, by Crispola's brother-in-law, Rui the carpenter, who had been working at the time on repairs at *Feitosa*. One evening, at twilight, Sr Sanches Lucena had gone down to the door of the gazebo when he met two labourers along the road, either drunkards or criminals, who picked a quarrel with that excellent gentleman. They started with sniggers and jokes and pranks. Sr Sanches patiently advised the men to be on their way, not go too far. Suddenly one of them, a big fellow, shook his jacket off his shoulders and raised his staff! Fortunately, his companion, who recognized Sr Sanches, called out, "Here, lad, he's our Deputy!" The boy rushed off in alarm. The other even went down on his knees before Sr Sanches Lucena . . . But the poor gentleman had such a shock that he had to take to his bed!

Gonçalo listened to the story, drying his hands slowly on the towel, and asked, impressed,

'When was this?'

'I told you, sir. When you were in Oliveira, sir. Just before or just after Senhora Dona Graça's birthday.'

The Nobleman dropped the towel and thoughtfully cleaned his fingernails. Then, with an incredulous half-smile, he remarked,

'Well, at least it's done Sanches Lucena some good being Deputy for Vila Clara . . .'

Dressed now, filling his cigar-case (because he had decided to spend the night in town and pour out his story to Gouveia) he again turned to Bento, who was tidying his clothes.

'So the drunkard, when the other one shouted, "Here lad, he's our Deputy!" came to his senses and fled, did he? Well I never! It's worth being a Deputy, then! At least it commands respect, man! At least more respect than being a descendant of the Kings of Lyons! . . . Well, well, let me have some dinner.'

During supper, mixing his plentiful supply of green wine and alvarelhão, Gonçalo did not stop thinking of Casco's audacious behaviour. For the first time in the history of Santa Ireneia, a farm worker from the villages which had grown up in the shadow of the illustrious House, which for so many centuries had held sway over hill and dale—had insulted a Ramires! And brutally, raising his crook in front of the walls of the historic estate! His father had re-counted that in the time of his great-grandfather Inácio, the men from Ramilde to Covinde had knelt by the roadside when the Noble-man of the Tower passed by. Now they raised their scythes! Why? Because he would not meekly lower his rents to benefit a ruffian! In the time of his ancestor Tructesindo, any villain who attempted such a thing would roast, like a wild pig, on a crackling bonfire in front of the barbican of the Manor. And as late as in the time of his great-grandfather Inácio he would have perished in a dungeon. Casco would not go scot-free. Impunity would merely increase his auda-city: impetuous and bitter, he would, when they met again, discharge his gun without further ado. Oh! He did not want him to suffer any permanent ill, poor fellow, with two little children, one of them still at the breast. But he ought to be dragged to the bench, handcuffed between two officers, and in that gloomy little room from which you could see the bars of the prison, receive a powerful admonition from Gouveia, the grave Gouveia, stiff and starched in his black frock-coat. In this way he would protect himself, by roundabout means— because he was not a Member of the House, and for all his talent

114

and his name—this extraordinary lineage stretching from those ancestors of his who had founded the Kingdom, he lacked the prestige of a Sanches Lucena, that powerful prestige which arrests staffs in mid-air!

When he had finished coffee, he told Bento to have the two farm-boys called—the one called Ricardo and the one with the horse's chin—and have them wait for him in the yard, armed. Because there still existed in the Tower an 'armoury'—a small, dark recess next to the archives with a collection of bent pieces of armour, a coat-of-mail, a Moorish buckler, halberds and heavy swords, powder-horns, 1820 blunderbusses, and among all these dusty pieces of black iron, three clean rifles from which the boys of the farm, on the pilgrimage of St Gonçalo, fired shots in honour of the Saint.

He stuck his revolver in his pocket, dug out, from the cupboard in the corridor, an old cane with a curved lead handle, and picked up a whistle. Thus armed, warmed inside by the green wine and the alvarelhão, and accompanied by his two men, stiff and important with their guns on their shoulders, he set off for Vila Clara, to find the District Administrator. The night enveloped the fields in coolness and peace. The new moon which had cleared up the weather, brushed the tops of the hills of Valverde like the shining wheel of a golden chariot. In the silence, the large, solid, nailed shoes of the two labourers echoed rhythmically. Gonçalo, further ahead, his cigar glowing, enjoyed that march in which a Ramires once more trod the roads of Santa Ireneia, accompanied by his men and armed vassals.

When he reached the town, however, he discreetly left his escort in Serena's tavern; while he cut up by the Erva Market, to Simões' Tobacconist's where Gouveia used, at that time, before going to the Club, to stop and buy a box of matches and thoughtfully examine the lottery tickets in the window. But that night the Administrator was not at the customary Simões. So Gonçalo set off for the Club; and there, downstairs, in the billiard-room, a bald-headed man, his collar unbuttoned, toothpick in mouth, and head raised forward contemplating the solitary caramboles of the scorer—informed the Nobleman that his friend Gouveia was ill.

'Nothing grave, just an inflammation of the throat . . . You are sure to find him at home, sir. He has not left his room since Sunday.'

Another gentleman, however, who was stirring his coffee at the corner of a table heaped with liquor bottles, assured him that the Administrator had been out that afternoon. He had seen him about five o'clock in the *Amoreira*, his throat well wrapped in a woollen scarf.

Gonçalo set off impatiently up the town. He was crossing Fountain Square when he caught sight of the sought-after Gouveia, at the door of the brightly-lit Ramos Drapery, talking to an enormous man with a thick jet-black beard and light grey dust-coat.

It was Gouveia, finger raised, who hurried towards Gonçalo.

'You've heard, then?'

'What?'

'Don't you know, man? . . . Sanches Lucena!'

'What?'

'He's dead!'

The Nobleman looked at the Administrator in amazement, and then at the other gentleman, who was pulling, with great effort, a short, tight, black glove on his vast hand.

'Good heavens! . . . When?'

'This morning. Suddenly. "Angina pectoris"—something or other to do with the heart . . . Suddenly, in bed.'

They looked at each other in silence, in ever-renewed awe of the death which was shaking Vila Clara. At last Gonçalo said,

'And I was talking about him only a short while ago in the Tower. And as usual, poor soul, with little respect.'

'What about me?' exclaimed Gouveia. 'I wrote to him only yesterday . . . A long letter about a favour Manuel Duarte wanted . . . And it was his corpse that received the letter.'

'That's a good joke,' grunted the fat gentleman, who was having a fierce struggle with his glove. 'The corpse received the letter . . . Good, that!'

The Nobleman twisted his moustache pensively.

'Tell me, how old was he?'

Gouveia had always imagined him really old, seventy years at least. But no! Only sixty, last December. But he was wasted, worn out. He had married late, to a strong young female . . .

'So now we have the beautiful Dona Ana a widow at twenty-eight, no children and the natural heir of the modest sum of two hundred *contos* . . . Perhaps more!'

'Nice bit of pocket-money!' snorted the swollen individual who had at last got his glove on, and was now grunting, his veins at bursting-point, as he did up the button.

The Nobleman felt ill at ease with this gentleman, anxious as he was to discuss with Gouveia the political vacancy in the constituency of Vila Clara so unexpectedly left by the brusque disappearance of the traditional leader. He could not control himself, but tugged the Administrator by the button of his frock-coat to the favourable shade of the wall.

'Oh, Gouveia! Now what, then? . . . We'll have a by-election . . . Who will be candidate?'

The Administrator, very simply, without dissembling in front of the big man in the dust-coat who, his gloves on at last, had lit a cigar and was approaching them familiarly, explained the facts:

'Now, my friend, with Cavaleiro's uncle Minister of Justice and José Ernesto Minister of Home Affairs, the seat will go to whomever André Cavaleiro says. That's obvious . . . Sanches Lucena kept his seat in S Bento by being the person naturally endorsed by the party. He was the first man here, the big man among the Historicals. Right! Now, as no one is naturally endorsed by the party, who is going to get the Government's support? Cavaleiro's personal choice. You know what a regionalist Cavaleiro is. In this constituency, then, it's logical that we'll have whomever Cavaleiro considers will follow in Lucena's steps—someone with influence and territorial stability. In another constituency one could still hastily arrange a deputy fabricated in Lisbon, in the offices there. But not here! The Deputy must be a local man and Cavaleirist. And Cavaleiro himself, let me tell you, is just now at a loss.'

The paunchy man murmured importantly through the enormous cigar he was smoking,

'I'm seeing him tomorrow so I'll know.'

But the Administrator had suddenly stopped, was scratching his chin and fixing Gonçalo with his bright glittering eyes as if a happy idea, almost an inspiration, had illuminated him. Suddenly he said to the other man who was stroking his black beard,

'Right, my friend, until the day after tomorrow. That's settled, then. I'll send the basket of cheeses direct to the Counsellor.'

He took Gonçalo's arm, which he squeezed impatiently. And paying no further attention to the large fellow, whom he profusely bade farewell, he pulled the Nobleman towards the silent road.

'Listen, Gonçalo, listen . . . You've got a superb opportunity here! If you wished, you could be deputy for Vila Clara within a few days!'

The Nobleman stopped short—as if a star had suddenly fallen there in the ill-lit street.

. . 'Now listen!' exclaimed the Administrator, freeing himself from Gonçalo's arm, so as to develop his idea more freely. 'You have no serious commitment to the Regenerators. You left Coimbra a year ago, you are now attempting to enter public life, you have never made any definitive acts binding you to either party. Just a letter or two to the newspapers—trifles!'

'But . . .'

'Listen, man! You want to get into politics, don't you? Of course you do. Well, then, as a Historical or a Regenerator, it doesn't much matter. They are both constitutional, both Christian . . . The question is getting in, breaking in. Now here you are, unexpectedly, with a door open before you. What is there to stop you? Your personal enmity with Cavaleiro? Rubbish!'

He flung out his arm in a broad, impatient gesture as if brushing aside such a childish obstacle.

'Rubbish! You haven't killed anyone, either of you. You're not really even enemies. Cavaleiro's a talented young fellow, a man of taste . . . I don't know of anyone else in the district who is nearer you in spirit, in education, in manners and traditions. In a small place like this, a reconciliation is bound to come sooner or later. So it might as well be now when such a reconciliation would take you to S Bento! And I repeat: the constituency of Vila Clara will elect whomever Cavaleiro commands!'

The Nobleman of the Tower breathed with effort, in the emotion that was suffocating him. Then, silently removing his hat and fanning himself with it, he remarked pensively, looking very crestfallen,

'But Cavaleiro, as you yourself said, is completely local, completely regional . . . He won't want anyone who is not a man like Lucena, with a large fortune and influence . . .'

His friend stopped, throwing wide his arms.

'What about you, then? What the devil! You have property here. You have the Tower. You have Treixedo. Your sister is rich now, richer than Lucena. And then there's the name, your family . . . You, the Ramires, are a well-established family, who've lived in Santa Ireneia for more than two hundred years.'

The Nobleman of the Tower raised his head sharply.

'Two hundred? . . . For a thousand years, nearly a thousand years!'

'There you are, then! For a thousand years. A house older than the monarchy. Contemporary with it, anyway. You're more aristocratic than the King himself! Isn't this a situation vastly superior to Lucena's? Not to mention your intelligence . . . Oh, confound it!'

'What's the matter?'

'My throat! A slight pricking. I'm still not quite cured.'

He decided to go home at once and gargle, because Dr Macedo had forbidden nights out. So Gonçalo would accompany friend Gouveia to his door. Wrapping his woollen scarf tighter, the Administrator resumed his train of thought.

'The constituency of Vila Clara, Gonçalinho, will elect whomever Cavaleiro decides. And Cavaleiro, believe me, would be greatly interested in choosing you, in introducing you into politics. If you therefore hold out your hand to Cavaleiro, the constituency is yours. Cavaleiro has the greatest, the very greatest interest, Gonçalinho!'

'I don't know about that, João Gouveia . . .'

'I do!'

Then, confidentially, in the deserted street, João Gouveia revealed to the Nobleman that Cavaleiro was yearning for the chance to resume his former friendship with his dear old Gonçalo! Only the week before Cavaleiro had stated (these were his very words), 'Of the young fellows of this generation, there is not one with a safer and greater future in politics before him than our Gonçalo. He's got everything! A great name, great talent, charm, eloquence . . . He's got everything! And I, who still have all the affection for Gonçalo that I had of old, would be delighted, absolutely delighted, to take him to the House!'

'His very words, my friend! Only six or seven days ago, in Oliveira, as we were both having coffee after dinner in the garden.'

Gonçalo's face beamed in the shadows, as he devoured the Administrator's revelations. Then, slowly, as if frankly revealing every cranny in his soul,

'To tell you the truth, I still retain my old affection for Cavaleiro. As for certain private matters, well, goodbye to them! They have grown old, worn thin, as obsolete today as the quarrels between the Horatii and the Curiatii. As you rightly mentioned just now, our hostility never led to any deaths. What the deuce! I was educated with Cavaleiro, we were like brothers! Believe me, Gouveia—every time I see him I feel a mad desire, a genuinely mad one, to run up to him and shout, "Oh André! The old clouds have passed—let's be friends again!" Believe me, it's only shyness that has prevented me doing this—only shyness! No, as far as I'm concerned, I'm willing for a reconciliation, with all my heart I am! But is he? . . . Because, you know, Gouveia, in my letters to the *Porto Gazette* I have been really cruel to him!'

João Gouveia stopped, his cane against his shoulder, considering the Nobleman with a smile of amazement.

'In your letters? What have you said in your letters? That the Civil Governor is a despot and a Don Juan? . . . My dear friend, every man likes the idea of being called a despot and a Don Juan by his political opposition. Do you suppose you hurt him? He was simply enchanted!'

The Nobleman murmured uneasily,

'Perhaps. But my allusions to his moustache and long hair . . .'

'Oh, Gonçalinho! Fine, curly hair and a handsome curled moustache are not defects of which a man is ashamed. On the contrary! All the women admire him. Do you suppose you made Cavaleiro look ridiculous? No! You merely announced to the matrons and the young ladies that read the *Porto Gazette* the existence of a splendid young fellow who happens to be the Civil Governor of Oliveira.'

Stopping once more (because ahead, on the corner, shone the open windows of his house), the Administrator pointed a firm finger for his final word of advice:

'Gonçalo Mendes Ramires, what you want to do is send for Torto's carriage and pair tomorrow, jump in, hurry over to the city, rush into the Civil Governor's offices with open arms and shout without any preliminaries, "André, what's past is past. Let me welcome you again with a hug! And as there's a vacancy in the constituency, let me welcome that with a hug, too!" And within five or six weeks you'll be Deputy for Vila Clara, with all the bells ringing . . . Will you have a cup of tea?'

'No, thank you.'

'Right, good luck, then! A carriage tomorrow to the Civil Governor's. Of course you'll have to arrange some sort of pretext.'

The Nobleman replied enthusiastically,

'I have one! No! What I mean is I have a real need, an absolute need, to speak to Cavaleiro or the Secretary-General. It's a matter concerning a tenant of mine . . . In fact, it was because of this unfortunate business that I came to see you here today, Gouveia.'

He babbled out the adventure of Casco, painting it in thicker colours to make it blacker. For weeks this wretch Casco had been obstinately and pertinaciously tormenting him to lease the Tower. But he had made a deal with Pereira, Pereira the Brazilian, for a splendid rent, far superior to what Casco had whiningly offered. After that, Casco had been grumbling and threatening in all the local taverns. That afternoon he had leapt out from a path and gone for him with his crook raised aloft! Thanks be to God, he had defended himself, shaken off the brute with his cane. But now, hovering over his tranquillity, over his life even, was the insult of that raised crook. And if he were attacked again he would shoot Casco, like a wild animal . . . So he urged his friend Gouveia to send for the man and severely reprimand him, even lock him up in prison for a few hours . . .

The Administrator, who had been feeling his throat as he listened, interrupted him, his hand upraised.

'The Civil Government, my friend, the Civil Government! These cases of preventive detention are up to the Civil Government! A reprimand is insufficient for such a brute! Only prison, a day in prison, on half-rations . . . The Civil Government will send me an official letter or telegram. You were really in danger, you know. There's not a moment to lose! Tomorrow, hop straight in a carriage to the Civil Governor. Even if only for the sake of law and order!'

Gonçalo, moved, his shoulders bent, yielded before the all-important reason of upholding law and order.

'Right, João Gouveia, I will! It is indeed a question of law and order. I'll go tomorrow and see the Civil Governor.'

'Excellent,' concluded the Administrator, tugging at the bell-pull. 'Give my regards to Cavaleiro. And let me tell you we'll get a phenomenal number of votes and we'll have fireworks and cheering and a superb supper in Gago's . . . You won't have a cup of tea? Really? Then good night . . . And listen! In a couple of years' time, when you're a minister, Gonçalo Mendes Ramires will remember this night conversation of ours in Vila Clara!'

Gonçalo went on thoughtfully past the Post Office, round the corner of the white steps of S Bento Church and then turned absent-mindedly down the acacia-lined road leading to the cemetery. From that high point of the town, with the street just below, where one could take in the rich expanse of fields from Valverde to Craquede, he felt that in his life, too, as solitary and confined as the dark street, a wide space had opened out full of interesting bustle and profusion. The wall, which he had always imagined irremediably closed, had suddenly split open. Here was the practicable crack! Beyond shone all the beautiful realities which he had yearned for since his days in Coimbra! But . . . But if he squeezed through that jagged crack he would surely tear his dignity or his pride. What was he to do?

Undoubtedly, by opening his arms to that animal Cavaleiro he would win his election. The constituency, a Historical domain, would meekly elect whichever member the Historical leader lazily decreed. But this reconciliation meant the triumphal entry of Cavaleiro into Barrolo's quiet home . . . He would thus be selling his sister's peace for a seat in S Bento! No! No, he could not, for Gracinha's sake! Gonçalo sighed, with a loud sigh, in the luminous silence of the road.

Not for three or four years would the Regenerators get into the government. He would remain here all that time, in his rural hole, playing soporific games of billiards in the town Club, idly smoking cigarettes on the verandahs of *Cunhais*, with no career, silent and at a halt in life, gathering moss, like his decrepit, useless Tower! By Jove! It would be shirking his most sacred duties towards himself and his name! . . . His friends from Coimbra would soon be securing high positions in rich companies, many would be in the House through fortunate vacancies, like the one Sanches had left; one or two, rather more or rather less daring or servile according to the individual, in the Government. Only he, with superior talent, and such brilliant lineage, lay forgotten and grumbling like a lame man in the gutter as a pilgrimage passes by. Why? For the childish fear of letting Cavaleiro's daring moustache come too near Gracinha's delicate lips . . . Such a fear was really an insult, a disgraceful insult, to his sister's seriousness. Because Portugal was not honoured with a more inflexibly serious woman, with graver and purer thoughts! That fragile body, which seemed light enough for a breeze to make tremble, contained a heroic soul. And Cavaleiro? His Excellency could shake his locks with the most fatal charm, and exude languor from his long-lashed eyes, but Gracinha would remain as inaccessible and firm in her virtue as if she were sexless and made of marble. Yes, really, as far as Gracinha was concerned, he could open all the doors of *Cunhais* to Cavaleiro, even the door of her boudoir, and wide open, too, like some well-prepared, secluded spot . . . this, moreover, was not the case of a maiden, or a widow. In the house in King's Square, thanks be to God, ruled an energetic, firm husband. It was his place, and his alone, to choose his household's friends—and therein maintain peace and quiet. No! The fear of any possible weakness in Graça, his most honourable, proud Gracinha—this mad, wicked fear of his should quite definitely be brushed aside with an easy, smiling heart. In the bright empty road, Gonçalo Mendes Ramires made a final sweeping gesture to conclude his argument.

There was still, however, his own humiliation to consider. For years now, both in talk and writing, in Coimbra, Vila Clara, in Oliveira and the *Porto Gazette*—he had vociferously attacked Cavaleiro. Was he now to climb the steps of the Civil Government Offices, his back bent and murmuring '*peccavi, mea culpa, mea maxima culpa*' . . .? What a laugh that would be in the city! 'The Nobleman of the Tower was in need, so off he went . . .' It would be Cavaleiro's greatest triumph. The only man in the District who held firm and who still fought and proclaimed the truth aloud—would be unarmed and reduced to silence, would quickly fall into line, in His Excellency's sycophantic retinue! That would be most disagreeable. But what the devil! The interests of the country came first! This reason seemed to him so admirable that he shouted aloud in the silent street: 'There's the country to consider!'

Yes, the country! So many reforms to be announced, to be carried out! In Coimbra, in the last year of his course, he had concerned himself with Education—an educational reform which would eliminate Latin and the idle arts to the benefit of industrial and colonial studies, thus helping to build a hard-working nation of producers and explorers. His companions, in their airy dreams of the Future, when they divided up the Ministry among themselves, always agreed, 'Gonçalo will look after Education!' It was because of these forceful ideas and his accumulated knowledge that he owed himself to the Nation—just as had the great armed Ramires of old, because of their might. For the Nation's sake he would allow his pride to yield to his duty as a citizen.

After that, who knew? A whole past of camaraderie passionately bound himself and Cavaleiro, a camaraderie which had merely cooled a little and which would probably revive at this meeting, would bind them in a close embrace, in which previous offences would disappear like a puff of smoke . . . But why conjecture like this, why keep going over things? What was patently necessary and all-important was his presence early tomorrow morning at the offices of the Civil Government, imploring Casco's restraint. His peace of mind and intelligence relied on his doing this in all haste. He would never be able to work on his novel nor tread, with an easy mind, the road to Vila Clara, knowing that near by the other fellow was lurking up some lane or in some shadow, waiting with his rifle. Rather than revert to the violent customs of his grandparents, travelling the district protected by his servants' guns, he needed Casco controlled, immobilized. It was therefore essential that he should go urgently to the Civil Government for the sake of law and order. Then, when he was with Cavaleiro in his office, standing in front of his table, Providence would decide the next move . . . 'Providence will decide!'

Firm in this resolve, the Nobleman of the Tower stopped and looked around him. This burst of intense thought had led him to the railings of the town's cemetery, which the moonlight illuminated like a spread sheet. At the end of the path which divided them, a livid, lean and wounded Christ, bright in the melancholy pallor of the moonlight, hung upon his tall black cross, more forlorn and paler than ever in the silence and solitude, with a desolate lamp flickering away at His feet. All round were cypresses, shadows of cypresses, white tombstones, the humble crosses on the poorer graves, a dead peace lying heavily upon the dead; and above, the still, yellow Moon. Then the Nobleman felt a spine-chilling fear of the Christ, of the gravestones, of the corpses there and the Moon and the solitude. He hurried back till he caught sight of the houses of the town from which he had ricocheted like a loose stone. When he stopped in Fountain Square, an owl hooted on the Tower of the Town Hall, and an air of melancholy settled over the peace of the still sleeping town of Vila Clara.

More nervous than ever, Gonçalo ran to Serena's tavern to collect his men who were whiling away the time playing cards. With them at his side, he crossed the town once more towards Torto's coach-house, to have him send a carriage and the chestnut pair to the Tower at nine o'clock the following morning.

Through the peephole of the metal-plated door which was opened with great caution, Torto's wife whined hesitantly,

'Oh, Lord above us, now, I don't know if he can . . . He's got a job at nine . . . Wouldn't it be better for your Lordship about eleven o'clock?'

'Nine o'clock!' shouted Gonçalo.

He wanted to arrive early at the door of the Civil Government, to avoid the curiosity of those gentlemen of Oliveira who, just after midday, used to meet in the Square and wander round beneath the Arcade.

But at half-past nine, Gonçalo, who had been up till the first light of dawn, pacing back and forth across the room in a flurry of hopes and fears—was still in his shirt, shaving himself before the enormous mirror with gilt columns. Then he availed himself of the carriage to leave his note of condolence to the beautiful widow, Dona Ana, at *Feitosa*. By midday he was famished and lunched in Vendinha while the horses rested. It was striking half-past two when he finally dismounted in Oliveira before the gate of the ancient monastery of San Domingos at the far end of the Square where his father, when he was Head of the District, had installed, with magnificence, the offices of the Civil Government.

At that hour, in the cool shade of the Arcade, which borders one side of the Square (formerly Silversmith's Square and now Liberty Square) the most leisured gentlemen of Oliveira, 'the boys', were already lounging in wicker chairs at the door of the Elegant Tobacconist's and Leão's shop. Gonçalo cautiously pulled down the green blinds of the calash. But in the square of the Civil Government, still ornamented with monumental benches from the time of the friars, he ran into his cousin José Mendonça, who was coming down the stairs in uniform. The gay captain, a slim youth with a short moustache and a slightly pitted face, was amazed to see Gonçalo.

'What are you doing here, Gonçalinho? And in a top-hat, too! By Jove, it must be something important!'

The Nobleman of the Tower bravely confessed. He had arrived that very moment from Santa Ireneia to talk to André Cavaleiro . . .

'Is he here, the good gentleman?'

His cousin took a step back in alarm.

'Come to talk to Cavaleiro?! You've come to talk to Cavaleiro?! . . . Holy Mary! Has someone set the Tagus on fire?'

Gonçalo flushed and answered in jest, no, no such misfortune had occurred. He could, however, reveal to his friend Mendonça what it was that led him to the august presence of the Civil Governor. There was a man from Bravais, a certain Casco, who was furious because he had not secured the lease of the Tower, had threatened him, and prowled round the Vila Clara road at night on the lookout for him with a rifle. He, not daring to administer the justice the man deserved at the hands of his men, as the Ramires had in feudal times, was modestly asking the superior authority for an order for Gouveia to restrain the audacious fellow from Bravais within the law and God's commandments.

'That's all, just a very small question of public order . . . Is the great man up there? Right, see you later then, Zèzinho . . . How's your wife? Well? I'll be dining at *Cunhais*, naturally. Come along!'

But the captain did not stir from the stone step, and leisurely opened his leather cigarette-case.

'What do you think of the latest news? Poor Sanches Lucena . . . ?'

Yes, Gonçalo had heard about it at the Club. An attack, wasn't it? Mendonça lit his cigarette and drew upon it.

'Suddenly, an aneurism as he was reading the *Daily News*! I and Maricas were dining with them only three days ago at *Feitosa*. I even played the quartet of *Rigoletto*, as a duet with Dona Ana. He was well enough then, chatting away, drinking his sugar-cane brandy . . .'

Gonçalo sketched a gesture of sorrow and pity.

'Poor fellow . . . I met him a couple of weeks ago, too, at the Holy Fountain. A fine fellow, well educated . . . And now we have our beautiful Dona Ana untenanted.'

'And the constituency!'

'Oh, the constituency,' murmured the Nobleman of the Tower with a disdainful smile. 'I'd rather have the widow. A Venus with two hundred *contos*! Unfortunately she has a horrible voice . . .'

Cousin Mendonça, at once interested, asserted with dedication:

'Oh, no! With intimate friends she loses that thickness . . . You can't imagine! A very natural, pleasant tone . . . And what a figure, my dear fellow, what a skin!'

'She must look splendid now in mourning!' decided Gonçalo.

126

'Right, I must be off! Drop in at *Cunhais* . . . I must run off now to Cavaleiro so the good man can protect me with his strong arm!'

He shook Mendonça's hand and leapt up the stone steps.

But the Captain, who had turned into S Domingos Street, was suspicious about his tale of threats and rifles . . . 'That's a likely story! There's something political mixed up here!' After a slow hour had passed, and he returned to the Square and saw the calash from the Tower still standing at the door of the Civil Governor's Offices, he rushed to the Arcade and at once burst out with his news to the two Vila-Velhas who were standing pensively, leaning, one on either side of the doorway of the Elegant Tobacconist's.

'Do you know who's in the Civil Governor's Offices ? . . . Gonçalo Ramires! With Cavaleiro!'

Everyone round stirred, as if awakening from the old wicker chairs into which they had been cast by the silence and sleepy indolence of the heavy summer's afternoon. Mendonça excitedly told them that, from half-past two, Gonçalo Mendes Ramires, 'in flesh and blood', had been shut up with Cavaleiro, in the Civil Governor's offices, having some vast discussion! The amazement and curiosity were so intense that everyone rose and hurried out of the Arches to peer at the monastery's bulging verandah above the doorway—which was where His Excellency's office was.

At that very moment, José Barrolo came round the corner of Vendas Street on horseback, in white riding-trousers and with a white rose in the lapel of his linen jacket. The attention of all these gentlemen was turned towards him, in the hopes of some revelation.

'Oh, Barrolo!'

'Oh, Barrolinho, come here!'

'Quick, man, it's important!'

Barrolo's horse, side-stepping, approached the Arcade; and his friends, huddled round his mare, immediately hurled the fantastic news at him. Gonçalo and Cavaleiro whispering together in secret all morning! The carriage from the Tower still waiting there with its sleeping pair! And the Cathedral's bells were already beginning to ring!

Barrolo leapt down at once. While a boy walked his horse up and down, he stood motionless amidst his friends, his whip behind him, gaping at the stone verandah of the Civil Governor's offices.

'I don't know anything about it! Gonçalo has not said anything to me!' he assured them in amazement. 'He hasn't been to the city for some days . . . But he hasn't said anything to me! And in fact the last time he was here, on Graça's birthday, he lost his temper over Cavaleiro!'

Everyone found it amazing! Then suddenly silence fell over the Arcade, heavy with emotion. From the slowly opening windows of the verandah, Cavaleiro appeared with the Nobleman of the Tower, and they were conversing together with smiles and lighted cigars. The large eyes of Cavaleiro immediately and maliciously alighted on 'the boys' gathered in wonder by the edge of the Arches. But it was the briefest of glances. He plunged again into the privacy of his office—the Nobleman too, after he had lent over the verandah to see if his carriage was still there. A cry broke out from the group of friends.

'Hooray! A reconciliation!'

'The War of the Roses has finished!'

'And the letters to the *Porto Gazette*? . . .'

'What a thing to happen!'

'Gonçalo's the new administrator of Oliveira!'

'More than that, good sir, more than that!'

But suddenly they fell silent. Cavaleiro and the Nobleman of the Tower reappeared, engaged in an absorbing conversation which made them, there on the verandah, open to public view, forget their surroundings for a moment. Then Cavaleiro, with affectionate familiarity, slapped Gonçalo on the back, as if proclaiming their reconciliation before the astonished Square. Once again they disappeared, chatting away together intimately, now in the shadows of the office, now on the sunlit verandah, their coat-sleeves rubbing together, the light smoke of their cigars mingling. Below, the crowd grew larger and more excited. Melo Alborim, the Baron of Marges and the local Delegate had passed by, and each of them had been anxiously called, had listened to the news wide-eyed, and gaped up at the old stone balcony lit by the sun. The thick hands of the clock of the Civil Government now pointed to almost four o'clock. The two Vila-Velhas and some more of 'the boys' had retired in exhaustion to the wicker chairs at the Tobacconist's. The Delegate, who suffered from his stomach and dined at four, disconsolately dragged himself away from the Arches, begging his neighbour Pestana 'to drop into the café and tell him what happened . . .'

Melo Alboim hurried off to his own house just in front of the Civil Government, at the corner of the Square, and from the windows, concealed behind his wife and sister-in-law, both in white dressing-gowns and their hair in paper curlers, studied the Civil Governor's office with his binoculars. Finally, with a great clatter, four o'clock struck. Then the Baron of Marges, nervously impatient, decided to go up to the Civil Governor's offices 'to see what was in the air! . . .'

But at that moment André Cavaleiro again appeared at the verandah—alone, with his hands stuffed into the pockets of his blue flannel jacket. Almost immediately the calash from the Tower set off from the doors of the Civil Government and crossed the Square, its green blinds half-drawn, revealing no more to those eager gentlemen than the Nobleman's light shoes.

'He's going to *Cunhais!*'

Barrolo would catch him there! Everyone urged the good Barrolo to mount his horse and hurry off home to hear his brother-in-law's explanation and details of the historic pact! The Baron of Marges even held the stirrups for him. Barrolo, all flustered, trotted to King's Square.

But Gonçalo Mendes Ramires did not stop at *Cunhais* and went straight on to Vendinha where he had decided to dine while his weary horses rested. As soon as he had passed the last houses of the city he pulled up the blinds, and his hat upon his knees, joyfully breathed in the luminous coolness of the afternoon—cooler and of a more comforting clarity than any afternoon in his life . . . He returned from Oliveira a conqueror! He had penetrated the wall, got through the gap! And without letting his honour or his pride be scratched on the rough edges of the crack! . . . Blessed Gouveia! Clever Gouveia! What a clever and blessed conversation theirs of the day before in the streets of Vila Clara! . . .

That moment, that silent moment when he had sat drily and stiffly on the edge of the armchair near the heavy administrative table of the Civil Governor, had indeed been painful. But he had maintained great dignity and great simplicity: 'I am obliged,' he had said 'to come to the Civil Governor, to the Administrator of authority, on a matter of law and order . . .' The first move had been made straightaway by Cavaleiro, who twisted the moustache on his pale face: 'I am profoundly sorry that it is not to the man, to his old friend, that Gonçalo Mendes Ramires comes . . .' But he had maintained his reserve, restraining himself and murmuring with coolness and sorrow: 'It is not, surely, my fault . . .' Then Cavaleiro, after a silence in which his lips trembled, replied, 'After so many years, Gonçalo, it would be kinder not to refer to faults but to remember only the friendship, which, at least as far as I am concerned has remained as loyal and serious as before.' To this moving supplication he had replied indulgently and affectionately, 'As my old friend André remembers our former friendship like this, I cannot deny that neither in me has it completely died . . .' They both stammered a few more confused laments about the capriciousness of life. Almost without noticing it, they began to address each other again as 'tu'! He told Cavaleiro about Casco's outrageous behaviour. And Cavaleiro showed his indignation as a friend, and still more as an administrator of authority, and at once sent a strong telegram to Gouveia to render the bully from Bravais impotent . . . Then they talked about the death of Sanches Lucena, which had so affected the county. Both of them praised the beauty of the widow and her two hundred *contos*. Cavaleiro recalled the morning in *Feitosa* when he had entered by the little gate of the garden, and caught her in a rose bower adjusting her suspender. A heavenly leg! Both of them refused, laughing, to marry Dona Ana, in spite of her two hundred *contos* and her heavenly legs . . . Already, the former intimacy which had existed between them at Coimbra, had been recovered. It was 'tu Gonçalo', 'tu André', 'oh, my dear boy', 'oh, my dear fellow'.

It was André, of course, who referred to the disappearance of the Government Deputy, to the unexpectedly vacant seat . . . Then, stretched out in the armchair and drumming on the edge of the table with his fingers, Gonçalo had murmured with an air of indifference,

'Yes, really, you must be in a difficult position, it happening suddenly like this . . .'

Not another word! No more than those lazily spoken words, murmured above the drumming fingers. Cavaleiro immediately, without any preliminaries, swiftly and earnestly, had offered him the seat! He had looked at him slowly and surely, as if wanting to penetrate him, to sound him—and then had gravely said,

'If you wished, Gonçalo, we should not be in a difficult position at all . . .'

He had answered, laughing and surprised,

'What do you mean, if I wished?'

André, his eyes fixed upon him all the time, those large, shining and so persuasive eyes of his, went on,

'If you wished to serve your country, Gonçalo, to be Deputy for Vila Clara, we should not be in a difficult position!'

If you wished . . . Before this pleading insistence, spoken with such fervour and sincerity, in the name of the country, he had consented, had bowed his shoulders.

'If I could be useful to you, and to the country, I am at your disposal.'

Thus was the crack in the wall already negotiated, the rough crack—without his dignity or pride torn in the least! Then they had talked together freely, walking about the office, from the paper-laden bookshelves to the verandah—which André had opened because of a persistent smell of paraffin which had been spilt the day before. André intended leaving for Lisbon that night, to discuss the consequences of Lucena's unexpected death with the Government. Now, in Lisbon, he would put forward the name of dear Gonçalo as the only possible person, completely safe and solid, for the place—by virtue of his name, his talent, his influence, his loyalty. There was the election over! Moreover, declared Cavaleiro, laughing, the constituency of Vila Clara was as much his property as Corinde! He could quite easily nominate and elect the office boy who stammered and drank. So he was doing the Government and the Nation a splendid service in offering them a young man of such high birth and such brilliant intelligence . . . Then he added,

'You don't have to worry about the election. You go back to the Tower. Don't tell anyone, except Gouveia, if you like. Just wait there, nice and quietly, for a telegram from me from Lisbon. When you receive it you'll know you are the Deputy for Vila Clara, you can tell your brother-in-law and your friends . . . Then on Sunday come and have lunch with me at Corinde, at eleven o'clock.'

Then they clasped each other in an embrace which once again united, for ever now, their two divided souls. Then at the top of the stairs to which he accompanied him, André, shyly returning again to the Past, murmured with a pensive smile, 'What have you been doing lately in our beloved Tower?' When he learnt of the novel being prepared for the *Annals*, he sighed as he remembered nostalgically the times of Imagination and Art in Coimbra, when he had fondly sketched the first canto of a heroic poem—*The Frontier Commander of Ceuta*. Then they had clasped each other again—and there he was returning as the Deputy for Vila Clara.

All these fields, these villages that he could see from the carriage window, were represented by him in the House, by him, Gonçalo Mendes Ramires . . . And well would he represent them, God willing. Because he was already being invaded by ideas—vibrant, fertile ideas. In Vendinha, while he waited for a smoked sausage fried with some eggs, and a couple of pieces of shad, he meditated upon his Reply to the Royal Speech—a severe, sharp outline of our Administration in Africa. Then he would deliver an exhortation to the Nation to arise and send some of their energy to this marvellous Africa, where they should build, from coast to coast, a greater Portugal as their supreme glory and supreme source of wealth! . . . Night fell, and other ideas were turning over in his head, vast, vague ideas—when the tired horses drew to a halt outside the Tower.

The next day, Tuesday, at ten o'clock, Bento came into the Nobleman's room with a telegram that had arrived in town at dawn. Gonçalo's heart leapt wildly and he thought 'It's the Government!' It was from Castanheiro, asking for the novel. Gonçalo screwed up the telegram. The novel! How could he work on the novel now, with the impatience and worry of the election hanging over him? He could not even eat his lunch calmly—only just restraining himself, as he pushed aside the various dishes, from a desperate urge to 'tell Bento everything'. Drinking his coffee with impatient gulps, he fled to Vila Clara to blurt out his news to Gouveia. The poor Administrator was once again lying on his wicker settee, a poultice on his throat. All evening, in the narrow, pale-green, papered room, Gonçalo praised the talented André, 'a statesman with ideas, Gouveia!', commended the Historical Government—'the only one capable of getting us out of this mess, Gouveia!' and developed brilliant policies which he had considered for Africa—'a magnificent opportunity for us, Gouveia!' While Gouveia, stretched out, only broke his silence and immobility to murmur feebly, feeling the heat of the poultice from time to time,

'And to whom do you owe all this Gonçalinho? To this chap here!'

When he woke, late on Wednesday, Gonçalo's thoughts at once flew to André Cavaleiro, who at this hour in Lisbon would be lunching at the Hotel Central (ever since he was a boy André had always remained faithful to the Hotel Central). All day long, in the silence of the house and garden, he followed Cavaleiro on his missions as Chief of the District, down town, along the Arcade, in the ministries . . . He would naturally dine with his uncle Reis Gomes, Minister of Justice. Another guest would of course be José Ernesto, Minister of Home Affairs, a friend of Cavaleiro's from University, and his political confident. So everything would be decided tonight!

'Tomorrow, by ten o'clock, I'll have a telegram from André.'

No news arrived at the Tower—and the Nobleman spent the whole of that long Thursday at the window, watching the dusty road along which the telegram boy would appear, a fat boy whom he knew by his oilskin cap and his limp. At dusk, intolerably anxious, he sent a lad to Vila Clara. Perhaps the telegram lay forgotten somewhere on the table of that 'fool of a Nunes in the Telegram Department'. There was no telegram for the Nobleman. Then he was sure that some difficulties had arisen in Lisbon! All that restless night, with an impatience that grew and grew, he imagined Cavaleiro feebly surrendering to other demands from the Minister—meekly accepting for Vila Clara the candidature of some imbecile from the Arcade, some common scribbler who worked for the Party.

In the morning he scolded Bento for bringing the papers and tea so late.

'Isn't there a telegram for me? Or a letter?'

'Nothing at all, sir.'

Very well—he had been betrayed. Well, never, never in his life, would that vile Cavaleiro enter the doors of *Cunhais*! What did the ridiculous election matter to him, anyway? Thank God he had other means of proving his worth—means far superior to a dirty old chair in S Bento. How wretched, honestly, to have to abase his spirit and name in the contemptible service of S Fulgêncio, that fat, horrible, bald-headed old man! He decided there and then to return to the pure heights of Art, nobly to devote the whole day to the elegant and elevated task of writing his novel.

After lunch, he did in fact settle down, with some effort, and nervously sorted through the sheets of paper. Then suddenly he snatched up his hat and rushed off to Vila Clara to get his telegram. Nunes had not received anything for his Lordship! He hurried, covered in dust and sweat, to see the District Administrator.

The Administrator had gone to Oliveira! . . . Some other arrangement had been preferred, quite obviously. He'd been taken for a ride!

He returned to the Tower determined to exact a fearsome revenge from Cavaleiro for such an affront upon his name, upon his dignity! All that sultry, hazy Friday was spent devising this revenge, which he wanted to be both public and bloody. The most appetizing and the simplest would be to tear the moustache off the infamous fellow, on the Cathedral steps one Sunday as he was coming out of mass! As night began to fall, after his dinner which he scarcely touched, so humiliated and disgusted was he, he slipped on his coat to go to Vila Clara again. He would not go to the Telegram office, he would feel too ashamed in front of Nunes. He would while away the evening in the Club, playing billiards, having a pleasant cup of tea, reading the Regenerator papers with a smile so that everyone should see how indifferent he felt—should they learn later about the false alliance into which he had slipped.

He went down to the yard where the trees increased the shadows of the dusk, darkened by lowering clouds. He was opening the gate when a boy came limping along, panting for breath and shouting, 'A telegram for you, sir!' How greedily did he snatch it from his hands! He rushed to the kitchen and scolded Rosa roundly because of the lack of light! And a match burning his fingers, he devoured in a flash the most blessed lines: 'Minister accepts, everything settled . . .' After which Cavaleiro merely reminded him he was expecting him at eleven o'clock on Sunday at Corinde for lunch and a talk . . .

Gonçalo Mendes Ramires gave the telegram boy five *tostões* and leapt back up the stairs. In the library, in the surer light of the lamp, he read the delightful telegram once again. 'Minister accepts, everything settled!' He felt such overwhelming gratitude to Cavaleiro that he immediately planned a superb dinner, given for him at *Cunhais* by Barrolo, to cement for ever the reconciliation between the two families. And he would advise Gracinha to honour the delightful banquet still more by exposing her shoulders and wearing her magnificent diamond necklace—the last historic piece of jewellery that the Ramires possessed.

'Ah, André! What a darling he is! What a grand fellow!'

*   *   *

The Chinese lacquered clock in the corridor struck nine o'clock throatily. Only then did Gonçalo notice the heavy rain that was beating down on the yard, which he, transported by his delight and

134

pacing back and forth across the library in a glorious cloud of fancy, had not heard falling on the stone verandah, or on the leaves of the lemon-trees.

To calm himself and occupy the night that was closing in on him, he decided to work on his novel. Now it was really convenient that he should finish this *Tower of Don Ramires* before all the bustle of the elections, so that in January, when Parliament opened, he could emerge into the world of Politics with his ancient name surrounded by a halo of Erudition and Art. He slipped on his flannel dressing-gown. At his writing-desk, with the customary pot of tea to inspire him, he carefully copied out the beginning of Chapter Two, which had not been to his liking.

It was in the Castle of Santa Ireneia, that August day when Lourenço Ramires had fallen in the valley of Canta Pedra, sore-wounded and captive to the Bastard of Baião. From the captain of his foot-soldiers, who, his arm pierced by a spear, had returned in desperate haste to the castle, Tructesindo learnt of the sorry outcome of the battle. At this point, Uncle Duarte, in his poem in the *Bard*, had depicted with frail lyricism the great, strong Nobleman in the armoury weeping profusely at the fate of his son, flower of the Knights of Riba Cávado, cruelly beaten to the ground and tied to a litter, at the mercy of the folk of Baião:

> 'Irrepressible tears burst forth
> And his coat-of-mail heaved with his sobs . . .'

Gonçalo, following in Uncle Duarte's harmonious tracks, had also portrayed, in the opening lines of the chapter, the disheartened old man seated on a bench, tears gleaming on his white whiskers, his hands drooping like those of some languid maiden—while on the stone floor, his two harriers wagged their tails and watched him with anxious, almost human sympathy. But now this tearful dejection did not seem consistent with such an indomitable and violent soul as that of great-grandfather Tructesindo. Uncle Duarte, from the house of Balsas, was not a Ramires, had not appreciated the heredi-tary fortitude of his race: and the mournful romantic of 1848 had at once drowned the intransigent face of a twelfth-century warrior, of a companion of Sancho I—in romantic weeping! It was up to him, however, to reinstate the character of the Lord of Santa Ireneia within the epic reality. Scratching out this spiritless and false beginning to the chapter, he began the episode again more energetically, filling the whole of the castle of Santa Ireneia with furious, intense excitement. Tructesindo's sublime and simple loyalty did not allow him to think of his son—he would postpone vengeance of this latest, bitter injury. Now all his efforts were combined to hasten the preparations of his vassals, so that they might reach Montemor and bring the help to the Royal Princesses which had been denied them through the ambush in Canta Pedra. But as the impetuous Nobleman was in the armoury giving his officer-in-command instructions regarding the expedition, the sentinels, sheltering from the August sun in the turrets, perceived, in the distance, beyond the copse of Ribeira, the flash of arms, a crowd of horsemen approaching Santa Ireneia. The bailiff, the fat, bustling Ordonho, climbed to the terrace of the barbican, puffing and wheezing, and recognized the pennant of Lopo de Baião, the sound of his Moorish trumpets wailing mournfully in the silence of the countryside. Then he raised his hairy hands to his mouth and shouted the alarm,

'To arms, men, to arms! It's the men of Baião! Cross-bowmen, to your places at the wall! And as many men as possible to the drawbridge over the moat!'

Gonçalo, scratching his forehead with the feather of his pen, was racking his brain for other realistic cries of the lusty Afonsine epoch, when the door of the library opened cautiously, making that awful creaking noise which nearly drove him to despair. It was Bento, in his shirt-sleeves.

'You couldn't come down to the kitchen a moment, sir, could you?'

Gonçalo looked at Bento in amazement, blinking, quite unable to understand.

'The kitchen . . . ?'

'Casco's wife is there making such a fuss. It seems they arrested her husband this afternoon . . . She's turned up in all this rain with her little ones, one of them still at her breast. She's determined to talk to you, sir. She won't be quiet, she's weeping away, on her knees, with the children, she looks like Inês de Castro herself!'

Gonçalo muttered, 'What a nuisance!' How annoying it really was! The woman, with agonized screams and shouts, dragging her children with her to the door of the Tower! And he, on the eve of the elections looking like some inhuman aristocrat to the whole of the sentimental parish! He flung down his pen furiously.

'What a nuisance! Tell the creature to leave me alone and not to upset herself. The Administrator will set Casco free tomorrow. I'll go to Vila Clara myself, before lunch, to speak for him. Tell her not to worry, and not to frighten the children . . . Go on, man, hurry!'

But Bento did not move from the door.

'Rosa and I have already told her. But the woman won't believe us, she wants to ask you yourself, sir. She came in all this rain. And one of the children is sick, too, he hasn't stopped trembling.'

Then Gonçalo, moved by this story, crashed his fist down upon the table with such a force that the papers of his novel flew apart.

'To have to put up with a thing like this! A man that tried to kill me! And now, on top of everything else, they bring their tears and their scenes and their sick children to me! You can't live in this place! One of these days I'll sell the house and the grounds and take myself off to Mozambique, to the Transvaal where there's none of this fuss and bother . . . Right, tell the woman I'll come down and see her.'

Bento showed his approval effusively.

'That's right, sir, it's no trouble . . . And as you'll be giving her good news . . . Something to console the poor woman!'

'I'm coming, man, I'm coming! Don't you start, too. It's impossible to work in this house! That's another night wasted!'

He stamped into his bedroom, slammed the doors—intending to slip two *ten-tostão* pieces into his dressing-gown pocket to console the children. But as he stood before the drawer he stopped in vexation. How brutal to fob off with money those little children whose father he had had removed in handcuffs and flung into prison! With a sudden inspiration, he picked up a box of dried apricots—some of those famous apricots from the Convent of Santa Brigida of Oliveira, which Gracinha had sent him the day before. As he slowly closed the door behind him, he was already regretting his rash severity which had destroyed the peace of their household. Then, in the corridor, with the rain pattering down from the rooftops on the stones of the yard, he was even more painfully affected by the thought of that poor woman, mad with worry, dragging her drenched, exhausted children along the pitch-black road in the teeth of the storm. By the time he entered the corridor leading to the kitchen he was shaking like a guilty man.

Through the glass door he could see Rosa and Bento consoling

137

the woman, chatting to her confidently, smiling. But her wailing and her noisy laments for her 'dear husband' rose sharply above the words of consolation, almost drowning them. When Gonçalo timidly pushed open the door, he almost recoiled in alarm and fear at the ear-piercing affliction which flung itself on him and his mercy! Clutching the ground and twisting her skinny hands above her head, the poor creature, who was all in black and seemed even blacker and more pitiful against the reddish glow of the sheet drying in front of the bright open fire, blurted out in a tumult of cries and supplication, 'Oh, my man, my man, have mercy on him, sir! They've arrested my man, they're going to send him into exile to Africa! Oh, Jesus, these children of mine will have no father! Ai, for the love of them, sir, for the love of them, have pity! I know he did wrong! He went mad! But have pity on these children! Ai, my poor dear husband's in prison! Ai, my dear, dear sir, have pity!'

Gonçalo felt tears in his eyes, and desperately clutching his box of apricots, he stammered through the emotion which was choking him.

'Oh woman, for goodness' sake calm yourself. They're going to set him free! Calm yourself! I've already given orders. They're going to let him go!'

On one side of her, Rosa, bending over the dark shape that was sobbing and groaning, insisted gently, 'There, see what I said, Aunt Mary! They're going to set him free first thing tomorrow morning!' On the other side, Bento, impatiently slapping his thighs, added, 'Oh, for goodness' sake, woman, stop that noise! The Doctor's promised, hasn't he? First thing tomorrow morning he'll be free!'

But she would not calm down, her kerchief awry, a strand of hair loose, she sobbed and cried above her sobs,

'Ai, I'll die if he's not set free! Oh, forgive him, dear, dear sir! . . .'

Then Gonçalo, who was tortured by that interminable, stubborn wailing which was like a nail piercing him again and again, stamped his slippered foot on the stone floor and shouted,

'Listen, woman! And look at me! But stand up! And look at me, look at me straight!'

She stood up stiffly, flinging her hands down to her sides as if escaping from handcuffs that threatened her, too, and stared at the Nobleman with terrified eyes, deep, black eyes with dismal, black shadows under them filling her lean, dark face.

'Good, exactly!' exclaimed Gonçalo. 'Now tell me! Do you think I could lie to you, when you're in such a state? Well then, calm yourself and stop this shrieking, because tomorrow, I give my word, early tomorrow your man will be free!'

Rosa and Bento triumphantly joined in,

'There, what did we tell you, you silly creature? If the Doctor's promised . . . Tomorrow you'll have your man with you!'

She slowly wiped her tears, silent ones now, on a corner of her black apron. But she was not yet convinced, and her shadowy eyes still stared at and devoured Gonçalo. Would the Nobleman have the order sent first thing the next morning? . . . It was Bento who convinced her, with a brutal,

'Good heavens, woman, you've got a cheek! I ask you! Are you doubting the Doctor's word?'

She let her apron fall, dropped her head, and murmured simply,

'Then thank you very much, sir, and may this be for your happiness . . .'

Gonçalo now looked round the kitchen, curious to see the little ones which she had carted from Bravais in all that heavy rain. The baby that was still being suckled was sleeping blissfully in the lid of a chest, where Rosa had tucked her up in pillows and blankets. But the boy of seven, huddled in a chair before the fire, drying out by the sheet that was also drying, sat with a fever-flushed face and a hacking cough, nodding sleepily and gasping for breath through his cough. Gonçalo put the box of apricots in the lid of the chest and felt the hand with which the child was incessantly scratching away, through the opening of his red shirt, at his still redder chest.

'But this child's feverish! . . . And you brought him here on a night like this, woman, all the way from Bravais?'

From the low chair into which she had sunk, she murmured, without raising her lean face, twisting a corner of her apron,

'It was so they could plead, too, because they'd lost their father, the poor things!'

'You're mad, woman! Do you intend going back to Bravais again tonight in all this rain, with the children?'

She sighed,

'I must, I must . . . I can't leave my man's mother alone, because she's eighty years old and confined to bed . . .'

At this the Nobleman crossed his arms despondently, at the

prospect of the journey which, through his ferocity, had endangered the lives of two children. But Rosa considered that the little baby girl would not suffer from the journey if she were well wrapped up in her mother's arms under a thick shawl. But the other, with the bad cough, the one that was feverish . . .

'He stays here!' said Gonçalo decisively. 'What's his name? Manuel . . . Right! Senhor Manuel stays here. Don't worry, Senhora Rosa will take care of him. He needs a good egg-nog, then a hot mustard-bath. You'll have him back in Bravais one of these days, cured of his cold and a few pounds heavier . . . Don't you worry!'

The woman sighed again, with the excessive tiredness that was exhausting her, weakening her. No longer resisting, she agreed, from her long habit of submission.

'All right then, sir, if your Lordship says so, that's all right . . .'

Bento opened the back door and said the weather was clearing, the black clouds lifting. Gonçalo encouraged an immediate return to Bravais.

'Don't be frightened, woman. One of the groundsmen will accompany you with a lantern and an umbrella to shelter the little girl . . . Listen! You had better take a rubber cape, too! . . . Oh Bento, run up and get my rubber cape. The new one I bought in Lisbon . . .'

When Bento brought the raincoat with its long cape, and wrapped it round the woman's shoulders, who was intimidated by the rich lining, by the rustle of silk—the folk in the kitchen were highly amused. The laments had ceased as the rain had done. Now it was an affable little visit, ending in cheerful hospitality. Rosa clasped her hands delightedly.

'You look a real lady like that! If it was daytime, you'd attract quite a crowd!'

The woman finally smiled half-heartedly.

'Oh, I can't think what I look like . . . A real sight!'

Gonçalo accompanied the group across the yard, its acacias gently dripping, to the orchard gate, and he was still calling out: 'See that baby's well wrapped up!' when the lantern which the boy was carrying disappeared into the humid darkness of the now calm night. Then, back in the kitchen, stamping his wet slippers on the stone floor, he felt Manuelinho again, who was sleeping, breathing hoarsely, curled against the back of the chair.

'He's not very feverish . . . But he needs a good mustard-bath . . . And before you tuck him up for good, a glass of hot milk, as hot as he'll drink it, with some brandy . . . And another thing he needs is a good scrub . . . What filthy people! Still, he can have that a bit later, when he's better . . . Now send me up something for supper, Rosa, something solid, because I didn't have any dinner and I've had an awful evening!'

In the library, after he had changed his slippers and rested, Gonçalo wrote Gouveia a letter, asking that Casco should be freed immediately. And he added, 'This is the first request made by the new deputy for Vila Clara (give me your congratulations!) because I have just received a telegram from our dear André, announcing "everything settled, minister agrees", etc. So we must get together. Would you, most worthy friend, care to have supper here tomorrow, at your Tower, in the shade of Tító and to Videirinha's playing. These two worthy gentlemen are indispensable if we are to have an appetite and a pleasant atmosphere. And I should be grateful, Gouveia, if you would let them know about the party to avoid my sending out eloquent invitations . . .'

He sealed the letter and leisurely picked up the manuscript of his novel again. Chewing the feather of his pen, he continued to think of typical cries with a true medieval flavour, for the part where the bailiff and the sentinels descried the Bastard's horsemen coming up Ribeira hill, with a flash of arms beneath the fierce August sun . . .

But his imagination, since that letter written to Gouveia from the 'Deputy for Vila Clara', restlessly fled the ancient Manor of Santa Ireneia—and fluttered stubbornly towards the hills of Lisbon—the Lisbon of S Fulgêncio. The terrace of the barbican, where the fat Ordonho shouted and gasped, kept disappearing like a fine mist, and in its place appeared a far more appetizing and interesting scene —a room in the Hotel Braganza, with a verandah overlooking the Tagus . . . It was a relief when Bento called him to supper. At table he let his imagination run free over Lisbon, through the corridors of the S Carlos Theatre, under the trees lining the Avenue, through the palaces of his relatives in San Vicente and Graça, in the more modern drawing-rooms of gay, cultured friends—stopping from time to time before these visions which he contemplated with a silent, delighted smile. He would hire a carriage by the month, of course. For the assemblies in S Bento, he would always wear pearl-grey gloves and a flower in his button-hole. And he would take Bento with him to make life easier, looking spick and span in a new dress-coat . . .

Bento entered with a bottle of brandy on a salver. He had given the letter to Joaquim da Horta, and told him to go first thing, at six o'clock, to the house of the Administrator, and to wait in the town in front of the prison till they set Casco free.

'We've already put the boy to bed in the green room. That way he's near me, and I sleep lightly if he should wake up and cry . . . But he's sleeping like a lamb already.'

'He's sleeping restfully, is he?' asked Gonçalo, sipping his glass of brandy quickly. 'Let's go and see the little gentleman!'

He took a candlestick and climbed up to the green room with Bento, smiling and walking softly up the narrow stairs. In the corridor, outside the door, on a faded green damask sofa, Rosa had carefully folded the little boy's tattered clothes, the frayed collar, the enormous trousers with only one button on them. Inside the room, the vast mahogany bed, a regal bed, took up the whole of the wall papered in an ancient velvety paper, decorated with green branches. Beside the two curved bedposts at the head of the bed hung two paintings of former Ramires—a fat Bishop leafing through a folio, and a handsome knight of Malta, with a fair beard, leaning on his sword and wearing a lace bow over his polished cuirass. On the high mattresses, Manuelinho snored away, no longer coughing but sleeping peacefully, snug under the thick blankets, damp with fresh healthy perspiration . . .

Gonçalo moved softly across the room and carefully pulled up the sheet a little. Then, worried about the decrepit windows, he felt to see that no treacherous draught was coming through the cracks. He sent Bento to fetch a lamp which he placed on the wash-stand, with the light shaded. Then he glanced attentively around the room again to make sure of the peace, the silence, the penumbra, the comfort. And he went out, still on tip-toe, smiling and leaving Casco's son guarded by the two noble Ramires—the Bishop with his book and the Knight of Malta with his immaculate sword.

* * *

Coming back from the Old Pool, at the bottom of the garden, where he had spent the hours after lunch in the cool of the trees, thumbing through a volume of *Panorama* to the murmur of running water, Gonçalo found on his library table, along with the mail from Oliveira, a letter which surprised him—an enormous letter on foolscap stuck down with a strip of paper. Inside, the signature was a flaming heart drawn in blue ink.

At a glance he devoured the words, written along pencilled lines in large, carefully rounded letters:

'Dear Sr Gonçalo Ramires,

The charming Civil Governor of the District, the gallant André Cavaleiro, has been passing constantly before *Cunhais* recently, looking fondly at the windows and at the honourable Barrolo arms. As it is hardly likely that he was studying the arquitecture of the mansion (which is not particularly noteworthy) responsible-minded people have concluded that the worthy head of the District has been waiting for you, sir, to appear at one of the windows of the Square or at one of the windows that give on to Weaver's Street, or above all *in the gazebo of the garden*, so that you could renew your former, severed friendship. So you acted most wisely in hastening to the offices of the Civil Government and proposing a reconciliation and opening wide your generous arms to your old friend, thus preventing the leading authority of the District wasting precious time on those rides back and forth, his eyes glued upon the mansion of the most honourable Barrolos. We therefore send you, sir, our most sincere congratulations on this most fit and proper action which will surely calm the impatience of the impetuous Cavaleiro and redund to the benefit of our public services!'

Turning the paper over in his hands, Gonçalo thought,

'This is the Lousadas' work!'

He continued to study the letter and the phrases used, discovering that *redound* was spelt *redund*, *architecture* with—*qu*—instead of—*ch*—. Furiously, he tore the thick sheet of paper in pieces, muttering to himself in the silence of the library,

'Drunken bitches!'

'Yes, it was from them all right, from the Lousadas sisters. This source alarmed him still more—because any slander spread by such zelaous disseminators of slander must surely by now have found its way into every house in Oliveira, even into the gaol and the hospital! And now the whole town, highly amused and relishing the scandal, would perfidiously relate André's prowling round *Cunhais* to his visit to the Civil Government, which had so surprised the Arcade. So it was the opinion of Oliveira, as suggested by the Lousada sisters, that it was he, he, Gonçalo Mendes Ramires, who had dragged Cavaleiro from his office and humbly led him to the King's Square and opened wide the door of the palace to him, till then walked around and gazed upon to no advantage. He who was calmly and shamelessly selling his own sister! Those insolent hags wanted their dirty old skirts pulled up in the middle of the square one morning after church and their bare, wrinkled bottoms flogged until the blood drenched the stones! . . .

The worst of it was that appearances had treacherously connived against him! This persistence of André's in prowling round Gracinha, the sound of his horse's hoofs echoing past the Mansion, had increased and had made a particular impression just now, in the month of August, on the eve of his appearance at the window of the Civil Government, which Oliveira was discussing as if it were a historic mystery. What an inopportune moment that animal Sanches Lucena had chosen to die! A few months before and not even the malicious-tongued Lousadas would have connected his reconciliation with André with an amorous siege which had not then begun or at least was not so talked about. Three or four months later, André, all hope lost before that inaccessible mansion, would certainly have abandoned his trots around the Square with his rose in his button-hole! But no! It unfortunately happens that when André is most obviously covetous, Gonçalo opens his arms to him, embraces the covetous one and throws open the door! So the Lousada sisters' malicious tongues found a basis on which to work, a basis which everyone in the city could see was real and undeniable, and upon this basis their gossip rose aloft like a great Truth! Infamous Lousadas!

But now what? Could he rigidly maintain his relationship with Cavaleiro within the field of politics and avoid the smooth familiarities which would make him the yearned-for guest in *Cunhais* as he had once been at the Tower? How could he? Now that he was reconciled to André it was natural, as natural as a shadow follows the movement of a branch, that Barrolo, his brother-in-law and shadow, should be reconciled as well. But how could he insist to Barrolo that their renewed familiarity with Cavaleiro should be kept within the limits of politics, as within an isolation hospital? 'I am once again André's close friend, and you are, too, Barrolo—but never invite him to your table, nor open your doors to him!' An extraordinary thing to insist, an impertinent demand, and one that, considering their frequent encounters and Barrolo's simple hospitality, would last no longer than a knot made with a piece of old worn string . . . What a ridiculous figure he would cut, standing erect before the door of the mansion, like the Archangel Michael, fiery cane in hand, to repel an intrusion by Satan, Chief of the District. But on the other hand, it was horrible to think of the whole city gossiping in corners, whispering Gracinha's name in connection with André's, while his own name, Gonçalo's, was involved, too, referred to as the thread that had succeeded in tying them together.

Losing his patience with this problem, with all the snares and difficulties which so hurt him, he thumped his fist upon the table in disgust.

'Ugh! What a confounded nuisance! Everything's a nuisance in these narrow-minded, gossiping towns . . .'

What would it matter in Lisbon if the Civil Governor frequented a certain square, and if a certain Nobleman of the Tower sought a reconciliation with the same Civil Governor? . . . Oh well, that was that! He would go forward undeterred, as if he lived in Lisbon, ignoring gossip and evil eyes on the alert for scandal. He was Gonçalo Mendes Ramires, of the house of Ramires! His name and manor were a thousand years old! He was superior to all Oliveira, to all its Lousadas: not only because of his name, thank heavens, but because of his noble spirit . . . André was his friend and he would enter his sister's house—and Oliveira could go and burst with its evil thoughts!

Nor would he allow the Lousadas' foul letter to disturb his quiet morning's work, for which he had been preparing himself ever since breakfast, reading bits of Uncle Duarte's poem, thumbing through articles in *Panorama* on sieges in the twelfth century. With an effort of erudite study, he sat down and dipped his pen in the bronze ink-pot which had served three centuries of Ramires. As he went over certain pages which he had written, the Castle of Santa Ireneia had never before seemed to him so heoric, of such lofty stature, on such a peak of history, set high above the Kingdom, which was spread out all round, covered with towns and fields of crops, acquired by the effort of its castellans!

In awe-inspiring majesty, the ancient Manor of Santa Ireneia stood out beneath the fierce sun of that Afonsine August morning, when the

Bastard's pennant appeared amid the flash of arms, beyond the woods of the Ribeira! The battlements were already thick with cross-bowmen peering out, their weapons at the ready. From the towers and parapets rose the thick black smoke from pitch boiling in the vats, to be poured upon the men of Baião should they attempt to scale the walls. The officer-in-command ran to the wall, reminding his men of the plans of defence, examining the bundles of arrows and boulders to be slung at the enemy. In the enormous courtyard, between thatched sheds, emerged old men of the Manor, serfs from the ovens, serfs from the stables, who crossed themselves in terror and seized the tunic of a hurrying scout for news of the approaching army. In the meantime the horsemen had crossed the Ribeira over the roughly-made wooden bridge, and were already calmly approaching, through the poplars, the granite Cross which had been erected on the boundary of the Manor by Gonçalo Ramires the Butcher. And in the quiet of the excessively hot morning, the trumpets of the Bastard sounded more clearly, with their slow, sad Moorish note.

But when Gonçalo, carried away by his work, tried to reproduce, with more sonorous phrases, enthusiastically sought in his Dictionary of Synonyms, the long drawn-out wail of the trumpets of Baião, he heard, from the direction of the Tower, lower-pitched notes of music approaching through the lemon grove. He held his pen still—and discovered it was the *Fado of the Ramires* arising from the garden, a serenade being played near the honeysuckle-covered verandah.

'Now he who behold you in solitude,
Tower of Santa Ireneia . . .'

It was Videirinha! He ran over to the window in delight. A bowler-hat bobbed among the branches, a shout rose, a shout of acclamation.

'Long live the Deputy for Vila Clara! Long live the illustrious Deputy Gonçalo Ramires!'

The guitar burst out triumphantly with the Anthem, and Videirinha, standing tip-toe in his patent leather shoes, shouted out, 'Long live the illustrious Ramires family!' And beneath a frenziedly waved bowler-hat, João Gouveia yelled, without sparing his throat, 'Long live the illustrious Deputy for Vila Clara! Hooray!'

Gonçalo, bathed in smiles, majestically stretched out an eloquent arm,

'Thank you, my beloved fellow-citizens! Thank you! . . . The honour you do me, coming here like this, in this famous group, the glorious Administrative Chief, the talented chemist, the . . .'

Then he noticed. Where was Titó?

'Hasn't Titó come? Didn't you tell Titó, João Gouveia?'

Replacing his bowler-hat over his ear, the Administrator, who was flaunting a scarlet satin tie, declared Titó 'a brute'.

'We'd arranged to come together. He was going to bring a dozen fireworks, too, to let off as we played the Anthem. We were to meet at the foot of the bridge . . . But the animal didn't turn up. Anyway, he was told, there's no doubt about that. And if he doesn't come, he's a traitor!'

'All right, come along up!' called Gonçalo. 'I'll only be a second getting dressed. And to whet our appetites I propose a vermouth and then a walk through the grounds as far as the pinewoods.'

At once, Videirinha, straight-backed, raised his guitar aloft and set off down the wide garden path under an arch of grape-vines. Behind him, João Gouveia paced along majestically, holding his sunshade aloft as if it were a banner. When Gonçalo went back into his room, shouting for Bento and hot water—the *Fado of the Ramires* was echoing in heroic harmony across the bean-fields, under the open windows where a bath-towel was drying out. They were the Nobleman's favourite verses, the ones in which his great-grandfather Rui Ramires, ploughing across the Gulf of Oman in a hooker, meets three powerful English men-of-war, and as he stands on the forecastle, dressed in vermilion, with his hand in his belt, inlaid with gold and precious stones, haughtily invites them to surrender:

> 'All at ease and hand in belt,
> Beside the Banner Royal,
> He calls to the men-of-war, "Strike sails,
> For the King of Portugal!"'

Gonçalo hurriedly fastened his braces and joined in the hymn of praise: 'All at ease and hand in belt, Beside the Banner Royal . . .' As he bellowed away unharmoniously, he considered that, with such a lineage, he could afford to despise Oliveira and the frightful Lousadas. But the slow rumble of Titó's voice echoed through the corridor:

'Where's our Deputy for Vila Clara, then? . . . Getting his uniform on?'

Gonçalo ran to the door, radiant.

'Come in, Titó! Deputies don't use uniform, man! But if they did, I can tell you I'd be in uniform today, with sword and tricorn, to honour such illustrious guests!'

His friend came slowly towards him, his hands in the pockets of his short, olive-green, velvet jacket, his enormous Braga hat pushed to the back of his head, uncovering his honest bearded face, ruddy with health and sunshine.

'When I said uniform I meant livery . . . Lackey's uniform!'

'What a thing to say!'

But the other thundered still louder,

'Well, what do you think you're going to be, man, but a servant, obeying the orders of S Fulgêncio, that disgusting, bald old man? You won't serve him tea when he calls, but when he tells you to vote, you'll vote! On the dot, vote as you're told! "Oh Ramires, vote as I tell you!" And Ramires, whoosh, in a twinkling, votes . . . Like a valet, man, a valet in livery.'

Gonçalo shrugged his shoulders impatiently.

'You're an uncivilized creature, a lake-dweller, almost pre-historic . . . You don't understand anything about social realities. In society there are no absolute principles!'

But Titó remained steadfast.

'How about this Cavaleiro? Is he a talented young fellow? Does he govern the District well, now?'

Gonçalo then became annoyed and protested, two spots of red on his cheeks. When had he ever denied André was talented or that he governed well? Never! He had only laughed and made fun of his vanity and his shiny moustache . . . Moreover, the country some-times demanded an alliance between men of different tastes, with different interests.

'Really, Sr António Vilalobos is a terrible moralist today, a Cato with whom it will be difficult to dine! You know it was always the cus-tom of the severest of philosophers to flee from the banqueting-room where the debauchees triumph, and take their protests to the kitchen!'

Titó calmly turned his majestic back.

'Where are you going, Titó?'

'To the kitchen!'

When Gonçalo laughed, Titó, who had reached the door, spun round like a tower to face his friend.

'I'm serious, serious, Gonçalo! Election, reconciliation, submission, and you in Lisbon at the service of S Fulgêncio, and in Oliveira with your arm through André's. It all seems out of place . . . Still, if Rosa is on form today, we won't refer any more to such sorry events!'

Gonçalo was gesticulating and protesting when the guitar again sounded in the corridor, with Gouveia's heavy marching tread, and the *Fado* began once more, softer now, more laudatory:

> 'Ancient house of the Ramires,
> Honour and flower of Portugal!'

6

CAVALEIRO'S HOUSE in Corinde was a construction built at the end of the eighteenth century, a house lacking elegance and art, a vast, yellow, flat-faced house, with fourteen windows at the front and situated almost in the middle of some flat farmland, all under cultivation. But a straight, elegant avenue of chestnut-trees led to a square in front which was decorated by two marble posts. The gardens still contained the splendid abundance of roses which had made them famous—and which, in the time of André's grandfather, Judge Martinho, had earned them an occasional visit from Queen Maria II. All the rooms gleamed with cleanliness and order under the care of the old house-keeper—a poor relation of Cavaleiro's, Senhora Dona Jesuina Rolim.

When Gonçalo, who had come from the Tower on his mare, went through the antechamber, he remembered one of the paintings on the wall, a smoky battle between galleons, which he had torn one afternoon when he had been fencing with André. Under this painting, a melancholy clerk of the Civil Government sat waiting on the edge of a straw-bottomed sofa, clasping his red file on his knees. From a distant doorway, at the end of the corridor, André, informed by his valet, the faithful Mateus, called out gaily:

'Oh, Gonçalo, come along to my room here! I've just got out of the bathtub. I'm still in my pants!'

Still in his pants he embraced him, a generous hug of congratulation. Then as he dressed, among the chairs still cluttered with the contents of travelling-bags—ties, silk socks, bottles of perfume—they talked of the heat, of the tedious journey, of deserted Lisbon . . .

'Terrible!' exclaimed Cavaleiro, heating a curling-iron at a petrol-lamp. 'All the roads in the Baixa are under repairs, there's dust and rubble everywhere. The Central Café is alive with mosquitoes. Masses of coloured people. Lisbon's just like Tunis at the moment! . . . Still we fought the good fight there!'

Gonçalo smiled from the edge of the divan where he had settled himself, between a pile of coloured shirts and a pile of pants with extravagant monograms.

'So, my dear André, everything's settled, is it?'

Cavaleiro stood before his dressing-table, curling the thick ends of his moustache with excessive care. Only after soaking them in brilliantine, after flattening the waves of thick, rebellious hair, studying himself and strutting in front of the mirror, did he assure Gonçalo, who was getting anxious, that the election was guaranteed . . .

'But just imagine! When I got to Lisbon, to the Ministry of the Interior, I found the place promised to Pita, Teotónio Pita, the famous fellow from *Verdade* . . .'

The Nobleman gave a start, knocking over a pile of shirts.

'And then what?'

Then he had shown José Ernesto how annoyed he was at the idea of disposing of the constituency as you would a cigar, without consulting him, the owner of the constituency . . . Then, when José Ernesto had got angry and declared that the country came first, he had pointed a finger at him and retorted immediately, 'Now look, Zèzinho darling, either I have Ramires for Vila Clara or I resign, and that's that!' Alarm, uproar, shouting—José Ernesto had given in, and everything ended with the two of them dining together in Algés with Uncle Reis Gomes, and at night the ladies had won fourteen *mil-reis* off them at bluff.

'To sum up, Gonçalinho, we need to keep our eyes open. José Ernesto is a loyal fellow and an old friend of mine. And he knows what my temper's like, too . . . But there are certain agreements and certain pressures . . . But let me tell you the most amusing piece of news. Do you know who's standing against you, for the Regenerators? . . Guess . . . Julhinho!'

'Which Julhinho? . . Not the photographer Julhinho?'

'The photographer Julhinho!'

'Heaven help us!'

Cavaleiro shrugged his shoulders derisively.

'He'll manage ten votes or so from his neighbours, and take photographs of all the tavern-keepers in the constituency, in their shirt-sleeves, and stay the same Julhinho . . . No, only Lisbon worries me a little, that political rabble in Lisbon.'

Gonçalo twirled his moustache disconsolately.

'I imagined everything more settled, less questionable . . . They'll find some complication, with all their plotting . . . I still won't get there!'

151

In front of the mirror, Cavaleiro opened his morning-coat which he had tried buttoned up, then unbuttoned and left open over his olive-green corduroy waistcoat, from which blossomed a light silk tie, pinned with a sapphire. Finally, soaking his handkerchief in essence of hay, he commented,

'We are good allies, aren't we? Well and truly reconciled? Then relax, my dear Gonçalo, and let's have a splendid lunch! I feel this morning-coat Amieiro made doesn't look at all bad, does it?'

'It looks magnificent!' agreed Gonçalo.

'Right. Let's go down to the garden, so you can have a look at all the old places again and get a Corinde rose for your buttonhole.'

In the corridor, decorated with large Indian pitchers and Chinese lacquered chests, André slipped his arm through the arm of his friend, his recovered friend.

'Well, my boy, here we are once again treading together the noble floors of Corinde, as we did five years ago . . . And nothing has changed, not a servant nor a curtain! Now one of these days I want to visit the Tower.'

Gonçalo replied ingenuously,

'Oh, the Tower's changed a lot . . . A lot!'

An embarrassed silence fell, as if between them rose the sad image of the old garden when love and hopes had reigned, when André and Gracinha had looked for the last violets of April under the protective eye of Miss Rhodes, down by the damp walls of Mãe d'Agua. In silence they descended the spiral staircase down which in former days they had slithered astride the banisters. Below, in a vaulted room lined with wooden benches with the Cavaleiro arms on their backs, André stood for a moment before the glass door leading to the garden, and made a languid, disconsolate gesture with his hand.

'I am not often in Corinde nowadays, anyway. You know well enough that it is not the cares of office that keep me in Oliveira . . . But this old house has grown cold, grown larger, since Mama's death. I wander round like a lost soul. Believe me, when I do stay for a while, my strolls round the garden and along the Rua Grande are far from happy . . . Do you remember the Rua Grande? . . I'm growing old in solitude, Gonçalo, my friend!'

Gonçalo murmured in sympathetic agreement,

'I get bored at the Tower, too . . .'

'But you've got a different nature from mine! I'm a melancholy at heart.'

He pushed back the stiff bolt of the glass door. Wiping his fingers on his perfumed handkerchief, he murmured,

'I think Corinde would only please me nowadays if it had high bare hills all round and great craggy rocks . . . Sometimes the soul within me calls out for the hermitage of S Bruno . . .'

Gonçalo smiled at his ascetic hunger, murmured with such affection from beneath the curled moustache gleaming with brilliantine. On the terrace, beside the stone, ivy-covered balustrade, he jokingly responded, taking in the orderliness, the resplendent fertility of the garden,

'Really, for a disciple of S Bruno, such a well-kept garden is a scandal! But for a sinner like myself it's magnificent! The garden at the Tower is a waste land.'

'Cousin Jesuina likes flowers. Don't you know Cousin Jesuina? She's an old relation of Mama's who looks after the house now. Poor old thing! So devoted and attentive! If it wasn't for the righteous creature, we'd have the pigs rooting in the flower-beds . . . My dear boy, where there's no skirt there's no order!'

They went down the curving steps between the blue china pots that were overflowing with geraniums and asters and lilies. Gonçalo remembered a St John's Eve when he had taken a terrific tumble down these steps, his arms full of rockets. As they wandered through the garden, memories of their old friendship came to mind. The trapeze was still there, from the time when they had both adopted the heroic religion of strength, gymnastics, and cold baths . . . Over there on that bench, one afternoon, under the magnolia tree André had read the first canto of his poem, *The Frontier Command of Ceuta*. But where was the target? The target where they had practised shooting for future duels which were inevitable in the campaign both had envisaged against the old Constitutional syndicate? . . . Oh, all that part of the wall, which adjoined the wash-house, had been pulled down after his mother's death, to enlarge the greenhouse.

'Anyway the target was no longer any use!' added Cavaleiro. 'That was about the time I joined the syndicate myself . . . Now you'll enter, too, through the door I've opened for you!'

Gonçalo, who had picked some leaves of lemon-scented verbena and was crushing them between his fingers to breathe in their perfume, agreed with a frankness accentuated by these recollections of a shared past,

'I want to join, I want to most desperately, as you know. But is the election safe, really safe? There won't be any little difficulties cropping up, André, old boy?... This Pita's clever.'

Cavaleiro merely murmured, his thumbs tucked in the armholes of his waistcoat,

'The strength of the Cavaleiros makes mock of the cleverness of the Pitas...'

They went down three tiled steps into the lower garden, free of trees and shade, where since May, the celebrated roses, the pride of Corinde, which had delighted a Queen had bloomed in splendour. His nonchalant disdain of Pita confirmed the safety of the election. Gonçalo, walking respectfully, as he would in a museum, showered dazzling compliments on Cavaleiro's roses.

'What exquisite beauty, André! They're marvellous! You have some absolutely sublime roses here... Those great open ones there, what splendour! And those yellow ones... Magnificent! Look at this delightful one! The pink flush just emerging, spreading out from the base of the white petals... Oh and that scarlet beauty there! What a divine colour!'

Cavaleiro crossed his arms in comic dejection.

'Just imagine! Such is my social and emotional isolation that, with all these roses blooming here, I have no one to send a bouquet to! I am reduced to presenting them to the Lousadas!'

A crimson flush, brighter than any of the roses he was praising, spread across the Nobleman's face.

'The Lousadas! Those shameless old hags!'

André turned his bright eyes upon his friend with an uneasy look of curiosity.

'Why?... Shameless old hags? Why?'

'Why? Because they are! They are by nature, by the will of God!... They are as shameless as these roses are red!'

Cavaleiro was reassured.

'Ah, generically... It's true they're full of malice. That's why I shower them with roses. In Oliveira, once a week I have a dutiful cup of tea with them!'

'Well, you're not taming them,' snorted the Nobleman.

But Mateus now appeared on the tiled steps, napkin in hand,

his bald head shining in the sun. It was time for lunch. Cavaleiro picked Gonçalo a 'triumphal rose' and for himself an 'innocent bud' . . . Thus adorned they were walking up to the terrace amid the brilliance and perfume of other rose-bushes, when Cavaleiro stopped short with an idea:

'What time are you going to Oliveira, Gonçalinho?'

The Nobleman hesitated. To Oliveira? He had not intended going there this week . . .

'Why? Is it urgent that I should to to Oliveira?'

'Certainly it is, my boy! We need to talk to Barrolo first thing tomorrow, arrange things to do with the votes from Murtosa! My dear Gonçalo, we can't sleep, you know. It's not for Júlio's sake, it's for Pita's!'

'All right! All right!' replied Gonçalo immediately, somewhat alarmed. 'I'll go to Oliveira.'

'In that case,' continued André, 'we can go at once and together, on horseback. It's a delightful ride through Freixos, shaded all the way . . . You'll want to send to the Tower, perhaps, for your clothes . . .'

No! In order to avoid the trouble of carrying suitcases around, Gonçalo kept a complete set of clothes in *Cunhais*, from slippers to dress-coat. He would enter Oliveira as the philosopher Bias had entered Athens—with a simple cane and infinite patience . . .

'Wonderful!' declared André. 'We'll make our official entry into Oliveira today, then. It'll be the beginning of the campaign.'

The Nobleman twirled his moustache in consternation at the thought of the spiteful laughter of the Lousada sisters, of all the city, at such an ostentatiously fraternal entry. When Cavaleiro told Mateus to have Rossilho and the Nobleman's mare saddled and ready for half-past four, Gonçalo exaggerated his fear of the heat and dust. Much better to go about seven, when it was cooler! (He thus hoped to enter Oliveira inconspicuously, effaced by the dusk.) But André protested:

'No, that would be a nuisance, we'd arrive at nightfall. What we want is to make a solemn entry, when the band's playing in the Square . . . Five o'clock—right?'

Gonçalo, his shoulders bowed before Fate, submitted,

'Five o'clock then, all right.'

In the dining-room, its floor covered with mats, its walls with blackened paintings of flowers and fruit on red wallpaper which was

155

an imitation of damask, André occupied grandfather Martinho's venerable armchair. The sparkling plates, the freshness of the roses in a Saxe bowl, revealed the attentions of Cousin Jesuina—who had to keep to her room with a stomach-ache. Gonçalo praised such elegant neatness, so rare in a bachelor's house, and lamented the absence of a Cousin Jesuina at the Tower. André smiled with delight as he unfolded his napkin, hoping that Gonçalo would let the Barrolos know about the comfortable luxury of Corinde. Then, spearing an olive with his fork, he commented,

'Well, there we are, my dear Gonçalo. I was in our great Capital for a day, and spent a day in Sintra . . .'

Mateus pushed the door ajar to remind the Governor of the Civil Government clerk, who was waiting to see him.

'Let him wait!' shouted Cavaleiro.

Gonçalo suggested that perhaps the worthy gentleman would grow impatient with hunger.

'Let him lunch then!' shouted Cavaleiro.

Such harsh comment for the poor clerk, neglected where he sat on the bench in the entrance-hall, his file upon his knees, made the Nobleman feel uncomfortable. But as he, too, speared an olive, he encouraged his friend to continue.

'You were saying, Sintra . . .'

'Dreary,' resumed André. 'Horrible amount of dust, the females mediocre . . . Oh, I nearly forgot. Do you know who I met there, on the Colares road? Castanheiro, our Castanheiro, Castanheiro of the *Annals*, of the top-hat. He flung his arms into the air in despair. 'Isn't our Gonçalo Mendes Ramires ever going to send me that novel?' It seems the first number comes out in December and he needs the manuscript by the beginning of October . . . He begged me to shake you up, to remind you of the glory of the Ramires. You ought to finish the novel . . . It would be useful if, before you entered the House, you could produce something serious, rich in erudition, something very Portuguese . . .'

'Of course it would be useful!' agreed Gonçalo quickly. 'All we need now is the fourth chapter. But it's this particular part that needs more preparation, more research. I need a calmer mind to finish it, the certainty of this infernal election . . . It's not this animal, Júlio that bothers me. But that scheming crowd in Lisbon . . . What do you think?'

Cavaleiro laughed, extending his fork towards the olives again.

'What do I think, Gonçalinho? That you're like a little child, frightened that the plate of rice pudding won't get round to you. Calm down, my boy, you'll get your rice pudding! . . . But really, I *did* find José Ernesto very stubborn. There were long-standing compromises with Pita. The *Verdade* has been siding with the Government very strongly. And this Pita, when he knows I've stopped him getting Vila Clara, will be seething, raging against me. Which is all utterly immaterial to me; Pita's little fits of temper and little jokes aren't likely to take my appetite away . . . But José Ernesto admires Pita, needs Pita, is under an obligation to Pita to pay him with a constituency . . . Only the last day I was there, he said to me in the office, and I even found it funny: "I see the deputies for Vila Clara have a habit of dying; now if your Ramires, following this good custom, should die in the near future, then Pita has the job." '

Gonçalo pushed back his chair.

'If I should die indeed! The animal!'

'Oh, he means, if you should die as far as the constituency's concerned!' put in Cavaleiro with a laugh. 'For example, if we should quarrel, if some disagreement arose between us tomorrow . . . But that's impossible, of course!'

Mateus entered with a tureen of delicious-smelling chicken soup.

'Go to it!' cried André, 'And don't let's talk any more of constituencies or Pitas, or Júlios, or wretched politics! . . . Tell me what your novel's about . . . History, eh? . . . Middle ages? Don João V? . . . If I were to try my hand at a novel I'd choose a splendid period like Portugal under the Filipes . . .'

*   *   *

A quarter to seven was striking on the permanently fast clock of the Church of St Christopher in Oliveira, when André Cavaleiro and Gonçalo, coming down Rua Velha, entered the Terreiro da Louça (now called Counsellor Costa Barroso Square).

Every Sunday, in a bandstand that the Counsellor had built on the site of an old pillory when he was President of the Town Hall, the brass band of the regiment, or the Lealdade Philharmonic Orchestra, turned that square into the most sociable centre in the quiet little town. Since the bazaar patronized by the Bishop had begun that afternoon in the Convent of Santa Brigida, there were a few ladies seated on the stone benches and the chairs scattered beneath the acacia-trees. The Lousadas were missing from their reserved seats, carefully selected for their view across the entire Square and the houses which confined it on the sides of St Christopher's and the Trinas, and also Rua Velha and Rua das Velas, the lemonade-stall and also the other retreat which was modestly concealed behind an ivy-covered trellice. But the only familiar group—Dona Maria Mendonça, the Baroness das Marges and the two Alboim sisters, were sitting talking with their backs to the Square, beside the iron railings built on the ancient wall—from which one could see fields, the grounds of the New Seminary, the whole Estevinha Pinewoods and the shining, twisting Crede River.

But the gentlemen who were wandering along the path called 'The Walk' across the square, enjoying the *March of the Prophet*, were once again astounded (although they all knew of the famous reconciliation at the Civil Government) when the two friends appeared, both wearing straw hats, both in high gaiters on their slowly-pacing mares—Gonçalo's mount a slender bay with a short tail in the English style, Cavaleiro's heavier and black, its chest arched, its thick tail sweeping the ground. Melo Alboim, the Baron of Marges and the Delegate halted in a startled row, which was joined by one of the Vila-Velhas, the Squire Pestana, and the fat Major Ribas, his uniform unbuttoned, rolling from side to side and joking about 'that fine friendship . . .' The notary Guedes, Guedes the Tufted, got up with such a start that he upset his chair, as, indignant but respectful, he bared his bald head with a deep, deep bow, while his hand holding the white hat trembled. And old Cerqueira, the lawyer, who had come out of the ivy-covered retreat and was adjusting himself, stood dumbfounded, his glasses perched on his tip-tilted nose and his fingers dangling at his trouser buttons.

Meanwhile the two friends gravely continued along the row of houses dominated by the palace of Dona Arminda Vilegas, with the heavy Vilegas arms on its cornice, its ten noble, iron-railed verandahs enriched with curtains of yellow damask. On the verandah at the corner, Barrolo and José Mendonça sat on straw stools, smoking. Hearing the slow trot of the horses, and seeing his brother-in-law so unexpectedly—the good Barrolo almost fell over the verandah:

'Oh, Gonçalo! Gonçalo! . . . Are you going home?'

Without awaiting confirmation he yelled again, waving his arms,

'We're just going! We've had dinner here today . . . Gracinha's upstairs with Aunt Arminda. We're off home now! Just a moment!'

Cavaleiro smilingly acknowledged Captain Mendonça. Barrolo had already fled enthusiastically behind the yellow damask curtains. And the two friends, leaving that wave of astonishment behind them in the Terreiro, entered Candle Street, where a policeman saluted—an incident most pleasing to the Nobleman of the Tower.

Cavaleiro accompanied Gonçalo to King's Square. In front of the mansion a man in a red beret was grinding away the wedding chorus from *Lucia* on his barrel-organ, looking hopefully towards the deserted windows. The doorman Joaquim ran from the yard to hold the Nobleman's mare. With a silent smile, the organist held out his beret. After flinging him a handful of copper, Gonçalo hesitated, and finally murmured with embarrassment and a blush:

'Would't you like to come in for a moment and rest, André?'

'No, thank you . . . So, two o'clock tomorrow, at the Civil Government, with Barrolo, to decide the question of the votes from Murtosa . . . Goodbye, my dear friend! We had a lovely ride and startled the townfolk!'

Cavaleiro, embracing the mansion with a long glance, turned down Weaver's Street.

In his room (which was always ready for him, the bed always made) Gonçalo had just finished washing and brushing his hair when Barrolo came rushing down the corridor, out of breath and impatient for news—and behind him, Gracinha, also breathless, nervously untying the scarlet ribbons on her hat. Ever since Barrolo 'had witnessed with his own eyes' the public conversation between André and Gonçalo on the verandah of the Civil Governor's Office, he and Gracinha had been seething with desperate impatience to understand the motive, the hidden story behind that amazing reconciliation. Then there was Gonçalo's flight to the Tower in the carriage, without stopping at *Cunhais*, and Cavaleiro's sudden journey to Lisbon; the silence, heavier than any iron lid, that had fallen over the case, had almost terrified them. Gracinha had murmured at night in the oratory in the midst of her prayers, 'Oh, dear Mother Mary, whatever can it be?' Barrolo had not dared go to the Tower, but he had even dreamt about the verandah of the Civil Government, which had appeared enormous, growing and growing till it overran Oliveira, reaching the windows of *Cunhais*, from which he had tried to push it away with a broom-handle. And now here were Gonçalo and André entering the town on horseback, most serenely, both wearing straw hats, like constant companions coming home from a friendly ride together!

Without even waiting to enter the room, Barrolo flung out his arms and shouted,

'What's all this about? . . . Everyone's talking about it! You and André together! . . .'

Gracinha stammered, as red as the ribbons on her hat,

'And you never come, never write . . . We've been so worried . . .'

Right there at the open door, without their sitting down even, the Nobleman explained the 'mystery', his towel still in his hands.

'A most unexpected but most natural thing. Sanches Lucena is dead, as you know. The constituency of Vila Clara is without a deputy. It's a constituency that can only accept a man born here, and with property and influence. The Government immediately sent me a telegram asking me if I wished to stand . . . And as I am, basically, on good terms with the Historicals, and am a friend of José Ernesto's . . . I wanted to enter the House . . . I accepted.'

Barrolo bruised his leg with a triumphal slap.

'I was right then, by Jove!'

The Nobleman continued, interminably wiping his hands.

'I accepted, but on conditions, of course, very rigid ones. But I accepted . . . In this case, as you know, it is desirable that the candidate should be on good terms with the Civil Governor. I did not want to renew our relationship at first. With Lisbon urging it, however, and urging it most strongly, and for higher political considerations, I consented to this sacrifice. Considering the difficulties the country has, everyone should make certain sacrifices. I did this. . . . André, moreover, was very pleasant, very affectionate. And the result is that we are friends again. Political friends: but very good friends, and loyal . . . I lunched with him in Corinde today, and we rode here together through Freixos. A beautiful afternoon! . . . So you see the former harmony has been reborn. And the election is safe.'

'Come here and let me hug you!' shouted Barrolo, in wild delight.

Gracinha slowly sank on to the edge of the bed with her hat in her lap, looking in fascination at her brother, in tender silence, her gentle eyes affectionate and smiling. The Nobleman, who had freed himself from Barrolo's arms, began to fold the towel slowly and absent-mindedly.

'The election is safe, but we need to work. You, Barrolo, must have a talk with Cavaleiro, too. I've already arranged it. Tomorrow in the Civil Government, at two o'clock. You must discuss the matter with him, because of the votes from Murtosa . . .'

'Right, my boy! Anything you wish! Votes, money . . .'

Gonçalo absent-mindedly sprinkled his jacket with eau-de-Cologne which splashed on the floor.

'From the moment I and André were reconciled, the entire past was over. You, Barrolo, will immediately be reconciled, too . . .'

Barrolo almost leapt to the air, such was his amazement.

'But of course I shall! And a very good thing too, because I like Cavaleiro immensely! I was always saying to Gracinha, "Oh, really, all this foolishness because of politics!" '

'Right,' concluded the Nobleman. 'Politics divided us, and now politics has reunited us . . . It's what's called the fickleness of times and empires.'

He caught Gracinha by the shoulders and gave her a playful kiss on each cheek.

'How's Aunt Arminda? Recovered from her scalding? Gone back to the exploits of Leandro the Handsome?'

Gracinha's face shone with the slow smile that had not left it, which lit her face with clarity and gentleness.

'Aunt Arminda's much better, she's already walking again. She asked after you . . . But Gonçalo, you must want some dinner!'

'No, I had an enormous lunch at Corinde . . . As you two dined early with Aunt Arminda, you'll be having a late supper, I suppose? Then I'll have some supper, too . . . All I want now is a cup of tea, very strong!'

Gracinha ran off, eager to serve her beloved hero . . . As he went down the stairs with Barrolo, who was watching him, the Nobleman of the Tower lamented the sacrifices he had made.

'It's true, my dear fellow, it's an awful bore . . . But what the deuce! We must all pull together to drag the country out of the mess it's in!'

Barrolo murmured in amazement,

'And you didn't say a word . . . So modest about it all! So modest . . .'

'One more thing, Barrolo. At the Civil Government tomorrow, you must invite André to dinner . . .'

'Of course!' exclaimed Barrolo. 'A large, sumptuous dinner?'

'No, no. A very quiet, very select dinner. Only André and João Gouveia. Send a wire to João Gouveia. You can ask the Mendonças, too . . . But a very discreet dinner, just so we can talk together, so we can seal our new friendship in a more sociable, more elegant way.'

The next day, at the Civil Government, Barrolo and Cavaleiro shook hands with such simplicity that it seemed as if they had spent the evening before playing billiards together and chatting in the Club in Pegas Street. Then they talked summarily about the election. As soon as Cavaleiro vaguely mentioned the votes from Murtosa, the good Barrolo almost choked in his anxiety to offer them.

'Anything you want . . . Votes, money, all you want! . . . You just say! I'll go along to Murtosa, there'll be a feast and a barrel of wine tapped, and the whole parish offering their votes amid the fireworks . . .'

Cavaleiro laughed and calmed down his eagerness for festivity.

'No, my dear Barrolo, no! We've prepared a very sober election, a very calm one. Vila Clara will elect Gonçalo Mendes Ramires deputy, naturally, as their best man. There's no fight, Julinho's only a shadow. Therefore . . .'

Barrolo persisted,

'Forgive me, André, forgive me! Of course we must have plenty of wine and food and fireworks and so on . . .'

But Gonçalo, embarrassed, anxious to stop Barrolo's chatter, and the affectionate slaps on the back with which he was demonstrating his intimacy with Cavaleiro, pointed to the Civil Governor's table.

'You have work to do, André. I can see a dreadful pile of papers there . . . Let's not take up more of the good gentleman's time. To work!

To work, my brother, for work
Is André, is virtue, is worth . . . !'

He picked up his hat and motioned to his brother-in-law. Then Barrolo, his fat cheeks shining with pleasure, stammered out the invitation which would seal that reconciliation in an elegant, sociable manner.

'Cavaleiro, perhaps we could talk things over better if you'd be kind enough to dine with us . . . Thursday, at six-thirty . . . When Gonçalo's here, we always dine a little later.'

Cavaleiro, who had blushed, thanked him with deliberate ceremony.

'That would be a great pleasure, a great honour . . .'

At the door of the antechamber, to which he had accompanied them, he begged Barrolo, as he held back the heavy scarlet baize curtain with the embroidered royal arms, to give his kindest regards to Senhora Dona Graça . . .

As Barrolo descended the large stone staircase, he wiped his forehead and his neck, damp with emotion. In the yard below, he blurted out,

'A charming fellow, your André! A frank fellow, I've always liked him . . . Really, I was dying for all this silliness to end . . . And for *Cunhais*, for company and for a bit of a chat, what a marvellous acquisition!'

★   ★   ★

After an early lunch on Thursday morning, when they were sitting having coffee on the terrace, Gonçalo advised Barrolo, 'that thoroughly to emphasize the simple intimacy of the dinner it would be better not to wear tails . . .'

'And you, Gracinha, nothing *décolleté*. Something light and cheerful.'

Gracinha smiled undecidedly, and continued to look through an *Almanac of Souvenirs*, as she lay stretched in a wicker-chair with a little white kitten in her lap.

After all the fuss and bustle of Sunday, she affected silent unconcern for the reconciliation which was still shaking Oliveira, for the election and for the dinner. But she had been restless these last few days—and so impatient and sensitive, that the good Barrolo was constantly advising her to take Mama's most excellent medicine for nerves—'rosemary flowers stewed in white wine'.

Gonçalo clearly understood how perturbed she was by this triumphant entry by André, the old André, into *Cunhais* and her married life. To appease his conscience, he reminded himself (as he had on the road to the cemetery in Vila Clara) of Gracinha's seriousness, of her strict and pure thoughts, of the nobility of her heroic little soul. This same morning, in his new anxiety and in the excitement of the election, all he feared was that Gracinha, through embarrassment or excessive care, might welcome Cavaleiro coldly, and thus chill him in his renewed enthusiasm for the Ramires family, in his political patronage. And he insisted, with a laugh,

'Did you hear, Gracinha? A white dress. A cheerful dress, which will smile at our guests . . .'

She murmured, absorbed in her *Almanac*,

'Yes, of course, with this heat . . .'

But Barrolo slapped his thigh. What a shame! What a shame he hadn't got, in Oliveira, 'for the toast of reconciliation' a famous port wine from his mother's wine-cellar, a magnificent, really ancient wine from the time of Don João II . . .

'Don João II?' snorted Gonçalo. 'Then that's no good now!'

'Don João II or Don João VI . . . One of those kings . . . A really unique wine, from the last century! Mama's only got nine or ten bottles left . . . Today would be the day for one, wouldn't it?'

The Nobleman slowly sipped his coffee.

'In the old days André used to be very fond of *ovos queimados*.'[1]

Gracinha abruptly closed her *Almanac*, and with a sudden, silent departure which dumbfounded Gonçalo, she shook off the sleeping cat from her lap, crossed the terrace and disappeared between the yew trees.

But that evening, as the Nobleman sat at the oval table beside his cousin Maria Mendonça, he at once noted between two compotiers a dish of *ovos queimados*. In spite of the informality of the dinner, they were using, with the China dinner service, Uncle Melchior's famous gold-plated cutlery. Two Saxe bowls were filled with white and yellow carnations, the heraldic colours of the Ramires.

Dona Maria, who had not seen her dear cousin since Gracinha's birthday, murmured with a smile, with grave courtesy, in the ceremonious silence as they were unfolding their napkins,

'I still haven't congratulated you yet, cousin Gonçalo . . .'

He interrupted her, fidgeting nervously with the glasses,

'Sh, cousin, sh! There's to be no talk of politics today . . . It's too hot for politics.'

She gave a feeble sigh, as if she were about to faint.

'Ah, the heat . . . How appallingly hot it was! Ever since she had

[1] *Ovos queimados*: sweet made of eggs.

entered *Cunhais* in the black dress "which was her Sunday evening best", she had not ceased envying Gracinha's cool white dress . . .

'How it suits her! She looks so lovely today!'

It was a simple dress in white *crépon* which emphasized her almost virginal charm and made her even younger. Never indeed had she been so fascinating, so pale and delicate, her green eyes shining like washed emeralds, a brighter wave in her thick locks, a soft, transparent blush in her cheeks—all the lustre and brightness of a freshly-watered flower, a refreshed flower, in spite of the awkwardness which numbed her fingers as she lifted her gold-plated silver spoon. At her side, large and robust, his chest arched like a cuirass and studded with two sapphires, and a full-blown white rose in his lapel, André Cavaleiro, who had refused soup (Oh, in summer he never ate soup!) dominated the table. He, too, was somewhat moved, and from time to time dabbed his shiny moustache with a handkerchief which was perfumed so strongly that it drowned the scent of the carnations. But it was he who kept their high spirits going with amusing complaints about the heat—the scandalous heat of Oliveira . . . Ah! what flaming Purgatory after his two days of paradise in deliciously cool Sintra!

Dona Maria Mendonça's beady eyes softened towards the Civil Governor. What had Sintra been like? Gay? Plenty of groups in Seteais in the afternoon? Had he met the Countess of Chelas, cousin Chelas? . . .

Yes, Cavaleiro had spoken a moment with the Countess of Chelas in the Pena Palace, when he had been visiting the Queen . . .

'Ah, how was the Queen? . . .'

'Oh, as enchanting as ever . . . The Countess of Chelas was looking rather thin. But so pleasant, so intelligent, so completely the *grande dame*—don't you think?' And as he leant towards Gracinha, with infinite sweetness in the simple movement of his head, she, disturbed and pinker-cheeked than before, mumbled that she did not know the Countess of Chelas . . . Dona Maria Mendonça immediately accused her Barrolo cousins of shutting themselves up in *Cunhais* and never venturing to Lisbon in the winter to have any social life, to get to know their relations . . .

'It's cousin José's fault, who hates Lisbon . . .'

Oh no! Barrolo did not hate Lisbon! If he could take all his conveniences to Lisbon, his room and his carriage and horses, his excellent water from the orchard, the magnificent verandah over-looking the garden—he would be delighted!

'But confined in those little rooms in the *Braganza* . . . And on top of that, bad food and the noise . . . Gracinha never sleeps when she's in Lisbon. And those boring mornings! There's never any-thing to do in Lisbon in the morning!'

Cavaleiro smiled at Barrolo as if enchanted by such wit and logic. Then he confessed that he, in spite of inhabiting a comfortable palace too (thanks to the state!), and enjoying excellent water, the superb water from the Well of St Domingos, he lamented the fact that his political duties and party discipline tied him to Oliveira. All his hopes lay in the fall of the ministry so that he could be free and spend three divine months in Italy . . .

On Gracinha's other side, João Gouveia (always shy and dumb in the presence of ladies) exclaimed, with an impetuous show of friendship, of conviction,

'Well, Andrézinho, you can give up your hopes! Because S Fulgêncio will not be brought down! You've still got to endure some three or four years yet!'

And he insisted, bending over Gracinha, in an essay of amiability which made him glow,

'S Fulgêncio won't be brought down! We've still got our André with us for another three or four years at least!'

André portested languidly, his thick lashes almost closed.

'Oh, João, my friend, don't wish me ill, don't wish me ill!'

He persisted. There was no doubt about it. He would even desert his party (what did a rusty lance matter to such a powerful host?)—he had been dreaming of passing the winter months in Italy, he was already making plans . . . Would Senhora Dona Gracinha allow him to pour her a little white wine?

Barrolo extended his arm effusively.

'Oh, Cavaleiro, I want you to try this white wine carefully. It's from my estate at Corvelo . . . I find it very special. But taste it carefully!'

The gentleman tasted it religiously—as if he were taking com-munion. With an air of appreciative conviction that made Barrolo glow with pleasure, he replied,

'It's magnificent! Absolutely magnificent!'

'It is, isn't it? Personally I prefer this Corvelo wine to all the

French wines, to the best of them . . . Even Father Soeiro, who's a saint, appreciates it!'

Silent and inconspicuous behind one of the tall vases of carnations, Father Soeiro coloured and smiled,

'Diluted with a lot of water, I'm afraid, Senhor José Barrolo. Taste craves but rheumatism does not allow.'

José Mendonça, who had no dread of rheumatism, always attacked the blessed Corvelo with the utmost enthusiasm.

'What do you think about it, João Gouveia?'

Oh, João Gouveia was already acquainted with it, thank Heavens! He had certainly never encountered any white wine in Portugal to compare with it for its freshness, its aroma, its fullness . . .

'I'm enjoying it as it deserves, Barrolo. This beautiful crystal decanter is fast losing its contents!'

Barrolo was thrilled. He was only sorry that Gonçalo did not enjoy 'that nectar'. No! Gonçalo could not tolerate white wines . . .

'Today I'm so thirsty only sparkling wines will satisfy me, with ice . . . Still, this Vidainhos wine's from Barrolo's lands, too. Oh, I don't despise family wines. Far from it. I consider this Vidainhos really sublime.'

Then Cavaleiro wanted to taste the superb sparkling wine from the Vidainhos estate in Amarante. The butler, at an enthusiastic sign from Barrolo, presented the Civil Governor with a slender glass, expressly for that sparkling wine. But Cavaleiro, caressing the cool glass without raising it to his lips, returned to the question of holidays, of travel, as if to stress his weariness and boredom in Oliveira. Did Dona Gracinha know where he was going this winter after Italy, if God and the Ministry allowed it? . . . To Asia Minor.

'A journey to tempt Gonçalo . . . So easy nowadays, with the railways! Venice to Constantinople is a mere step. Then from Constantinople to Ismir, one or two days in an excellent boat. Then, with a good caravan via Tripoli and ancient Sidon, we would enter Galilee . . . Galilee! Eh, Gonçalo? How beautiful!'

Father Soeiro, his fork suspended in mid-air, reminded them timidly that, in Galilee, Sr Gonçalo Ramires would be treading ground that in former times had belonged to his family.

'One of your ancestors, Gutierres Ramires, Tancredo's companion in the first Crusade, refused the dukedom of Galilee and Trans-Jordan.'

'What a thing to do!' laughed Gonçalo. 'What a stupid thing grandfather Gutierres did! There wouldn't be anything more amusing today than for me to be Duke of Galilee! Senhor Gonçalo Mendes Ramires, Duke of Galilee and Trans-Jordan!... A magnificent joke!'

Cavaleiro made a friendly protest.

'No, really! Why?'

'Don't you believe what he says,' said Dona Maria Mendonça, her bright eyes shining. 'Cousin Gonçalo, for all his jokes, is profoundly aristocratic at heart. Oh, terribly aristocratic!'

The Nobleman of the Tower put down his glass of Vidainhos, after a long appreciative draught.

'Aristocrat... Of course I'm an aristocrat. I would, I don't deny it, feel a certain distaste at having been born, like a weed, from other weeds. It gives me pleasure to know that I am the son of my father Vicente, who was the son of his father Damião, who was born of Inacio and so on, back to I don't know which Suevian king...'

'Recesvinto!' Father Soeiro respectfully informed him.

'As far back as Recesvinto, then. The worst of it is that the blood of all these ancestors of mine is no different, really, from the blood of the ancestors of doorman Joaquim. And if we go back beyond Recesvinto, back to Adam, I find I haven't got any more ancestors!'

As they all laughed, Dona Maria Mendonça leant towards him and from behind her wide-open fan murmured,

'You're feigning contempt for these things, cousin. But I know of a lady who has the highest admiration for the house of Ramires and its representative.'

Gonçalo filled his glass again, lovingly, carefully watching the bubbles.

'Bravo! But "one must be precise", as Manuel Duarte says. Who is it she really admires, me or the Suevian, Recesvinto?'

'Both of you.'

'Heavens!'

Then putting down the bottle, he asked more seriously,

'Who is it?'

Oh, she could not confess. She was not yet the age to go round carrying *billets-doux*. Gonçalo would not bother about the name then—all he wanted to know was her virtues. Was she young? Was she pretty?

168

'Pretty?' cried Dona Maria. 'She is one of the most beautiful women in Portugal!'

Gonçalo blurted out the name in astonishment.

'Dona Ana Lucena!'

'Why?'

'Because a woman so beautiful, living in this area, and so familiar with you, cousin, that she confides in you, must be Dona Ana.'

Dona Maria, straightening the two roses that brightened up the black silk bodice, smiled,

'Perhaps it is, perhaps . . .'

'Then I am immensely flattered. But I must still be precise, like Manuel Duarte. If this kindness of hers is directed towards the honourable goal, then no! Heaven help me, no! . . . But if it is for some more perverse reason, then naturally, cousin, I shall do my duty honourably, within my ability of course . . .'

Dona Maria hid her face behind her fan, scandalized. Then glancing sharply around, her bright eyes gleaming, she remarked,

'Oh, cousin, it's the honourable goal that would be most profitable, because it all comes to the same and you'd be two hundred *contos* better off!'

Gonçalo shouted out in admiration:

'Oh, really, cousin Maria! There's no one more intelligent in all Europe!'

Everyone was eager to hear Sra Dona Maria's latest sally. But Gonçalo would not satisfy their curiosity.

'It can't be told. It's about marriage.'

Then José Mendonça remembered the delectable news that had set Oliveira talking since yesterday.

'About marriage! . . . What do you think about Dona Rosa Alcoforado's marriage?'

Barrolo, then Gouveia, and even Gracinha, all declared it was awful. That perfect girl, with the peaches-and-cream skin and golden hair, tied to Teixeira de Carredes, a patriarch with innumerable grandchildren . . . What a dreadful affair!

But the marriage did not strike Cavaleiro as dreadful. Teixeira de Carredes, apart from being very distinguished and very intelligent, was a very youthful old man, with hardly a wrinkle,—even handsome, that dark moustache contrasting with his thick, curly white hair. As for Dona Rosa, despite the roses of her skin and gold of her hair, there was something strangely lifeless and listless about her ... And she wasn't very bright. Nor very particular about her appearance—her hair was always untidy.

'So, excuse me, ladies and gentlemen, but I consider it's poor Teixeira de Carredes who's made a poor marriage.'

Dona Maria Mendonça studied the Civil Governor with polite astonishment.

'If Senhor Cavaleiro does not admire Rosinha Alcoforado, I really can't imagine which girl he can admire within his District ...'

He at once answered gallantly,

'Apart from yourself, madam, there is no one I admire! Really, I must govern the district most lacking in beauty in all Portugal!'

Everyone protested. What about Maria Marges? And the young Reriz, from Riosa? And Melozinho Alboim, with those magnificent eyes of hers? But Cavaleiro would not agree, he crushed them all with a sarcastic comment either about their lustreless skin or their ungainly walk, their provincial taste and manners, in every case for the lack of beauty and charms which embellished Gracinha—thus indirectly casting at her feet a number of crumpled and defeated ladies. She perceived his subtle flattery, and her eyes lit with a tender glow the blushes which brought the pink to her cheeks. She wished to share this excessive devotion—and timidly suggested another beauty of which the District was proud:

'The Viscount of Rio Manso's daughter, Rosinha Rio Manso ... She's lovely!'

Once again Cavaleiro triumphed easily:

'But she's only twelve years old, madam! She's not a rose yet, only a rose-bud!'

Almost humbly, Gracinha suggested Luisa Moreira, a shop-keeper's daughter, a girl very much admired on Sundays at mass in the Cathedral and in the Terreiro da Louça:

'She's a beautiful girl. And her figure especially ...'

'Yes, but her teeth are crooked, Senhora Dona Graça!'

'All over the place! Haven't you ever noticed? Oh, a most unpleasant mouth! And apart from her teeth, there's her brother, Evaristo, with his face even flatter than his soul, and his dandruff and dirtiness and Jacobinism. No beautiful woman can have so ugly a brother!'

Mendonça stuck out his hand to mention another point that was occupying Oliveira.

'Talking about Evaristo! Did he start that new republican paper he was planning, *The Alarm*?'

The Civil Governor shrugged his shoulders with an air of smiling, superior ignorance. But João Gouveia, red and glowing after his bottle of Corvelo and his bottle of Douro, confirmed that *The Alarm* would be appearing in November. He even knew the patriot who was putting up the money. The campaign in *The Alarm* was to begin with five resounding articles on the Storming of the Bastille.

Gonçalo was amazed at the way in which Republicanism was spreading through Portugal—even in dear, devout old Oliveira.

'When I was starting at University there were only two Republicans in Oliveira, old Salema, teacher of Rhetoric and myself. Now there's a party, there's a committee, there are two papers . . . And there's even the Baron of Marges holding *The Public Voice*, under the Arcade . . .'

Mendonça did not fear a Republic and jested,

'They're still a long way off, a long way off . . . We've still got time to eat these beautiful *ovos queimados*.'

'Delicious,' murmured Cavaleiro.

'Yes,' agreed Gonçalo. 'We still have time for the eggs . . . But if a revolution breaks out in Spain, or the young king dies before he reaches his majority, as he surely will . . .'

'Oh, no! Poor little thing! And his poor mother!' murmured Gracinha, moved by such an idea.

Cavaleiro calmed her. Why should the little King of Spain die? The republicans were merely spreading gloomy tales about the health of the excellent child. But he knew the truth—he assured Sra Dona Gracinha that, fortunately for Spain, an Afonso XIII and even an Afonso XIV would yet reign. As for our Republicans, well . . . Good gracious, it was merely a question for the municipal guard! Portugal remained, in the depth of its masses, basically monarchic. Only in the upper strata, among the bourgeoisie and in the schools, floated a light but dirty scum, which would be cleaned off easily with a sabre . . .

'You, Senhora Dona Graça, who are a perfect housewife, obviously know of this operation which is carried out in the broth-pot . . . Skimming the pan, it's called. You do it with a spoon. Here it's done

with a sabre. This, in all simplicity, is how Portugal must be puri-
fied. Which is what I remarked only recently to the King.'

He raised his head—and his breast gleamed, broader, like a
cuirass strong enough to defend the monarchy. In the respectful
silence that spread over the table, two champagne corks popped in
the pantry behind the partition.

As soon as the butler had hastily filled the glasses, the Nobleman
of the Tower, with a seriousness lightened by his smile, toasted,

'To your health, André. Not the Civil Governor, but the friend!'

All glasses were raised with friendly murmurs. João Gouveia
waved his with particular effusiveness and cried, 'Andrèzinho, my
dear old friend!' The good gentleman merely brushed his glass
against Gracinha's. Father Soeiro murmured grace. And Barrolo
asked, flinging down his napkin,

'Coffee here or in the drawing-room? . . . It's cooler in the
drawing-room.'

The large drawing-room, the crimson, velvet room, shone in
solitary splendour; the serene, warm night, the restrained silence of
Oliveira entered through the three open windows; below, in the
Square, certain persons, including two ladies with white woollen
shawls round their heads, stared in astonishment at that bright air
of festivity which poured out of *Cunhais*. Cavaleiro and Gonçalo lit
their cigars on the verandah, breathing in the welcome cool air.
And Cavaleiro remarked blissfully,

'There's no doubt about it, Gonçalo, one dines sublimely in your
brother-in-law's house! . . .'

Gonçalo invited him to dine at the Tower on Sunday. There were
still a few bottles of Madeira left, from Grandfather Damião's time
—upon which, with the help of Gouveia and Titó, they would make
a heroic assault.

Cavaleiro promised, already delighted with the idea, as he took
his coffee without sugar from the heavy silver tray.

'And now you, Gonçalo, really shouldn't stir from the Tower.
Your role is to remain in the locality. The Nobleman of the Tower is
in the midst of his lands, from which he will be elected to the House.
This is your role . . .'

Barrolo, with a fascinated smile, came between the two friends,
whom he clasped affectionately round the waist.

'And we'll both stay here, working, Cavaleiro and myself!'

But Dona Maria, from the deep sofa in which she was sitting, called cousin Gonçalo over 'to talk business'. Beside a console-table, João Gouveia and Father Soeiro sat and stirred their coffee and agreed on the need for a strong Government. And Gracinha, with cousin Mendonça, went through the music on top of the piano, looking for the *Fado of the Ramires*. Medonça played with easy brilliance, and had composed waltzes and a hymn to Col Trancoso, the hero of Machumba—and even the first act of an opera, *The Shepherd*. As they could not find the *Fado* with Videirinha's verses, he sat down without bothering to put down his cigar, to attack one of his own waltzes, *The Pearl*, a piece with a lazy gentle rhythm that reminded one of the waltz from *Faust*.

Then Cavaleiro, who had come back into the room, gave a tug to his waistcoat, smoothed his moustache, and approaching Gracinha in semi-serious, semi-playful mood, asked,

'Would you do me the great honour, madam? . . .'

He invited her, and opened his arms. Gracinha, crimson all over, yielded, carried away at once in the long gliding steps made by Cavaleiro on the carpet. Barrolo and João Gouveia hastened to move away the armchairs, clearing a space where the waltz was unfolding to the soft, white bobbing of Gracinha's dress. Small and light, she was completely lost, as if she had merged with the masculine strength of Cavaleiro, who bore her off in slow turns, his head inclined, breathing in the freshness of her magnificent hair.

From the edge of the sofa, Dona Maria Mendonça gasped in astonishment, her fine eyes flashing.

'But how well he waltzes, how well the Civil Governor waltzes!'

At her side, Gonçalo twisted his moustache nervously, surprised at such familiarity, re-adopted by Cavaleiro with such calm confidence, and by Gracinha with such abandon . . . They turned, clasped together. From Cavaleiro's lips came a smile and a murmur. Gracinha was panting, her varnished shoes shining beneath her skirt which twirled round Cavaleiro's trousers. Barrolo clapped delightedly as they brushed by him, and cried ecstatically,

'Bravo! Bravo! Lovely! . .·. Magnificent!'

7

GONÇALO WAS COMING home to lunch after a walk in the orchard, glancing through the *Porto Gazette*, when he saw, sitting on the stone bench beside the kitchen door, where Rosa was putting fresh millet in her canary's cage, Casco, José Casco of Bravais, who was waiting, thoughtful and dejected, his hat on his knees. Hoping to avoid the man, he hastily plunged into his newspaper again. But he saw the man's leanness as he emerged from the shade of the trellis-work, advanced into the brilliant light of the yard, and hesitated, as if afraid . . . Encouraged by Rosa's presence, Gonçalo stopped and forced his lips into a smile, while Casco rotated the hard brim of his hat in his trembling fingers and stammered,

'If your Lordship would be kind enough to let me have a word with you . . .'

'Oh, it's you, Casco! I didn't recognize you, man! What is it then?'

He folded his newspaper, at ease now, even enjoying the sub-mission of the ruffian who had so terrified him when he had risen up, tall and black as a pine-tree, in the solitude of the pinewood. Casco spluttered and faltered, drew up his head and stretched his neck between the thick embroidered collar—until at last he blurted out, from the bottom of his heart in plaintive entreaty, holding back the tears which were filling his eyes,

'Oh, my Lord, forgive me for the love of God! Forgive me, because I don't know how to ask your pardon!'

Gonçalo interrupted him with generosity and kindness. Hadn't he warned him? There was nothing to be gained in shouting and raising his crook . . .

'Now look here, Casco! When you went for me in the pinewood I had a revolver in my pocket. I always carry a revolver. Ever since a night in Coimbra, in the Poplar Grove, when two drunkards attacked me, I've always taken the precaution of carrying a revolver . . . Think what a disaster it would have been if I'd drawn my revolver, if I'd fired! What a disaster, eh? Fortunately I at once saw that I would lose control of myself, that I'd kill you, so I fled. That's why I fled, so as not to fire my revolver . . . Still, that's all over. And I'm not a man to bear a grudge; I've forgotten it. So now you,

174

too, now you're calm and clear-headed, had better forget it as well.'

Casco was kneading the brim of his hat, his head down. Without looking up, without daring to, hoarse from the sobs choking him, he stammered,

'It's now I realize, your Lordship! Now I curse my stupidity! Now! After what you did for my wife and little boy, your Lordship!'

Gonçalo smiled and shrugged his shoulders.

'What nonsense, Casco! Your wife turned up here one raining night . . . And the little boy was ill, poor little fellow, feverish . . . How is Manuelzinho?'

Casco murmured from the depths of his humility,

'Thanks be to God, sir, he's very well, very healthy.'

'Good . . . Put your hat on. Put your hat on, man. And goodbye! There's nothing to thank me for, Casco! . . . And listen, bring the little boy along one day. I liked him. He's a bright little lad.'

But Casco did not move, as if fixed to the ground. Finally he burst out with a sob,

'I just don't know how to tell you, your Lordship . . . The day in prison I got is over and done with. I've a bad temper, I did something foolish, and I paid for it. And it cost me very little, thanks to you, sir . . . But then when I was let out, when I heard my wife had come to the Tower, and that the Nobleman had even wrapped her up in a cape, and hadn't let the little boy leave the house . . .'

He stopped, choked with emotion. When Gonçalo, also moved, clapped him affably on the shoulder, 'to stop all this talk, not to say another word about such trifles,' Casco blurted out in a painful, broken voice,

'But your Lordship doesn't know what that boy means to me! . . . Ever since God sent him I've felt such a passion for him, here inside me—you can' imagine! . . . You know that night I spent in prison, I couldn't sleep . . . And God forgive me, I didn't think of my wife, or my poor old mother, or the little bit of land I cultivate, all deserted. All night long I was moaning, "Ai, my dear little boy! my dear little boy! . . ." Then when my wife told me along the road that the Nobleman had kept him at the Tower and put him in the best bed and sent for the doctor . . . And later on, when I heard from Sr Bento how your Lordship had gone up that night to see if he was well covered and had tucked him up, poor little fellow . . .'

Impetuously, crying out, 'Oh your Lordship! Oh your Lordship!'

Casco caught hold of Gonçalo's hands and kissed them again and again, as the tears poured from his eyes.

'Really Casco! How foolish! . . . Stop it, man!'

Pale, Gonçalo shook off such effusive gratitude—until they both stood facing each other, the Nobleman his eyelashes moist and tremulous, the farmer from Bravais sobbing in confusion. It was the latter who, finally, checking a further sob, recovered his composure and surfaced with the idea that had brought him there, that had deeply moved him, and that now constricted his face and gestures in a determination that would never waver.

'Your Lordship, I don't know how to speak, how to say this . . . But if at any time in the future your Lordship needs a man's life, whatever it might be for, you have mine!'

Gonçalo gave his hand to the farmer, very simply—just as a Ramires of former times would have received the homage of a vassal.

'Thank you, José Casco.'

'That's a deal, then, your Lordship, and may our good Lord bless it!'

Gonçalo climbed swiftly up the verandah steps, while Casco slowly crossed the yard, his head held high, like a man who had owed a debt and had paid it.

Upstairs, in the library, Gonçalo thought, in alarm, 'So that's how one gratuitously earns devotion in this sentimental world of ours! . . . Why indeed ? . . . Who would not have stopped a feverish child facing a night on a black road with a storm blowing ? Who wouldn't have put him to bed, made him a hot drink and tucked him up snugly in the blankets ? And for this bed and hot drink, the father comes running, trembling and weeping, to offer up his life! Ah, how easy it was to be a King—and a popular King, too!'

This conviction encouraged him still more to obey Cavaleiro's recommendations—to begin at once his visits to the most influential of his electors—those adulatory visits that would enable the election to be won with arrogant unanimity. First thing after lunch, while still at table, he pushed aside the plates and copied out a list of such magnates, from a rough draft with which João Gouveia had supplied him. There was Dr Alexandrino; old Gramilde of Ramilde; Father José Vicente of Finta; and other less important names. Gouveia had marked with a cross, as being the most powerful and most difficult to win round, the Viscount of Rio Manso, who carried with him the very large parish of Canta Pedra. Gonçalo knew these gentlemen, men with property and money (Papa had in former days been indebted to all of them)—but he had never met the Viscount of Rio Manso, an old Brazilian gentleman, owner of the Varandinha Estate, where he lived along with a grandchild of eleven, the lovely Rosinha whom they called 'the rose-bud', the richest heiress in the whole county. First thing that afternoon, in Vila Clara, he asked João Gouveia for a letter of introduction to Rio Manso.

The Administrator hesitated.

'You don't need a letter. What the deuce! You're the Nobleman of the Tower! You go there, you enter and you talk . . . Moreover, in the last election Rio Manso helped the Regenerators; so we're a bit cool. Rio Manso is a dour old fellow . . . But there's no doubt about it, Gonçalinho, you ought to start your canvassing!'

That night, in the Club, the Nobleman began his canvassing by accepting an invitation from the honoured Romão Barros, (the boring, ridiculous Barros) for the great party he was giving on his Roqueira estate to celebrate the feast of Saint Romão. He spent all this week and the next in the same way, in Vila Clara, courting the electorate—to the extent of buying horrible calico shirts in Ramos's shop, ordering a sack of coffee from Telo the grocer's, offering his arm in Fountain Square to the nauseating wife of the drunkard Marques Rosendo, and frequenting, his hat pushed to the back of his head, the Billiard Room in Pretas Street. João Gouveia did not approve of such excessive measures, and advised him rather to make 'formal visits, with all due ceremony, to the serious, influential people'. But Gonçalo yawned and prevaricated, with ungovernable inertia at the thought of having to face old Gramilde's grumpiness or the judicial solemnity of Dr Alexandrino.

August came to an end; and occasionally, as he sat in the library, scratching his head disconsolately, Gonçalo contemplated the white sheets of foolscap, the third chapter of the *Tower of Don Ramires*, now at a standstill . . . But really, he couldn't, not in that heat and with all the worry of the elections, immerse himself in the Afonsine era again!

When the long afternoons began to grow colder, he would mount his horse and prolong his ride round the parishes, not forgetting Cavaleiro's recommendations—always filling his pocket with sweets to throw to the children. But in a letter to dear André, he had to confess that his popularity was not increasing, was not expanding.

'No, really, old friend, I just haven't the knack! I only know how to chat familiarly with the men, greet the old women who sit in the sun in their doorways by their names, and joke with the youngsters; and if I meet a little ox-driver in a torn skirt, give her five *tostões* for a new one. But all these things come naturally to me, I've always done them, ever since I was a boy, and they've never brought me any special influence . . . So you see, I need this good gentleman of Authority to give me a more skilful helping hand!'

However, one afternoon, when he met old Cosme from Nacejas near the Tower, and then later, one Sunday, Adrião Pinto from the hamlet of Levada, saying his Ave Marias at the Holy Fountain—both of them significant and active participators in elections—he asked them for their votes with a laugh and apparent indifference. He was almost amazed at the promptness and fervour with which they both offered them: 'Vote for the Nobleman? But of course! Even if it meant voting against the Government; you're like a father to us!' Discussing this with João Gouveia, in Vila Clara, Gonçalo claimed that such heart-felt offers showed 'the political intelligence of country folk'.

'Obviously they're not carried away by my looks! They know I'm the man to speak up, to fight for their interests . . . Sanches Lucena was no more than a very rich and very dumb Counsellor! These people want a deputy who will shout out, fight, insist . . . They vote for me because I'm rather intelligent . . .'

Gouveia, looking thoughfully at the Nobleman, replied,

'Who knows, my dear fellow! You've never tried, Gonçalo Mendes Ramires. Perhaps it really is because of your looks!'

*　　*　　*

On one of these rides, one scorching Friday, with the sun still high, Gonçalo passed through the little hamlet of Veleda, on his way to Canta Pedra. At the end of the row of poor cottages which straggled along the road, stood the famous Pintainho's Tavern, very brightly white-washed, on a piece of ground in front of the church. The trellised bowers in its garden and the fame of its rabbit stew attract vast numbers of people on holidays in Veleda. That morning Titó, after an early morning out shooting partridge in Valverde, appeared at the Tower for lunch, bellowing that he was starving. It was Friday and Rosa had prepared a delicious meal of hake with tomatoes followed by baked codfish. Gonçalo, tortured all afternoon with thirst, which had been aggravated by the dusty road, stopped eagerly at the door of the shop and called for Pintainho.

'Oh, your Lordship!'

'Oh, Pintainho! Hurry and bring me a sangria! A huge cold sangria, I'm dying of thirst!'

Pintainho, a stout old man with yellowish hair, was not long bringing the deep, appetizing glass with a slice of lemon floating on top. Gonçalo was enjoying his sangria with inexpressible pleasure when from the ground-floor window of the tavern came a slow whistle, a high-pitched trill like the kind muleteers used to encourage their beasts to drink at the rivers. Gonçalo stopped drinking in amazement. A strong, handsome young fellow with a fair complexion and side-whiskers was leaning out of the window, his hands on the window-sill and his head held high, and looking at him challengingly, with an insolent, provocative air. In a flash the Nobleman recognized the hunter who, one afternoon, in the village of Nacejas, near the glass factory, had stared at him arrogantly, had brushed his leg with his rifle, and then later, as he had stood under the window of the girl in the blue jacket, had waved to Gonçalo mockingly as he went down the hill. It was him! As if he did not understand the insult, Gonçalo hastily drank his sangria, threw a coin to the embarrassed Pintainho, and spurred on his fine mare. But then, from the window, came a chuckle and a jeering, contemptuous laugh which struck his back like the crack of a whip. Gonçalo spurred the mare on to a gallop. A little further on, slowing down his mount in the shelter of a narrow lane, he thought, still trembling, 'Who can the shameless wretch be? And what have I done to him, dear Lord, what have I done to him?' At the same time, his entire being raged at that disgraceful fear, that shrinking of the flesh, that creeping of the skin, which always, in the face of any danger, any threat, any figure emerging from the shadows, hypnotized him, urged him to run away and escape! For his soul, thank God, did not lack courage. It was his body, his treacherous body, which in horror, in alarm, fled, rushed away, dragging with it his soul—which fumed inside.

He entered the Tower in mortification, envying the boldness of his farm lads and feeling a sullen hatred for the brute with the golden side-whiskers whom he would quite definitely denounce to Cavaleiro and have locked up in a dungeon! But as soon as he entered the corridor, Bento banished such thoughts by handing him a letter which a boy had brought from *Feitosa*.

'From *Feitosa*?'

'Yes sir, from the estate of Senhor Sanches Lucena, may God preserve his soul. He said that it came from the ladies . . .'

'From the ladies? Which ladies?'

With no black edging, the letter could not have come from the beautiful Dona Ana, but it was from Dona Maria Mendonça, who signed herself, 'your affectionate cousin, Maria Severim'. He read it at a glance, affected by this new surprise, immediately distracted from Pintainho's Tavern and the insult.

'My dear Cousin,

I have been here three days with my friend Ana, and as the month of full mourning is over and she can go out again (and needs to, too, because she's been rather weak), I am taking advantage of the opportunity to travel round this area which they say is pretty and which I scarcely know. We intend to visit Santa Maria de Craquede this Sunday, where the tombs of my Ramires great-uncles lie. How impressed I shall be! . . . But it seems that apart from the tombs in the cloister, there are others, older still, that were open in the time of the French invasion, and are now in an underground chamber, which you cannot enter except by special permission and with a key. I am therefore asking you, dear Cousin, to give the necessary orders so that we may go this Sunday down to the underground chamber which everyone assures us is very interesting because there are still bones and weapons there. If there were a woman in the Tower, I would have come myself with this request . . . But one may not visit such a dangerous old bachelor! Get married quickly! . . . Everyone is well in Oliveira. I am, as always, etc. . . .'

Gonçalo turned to Bento, who was waiting, intrigued by his master's astonishment.

'Do you know if there are other tombs in Santa Maria de Craquede, in an underground chamber?'

His astonishment now spread to Bento.

'In an underground chamber? . . . Tombs?'

'Yes, man! Apart from the ones in the cloister, it seems there are others, older ones, underground . . . I have never seen them, as far as I can remember. Though it's years since I've been to Santa Maria de Craquede! Not since I was a boy! . . . Don't you know ?'

Bento shrugged.

'Wouldn't Rosa know ?'

Bento shook his head doubtfully.

'No one ever knows anything! Right! Tomorrow early, go to Santa Maria de Craquede and ask in the church there, ask the sacristan if there's an underground chamber. If such a thing exists, tell him to let some ladies see it on Sunday—Senhora Dona Ana Lucena and Senhora Dona Maria Mendonça, my cousin Maria . . . And to have it all swept out and made decent!'

But as he went through the letter again, he noticed a postscript in smaller writing, in the corner of the page: 'On Sunday, don't forget, our visit will be between five and five-thirty!'

Gonçalo thought, 'Is this a rendezvous!' In the library, throwing his hat and whip on a chair, he decided it was a rendezvous, time and place quite clear! Possibly the underground chamber did not even exist! Maria Mendonça, with her tortuous cunning, had invented it as an excuse for writing, and for announcing that, on Sunday, at half-past five, the beautiful Dona Ana and her two hundred *contos* would be waiting for him in Santa Maria de Craquede. So Cousin Maria had not been joking, then, in Oliveira ? Did Dona Ana really like him ? A voluptuous curiosity passed through Gonçalo at the idea of such a beautiful woman desiring him. Ah, but surely she wanted him for a husband, because if she fancied him as a lover, she would not have recourse to the services of Dona Maria Mendonça—and neither would cousin Maria, in spite of her toadying to rich friends, offer her services so shamelessly, like a procuress in a play! By Jove! Marry Dona Ana! Never!

Suddenly he longed to know more of Dona Ana's life. Had she put up with old Sanches for so many years in strict fidelity ? Yes, perhaps, in *Feitosa*, in the solitude of the great walls of *Feitosa*—because there had never been the slightest rumour about her in such a small-minded place, so avid for spiteful gossip. But in Lisbon ? Those 'esteemed friends' of whom poor Sanches Lucena had been so proud, Don João something-or-other, the pompous Arronches Manrique, Filipe Lourençal of the trumpet ? . . . Surely one of

181

them had approached her—perhaps Don João, in traditional duty
to his name. And her? Who could give him information about the
emotional life of Dona Ana?

Then at supper he remembered Gouveia. A sister of Gouveia's,
married to a certain Cerqueira (a producer of plays, employed in
Misericordia Hospital), lived in Lisbon and was in the habit of
sending her brother, the Administrator, intimate reports on all the
people known in Oliveira and Vila Clara, who stayed in Lisbon—
and who interested her brother politically or for reasons of gossip.
Surely dear Gouveia, through his sister Cerqueira, must know all
the details of Dona Ana's life during her winters in Lisbon, her
pleasures among the 'select circle'.

But that night the Administrator did not put in an appearance at
the Club. Gonçalo was returning disconsolately to the Tower when
he met him in Fountain Square with Videirinha—both of them
seated on a bench under the dark Judas trees.

'You've come at just the right moment!' cried Gouveia. 'We were
just off to my house for a cup of tea. Won't you come? You usually
like my toast.'

The Nobleman accepted, in spite of his tiredness. Immediately,
in the Calçadinha, he slipped his arm through the Administrator's
and told him that he had received a letter from Lisbon, from a
friend, with some fantastic news . . . What? Dona Ana was going
to get married again!

Gouveia stopped in astonishment, pushing his bowler-hat to the
back of his head.

'To whom?'

Gonçalo, having invented the letter, invented the bridegroom, too.

'To a distant relative of mine, it seems, a Don João Pedroso, or
Pedrosa. Sanches Lucena often spoke to me about him . . . They
spent a lot of time in each other's company in Lisbon.'

Gouveia tapped his stick against the stones.

'It can't be true! . . . What nonsense! Dona Ana would not
arrange another marriage seven weeks after her husband's death . . .
Lucena only died in the middle of July, man! He hasn't even had
time to get used to his grave yet!'

'That's true,' murmured Gonçalo.

He smiled, with a little rush of vanity, at the thought that, seven
weeks after her widowhood, she had irresistibly, casting aside her

modesty along with her mourning, arranged a rendezvous with him in the ruins of Craquede.

Such a suggestion, however, although it seemed nonsense, seemed to be accepted, because when they were up in the Administrator's green drawing-room, amazement broke out once again. Videirinha rubbed his hands together, highly amused.

'Oh, sir, it's really funny, you know! . . . If Dona Ana hooks a young chap a few weeks after getting the old man's two hundred *contos* . . .'

No, no! Gonçalo, now he thought about it, found the story absurd with poor Sanches still warm, almost . . .

'There must have been some affair between her and this Don João, a few stolen glances . . . That's why they imagined there'd be a marriage. Actually, someone told me, some time ago, that this Don João had wooed her persistently, as befits a Don João, and she . . .'

'A lie!' interrupted the Adminstrator, as he bent over the petrol lamp to light his cigar. 'A lie! I'm sure of that, and from an excellent source . . . From my sister, in fact! Never did Dona Ana ever give any reason to gossip in Lisbon. She's a very serious woman, very serious indeed. Naturally there's always some rogue prepared to attempt flirtation . . . Perhaps this Don João, or some other friend of her husband's, according to tradition. But not her! Not the merest glance! A Roman wife, my friend, and of the best ages of Rome!'

Gonçalo, deep in the sofa, slowly twisted his moustache, welcoming these revelations delightedly. Gouveia continued from the middle of the room, with a superior, convinced gesture,

'You shouldn't be surprised! These beautiful women are insensitive. Beautiful pieces of marble, but cold marble, all the same . . . No, Gonçalinho, where sentiment's concerned, and soul, and all the rest, give me little women, thin ones, dark ones! They're the best! Those tall, white women, the Venus type, are only fit for show, fit for museums.'

Videirinha dared to doubt.

'But a woman as lovely as Senhora Dona Ana, and with her blood, married to an old man . . .'

'There are women who like old men precisely because they have old sentiments, too!' declared Gouveia, pointing his finger, with immense authority and philosophy.

But Gonçalo's curiosity was not satisfied. How about in *Feitosa*? Had there never been any murmurs of a secret affair? It seems that, with Dr Júlio . . .'

Again the Nobleman was inventing. Again Gouveia refuted the lie.

'Neither in *Feitosa* nor in Oliveira, nor in Lisbon . . . Anyway, it's as I said, Gonçalo Mendes. She's a woman of marble.'

Then, in humble admiration, he acknowledged,

'But what marble . . . You, my boys, can't imagine the beauty of that woman in *décolleté*!'

Gonçalo gasped in surprise,

'Where did you see her in *décolleté*?'

'Where? In Lisbon, at a ball in the Palace . . . It was Lucena in fact who got me the invitation to the Palace. I cut quite a dash in breeches there. Most boring. Even disgraceful, I should say, all that crowd trampling on each other to get at the buffet tables, and shouting and grabbing little bits of turkey . . .'

'But what were you saying about Dona Ana?'

'Dona Ana's a beauty! You can't imagine! . . . Holy mother of God! What shoulders! What arms! What breasts! So white and perfect. Enough to drive one out of one's senses! At first, because there were lots of people there and she was hiding away shyly in a corner, she did not attract much notice. But then they discovered her. People were hurrying about, crowds staring open-mouthed . . . "Who is she?" everyone was asking. "What a beauty!" Everyone fell for her, even the King!'

For a moment the three men were silent as they evoked the image of that magnificent body which rose there in their midst, almost nude, dazzling the modest, ill-lit room with the splendour of its white skin. Then Videirinha moved his chair forward confidentially, to pass on his little bit of information.

'Well, personally, I know that Senhora Dona Ana is very clean and fond of washing . . .'

As his companions looked at him in amazement and laughed at his positiveness which revealed such familiarity—Videirinha told them how, every week, a boy came from *Feitosa* to Pires' Pharmacy to buy three or four bottles of Portuguese eau-de-Cologne, made by Pires.

'Pires always used to say, rubbing his hands, that they must water their lands in *Feitosa* with eau-de-Cologne. Then we learnt through the maid . . . Senhora Dona Ana has a full bath every day, which isn't simply for washing herself but also for pleasure. She stays a whole hour in the tub. She even reads the newspaper while she's there. And every bath she has, Whoosh! in goes half a bottle of eau-de-Cologne . . . That's what I call real luxury!'

Then Gonçalo suddenly felt irritated by all these revelations from the Administrator and the Chemist's assistant, about the *décolletés* and baths of the lovely woman who awaited him among the tombs of the ancient Ramires. He shook the newspaper with which he had been fanning himself and cried,

'Right! Now to go on to a more serious subject . . . Have you heard anything about Dr Júlio, Gouveia? Has he started his campaign yet?'

The maid entered with the tea-tray. Seated round the table, munching the famous toast, they talked about the election, about the local officers' information, about the non-commitment of Rio Manso and about Dr Júlio, whom Videirinha had met in Bravais begging for votes from door to door, accompanied by a boy with a camera slung over his shoulder.

After tea, Gonçalo, tired and sated with 'revelations', lit his cigar before returning to the Tower.

'You're not coming, Videirinha?'

'Today I can't, sir. I'm leaving for Oliveira early tomorrow morning in the stage-coach.'

'Why the deuce are you going to Oliveira?'

'About a pair of beach-shoes and a bathing costume belonging to my employer's wife, Dona Josefa Pires . . . I have to change them in Emílios, give them the measurements.'

Gonçalo raised his arms in horror.

'What a country! A great artist like Videirinha, carting beach-shoes to Oliveira for Senhora Pires, his employer's wife! Oh, Gouveia, when I become deputy we must find a good post for Videirinha in the Civil Government. An easy position with lots of free time so he won't neglect his guitar!'

Videirinha flushed with pleasure and expectation and ran to take down the Nobleman's hat off the peg.

Along the road to the Tower, Gonçalo's thoughts immediately flew, with irresistible temptation, to Dona Ana—to her *décolletages* and her lazy baths in which she lay and read the newspaper. Really, he thought, what the deuce! This Dona Ana was so honest, so perfumed, so magnificently beautiful, that she had only one drawback—even contemplated as a wife—her papa the butcher! And her voice, too—the voice that had repelled him so much at the Holy Fountain . . . But Mendonça had assured him that she lost that thick, grating tone among intimates, and her voice became smooth, almost sweet . . . And anyway, after months of living together, one got accustomed to the most unpleasant of voices—he himself, now did not even notice Manuel Duarte spoke nasally! No, the only really irreparable defect was the butcher father. But with mankind descended as it was from one man, who didn't have a butcher grandfather among the thousands of his ancestors stretching back to Adam? Even he, a wellbred nobleman, offshoot of a house of Kings from which dynasties had been founded, would surely come across a butcher Ramires if he inquired diligently enough into the past. Whether the butcher appeared prominently in the last generation, in a butcher's shop which still had clients, or was only vaguely discerned through the veil of centuries, among his ancestors thirty generations ago—he was there, all the same, with his knife and his chopping-block, and the blood-stains on his sweaty arm . . .

This thought did not leave him until he reached the Tower—or even afterwards, as he stood at the window of his room, finishing his cigar and listening to the chirping of the crickets. Even after he had lain down and his eyes were closing, he felt his impatient steps probing the past, the dim past of his House, amid the tangled webs of History—in search of the butcher . . . He was already far beyond the Visigoth Empire, when his bearded ancestor Recesvinto, golden orb in hand, had reigned. Exhausted, panting for breath, he had traversed civilized cities peopled with men of culture, and had penetrated the forests where the mastodon still plodded. Amid the thick, humid foliage he had already come across vague Ramires, grunting as they carried bundles of wood or a dead beast. Others emerged from smoky holes, baring their sharp, greenish teeth to smile at their great-grandson who was passing by. Then, across gloomy wastes, in gloomy silence, until he arrived at a misty lagoon. At the edge of the muddy water, among the clumps of reeds, a monstrous man, hairy as a beast, was crouching in the mud and, with hefty strokes of his stone axe, chopping off slabs of human flesh. It was a Ramires. In the grey sky above hovered the black goshawk. Then, across the mist of the lagoon, he waved towards Santa Maria de Craquede, towards the beautiful, perfumed Dona Ana, shouting above Empires and Centuries: 'I have found my butcher ancestor!'

★　　★　　★

On Sunday, Gonçalo woke with a bright idea. He would not rush to Santa Maria de Craquede with fervent punctuality, at five o'clock (the five o'clock named in Cousin Maria's postscript)—thus revealing his enthusiasm to meet the so beautiful and so rich Dona Ana Lucena! But at six o'clock, when the ladies' pilgrimage to the tombs was over, he would put in a casual appearance as if, returning from a ride through the cool, neighbouring countryside, he had suddenly remembered, and called by to have a word with Cousin Maria.

But at four o'clock, he began to dress with such fastidiousness that Bento, tired of seeing his master try on so many ties and throw them all crumpled on to the divan, could contain himself no longer and suggested,

'Put the white silk one on, sir! Put the white silk one on, it suits you best! And it's cooler, too, in this heat.'

When selecting a button-hole he decided impeccably upon a yellow carnation and a white one—the heraldic colours of the Ramires. As he mounted his mare at the gate, he feared the ladies (not finding him at the cloister) would cut their visit short, and he spurred his mount on to a trot along the short-cut to Portela. Then, further on, as he came out on to the main road, he went into an impatient gallop which covered him in white dust.

He only slowed down again to a nonchalant amble when he was approaching the Railway, where a cart of wood and two men were waiting at the level-crossing, which had closed to allow a slow train laden with casks to pass. One of these men, knapsack on back, was the Beggar—the conspicuous Beggar who flaunted the remunerative majesty of his beard in the local villages like some river-god. Gravely raising his broad-brimmed hat, he expressed his wish that God should go with the Nobleman.

'Earning your livelihood round Craquede today?'

'I make my way there at times, your Lordship, when the Oliveira

187

train goes by. The passengers like to see me standing there on the slope, they always rush to the windows . . .'

Gonçalo laughed and remembered that a meeting with this ancient always preceded a meeting with the beautiful Dona Ana. 'Who knows ?' he thought. 'Perhaps he's Destiny! In olden days Destiny was portrayed with long whiskers and hair, the bag on his back containing the fates of men . . .' Indeed, at the far end of the silent pinewood, softly gilded by broad beams of sunlight, he noticed the *Feitosa* carriage standing under an oak-tree, with the coachman dressed in mourning, dozing on the cushion. Here the main road to Oliveira passes by the ancient yard of the Monastery of Craquede, burnt by heaven-inspired fire in the raging storm called the Storm of San Sebastian, which alarmed Portugal in 1616. Grass now carpets the ground, thick and green, beneath the powerful trunks of the ancient chestnut-trees. The new little whitewashed church stands out at the end of the leafy avenue; and connected to it by a broken wall, clothed in thick ivy, which runs the whole of the eastern side of the Square—rises, splendidly filling the brilliant sky, the façade of the church of the old monastery, softly yellowed and bronzed by the weather, with its magnificent doorless portal, its broken rose-window, its burial niches empty, where in former times stood the images of its founders, Freitas Ramires and his wife Estevaninha, Countess of Orgaz, known as the Griever. Two single-storey houses occupy the front of the square—one clean with its window-mouldings painted a vivid blue, the other deserted, almost roofless, lost amid the foliage of a wild flower-bed where sunflowers bloomed. A meditative silence enveloped the trees and the tall ruins. Yet this was not broken but rather serenely lulled by the murmur of a fountain, which the drought had reduced to a slow trickle that scarcely filled the stone bowl, and which was shaded by the pale, sparse foliage of a tall weeping-willow.

The *Feitosa*'s footman, who had been sitting on the edge of the fountain cutting up tobacco, jumped up with a smile, when he saw the Nobleman, to hold his mare. Gonçalo, who had not entered the ruins of Craquede since he was a boy, was pensively following a path cut through the lawn, enchanted by the romantic, poetic solitude, when he saw, in the arch of the doorway, the two ladies who were returning from the ancient cloister. Dona Maria Mendonça, with her impetuous vivacity, immediately waved her sunshade at him, of a check material like her dress, the sleeves of which puffed out exaggeratedly at the shoulders and enhanced the slim elegance of her figure. At her side, in the sunlight, stood Dona Ana, a slim, silent, black figure in black wool and black crepe, against which stood out, softened by the black veil, the splendid whiteness of her serious, sensual face.

Gonçalo ran up, raising his straw hat and stammering his 'pleasure at such a meeting'. But Dona Maria was already rebuking him, refusing to accept the fiction of a chance encounter.

'You're not at all kind, cousin, not at all kind . . .'

'Oh, cousin!'

'You knew we were coming, from my letter! And you did not come at the time arranged, to do the honours, as was fitting.'

He laughed, with his customary, elegant ease, and disclaimed any such duty. That house was not his, but the Good Lord's! It was therefore fitting that the Good Lord should do the honours—welcome such gentle pilgrims with some nice little miracle . . .

'Did you enjoy it, then? Did you enjoy the ruins, madam, Senhora Dona Ana? They are very interesting, aren't they?'

Through the veil, with a slowness that the thick, black veil made graver, she murmured,

'I already knew them. I came here one afternoon with poor Sanches who is now with God.'

'Ah . . .'

At this mention of the poor dead husband, Gonçalo's smile disappeared, to be replaced by polite sorrow. But Dona Maria Mendonça now broke in, flinging out her thin arms in a gesture, as if to drive away this importunate shadow,

'Ah, you can't imagine how I enjoyed it, cousin! The whole cloister's fabulous . . . First, there's that rusty sword fixed over the tomb . . . There's nothing so impressive as these things of the past . . . Oh, cousin, and to think there are ancestors of ours here!'

Gonçalo's smile flashed again, gay and welcoming, as always when Maria pushed her way greedily, desperately, into the Ramires family. And he joked with her affably. Oh, ancestors . . . No more than a few handfuls of worthless dust! Wasn't that so, Dona Ana? . . . Really! Who would ever imagine that Cousin Maria, so lively and sociable and witty, was descended from a gloomy little pile of dust preserved inside a stone tomb. No, one could not connect so much being with so much non-being . . . And as Dona Ana smiled, with a vague nod of agreement, resting her two strong hands in their tightly-fitting black skin gloves on the long pearl handle of her sunshade, he asked feelingly,

'Perhaps you are tired, Senhora Dona Ana?'

'No, I'm not tired. We even mean to go into the chapel for a little while. I don't ever get tired.'

It seemed to Gonçalo as if the beautiful creature's voice was not so deep-throated and coarse and flat, but was more refined, sweetened and softened by the mourning wool and crepe, like those coarse, strident noises that night and trees render beautiful. But Dona Maria confessed that she was extremely tired! Nothing exhausted her more than visiting curiosities . . . And apart from the visit, there was the emotion, the idea of such ancient heroes!

'Suppose we sat down on that bench, eh? It's too early to go back, don't you think, Anica? And it's so cool and pleasant here.'

It was a stone bench under the broken wall which was covered with ivy. Around it, the lawn flourished more wildly, abloom with the last daisies and celandines spared by the August sun. A faint aroma, of jasmine mingled with ivy, wafted across and sweetened the calm afternoon. From the branch of a poplar opposite the chapel door, a thrush sang twice. Gonçalo dusted down the bench carefully with his handkerchief. Sitting on one end, next to Dona Maria, he, too, praised the coolness and the privacy of that charming corner of Craquede . . . Yet he had never availed himself of the holy refuge which belonged to him—not even for a bucolic lunch! Now he would certainly return and smoke a cigar there, meditate upon peaceful ideas in the peaceful shade of the oak-trees, near his dear, dead ancestors . . . Then he added, with curiosity,

'But tell me, cousin, what about that underground chamber?'

Oh, there was no underground chamber! . . . Yes, one did exist, but it was blocked up and there were no tombs there, no ancient remains. The sacristan had hastily assured them that it was not worth soiling their skirts . . .

'Oh, that reminds me, Anica, did you give the sacristan something?'

'I gave him five *tostões*, my dear . . . I don't know if that was enough.'

Gonçalo assured them that they had paid the sacristan most

royally. And if he could have expected such generosity from Senhora Dona Ana, he would have snatched up a bunch of keys, slipped on a black surplice, shown them the place and been reimbursed . . .

'Well that's what you ought to have done!' exclaimed Dona Maria, her bright eyes sparkling. 'You would surely have got your five *tostões*! Because you would undoubtedly have been more instructive than that little fellow who mumbled away and didn't know anything! Sluggish individual he was! I was so curious about that open tomb with the split lid. And all the silly ape could mutter was that "they were very ancient stories of the Nobleman of the Tower . . ." '

Gonçalo laughed.

'Well, actually, I do happen to know this particular story, Cousin Maria! I know it through the Fado of the Ramires, Videirinha's fado . . .'

Dona Maria Mendonça raised her slender hands to heaven, horrified at such indifference towards the heroic traditions of his House. To know one's history only after it had been strummed out on a fado! . . . Wasn't Cousin Gonçalo ashamed of himself?

'But why, cousin, why? Videirinha's fado is based upon authentic documents which Father Soeiro has studied. All the historical matter was supplied by Father Soeiro. Videirinha only put it into verse. Moreover, cousin, in former times, History was perpetuated in verse and sung to the sound of a lyre . . . Anyway, do you want to know this story of the open tomb, according to Videirinha's verses? I'll tell you the story! But only to Senhora Dona Ana, who doesn't suffer from such scruples . . .'

'No!' cried Dona Maria. 'If Videirinha has the authority of history, then you can tell me, too, for I belong to the House!'

Gonçalo coughed playfully and wiped his lips with his handkerchief.

'Well, then, this is what happened! In this tomb lay, dead, of course, one of my great great-grandfathers . . . I can't remember his name, Gutierres or Lopo. I think it was Gutierres . . . Anyway, he was already there when the Battle of Navas de Tolosa was being fought . . . Cousin Maria knows about the Battle of Navas, with the five Moorish kings, etc. . . . How this Gutierres knew of the battle Videirinha's verses do not say. But no sooner did he smell, there, from inside his tomb, the carnage, than he broke out of it, rushed

191

like a desperate man across the yard here, digs up his horse which had been buried in the yard where those oaks are now growing, mounts him fully armed and, a dead horseman on dead horse, goes galloping across Spain, arrives at Navas, draws his sword and slaughters the Moors . . . What do you think of that, Senhora Dona Ana ?'

He had dedicated this story to Dona Ana, searching her beautiful eyes for a sign of attention and interest. She, secretly drawn behind the decorous melancholy which she had adopted, and smiling tenderly, merely remarked, 'Amusing!' Dona Maria, however, almost fluttered over the stone bench in ecstasy: 'Lovely! Lovely! How poetic! . . . Oh, such a jolly legend!' And so that Gonçalo should exhibit his narrative powers still more and recount further marvels from his chronicles, she pleaded,

'Go on, cousin, tell us . . . Did he return to Craquede, this Uncle Ramires ?'

'Who, cousin ? Gutierres ? . . . He wasn't that foolish! Once he'd got out of that wretched tomb he wasn't seen in Santa Maria de Craquede again! The tomb was empty, as it still is, and he was off across Spain on a heroic spree! . . . Just imagine! A corpse that by a miracle manages to sneak out of its tomb, from its eternal position, so stretched out and yet confined . . .'

He stopped, suddenly remembering Sanches Lucena, also stretched out in his leaden coffin, beneath his grand tomb in Oliveira . . . Dona Ana lowered her head, her face even less discernible beneath the veil, digging into the grass with the point of her sunshade. The quick-witted Dona Maria, to drive away the impertinent shadow that was once again touching them, remembered yet another curious detail connected with the noble Ramires.

'Ah, yes! I always forget to ask you. You still have lots of relations in France, cousin . . . Or didn't you know that, either ?'

Yes, Gonçalo did happen to know the story of his relations in France—although Videirinha did not sing of them in his Fado.

'Then tell us! But a more cheerful story this time!'

Oh, it wasn't exceptionally amusing! A Ramires ancestor, Garcia Ramires, had accompanied Prince Don Pedro, son of His Majesty Don João I, on his famous journeys . . . Cousin Maria knew him —the Prince Don Pedro who had visited all four corners of the earth . . . Well, Prince Don Pedro and his nobleman, on their return from Palestine, stayed a whole year in Flanders with the Duke of Burgundy. They had magnificent celebrations there, with a banquet that lasted seven days, which is recorded in the Histories of France. Where there is dancing, there is love ... Great-grandfather Ramires had an excess of imagination and courage ... It was he who, as they stood in the Valley of Jehosaphat before Jerusalem, suggested that they should put up a sign there so that the Prince and his companion should, on the great Day of Judgment, recognize each other. Of course, he was a handsome youth with a thick, black beard in the Portuguese style ... He married a sister of the Duke of Cleves, an awesome lady, niece of the Duke of Burgundy and Brabant. Later, through these connections, another Ramires, who was a widow, also married in France, with the Count of Tancarville. These Tancarvilles, Grand Masters of France, owned the most formidable castle in Europe, and ...

Dona Maria clapped her hands, laughing.

'Bravo! Wonderful! That's the way, sir! ... So you boast that you know nothing about your lineage, cousin ... See how he knows every detail of these great marriages! Eh, Anica? ... He's a walking chronicle!'

Gonçalo bowed his shoulders and confessed that he had concerned himself with all this heraldic history for a very sordid reason —for lucre!

'For lucre?'

'Yes, cousin, for cash!'

'Tell us! Tell us! Look, Anica's dying to know ...'

'Do you want to know, Senhora Dona Ana? Well, it was in Coimbra, in my second year in Coimbra. My companions and I hadn't a farthing between us. Not even the price of a cigarette! Not even the price of a sacred glass of cheap wine and the customary three olives ... So one of them, a delightful fellow from Melgaço, had the brilliant idea that I should write to my relations in France, to these Cleves, these Tancarvilles, obviously very rich persons, and ask them, without a trace of embarrassment for a loan of three hundred francs!'

Dona Ana, frankly amused, could not repress a smile,

'Oh, it's so funny!'

'But it bore no results, madam ... There are no longer any Cleves nor Tancarvilles! All these great feudal families have come to an end, have fused with other houses, even with the French royal family. And Father Soeiro, in spite of all his genealogical learning, never succeeded in discovering who represented them—a near enough relation to loan me, a poor Portuguese relation, three hundred francs.'

Such penury on the part of Gonçalo, of so great a nobleman, moved Dona Ana.

'None of you had a sou! Who would imagine it! But it's rather funny, really! These stories from Coimbra are always very amusing. Don João da Pedrosa, in Lisbon, used to tell a lot of them . . .'

But Dona Maria Mendonça discovered, behind these student jokes, another unexpected proof of the greatness of the Ramires family. She at once laid it skilfully before Dona Ana.

'There, do you see ? All those great houses of France, so rich and powerful, have come to an end, have disappeared. Yet here, in our little Portugal, the house of Ramires still stands!'

Gonçalo interrupted her.

'It's all over now, cousin! Don't look at me in amazement like that. It's all over now. Because I shan't marry!'

Dona Maria drew in her flat chest—as if her cousin's marriage depended on the right sort of tender pressure, which would be better exerted at closer quarters, without Maria Mendonças between them on the narrow bench, in her puffed sleeves, hindering the waves of effluvia. She smiled, almost languidly,

'What do you mean, won't marry ? Why not, cousin, why not ?'

'Because I'm not the sort, cousin. Marriage is a very delicate art which needs a vocation, a special temperament. The Fates did not grant me such a temperament. If I devoted myself to such a task, alas! I fear I'd ruin it.'

As if thinking of something else, Dona Ana slowly pulled her watch, attached by a hair chain from her belt. Dona Maria insisted, refused to accept these excuses from the Nobleman.

'That's nonsense. You are so fond of children, cousin.'

'Yes, I'm fond of children, very fond of them, even little babies. Children are the only divine beings known to wretched humanity. The other angels, those with wings, never put in an appearance. The saints, once they've become saints, spend an idle life in Paradise, and you don't catch another glimpse of them. The only things we have to give us some idea of Heaven are little children . . . Yes, you're right, cousin, I am very fond of children. But I'm also fond of flowers, yet I'm not a gardener, nor do I have a flair for gardening.'

Dona Maria, a glint in her eyes as she gave him a knowing look, commented,

'Don't worry—you've still got time to learn!'

Then she asked Dona Ana, who was still absent-mindedly studying her watch,

'Do you think it's time to go? Then if you like, we'll just have a look in the chapel . . . Oh, cousin, see if it's open, will you?'

Gonçalo hurried over and pushed open the door of the chapel. He then accompanied the ladies along the little flagged nave, between some slim, roughly whitewashed pillars—which also covered the smooth walls whose uncompromising bareness was relieved only by some lithographs of saints in pinewood frames. Before the altar, the ladies knelt—Cousin Maria burying her face in her clasped hands like a carving of Mercy. Gonçalo knelt briefly and mumbled a Hail Mary.

Then he went out into the square and lit a cigarette. As he lightly trod the grass he considered how widowhood had improved Dona Ana. Beneath her mourning black, like dusk which mellows the coarse ungainliness of things, all her flaws were dissolved—the flaws which had horrified him so much that afternoon at the Holy Fountain, the thick, throaty voice, the jutting bosom, the ostentation of a rich bourgeoise abundantly supplied with the good things of life . . . She didn't even address him as kind gentleman any more. There, in the melancholy square of Craquede, she definitely appeared interesting and desirable.

The ladies were coming down the two steps from the chapel. A blackbird fluttered in the branches of the poplars. Gonçalo caught the glitter of Dona Ana's serious eyes seeking his.

'My apologies for not having offered you holy water as you left, but the shell was empty.'

'Lord, cousin, what an ugly church!'

Dona Ana ventured timidly,

'After the ruins and the tombs, it seemed almost irreligious.'

The observation impressed Gonçalo as very subtle. As he walked beside her, pleasurably slowing down his steps, he noticed, diffused by her movements, by the swish of her skirts, a perfume which was subtle, too, and was definitely not from the awful eau-de-Cologne produced at Pires' Chemist's. In silence, under the branches of the cak-trees, they made their way to the carriage where the coachman had drawn himself erect, well trained, doffing his hat. Gonçalo noticed that he had shaved off his moustache. The pair of horses gleamed, harnessed to perfection.

'Well, Cousin Maria, are you staying long in the neighbourhood?'

'Yes, cousin, another couple of weeks . . . Anica is so kind, she told me to bring the children. And what a wonderful time they've had in the garden, you can't imagine!'

Dona Ana murmured in the same serious tone,

'They are delightful, and excellent company . . . I am very fond of children too.'

'Oh, Anica adores children!' put in Dona Maria eagerly. 'How she puts up with them! She even plays at Bogeyman with them.'

As they approached the carriage, it occurred to Gonçalo that another turn round the square, slower this time, with Dona Ana and her subtle perfume, would be pleasant in the calm of the dying afternoon, tinged with such lovely rosy hues above the darkening pines. But the footman was already approaching, bringing up his mare. Dona Maria, after admiring and stroking the mare, called her cousin aside discreetly—to know how far it was from *Feitosa* to *Treixedo*, the other historic estate of the Ramires.

'To *Treixedo*, cousin? . . . A good five leagues, and a bad road.'

At once he regretted his reply, envisaging a ride there, another meeting.

'But they've been improving the road lately. And it's a pretty spot, high on a hill, with part of the old walls still standing . . . *Treixedo* used to be an enormous castle . . . There's a little lake in the grounds in an ancient grove. Oh—a delightful spot for a picnic!'

Dona Maria hesitated.

'It's rather far, we'll see perhaps.'

As Dona Ana waited in silence, Gonçalo opened the carriage door and took the reins of his mare from the footman. Dona Maria Mendonça, satisfied at such a profitable afternoon, shook her cousin's hand fervently, and assured him she 'was thrilled with Craquede!' Dona Ana, shy and blushing, merely brushed Gonçalo's finger-tips.

Alone, the reins slipped over his arm, Gonçalo smiled. Really, this afternoon, Dona Ana had not displeased him at all. Different manners, a graver simplicity, a gentleness in the robust beauty of that country Venus . . . And that observation of hers on the chapel, 'almost irreligious', after the ancient ruins of the cloister, was a subtle observation. Who knew? Perhaps a delicate nature was hidden beneath that sensual flesh. Perhaps the influence of another man, different from the stupid Sanches, would bring out qualities of great charm in the splendid butcher's daughter . . . Oh, definitely, that observation on the tombs and their religiousness emanating from Legend and History was subtle.

But then he, too, was filled with curiosity to visit the cloister that he had not entered since a boy—when the Tower still had its carriages in use and the romantic Miss Rhodes always chose Craquede for her pensive, autumn afternoon rides. He pulled his mare round, passed through the gateway, crossed the open space which had formerly been the nave—strewn with rubble, with stones fallen from the vaulted roof and buried amid the weeds. Through a gap in the wall to which still clung a piece of the altar, he entered the silent Afonsine cloister. All that remained of it were two squat, interlinked arcades, supported by rough pillars, and paved with solid but worn stone slabs which the sacristan had carefully swept that morning.

Against the wall, where thick ribs indicated other arches, rose the seven immense tombs of the ancient Ramires, blackened, smooth, without any carvings, like rough granite chests, some heavily imbedded in the stones, others balanced on spheres chipped away by the centuries. Gonçalo followed a brick path beside the arches and remembered how he and Gracinha had once leapt noisily over these gravestones, while in the cloister square the good Miss Rhodes was crouched in search of wild flowers. There in the vault, above the largest tomb, was fixed the blackened sword, the famous sword with the iron chain hanging from its hilt, its blade rusted through the ages. Over another burnt the lamp, the strange Moorish lamp which had not gone out since the remote afternoon when some monk had silently lit it from a funeral candle. When had it been lit, that eternal lamp? Which Ramires lay in these granite tombs which time had erased of inscriptions and dates, so that History should vanish into them and more darkly transform those proud, valiant men into light, nameless dust? . . . Further on, at the end of the cloister, was the open tomb, and beside it, in two pieces, the lid which the skeleton of Lopo Ramires had broken off in order to rush to Navas de Tolosa and conquer the five Moorish kings. Gonçalo peered in curiously. In one corner of the deep cavity gleamed a little pile of bones, clean and neatly arranged! Had old Lopo, in his heroic dispatch, forgotten these few bones, already separated from the rest of his skeleton? . . . Dusk was falling, and with it gloomy shadows which were darker among the vaults of the cloister and covered this resting-place for corpses with mortal sorrow. Then Gonçalo felt the desolate solitude which enveloped him and cut him off from life, lost and helpless there amid the dust and errant souls of his fearful ancestors! Suddenly he shuddered, in hair-raising alarm that another lid might burst open with a crash, livid, fleshless fingers appear from the crack! He pulled his mare desperately through the broken wall again, and in the ruins of the nave, he leapt into the saddle and trotted through the gateway, anxious to reach the yard—and he felt calmer only when he saw, at the end of the pine wood, the level-crossing gate open, and an old woman passing through, driving her grass-laden donkey.

8

AT THE END of the week, Gonçalo, who ever since his visit to Santa Maria de Craquede had been troubled by uncomfortable remorse at his laziness, at deserting his novel for so long, received, one morning, when he got out of his bath, a letter from Castanheiro. It was short: it informed friend Gonçalo that if three chapters of his manuscript did not reach Lisbon by mid-October he would have to publish, although he and Art regretted it, instead of *The Tower of Don Ramires* in the first number of the *Annals*, a drama by Nuno Carreira in one act, entitled *In the House of the Reckless One* . . .

'In spite of its dramatic medium and fictitiousness [he added] it is suitable for the erudite character of the *Annals* because this Reckless One is Carlos the Reckless, and the whole action, cleverly developed, takes place in the Castle of Peronne, where we meet none other than Luis XI of France and our wretched Afonso V, and Pêra da Covilhã who is accompanying him, and other famous bigwigs in history . . . Just imagine it! Of course the supreme contribution would be *Tructesindo Mendes Ramires* told by our own Gonçalo Mendes Ramires! But as far as I can see this supreme contribution is hindered by supreme laziness. Sunt lacrymae Revistarum!'

Gonçalo flung down the letter and called for Bento.

'Bring along some strong green tea to the library, and some toast. I won't lunch till late today, about two o'clock . . . Perhaps I won't lunch at all!'

Slipping on his working dressing-gown, he decided to sit tight at his work-table, like a captive at his oar, until he had finished off that difficult Chapter III, which included the most barbarous and sublimest action by ancestor Tructesindo. No, what the deuce! It wouldn't do to miss publication of the novel at such a beneficial moment, on the eve of his arrival in Lisbon, when he needed such glory for his political influence and social prestige; and according to old Vigny, 'a steel pen adds to a nobleman's crest'. Fortunately, this luminous morning, with the waters in the garden gurgling for joy, he felt his talent alive, too, glad to be set free and to plunge on. After his visit to the cloister of Craquede, he was able to conceive in his imagination a less hazy picture of his Afonsine ancestors—it was as if he could feel them in his being and thinking, ever since he had contemplated those vast tombs where their great bones lay crumbling to dust.

In the library he avidly picked up, after shaking off the dust, the pages of the novel where he had got stuck, at the fear-inspiring event of great moment, when the bailiff, old Ordonho, had recognized the Bastard's pennant which appeared on the bank of Horse-Kick Stream among the upraised, flashing lances, as they crossed the ancient wooden bridge. For a moment it disappeared among the green foliage of the poplars, to appear once more raised high and taut, advancing towards the rough-hewn stone Cross of Gonçales the 'Butcher'. Then, Ordonho crying aloud, 'To arms! To arms! The Bastard's host approaches!'—rushed down the steps of the wall like a rolling bundle.

Meanwhile Tructesindo Ramires, in his efforts to speed his vassals and reach Montemor, had already given his officer-in-command instructions about the journey, charging him that the trumpets be sounded as soon as the sun's rays coloured the wall of the large well. Now, in the lofty hall of the Castle, he sat talking with his cousin from Riba Cávado and his usual comrade-in-arms, Don Garcia Viegas—both of them seated on the stone seat of a deep-set window where a pitcher of water and its cup, between vases of basil, offered refreshment. Don Garcia Viegas was an old, lean, agile man, with a large, dark, clean-shaven face and small, gleaming eyes—who had earned the nickname of The Wise, through the quickness and acumen of his remarks, his infinite dexterity in war, and his gift of speaking Latin more correctly than a churchman of the Curia. Called by Tructesindo, as other relations of the house had been called, to swell the numbers of the Ramires host in their duty to the Princesses, he had at once hastened loyally to Santa Ireneia with his small force of ten lances—beginning by sacking en route the estate of Palha Cã, those of Severosa, who raised their banner aloft with the men of the Royal host against the oppressed ladies. So unsparingly had he sped, that all he had had since dawn was two slices of stolen sausage eaten in the saddle at Palha Cã. Thirsty from his scorching ride, and still overcome by the bitter news of the defeat of his godson, Lourenço Ramires, he was once again filling his cup with water from the pitcher when, through the door of the armoury dominated by three wild boars' heads, burst old Ordonho, panting wildly,

200

'Senhor Tructesindo! Senhor Tructesindo Ramires! The Bastard of Baião has crossed the River and is coming upon us with a vast number of lances!'

The old nobleman leapt up from his seat, and shaking a hairy fist clenched tight with wrath, as if he were already grasping the Bastard's throat, he cried,

'By God's blood! They do well to come for they save us the journey! Eh, Garcia Viegas? Shall we mount and at them?'

But at the unsteady heels of Ordonho came a captain of cross-bows who shouted from the doorway, brandishing his leather helmet,

'Senhor! Senhor! The Baião's host has stopped at the Cross! And a young horseman with a green branch is standing outside the barbican as if he brings a message . . .'

Tructesindo stamped his iron shoe on the stone floor, indignant at such an embassy, sent by such a villain. But Garcia Viegas, who had emptied his mug at a single draught, calmly and loyally reminded him of the rules.

'Stay, stay, cousin and friend! For it is rule and custom both far and near that a messenger with a branch should always be heard.'

'Let is be so, then!' shouted Tructesindo. 'Go to the bail with two lances, Ordonho, and hear the message!'

The bailiff waddled down the blackened, spiral stairway to the steps outside the keep. Two liegemen, their lances at their shoulders, returning from a round, were talking with the armourer who was painting the handles of new javelins yellow and scarlet and lining them up against the wall to dry.

'By our Lord's command!' shouted Ordonho. 'Raise your lances and come with me to the barbican to receive a message!'

Escorted by the two men who walked stiffly beside him, he crossed the bailey; through the postern of the barbican guarded by a swarm of cross-bows, he went out into the Manor land beyond— a wide stretch of paved land without grass or tree, where still remained the worm-eaten posts of an ancient scaffold, and where planks of wood and huge whitewashed ashlars were piled up for repairs to the keep. Then, without leaving the gateway, thrusting out his belly between the two liegemen, he called to the young horseman who was waiting beneath the fierce sun, swatting the horse-flies with a bramble-branch.

'Say whence you come! And why you come! And what credentials you bring!'

Since he had raised a nervous hand to his ear, the horseman, calmly sticking the branch between his cuisse and his saddle-bow, also raised his two shiny mail gauntlets to the mouth-piece of his helm and shouted,

'I am a Knight of Baião's! Credentials I do not bring for I bring no proposal. Don Lopo is beyond the Cross and desires that the noble lord of the Manor, Senhor Tructesindo Ramires, hear him from the top of the barbican . . .'

The bailiff acknowledged him and returned through the vaulted postern of the barbican tower, murmuring to the two yeomen,

'The Bastard is coming to discuss ransom for Senhor Lourenço Ramires . . .'

They both snorted,

'An ugly deed.'

But when Ordonho hurried breathlessly towards the keep, he met Tructesindo Ramires, who, in his irate impatience at the dallying of the Bastard, had already descended, armed, into the court-yard. Against the long, dark green, woollen tunic which he wore over his coat-of-mail, his beard shone whiter, tied in a thick knot like a charger's tail. From one side of his silver inlaid belt hung his curved dagger and his ivory horn, and from the other, his Gothic sword with its wide blade and long gilt handle in which glittered a rare stone brought back from Palestine in earlier days by Gutieres Ramires, the Overseas Ramires. A man-at-arms carried his gauntlets on a leather cushion and his round helm with its barred visor like the one Don Sancho had used; another brought his enormous heart-shaped cuirass, covered in scarlet leather, with the black goshawk roughly painted on it, its claws curved in fury. The standard-bearer, Afonso Gomes, followed, with the standard rolled in its canvas sling.

With the nobleman had descended Don Garcia Viegas, and other relations of the family—the decrepit Ramiro Ramires, a veteran of the capture of Santarém, now twisted with rheumatism like the roots of an oak-tree, and supporting his trembling steps not with a staff but with a spear; and the handsome Leonel, the youngest of the Samoras of Cendufe, who had killed two bears on the moors of Cachamuz and was famous for his ballads; Mendo de Briteiros of the red beard, great burner of witches, gay inventor of dances and entertainments; and the gigantic Lord of the Manor of Avelim, all covered, like some fantastic fish, with the shining mesh of his mail. As the sun approached the wall of the great well, the appointed hour for the expedition to Montemor, the stable-boys were already pulling out the war-horses, their high saddles studded with silver, their haunches and breasts protected by covers of fringed leather which reached to the ground, from the deep sheds which concealed the jousting fields. All over the castle, the news had spread that the Bastard, after the battle, fatal to the Ramires, was hurrying from Canta Pedra to threaten the manor; leaning over the galleries that joined the wall to the counterforts in the keep, or in among the slings that crowded the battlements, the serfs that tended the gardens, the pantry-boys, the villeins hiding in the barbican, watched the lord of Santa Ireneia and his sturdy knights anxiously, trembling in fear of an assault from the Baião host and those dreadful balls of fire-filled lead which nowadays the Christian bands flung as skilfully as the Saracen hordes. Meanwhile, Ordonho, his cap crushed against his breast, panted out to Tructesindo the Bastard's message.

'He's a young knight, and brings no credentials . . . Senhor Bastard is waiting by the Cross . . . He begs you to give ear to him from the top of the barbican.'

'Let him come then!' shouted the old man. 'And with as many of his knaves that care to accompany him!' But Garcia Viegas, the Wise One, ever prudent, gently and astutely suggested,

'Wait, cousin and friend, wait! Don't go up to the barbican until I have made sure that the Baião does not come with trick and guile.'

Then, handing his heavy beech lance to a squire, he entered the dark stairway of the barbican tower. Above, on the top, he hissed, 'Sh! Quiet!' to the line of arbalesters guarding the battlements, on the alert with their cross-bows curved; he entered the look-out place and peered through an embrasure. The Baião's herald had galloped back to the Cross, which was now surrounded by a moving sea of gleaming lances. A brief message he must have given—for immediately, Lopo de Baião, on his sorrel horse covered by a net of mail laced with gold, left the dense body of horsemen, with his visor raised, and bearing no lance or javelin but with his hands idle upon the Moorish saddle-bow and merely holding the scarlet, leather reins. Then, at a protracted note on the horn, he advanced slowly towards the barbican as if he were accompanying a funeral procession. His yellow and black pennant did not stir. Only six squires accompanied him, also without lance or cuirass, purple garments over their coats-of-mail. Behind, four robust cross-bows carried a litter on their shoulders, roughly constructed from tree-trunks, on which a man lay stretched like a corpse, and protected against the heat and gadflies by light branches of acacia. A monk followed on a white mule holding in his hands, together with the reins, an iron crucifix, over which hung the edge of his hood and the tip of a black beard.

From the embrasure, without being able to see the face of the man lying in the litter beneath the layer of branches, the Wise One divined Lourenço Ramires, the gentle godchild whom he loved so dearly, whom he had taught to cross lances and train hawks. Clenching his fists and crying hoarsely, 'Be ready, cross-bows, be ready!' he went down the dark stairway, so stung with wrath and pain that his helmet clanged hollowly against the archway over the door, where Tructesindo Ramires awaited him with the knights his relatives.

'Cousin, my Lord!' he shouted. 'Your son Lourenço is before the bail, lying upon a litter!'

With a gasp of alarm, a rush of iron-clad feet sounded upon the stone slabs as they all followed the nobleman through the postern of the barbican tower, to the heavy wooden ladder which had been pushed against the outer wall. When the enormous old man appeared on the terrace, a heavy, anxious silence fell, so complete that one could hear beyond the garden the slow, mournful creak of the scoop-wheel and the barking mastiffs.

On the space in front of the iron-barred postern, the Bastard waited, motionless upon his jennet, his handsome face raised high, the face of the Fair Sun, his curly beard falling upon the metal cuirass shining like new gold. Bowing his brass helmet, he greeted Tructesindo gravely and respectfully. Then he raised the hand from which he had taken the gauntlet. And in a calm, careful tone, he spoke.

'Senhor Tructesindo Ramires, on this litter I bring you your son Lourenço, whom in loyal battle in the valley of Canta Pedra I took prisoner, and who therefore belongs to me according to the traditional rules of Spanish[1] noblemen. From Canta Pedra I have brought

---

[1] Spain then referred to the whole Iberian Peninsula, including Portugal.

him to beseech you that these murders and ugly quarrels between us should cease, for the blood of good Christians is thus wasted . . . Senhor Tructesindo Ramires, I, like you, descend from kings. From Don Afonso of Portugal I received my knighthood. All the noble race of Baião is proud of me. Consent in giving me the hand of your daughter Dona Violante, whom I love and who loves me, and have the drawbridge lowered so that the wounded Lourenço may enter his home and I may kiss my father's hand.'

From the litter, which trembled upon the shoulders of the crossbows, a desperate shout rang out:

'No, father!'

Standing stiffly on the edge of the terrace, without uncrossing his arms, old Tructesindo took up the shout—which echoed over the entire ground, more arrogant and cavernous than ever:

'My son has answered you first, knave!'

As if a lance had struck him in the chest, the Bastard tottered in his high saddle; at the tug on the reins his bay moved backwards, its golden brow raised high. But with a further jerk he moved again towards the gate. Lopo de Baião, erect in the stirrups, shouted anxiously, furiously,

'Senhor Tructesindo Ramires, don't tempt me! . . .'

'Begone, knave, and son of knaves, begone!' proudly cried the old man, without unfolding his arms from his arrogant chest, in stern immobility and obduracy, as if all his body and soul were of inflexible iron. Then the Bastard, flinging his gauntlet against the wall of the barbican, roared in a wild, hoarse voice:

'By the blood of Christ, and by the souls of all my family, I swear to you that if you don't give me this woman that I love and who loves me, this instant, you will lose your son, for with my own hands, before you here, and though all Heaven should help you, I shall finish off his life!'

A dagger flashed in his hand. But in an impulse of sublime pride, a superhuman impulse, when he grew like another black tower among the towers of the Manor, Tructesindo drew his sword.

'Then do it with this, coward! With this! So that it should be with pure metal, not vile like yours, that my son's heart be pierced!'

Furiously, with his two powerful hands, he flung down his sword which whistled and glittered as it spun and embedded itself in the hard ground, where it shuddered and still glittered, as if some heroic wrath were animating the weapon, too. At the same moment, the Bastard roared, his jennet sprang into the air, and leaning down from the saddle, he thrust his dagger into Lourenço's throat—with such a deep, fierce thrust that the blood spurted out and spattered his fair face and golden beard.

Then there was a mad flight. The four cross-bows dropped the litter to the ground, with the corpse entangled in the branches—and shot off across the open space, like hares in a clearing, after the monk who crouched, clutching the mane of his mule. Swiftly, the Bastard and his six knights, giving the alarm, covered the short distance to the rest of the band which had halted beside the Cross. Tumult whirled round the holy pillar, and the band spurred on their horses post haste to the river bank, swept across the old bridge and were straightaway enveloped in dust, and lost beyond the wood, in a fleeting glitter of helmets and massed lances.

A clamour meanwhile echoed through the walls of Santa Ireneia! A volley of shafts and bolts and shot from slings whistled out, discharged in the same furious instant upon the Baião's band, but only one of the cross-bows who had carried the litter fell, writhing, a shaft in his hip. Through the gate of the bails, knights and pages rushed out desperately to bring in the body of Lourenço Ramires. Garcia Viegas and other relatives ran up to the terrace of the barbican where Tructesindo still stood motionless, stiff and silent, staring at the litter and his son which lay together on the Manor ground. When he slowly turned at the noise behind him, everyone was rendered speechless by the serenity of his face, white as a tombstone, whiter than his white beard, while his dry, coal-black eyes flashed and glittered like two holes in a furnace. With the same fatal serenity, he touched old Ramiro, who leant trembling on his spear, upon the shoulder.

'Friend, look after my son's body, for his soul shall be quiet today, I swear to God!'

He moved away from the gentlemen who stood speechless with awe and emotion—and went down by the worn wooden staircase which creaked under the weight of the enormous nobleman oppressed by grief and wrath.

At that moment, among jostling cross-bows and serfs, the body of Lourenço Ramires passed through the gateway of the barbican, carried by the handsome Leonel and Mendo de Briteiro, both of them weeping profusely and uttering furious threats against the race of Baião. Behind moaned the tottering Ordonho, clasping Tructesindo's sword, which he had picked up from the ground and was kissing to console himself. At the edge of the moat, a hazel-tree spread its tenuous shadow upon rough-hewn planks nailed to stumps of trees—where, on Sundays, Lourenço, with the captain of cross-bows, directed long-bow and cross-bow games, afterwards handing out generous prizes of honey-cakes and tankards of wine. Upon these planks they laid him, and stepped back in awe as they crossed themselves. A knight from Briteiros, fearful for his abandoned and unconfessed soul, ran to the Castle chapel in search of Friar Múncio. Others, running round the walls to the Old Bastion, shouted and made desperate signs to the damaged tower in which the physician lived like an owl. But the well-directed thrust of the Bastard's dagger had put an end to the courageous Lourenço, flower and model of knights throughout the land of Riba Cávado . . . And what a sorry, disfigured sight—dirt and mud on his face, his throat plastered with black blood, his coat-of-mail torn at the shoulders and embedded in his stabbed flesh, and the leg wounded at Canta Pedra naked, without greaves, all swollen and purple and besmeared with more blood and mud!

Tructesindo descended slowly and stiffly. His eyes, like dry coals, blazed more brightly as he approached the body of his son in painful silence. Before the bench he knelt and clasped the cold hand which hung down; beside the face stained with earth and blood, he whispered, soul to soul, in a hushed whisper, not a farewell but a supreme promise, ending with a long kiss upon his forehead on which a ray of sunlight shone brightly down through the leaves of the hazel-tree. Then, jumping up and throwing out his arm as if to gather up all the strength of his race, he shouted,

'And now men, on your horses, and a fitting revenge!'

Already across the courtyards around the keep sounded a rush and clatter of arms. To the barked orders of the captains, rows of cross-bows and archers and slingers ran from the battlements of the wall to draw up their ranks. Swiftly the stable-boys strapped boxes from the stores, fat wine-skins, on the mules' backs. At the low doors of the kitchen, foot-soldiers and attendants hurriedly drank down a bowl of beer before setting out. And in the outer bailey, the knights, clad in iron, ponderously hoisted themselves, with the help of their pages, into the high saddles of their jennets—immediately flanked by their squires and men-at-arms who raised aloft their lances above their thighs and whistled to their harriers.

Finally the standard-bearer, Afonso Gomes, drew out from its sheath and unfurled with a flourish the standard on which the goshawk's wings shone black, wide open, as if taking off in angry flight. The high-pitched shout of the officer-in-command sounded over the entire Manor—ala! ala! From the top of a stone post, near the barbican door, Friar Múncio raised his lean, still-trembling hands above the host and blessed them. Then Tructesindo, on his black horse, received from old Ordonho the sword from which he had been so horribly parted. Then, stretching forth the shining blade towards the towers of his Manor as if towards an altar, he cried,

'Walls of Santa Ireneia, never shall I see you again if in three days, from sunrise to sunset, there yet remains cursed blood in the veins of the traitor of Baião!'

The gate of the bail was thrown wide open and the knights clattered out around the open standard—while in the watch-tower, beneath the still splendour of the August afternoon, the great bell began to toll the death-knell.

★ ★ ★

When Gonçalo sat one afternoon ensconced in his armchair on the verandah, reading this chapter of blood and fury over which he had toiled for a week, he decided 'the piece was impressive!'

Then he longed to receive the praises due at once—and show Gracinha and Father Soeiro the three complete chapters before sending the manuscript to the *Annals*. It might be useful, because Father Soeiro's archeological erudition might provide some new, really Afonsine touch that would bring the Manor of Santa Ireneia and his formidable ancestors more clearly to life. He therefore decided to leave the next day for Oliveira, with his work—which, after being scrutinized by Father Soeiro, he would entrust to Dona Arminda Viegas' steward to copy out in his beautiful handwriting which was famous all over the Country, and which was equalled (and then only in the capitals) by no one save the clerk of the Church Council.

He was already shaking the dust off an old morocco leather case in which to carry his beloved work when Bento pushed open the door, weighed down by a wicker-basket covered with a lace cloth.

'A gift, sir.'

'A gift?... From whom?'

'From *Feitosa*, from the ladies.'

'Bravo!'

'With a letter that was attached to the cloth.'

With what curiosity did Gonçalo tear open the envelope! But in spite of the pompous seal with its coat-of-arms, all it contained was a few lines pencilled on a visiting card of Cousin Maria Mendonça's.

'Yesterday at supper I mentioned how much you like peaches, Gonçalo, especially prepared in wine. So Anica took the liberty of sending you this little basket of peaches from *Feitosa* which, as you know, are spoken of throughout Portugal . . . Regards.'

Gonçalo at once imagined, at the bottom of the basket, sweetly concealed beneath the peaches, a letter from Dona Ana!

'Right! They're peaches . . . Leave them here on a chair . . .'

'I'd better take them down to the pantry, sir, to put on the shelves there.'

'Leave them on the chair!'

As soon as Bento had shut the door, Gonçalo spread the cloth on the floor and carefully tipped out onto it the beautiful peaches which filled the room with their fragrance. At the bottom of the basket all he found was a few vine-leaves. Slightly disappointed, he inhaled the aroma of one of the peaches. Then he decided that the fruit, packed by her, on the vine-leaves which she had picked from the trellis, under the cloth which she had selected from the cupboard, contributed, in their fragrant silence, a sentimental message on their own. Still crouching on the mat, he ate the peach—and put the others back in the basket to take to Gracinha.

The following day, at two o'clock, with Torto's pair already hitched to his carriage, and his gloves on ready for the journey to Oliveira, he received an unexpected call from the Viscount of Rio Manso. Pulling off his gloves, the Nobleman thought, 'Rio Manso! What does that dour fellow want with me?' In the drawing-room, perched on the edge of the green velvet sofa, rubbing his knees, the Viscount explained how, passing by the Tower on his way back from Vila Clara, he had overcome his usual timidity and stopped to pay his respects to Senhor Gonçalo Ramires. Not only for this most pleasant duty—but also (since he had learnt that he was standing as Deputy for the District) to offer him, from the parish of Canta Pedra, his services and the votes he commanded there . . .

Gonçalo, smiling and surprised, thanked him and twisted his moustache in embarrassment. The Viscount of Rio Manso could understand his surprise, because of course Senhor Gonçalo Ramires knew him to be an intransigent Regenerator . . . But really! He belonged to that generation who, now greatly reduced, put the duties of gratitude before Political ones;—and apart from the sympathy Senhor Gonçalo Ramires deserved (and the whole District spoke about his talent and charm and generosity), he also owed the Nobleman a debt of gratitude, still outstanding through timidity rather than indfference . . .

'Can't you guess, Senhor Gonçalo Mendes Ramires ? . . . Don't you remember ?'

'No, really, my Lord, I can't . . .'

Well, one afternoon, Senhor Gonçalo Mendes Ramires was riding his horse past his estate *Varandinha* when his granddaughter, playing on the terrace (that fenced-in terrace from which bowed a magnolia tree) had let a ball fall into the road. Senhor Gonçalo Mendes Ramires had laughed, dismounted and picked up the ball, and in order to return it to the little girl leaning through the railings, had mounted again and drawn his mare alongside the wall—how prompt and charming he had been!

'Don't you remember now ?'

'Yes, yes, now I do . . .'

On the ground of the terrace, beside the railings, there had been a pot of carnations. Senhor Gonçalo Mendes, after joking with the little girl (who, thank heaven, was not awkward and shy!) had asked her for a carnation which she had picked and given to him as seriously as a young woman! The Viscount, who had been watching from the window of his room, had thought, 'Well, I never! This Nobleman of the Tower, such an aristocrat, and so charming!' No, his Lordship need not laugh and blush—his kindness had been very great, and had struck him, the grandfather, as exceptional! He had not just returned the ball and left it at that . . .

'Don't you remember, Sr Gonçalo Mendes Ramires ?'

'Yes, my Lord, I remember now . . .'

The next day, Senhor Gonçalo Mendes Ramires had sent a

beautiful basket of roses from the Tower, with his card and a playful note: 'Roses for Senhora Dona Rosa in gratitude for a carnation.'

Gonçalo almost jumped from his chair, and laughingly answered, 'Ah yes, Viscount, that's right! Now I remember perfectly!'

Well, ever since that afternoon he had been longing to show Sr Gonçalo Mendes Ramires his gratitude, his appreciation. But it was no good—he was shy and led a very solitary life. That morning, however, in Vila Clara, he had learnt from Gouveia that the Nobleman was standing as Deputy for the District. Although the election was so safe, both on account of Sr Ramires and of the government, he had thought immediately, 'Right, here's the opportunity!' Now he was offering him from Canta Pedra his services and the votes which he commanded there.

Gonçalo was moved and murmured,

'Really, Viscount, there's nothing that could move me more than such a spontaneous offer, such a . . .'

'It is I who am moved that you should accept. Now let us talk no more of my poor services and my poor votes . . .You have a most venerable home here.'

Since the Viscount mentioned the desire that he had had for years to admire, at close hand, the famous Tower, older than Portugal itself, they both went down to the orchard. The Viscount, his sunshade at his shoulder, stood looking in awe at the Tower; he recognized (although a liberal) the prestige that so formidable a lineage as the Ramires brings; and he praised the orange grove most sincerely. Then, knowing that Pereira da Riosa had leased the farm, he congratulated Senhor Ramires on having so careful and honest a lessee . . . Outside the gate, the Viscount's carriage waited, hitched to two sleek, shining mules. Gonçalo admired the mules. Opening the door, he asked the Viscount to kiss Sra Dona Rosa's little hand for him. Touched, the Viscount expressed his hope, his profound desire, that the Nobleman would stop in Canta Pedra when he wished one day and dine in his home, so that he should get to know the young lady of the ball and the carnation better . . .

'I should be extremely honoured! . . . And here and now let me offer to teach the Senhora Dona Rosa, if she does not already know it, the ancient Portuguese way of playing *péla*[1].'

[1] *Péla*: an ancient game reputedly the precursor of tennis.

The Viscount thanked him, hand on heart and bathed in pleasure and smiles.

Gonçalo murmured to himself as he climbed up the steps, 'What a charming man! And how gorgeous, to pay for roses with votes! Just imagine how, at times, a tiny attention earns one a friend! Next week I'll definitely dine at Canta Pedra! . . . Delightful man!'

It was in a happy frame of mind that he laid the morocco-bound case containing his manuscript in the carriage together with the romantic basket of peaches from Dona Ana—lit a cigar and jumped up on to the cushion to take the reins and drive Torto's white pair to Oliveira at a gay trot.

*　　*　　*

In King's Square, before he dismounted, he immediately asked doorman Joaquim after his master and mistress. They were very well, thanks be to God. Sr José Barrolo had left that morning on horseback for the Baron of Marges's estate, and would only be back that evening.

'And Father Soeiro?'

'Father Soeiro is at Dona Arminda's house, I believe.'

'And Senhora Dona Graça?'

'Senhora Dona Graça went down to the gazebo a little while ago, with her hat on . . . I presume she was going to the Church of the Monicas.'

'Right. Take this basket of peaches and tell pantryman Joaquim to put them on the table just as they are, in their basket, with the leaves. And have some hot water sent up to my room.'

The clock on the wall in the waiting-room lazily wheezed out five o'clock. The mansion was enveloped in a luminous silence. After the dust and bumps of the road, the freshness of his room seemed still more agreeable to Gonçalo, with the four windows open on to the well-watered garden and yard of the Monicas. He carefully put away the precious morocco-bound case into a drawer of the chest-of-drawers. A maid with big round eyes entered with the large jug of hot water: and the Nobleman, as always, teased her about the handsome cavalry sergeants whose tempting barracks overlooked the wash-house in the garden and kept the girls of the house passionately soaping all day. Still he dallied, changing his dusty suit, whistling vaguely, leaning against the verandah overlooking silent Weaver's

Street. The bell of the Monicas chimed prettily . . . Gonçalo, bored with his solitude, decided to go down through the terrace of the garden and surprise Gracinha in her devotions in the little church.

Below in the corridor he met pantryman Joaquim.

'Isn't Senhor Barrolo dining at home today?'

'Senhor Barrolo has gone to dine with the Baron of Marges, on his estate . . . It's the little girl's birthday. He won't be coming home till tonight.'

Gonçalo dawdled among the flower-beds in the garden, selecting a sprig of light flowers for his buttonhole. Then he wandered round the greenhouse, smiling at the door with which Barrolo had embellished it, an arched, glass door decorated with ironwork and a monogram in brilliant colours; he went down the path which led to the fountain, covered with shade and silence by the intertwining branches of the tall laurels. A little further on, surrounded by stone benches, and sweet-scented flower-laden trees, the small fountain murmured sleepily in its round, wide-edged pool, where large white china pots stood, with the branching coat-of-arms of the Sá's. Surely they had cleaned the pool that morning or the day before, because, in the quite transparent water above the bright stone slabs, the fish, that Gonçalo frightened by poking in his cane, darted around with uncommon vivacity in scarlet flashes. From the edge of the pool he could see, at the bottom of another path, bordered by blooming dahlias, the gazebo—an eighteenth-century construction made in imitation of a little Greek temple of a faded pink colour with a fat Cupid on the cupola, and a row of little windows between the grooved columns in half-relief, up which crept sweet-smelling jasmine.

Gonçalo picked some leaves off a branch of lemon-scented verbena, as he often did, to crush between his fingers and perfume his hands; and he continued on his way to the gazebo, wandering slowly between the thick blooms of dahlias. His fine, patent-leather shoes trod noiselessly upon the soft stones of the freshly-gravelled path. So he approached, quiet as an idle shadow, one of the little windows of the gazebo which was not quite shut but had its green blinds pulled down inside. Beside this window were the stone steps which led, from the long high terrace on which the garden was built, down to Weaver's Street, almost in front of the Chapel of the Monicas. Gonçalo was walking leisurely down, when he heard, through the thin blind inside the gazebo, a murmur, a disturbed whispering. He smiled to himself, supposing a maid from the house were hiding in this little temple of Love with one of the terrible cavalry sergeants! But no, that was impossible! Only a few moments before Gracinha had brushed by that window and descended those steps on her way to the Monicas! Then another idea struck him like a sword-blow— so painful was it that he stepped back in horror from the edge of the gazebo where it had cruelly attacked him. But now a desperate curiosity caught hold of him and was urging him on—and he bent his face to the blind as cautiously as a spy. The gazebo had resumed its silence, and Gonçalo feared his heart-beats would betray him. Dear Lord above! The murmuring had begun again, more breathless, more disturbed. Someone was pleading, was stammering, 'No, no! This is madness!' Someone was urging, impatient and ardently, 'Yes, my love! Yes, my love!' He recognized both voices—as clearly as if the blind had suddenly lifted and all the bright light of the garden had streamed in. It was Gracinha! It was Cavaleiro!

Overcome with immense shame, in confusion and fear that he should be surprised beside the gazebo and the depravity concealed there, he went back down the dahlia path, hunched up, treading lightly on the soft gravel, circled the fountain under the branches of the bushes, plunged into the dark shadows of the laurels and slipped stealthily behind the greenhouse and back into the calm of the palatial house. But the whispers from the gazebo still followed, feebler now, more compliant—'No, no! This is madness! . . . Yes, yes, my love! . . .'

He hurried through the deserted rooms, like a hunted shadow, slipped silently up the stone staircase, and dashed straight out of the gate, looking around, afraid he might see doorman Joaquim. In the square he stopped before the railings round the sun-dial. But the murmuring from the gazebo rustled throughout the square like a whirling wind, rasping against the paving stones, flapping the beards of the saints over the doorway of St Mateus' Church, whistling round the mossy roofs of the rope-factory . . . 'No, no! This is madness! Yes, yes, my love!' Then Gonçalo felt an urgent desire to run a long way off, miles from the square and the mansion and the city, from all the shame that tortured him. But what about a carriage? He remembered Maciel who hired out horses, the place furthest away, way beyond the last houses on the road to the Seminary.

Hugging the low walls bordering the poor roads, he ran and ordered a closed carriage to be got ready.

As he waited by the door on a bench, a cart trundled by loaded with furniture, kitchen pans, and a large mattress with a stain on it. Gonçalo suddenly thought of the divan which furnished the gazebo. It was enormous, made of mahogany, covered with a striped material, and had slack springs that squeaked. Suddenly the whispering began again, and grew until it thundered out loud over the rooftops of the poor houses, over the Seminary yard, over all horrified Oliveira: 'No, no! This is madness! Yes, yes, my love!'

Gonçalo leapt up and shouted into the darkness of the coach-house,

'What the devil are you doing? Isn't this carriage ready yet?'

'Just coming out, your Lordship.'

On the clock of the Piedade, seven o'clock was striking when he jumped into the calash, pulled down the stiff blinds and sat himself well back, well hidden, crushed, with the feeling that the earth was shaking and the bravest souls were cast down, and that his own Tower, old as the kingdom itself, was split apart, revealing an unexpected pile of rubbish and dirty skirts.

9

AT THE DOOR of the kitchen, Gonçalo shook a screwed-up envelope at Rosa the cook and shouted, 'Oh, Rosa! Didn't I ask you not to write to my sister Graça? How stubborn you are! Can't we take care of the girl without all this whining to Oliveira? Thank heavens the Tower is large enough to take in another child.'

Crispola had died: the poor widow, who was a neighbour of the Tower, with a little family of two boys and three girls, had lain wasting in her humble bed since Easter. And now Gonçalo, who had kept the wretched house abundantly supplied was arranging for care of the children—already very neatly attired in mourning by him. The eldest girl (also Crispola), always tucked away in the kitchen of the Tower, naturally became 'Rosa's paid assistant'. One of the boys, a twelve-year-old, a tall, bright fellow, was also employed by Gonçalo in the Tower, as a messenger-lad in a uniform with yellow buttons. For the other—a sluggish, snivelling boy, but with a knack for and interest in carpentry, Gonçalo had found a place under Aunt Louredo's patronage, in the S José Workshop. One of the other girls was taken in by Manuel Duarte's mother—a charming lady who lived on a beautiful estate near Treixedo, and adored Gonçalo, whose vassal she considered herself. But for the youngest and weakest he had not yet found a stable home. Rose had then suggested 'that surely Senhora Dona Maria da Graça would take the poor little creature in . . .' Gonçalo snorted drily, 'Oh, there's no need to worry the city of Oliveira for another crust of bread!' Rosa, however, carried away by her good works, and wanting a woman's warmth for the little, fair, delicate child, had written to Gracinha, in Bento's impeccable hand, a verbose letter with the request and the whole lamentable story of Crispola with much praise for her master's charity. It was Gracinha's reply, belated but compassionate, with the request that they should send the poor child to her at once, that had annoyed the Nobleman.

Since that dreadful afternoon at the gazebo, a strange repugnance to communicate with *Cunhais* had taken hold of him. It was as if the gazebo and the depravity harboured within its pink walls had contaminated the garden and the mansion, King's Square and the whole city of Oliveira, and now he, through moral scruples, recoiled from this contaminated region where his heart and his pride felt suffocated . . . Immediately after his flight, he had received an astonished letter from the good Barrolo:

'What whim of yours was this? Why didn't you wait? I was even rather worried when I got back from Marges' estate. And you can't imagine how upset Gracinha is! We heard of your departure, as it happened, through a driver from Maciel's. We are already eating the peaches, but we don't understand!'

Gonçalo replied drily on a card, 'Business'. Then he remembered that he had left the manuscript of his novel in the drawer in his room, and early in the morning he sent one of his farm-boys almost secretly to Father Soeiro, 'asking him to give the case well wrapped to the bearer without saying anything to the lady and gentleman'. All he wanted between the Tower and *Cunhais* was silence and separation.

During those secluded days which he spent in the Tower (not daring to risk a visit to Vila Clara, afraid that his sullied name was already being bandied about in Simões' Tobacconist's or in Ramos's store) he was assailed by a fury that struck out at everyone . . . Fury with his sister that had trampled upon modesty, pride of race and fear of Oliveira's scorn, as simply and rashly as if she had been treading on the faded flowers of a carpet, and had run to the gazebo and to the mustachioed male as soon as he had signalled to her with his musk-scented handkerchief! Fury with Barrolo, the chubby-cheeked simpleton, who spent all his foolish days praising Cavaleiro, dragging Cavaleiro to King's Square, choosing the finest wines from his cellar to heat Cavaleiro's blood, plumping up the cushions on all the sofas so that Cavaleiro could stretch out and enjoy his cigar and the charm of Gracinha's presence! Finally, fury with himself who, through his base desire for a seat in S Bento, had broken down the only secure wall between his sister and the man with the gleaming locks—which was his enmity, that uncompromising enmity which he had so rigidly reinforced and renewed since Coimbra! . . . Ah! All three of them horribly guilty!

Then, one afternoon, bored with his solitude, he chanced a ride to Vila Clara. He realized that, in the Club, in Simões' Tobacconist's, in Ramos's shop, Gracinha's love-affair was as little known as if it had taken place in the depths of Tartary. Immediately, his lenient soul, now that it was calm again, abandoned itself to the sweet task of inventing subtle excuses for all those to blame in the sorry affair . . . Gracinha, poor girl, childless and with such a dull, sluggish husband, cut off from all intellectual pursuits and too lazy even to do sewing or embroidery—had yielded, what woman would not have done? She had yielded to the simple, primitive passion which had sprung up in her soul and taken root there, given her the only pleasures in her life and (still more important!) wrung from her her only tears! Barrolo, poor thing, was the simpleton, and like the hawthorn in the song, unable to produce anything nobler than hawthorn berries, could bear only the fruits of his foolishness. He, Gonçalo, had stupidly and irresistibly succumbed to the fatal Law of Increase, which had led him, as it leads everyone in their desire for fame and fortune, to pass rashly through the first door that opened to him, without noticing the dung that cluttered up the doorway . . . Yes, really, all of them were so little guilty before God, who had created man so variable, so weak, so dependent on forces that were less governable than the wind or sun!

No, there was only one who was unpardonably guilty—the scoundrel with the wavy mane! This fellow, through all his dealings with Gracinha, ever since his student days, had been brazenly selfish, punishable only in the manner in which the Ramires of old had punished their enemies—with death after torture, the corpse flung out to the crows. When it pleased him, in the idle hours of a long summer, to enjoy a bucolic love affair in the groves of the Tower —he did so. When he considered that a wife and children would constrain him—he betrayed her. As soon as his former sweetheart belonged to another man—he reopened his indolent siege to reap, without the responsibilities of fatherhood, the pleasures of his emotions. As soon as the husband opened his door a little—he did not wait, but seized his prey brutally! Ah, just think how great-grandfather Tructesindo would have treated so villainous a villain! Without any doubt he would have roast him on a crackling bonfire in front of the barbican—or would have filled his false throat with good molten lead in the dungeons of the Castle!

He, however, a descendant of Tructesindo, could not even pass Cavaleiro without raising his hat when he met him in the streets of Oliveira! The slightest cooling of this so disastrously renewed friendship would be proof of the still undivulged lewdness in the gazebo. All Oliveiro would whisper and laugh. 'Look, there's the Nobleman of the Tower! He lets Cavaleiro into *Cunhais* with his sister and a few weeks later breaks with him again! There was a nice juicy scandal there, I bet!' What fun for the Lousadas! No, what he must do now was display so close and obvious friendship with Cavaleiro—that its very closeness and obviousness would quash any suggestions of the vile affair. A tortuous simulation imposed by the honour of his name. The filthy affair carefully concealed among the thick bushes in the garden, in the darkest shadows of the gazebo! And outside, in the sunshine, in the squares of Oliveira, he with his arm affectionately slipped through Cavaleiro's!

The days rolled by, and no peace had yet settled in Gonçalo's heart. What embittered him above all was to feel that he was compelled to act out this public intimacy with Cavaleiro—both for the sake of his name and for thè convenience of the election. All his pride rebelled at times: 'What does the election matter? What's a dirty chair in S Bento worth?' But immediately grim reality silenced him. The election was the only crack through which he could escape from his rural hole; if he broke with Cavaleiro, this scoundrel, this habitual scoundrel would immediately arrange, with the support of the intriguing horde in Lisbon, another candidate for Vila Clara . . . Unfortunately he was one of those spineless souls who depended on others. And this pitiful dependence stemmed from what? From poverty—the meagre income from two estates, plenty for a simple man, but poverty for him, with his education, his tastes, his duties as a nobleman, his sociable temperament.

These thoughts slowly and subtly impelled him towards another idea—to Dona Ana Lucena and her two hundred *contos* . . . Until, one morning, he courageously faced a disturbing possibility—that of marrying Dona Ana! Why not? She had patiently showed an inclination towards him, almost consent . . . Why not marry Dona Ana?

Yes, there was the father who had been a butcher, the brother a murderer! But he, too, somewhere among his numerous ancestors that went back to the fierce Suevians, could discover a butcher; and the occupation of the Ramires, throughout the heroic centuries, had in fact consisted of murder. Moreover, the butcher and the murderer, both dead, were remote shadows and already belonged to a fading legend. Dona Ana had risen by her marriage from the

Populace to the Bourgeoisie. He had not found her in her father's butcher's, nor at her brother's hide-out—but on the *Feitosa* estate, already an heiress with her own steward, her chaplain and lackeys, like an ancient Ramires. Ah, really, any further hesitation would be childish—since she was bringing those two hundred *contos* of very clean money, good rural money, with her body, the body of a beautiful and serious woman. With such pure gold, his name, and his talent, he did not need the deceitful hand of Cavaleiro to win in Politics. Then what a noble and complete life his would be! The old Tower restored to the solemn splendour of former eras; the best type of cultivation for the historic lands of Treixedo; fruitful journeys to lands that educate! . . . And the woman who supplied these delights would not sour the pleasure, as in so many rich marriages, by her ugliness, her protruding bones, her coarse skin! No! After the social splendour of the day, no scarecrow would await him in the bed-chamber—but Venus.

Thus, slowly overcome by these temptations, he sent a card one afternoon to Cousin Maria at *Feitosa* asking whether they 'could meet privately, at some spot in the neighbourhood, because he wanted to have a very serious and intimate little talk with her . . .' But three long days elapsed and the longed-for letter from *Feitosa* did not appear. Gonçalo concluded that Cousin Maria, intelligent as she was, had sensed the nature of the 'little talk', and not being sure she could make him happy, was prevaricating, was refusing to see him. He then spent a desolate week, pondering on the sadness of a life that seemed hollow and full of uncertainty. Pride, and a complicated form of modesty, would not allow him to return to Oliveira, to his room there where the cupola of the gazebo with its fat Cupid was relentlessly above the bushes; and he almost shuddered at the thought of kissing his sister on the cheek over which the other had slobbered! A tomb-like silence had descended over the elections— and a bitterer repugnance prevented him from writing to Cavaleiro. João Gouveia was enjoying his holidays on the coast, in white shoes, collecting little shells on the beach. He could not tolerate Vila Clara these scorching September days, with Tító in Alentejo, where he had been called by an illness of the old squire of Cidadelhe, Manuel Duarte on his mother's estate supervising the grape-harvest, and the Club deserted and sleepy amid the interminable buzzing of flies.

*   *   *

To occupy his hours, to kill time, more than through any duty or feeling for Art, he picked up his novel. But without enthusiasm, or inspiration. Now it was Tructesindo and his knights' grim pursuit of the Bastard of Baião. A difficult chapter—calling for panache and lots of medieval colour. And he was so limp and worn-out! . . . Fortunately Uncle Duarte had filled this violent passage in his poem with detailed descriptions of scenery and interesting glimpses of battle.

On the bank of Horse-Kick Stream, Tructesindo found the ancient bridge chopped down, and the worm-eaten planks and supports cluttering up the shallow stream below. The Bastard had prudently demolished it to stop the avenging horsemen pursuing him. Then the slow host followed along the narrow bank, skirting the rows of beeches in search of the Espigal Ford. But what a time it took! When the last pack-mules stepped on to the far bank, the evening was coming to an end, and the stepping-stones did not shine so brightly, some still a pale gold, others now a pink shade. Immediately, Don Garcia Viegas, the Wise One, proposed dividing the party: the foot-soldiers and beasts-of-burden to advance stealthily and silently to Montemor, to avoid clashes; the lances and mounted cross-bows to hurry and do their utmost to catch up with the Bastard. Everyone praised the Wise One's guile and the horsemen, no longer hampered by the halberdiers and slingers, gave their horses the rein, set off across the waste land, and then through a craggy region till they reached the Three Ways, desolate, flat country where an ancient oak grew in solitude, which once, before its exorcism by S Froalengo, had sheltered, on the darkest Saturday in January, by the light of sulphur-torches, the Great Circle of all the witches in Portugal. Near this oak-tree, Tructesindo called the party to a halt; raising himself in his stirrups, he sniffed the three paths which branched off between gloomy hills of wild, gorse-covered land. Had the evil Bastard passed by this way? . . . Ah, surely he and his evil had passed this way—for at the back of a rock, near three thin goats which were grazing in the brush, lay a poor dead goatherd, his arms outstretched, pierced by an arrow! So that the unhappy fellow should not breathe news of the people of Baião, a brutal arrow had pierced the lean, hungry, rag-covered breast. But which of these paths had the wicked men penetrated? On the loose soil, blown by the hot south wind which came from the hills, there was no sign of earth churned up by the fleeing band. And in such a solitary place there was no thatched hut or shack from which some villein or crouching old woman might have peeped out and caught sight of the fleeing band . . . So, at a command from standard-bearer Afonso Gomes, three scouts set out down the three paths to reconnoitre—while the horsemen, without dismounting, undid their morions to wipe the dripping sweat from their bearded faces, or guided their jennets towards a thin trickle of water that wound between stunted reeds. Tructesindo did not move from beneath the branches of S Froalengo's oak, motionless upon his motionless black horse, enclosed in his black armour, his hands together upon the saddle and his helm bent low in prayer and pain. At his side, with their spiked collars and lolling, pink tongues, his two mastiffs lay stretched out, panting.

The men waited, were growing restless and impatient—when the scout who had set out down the western path reappeared in a cloud of dust, waving from afar, his javelin held high. An hour's ride away he had discerned an encampment on a hill-top, on a safe camping-ground, surrounded by stakes and ditches!

'What's their pennant?'

'Thirteen torteaux.'

'Praise be to God!' shouted Tructesindo, who trembled as if awakening from sleep. 'It's Don Pedro de Castro, the Castilian, who has come with the Leonese in succour of the Princesses!'

So the Bastard had not dared ride that way. And now, from the path leading eastwards, came back another scout to tell that in a pine-grove in the hills, he had come across a band of Genoese pedlars, delayed there since dawn because one of them had been struck down by fever. What then? Then no one had passed by the pine wood all that day, according to the Genoese, except a group of clowns on their way home from the fair at Grajelo. So that left only the path in the middle, a steep, stony path along a dry river-bed. Down it, at a shout from Tructesindo, trooped the band. But the melancholy gloom of dusk was falling and the path went on and on, a rough, dismal, interminable trail between gorse-covered slopes and rocks, with not a cabin in sight, nor a wall nor a hedge nor a path nor sheep-track. Far off, away in the distance, they could still see the arid countryside covered in solitude and shadow, stretching mutely to a remote sky, where the last copper-coloured, blood-coloured ray of the setting sun was fading. Then Tructesindo stopped his fleet-footed band beside the brambles which were bending under the stronger gusts of the southern wind and cried,

'By God, my Lords, we are embarked on a futile and hopeless chase, it would seem! What think you, Garcia Viegas?'

All the band crowded round; steam rose from the jennets panting under their mail coverings. The Wise One stretched out his arm.

'My lords! The Bastard has fled from us beyond the distant horizon and reached Vale Murtinho to spend the night in the Agradel Manor, which is well fortified and belongs to relations of the Baião's . . .'

'So what must we do, Don Garcia?'

'What we must do, my lords and friends, is rest the night, too. We'll return to the Three Ways. From there, all concurring, to Don Pedro de Castro's encampment, to beg shelter. With such a lord we shall have in greater abundance than in our saddle-bags what all of us, Christians and animals need—barley and a chunk of meat and three good draughts of wine! . . .'

They all shouted aloud, 'A good plan! An excellent plan!' And they set off back laboriously along the steep, stony path towards the Three Ways—where two crows were avidly feeding on the corpse of the dead goatherd.

Soon, at the far end of the eastern path, on a high hilltop, the white tents of the encampment stood out in the light of the bonfires burning all over the site. The officer-in-command of Santa Ireneia blew three slow blasts on the horn, announcing the arrival of a nobleman. Immediately, within the barricade, others sounded, clear and welcoming. Then the officer-in-charge galloped as far as the surrounding ditch and announced, to the sentinels posted along it between the glowing watch-fires, the friendly band of Ramires. Tructesindo had stopped at the dark stream which the thick pine-wood darkened still more as it waved and moaned in the wind. Two knights dressed in black, hooded tunics immediately hurried down the slope announcing that Senhor Don Pedro de Castro awaited the noble lord of Santa Ireneia and was greatly pleased to help and serve him. Silently, Tructesindo dismounted, and with Don Garcia Viegas, Leonel de Samora, Mendo de Briteiros and other relations from the Manor, all of them without lance or cuirass and un-gauntleted, climbed up the hill to the barriers, the gates of which were wide open, revealing beyond, in the uncertain light of the low bonfires, crowds of infantry, and among the steel bascinets appeared the yellow bonnet of a camp-follower or the long cap of a jester. As soon as the old man appeared near the logs, two squires waved their swords and shouted,

'Honour! Honour to the noblemen of Portugal!'

The harsh blare of trumpets mingled with the soft rolling of the drums. Between the crowd, which silently opened a path for him, preceded by four knights bearing aloft lighted torches, came old Don Pedro de Castro, the Castilian, a man of many a long battle and vast property. He wore a silver ornamented skin bodice on the upper part of his body which was bowed as if exhausted by so much fighting and such great craving to rule. Without helmet, or armour, he rested his hairy, large-veined hand on an ivory cane. His sunken eyes shone with friendly curiosity in his lean, dark-tanned face, its nose more curved than a falcon's beak, drawn to one side by a deep scar which disappeared into his curly, pointed beard, now almost white.

Standing before the Lord of Santa Ireneia he slowly opened wide his arms. With a grave smile that made his rapacious nose curve still more sharply over his pointed beard, he spoke words of welcome.

'God be praised! Joyful is the night that brings you to us, cousin and friend! I was not expecting such an honour, nor so great a pleasure! . . .'

*   *   *

After bringing this difficult chapter to an end, after three mornings of work, Gonçalo flung down his pen with a sigh of exhaustion. Ah! how tired he was getting of this interminable novel, all unravelled like a loose skein of yarn, and he unable to trim the threads because Uncle Duarte, upon whose heels he was breathlessly following, had so thoroughly entangled it. Then he did not even have the consolation that he was composing a substantial work. These Tructesindos, these Bastards, these Castros, these Wise Ones, were they really Afonsine men of real historical substance? . . . Perhaps they were merely hollow puppets, enclosed in borrowed armour, inhabiting unrealistic camps and castles, without a word or gesture relating them to bygone days!

The next day he could not muster the courage to pick up the

threads of that impatient pursuit by the men from Santa Ireneia of Baião's fleeing band. Anyway, he had already sent in three chapters of the novel, he had already calmed the persistent Castanheiro. But idleness weighed more heavily upon him this week, moving dully from one sofa to another or wandering among the box-trees in the garden, smoking and sadly contemplating that life was ebbing away from him. To increase the nervous tension came the additional problem of money—a promissory note for 600 *mil-reis* borrowed in his last year in Coimbra—a debt that had been renewed and had grown; and now the lender, a certain Leite from Oliveira, was insisting on the payment of the money. His Lisbon tailor was also pestering him for a fantastic sum—a bill filling two sheets of paper. But what depressed him above all else was the solitude of the Tower. All his cheerful friends scattered about their estates or on some beach. The election at a standstill, like a boat stuck in the mud. His sister surely in the gazebo with 'the other one'. Even Cousin Maria ungratefully ignoring his timid request for a little talk. And he in his enormous hot-house, with no energy, and paralysed by growing inertia as if cords were binding him, each day tighter—and the man was turning into a mere bundle.

One afternoon, in his room, feeling dull and gloomy without even a word for Bento, he had just dressed to go for a horse-ride, a gallop round Valverde, when Crispola's little boy (already established at the Tower as a page, in a little uniform with yellow buttons) knocked urgently at the door. A lady had stopped at the gate, in a carriage, and had asked the Nobleman to go down for a moment.

'Didn't she give her name?'

'No, sir. She's a thin lady, and the carriage was drawn by a pair with nets . . .'

Cousin Maria! How excited he was as he ran out, snatching an old straw hat off a hook in the corridor as he passed! Down below he stood as if contemplating the Goddess of Fortune, in her light chariot.

'Oh, Cousin Maria! What a surprise! . . . What a pleasure!'

Leaning out of the window of the carriage (the blue calash from *Feitosa*), Dona Maria Mendonça, in a new hat adorned with lilacs, laughingly excused her silence with a certain embarrassment. She had received her cousin's letter very late . . . The same wretched postman, always drunk and hobbling . . . And then some awfully busy days in Oliveira with Anica who was getting her house in Velas Street ready for the winter.

'Then as I owed poor Venancia Rios in Vila Clara a visit, who's been ill, I thought the simplest and best thing to do was to stop at the Tower . . . So what is it, then?'

Gonçalo smiled embarrassedly.

'Oh, nothing serious, but . . . I just wanted to have a talk with you. Why don't you come in?'

He opened the door. She preferred to walk along the road. So they walked to the old stone bench which was shaded by poplars opposite the gate of the Tower. Gonçalo flicked the dust off the edge of the bench with his handkerchief.

'Well, Cousin Maria, I did want to have a talk with you . . . But it's difficult, so difficult! . . . Perhaps the best thing to do is attack the question brutally.'

'Attack, then.'

'Here goes, then! Do you think I should be wasting my time, cousin, if I devoted myself to your friend, Dona Ana?'

Sitting perched on the edge of the bench, carefully rolling up her black silk sunshade, Maria Mendonça took her time replying, and then murmured,

'No, I don't think you'd be wasting your time, cousin . . .'

'Ah, you don't think so?'

She studied Gonçalo, enjoying his anxiety and discomfort.

'Lord Jesus, cousin! Say something more!'

'But what more do you want me to say to you? I already told you in Oliveira. I'm still too young to be a messenger in love affairs. But I think Anica is pretty, and rich and a widow . . .'

Gonçalo got up from the bench, and raised his arms in desolation. When Dona Maria also got up, they wandered together over the strip of grass which ran along the edge of the poplars. He almost moaned in his distress.

'Pretty and rich and a widow indeed! I wouldn't have bothered you, cousin, to discover such great secrets. What the deuce! Be a good girl, cousin, be frank. You must know, you've surely talked together. Be frank. Does she like me at all?'

Dona Maria stopped, and murmured, as she scratched the yellowed path through the grass with the point of her sunshade,

'Of course she does . . .'

226

'Bravo! Then, in a little while, after these first months of mourning are over, if I made her a proposal . . .'

She darted her bright eyes at Gonçalo,

'Lord above, how you gallop on, cousin. Is this a passion, then ?'

Gonçalo took off his old straw hat and ran his fingers slowly through his hair. Suddenly opening his heart, he admitted,

'Look, cousin! It's mainly a need to establish myself in life! Don't you agree ?'

'So much so that it was I who pointed out the way to you . . . And now goodbye to you, for it's past five o'clock. I mustn't delay because of the children.'

Gonçalo protested, begged her,

'Just a few minutes more! . . . It's so early! Just one more thing, and in all sincerity. Is she a good girl ?'

Dona Maria turned at the end of the avenue of poplars to go back to her calash.

'A little bit of temper, to liven things up. But a good girl! And an admirable housewife! You can't imagine how excellently *Feitosa*'s kept. The order, the discipline, the cleanliness and punctuality . . . She keeps her eye on everything, even the wine-cellar and the coach-house!'

Gonçalo rubbed his hands together in delight.

'Well, if the great event takes place in a year's time, I must proclaim throughout the realm that it was Cousin Maria who saved the house of Ramires!'

'That's what I work for, to serve your name and coat-of-arms!' she exclaimed, jumping up lightly into the calash, as if in flight after such a frank confession.

The servant climbed up to his cushion. As the rested horses set off at a trot, Dona Maria called out,

'Do you know who I met in Vila Clara ? Titó!'

'Titó!'

'He's just got back from Alentejo. He's coming to you for dinner. I didn't bring him in the carriage for decency's sake, so as not to ruin his reputation . . .'

The calash rolled off—amid smiles and friendly waves exchanged in the new, warmer feeling of a shared romantic conspiracy.

Gonçalo set off gaily to Vila Clara to meet Titó. He was already excited at the thought of getting from Titó, an intimate friend of

Feitosa, information on Dona Ana, her temperament and her ways. Cousin Maria, for love of the Ramires (especially, poor soul, for the benefit of the Mendonças!) idealized the lady. But Titó, the most truthful man in the kingdom, worshipping truth with the ancient devotion of Epaminondas, would describe Dona Ana without embellishing or denigrating her unjustly. And Titó . . . Ah! Beneath that thundering voice, that bovine indolence, Titó possessed a most attentive, amost penetrating mind.

The two friends met at Portela. In spite of the brevity of their separation, they clasped each other with noisy affection.

'Oh, Gonçalo, you old rascal!'

'Oh, Titó, my dear! I've missed you terribly. How's your brother?'

His brother was better, but worn out. Too many parchments and too many females for an old man of sixty. As he had warned him, 'Brother João, brother João! If you spend all your time stuck with old papers and young wenches, you'll burst!'

'And what's happening here? How's the election going?'

'The election's set for October, the beginning of October. Apart from that, no interest anywhere. Gouveia's at the seaside, Manuel Duarte's looking after the grape-harvest. I myself am bored, dull, lifeless and without any appetite even.'

'I'm coming to you for dinner and I've invited Videirinha along.'

'I know. Cousin Maria's just told me—she dropped in at the Tower for a moment . . . She's at *Feitosa* with Dona Ana.'

For a moment he spoke about Cousin Maria's intimacy at *Feitosa* and felt tempted to open his heart there and then on the roadside about the unexpected romance that had blossomed. But he did not dare! He felt an embarrassed shyness—a sort of shame as if he were lusting after all poor Lucena's remains—both his constituency and his widow.

Then, talking about Alentejo and brother João (who had told a lot of boring old tales about the genealogy of the Ramires), they made their way from Portela to the Tower with the intention of prolonging their walk as far as Bravais. But at the Tower, Gonçalo stopped to warn Rosa of the two unexpected guests, both of whom wielded a fork most competently. They went in by the orchard gate, where a thin trickle of water was dribbling among the irrigation ditches. At the Nobleman's merry shouts, Rosa hurried out, wiping her hands on her apron. What? Two guests? Even with four, and the hungriest, there would be more than enough, thank the dear Lord! That very afternoon she had bought a basket of sardines from a woman from the coast, great fat ones that were a treat. Titó immediately insisted on an enormous fried dish of eggs and sardines. The two friends were crossing the yard when Gonçalo noticed Bento, seated astride a bench by the trellis in front of a bowl, enthusiastically cleaning a carved silver knob which emerged from a towel rolled round it like a sheath.

'What's that the top of, Bento? All wrapped up like that?' Bento slowly shook out a whip from the twisted towel, a long, dark whip with three sharp edges, keen as a rapier.

'You didn't know about it, did you, sir? It was in the attic. I was raking around there this afternoon because of a litter of kittens, and behind a trunk I found some ornamental spurs and this weapon.'

Gonçalo studied the solid silver head of the handle and the fine switch which hummed as he twitched it.

'Splendid whip, eh, Titó? Sharp as a dagger. And old, very old, like my coat-of-arms . . . What the devil's it made of? Whale?'

'Hippopotamus. A terrible weapon. Could kill a man . . . Brother João has one, but with a metal handle . . . Could kill a man!'

'Right,' Gonçalo closed the subject. 'Clean it and put it in my room, Bento! It'll be my war whip!'

At the orchard gate, they met Pereira da Riosa with a drill jacket slipped round his shoulders. Very soon, on Michaelmas Day, Pereira would be taking over cultivation of the land belonging to the Tower. Gonçalo laughed and joked, as he pointed out to Titó the famous farmer. That was the man! There was the great man who was preparing to turn the Tower into a splendid stretch of cornfields and vineyards and vegetable-gardens! Pereira scratched his thin beard.

'And sink good money in it too! Still, something you take pleasure in is worth paying a bit for. And the Nobleman is landlord, and he deserves to have land that delights the eyes.'

'Oh, Senhor Pereira!' thundered Titó. 'Then don't forget to look after the melons. It's a real disgrace! You never get a good melon at the Tower!'

'Well, next year, if God grants it, you'll taste a good melon at the Tower, sir!'

Gonçalo gave the capable farmer a hug, and hurried out to the road, resolved to tell Titó the whole story in the favourable solitude of the Bravais wood. But no sooner had they set out again than he was constrained by the same embarrassment, and he almost feared the information Titó, so stern a man, with such strict moral values, might give him. Their long tour round Bravais came to an end without Gonçalo disclosing his secret. Twilight had descended, soft and warm, when they returned, discussing the fishing of shad in the Guadiana River.

Outside the gate of the Tower, Videirinha was waiting, plucking the strings of his guitar in the shade of the poplars. As the night was close, not a breath of wind stirring, they dined on the verandah with two lighted lamps. As he unfolded his napkin, Titó red-faced and slumped in his chair, declared that 'thanks to the Lord of Health, he had a good thirst!' He and Gonçalo performed their usual feats with fork and glass. When Bento served coffee, an enormous, shining, full moon was rising at the far end of the dark garden, behind the hills of Valverde. Gonçalo, sunk in a wicker chair, lit his cigar blissfully. All the tedium and uncertainties of the past weeks fell from his soul like burnt ash being gently flicked away. He was thinking less of the softness of the night than of the renewed suavity of his own life, when he exclaimed,

'Well, now, gentlemen, this is delightful!'

Videirinha, after a brief cigarette, picked up his guitar again. Across the grounds, sections of whitewashed wall, a stretch of road more open than the rest, and the water of the great reservoir shone in the moonlight which fell upon the hills; and the quietness of the wood, of the clarity, and of the night, filtered into the soul like a soothing caress. Titó and Gonçalo tried the famous Muscatel brandy, a precious antique of the Tower, as they sat listening in silent rapture to Videirinha who had withdrawn to the back of the verandah where he was engulfed in shadows. Never had that excellent singer plucked his strings with more tender inspiration. Even the fields, the tilted sky, the full moon over the hill tops, listened to the complaints of the Fado of Areosa. In the dark, under the verandah, the sound of Rosa clearing her throat, the muffled steps of the servants, the soft laugh of a girl, the flapping of a setter's ears—were like the presence of persons gently attracted by the beautiful music.

So the night went on, and the moon climbed the sky in solitary splendour. Tító, prostrated by the feast, had dropped off. As always, by way of conclusion, Videirinha enthusiastically attacked the Fado of the Ramires:

> 'Who can see you without a shiver,
> Tower of Santa Ireneia,
> So dark and still and silent,
> On nights of the full moon . . .'

Then he broke into a new verse, which he had been lovingly working on all week, based on an erudite note by Father Soeiro. It was about the glory of Paio Ramires, Master of the Temple—whom Pope Innocent and Queen Branca of Castile and all the Princes of Christendom had beseeched to arm himself and hasten to liberate St Louis, King of France, a captive in the lands of Egypt:

> 'For only in Paio Ramires
> Does the world feel there's a chance.
> 'Won't he gather together his knights
> And save the King of France?'

Even Gonçalo was interested in this ancestor and his adventure, accompanying the song in a wavering tremolo, his arm raised high:

> 'Won't he gather together his knights
> And save the King of France?'

At the loudest note in the chorus, Tító opened his eye-lids, and dragging his enormous body out of the sofa, declared that he must be making his way back to Vila Clara.

'I'm worn out! All that journey and not a wink of sleep since four o'clock yesterday morning when I left Cidedelhe . . . By Jove, I'm like that Greek king—I'd give a *cruzado*[1] for a donkey!'

Then Gonçalo, encouraged by the brandy, also got up, almost gaily resolved,

'Oh, Tító, before you go, come in here a minute! I want to talk to you about a certain matter!'

He picked up one of the lamps and entered the dining-room, where the smell of magnolias dying in a vase filled the air. There, without any preparation, with decision in his eyes fixed upon Tító,

---

[1] *Cruzado*: ancient Portuguese gold coin.

who was slowly following him, still stretching himself, he blurted out,

'Oh, Titó, listen and be frank. You used to go to *Feitosa* a lot. What do you think of Dona Ana ?'

Titó, who had woken up as if a bomb had exploded, contemplated Gonçalo in amazement.

'What a thing to ask! Why on earth do you ask ?'

Gonçalo hurried on, anxious to be reassured.

'Listen! I haven't any secrets from you. There have been some little talks these last few weeks, and meetings . . . Anyway, to cut a long story short, if I were to think of marrying Dona Ana some time in the future, I don't think she would refuse. You used to go to *Feitosa*. You know . . . What sort of girl is she ?'

Titó crossed his arms indignantly.

'So you're thinking of marrying Dona Ana ?'

'I'm not marrying her right now, man. I'm not going to the Church this very night. I just want some information . . . And who could give me more correct information than you, who is my friend and who knows her well ?'

Titó did not uncross his arms and raised his severe, honest face to the Nobleman of the Tower.

'Do you really mean that you are thinking of marrying Dona Ana, you, Gonçalo Mendes Ramires ?'

Gonçalo gave an impatient shrug.

'Oh, if you're going to start on about the aristocracy and Paio Ramires . . .'

Titó almost shouted at him with indignation.

'Aristocracy! The fact is a good man like you doesn't consider marrying a creature like her! . . . Aristocracy ? Yes! But aristocracy of the heart and soul!'

Gonçalo was silent, impressed by this speech. Then, with a serenity achieved by great effort, he deduced,

'Right! You obviously know other things about her . . . I only know she is pretty and rich; I also know that she is serious, because there's never been the faintest murmur about her behaviour either here or in Lisbon; these are qualities that recommend a woman for marriage . . . Now you say one can't marry ·her. Therefore you know something else . . . Tell me.'

Then it was Titó's turn to grow silent, standing motionless before

232

the Nobleman, as if a cord had caught and bound him. Finally, sighing, with an enormous effort he said,

'You didn't call me to give testimony . . . On principle, without any explanation, you ask if you can marry this woman. And I, too, without any explanation, on principle say you can't . . . What the deuce more do you want?'

Gonçalo exclaimed in annoyance,

'What do I want? For heaven's sake, Titó! Suppose I were madly in love with Dona Ana, or that I had a particular interest in marrying her . . . I'm not, and I haven't, but just suppose! In that case a friend wouldn't put a friend off an action he's so keen on performing without giving a reason, some proof . . .'

Cornered, Titó lowered his head and scratched it desperately. Then, in a cowardly manner, to get out of the awkward position he was in, he postponed the argument.

'Look, Gonçalo, I'm worn out. You're not off to the Church just yet, are you? And she's obviously not, with her other husband still not cold in his grave. We'll talk tomorrow.'

Two enormous strides and he pushed open the verandah door and shouted to Videirinha:

'Time to go, Videira! Get a move on because I haven't slept since Cidadelhe.'

Videirinha, who was carefully preparing himself a cold 'grog', emptied his glass in a hurry and picked up his precious guitar. Gonçalo did not detain them, but stood silently rubbing his hands together, annoyed by Titó's stubborn and unfriendly refusal to speak. Like shadows they crossed a drawing-room where a Chinese lacquer spinet slept, neglected since the Ramires of the eighteenth century. On the landing of the stairs which led to the little green door, Gonçalo picked up a candlestick to light their way. Titó lit his cigar at the candle. His hairy hand trembled.

'Right, then . . . I'll come along tomorrow, Gonçalo.'

'Whenever you want, Titó.'

There was such contempt in the Nobleman's dry assent that Titó hesitated on the narrow steps which he was blocking. Finally he moved heavily down the steps.

Videirinha, who had already reached the road, contemplated the sky, the luminous serenity.

'What a lovely night, sir!'

233

'Lovely, Videirinha . . . And thank you. You played divinely tonight.'

Gonçalo had entered the picture-gallery and was just putting down the candlestick, when he heard beneath the open verandah Tító's gusty voice boom out:

'Oh, Gonçalo! Come down here a minute.'

Gonçalo slipped down the steps eagerly. Beyond the poplars, in the moonlight on the road, Videirinha was tuning his guitar. No sooner had the Nobleman's face emerged in the bright doorway than Tító, who was waiting there with his hat pushed to the back of his head, burst out,

'Oh, Gonçalo, you were annoyed . . . This is silly! I don't want any unpleasantness between us. So I'll tell you! You can't marry this woman, because she's had a lover. I don't know whether she had any others before or after that one. There's no craftier nor more hypocritical creature alive. Don't come asking me any more questions now. But there's no doubt that she's had at least one lover. I am telling you this, and you know I never lie!'

He turned abruptly towards the road again, his powerful shoulders bent. Gonçalo did not move from the stone steps, in front of the silent poplars, as motionless as himself. A few brief words had passed, irremediable words, in the soft silence of the night and the moon—and there was the lofty dream which he had built about Dona Ana and her beauty and her two *hundred* contos, flung into the mud! He went slowly up the steps and entered the drawing-room again. Above the tall flame of the candle, from a dim panel, a face had awoken, a dry, yellowed face with an arrogant, black moustache, which bent forward as if watching and listening. Far away, Videirinha scattered over the sleeping fields the naïve verses celebrating the incomparable Glory of the illustrious House:

> 'For only in Paio Ramires
> Does the world feel there's a chance.
> Won't he gather together his knights
> And save the King of France?'

10

GONÇALO PACED HIS ROOM until the early hours, brooding over the bitter certainty that always, throughout his life (almost since his time at the College of S Fiel), he had never been spared humiliations. All of them had derived from simple enough plans—as safe for any other man as flight for a bird, and only for him frustrated by pain or shame or loss! When he had entered upon life, he had enthusiastically chosen a confidant, a brother, whom he had brought into the quiet intimacy of the Tower—and immediately this man had lightheartedly taken possession of Gracinha's heart and then outrageously abandoned her! Then he conceives the normal enough idea of entering politics—and chance compels him to surrender himself and accept the influence of this same man, now a powerful authority, who had been loathed and jeered at by him throughout those years of disdain. Then he opens the door of *Cunhais* to this friend, now accepted once again in their midst, confident in his sister's seriousness and pride, and the sister at once gives herself to her former deceiver, without the least struggle, the very first afternoon that she finds herself with him in the favourable shade of a summer-house! Now he thinks of marrying a woman who is offering him a great fortune and beauty—and a companion from Vila Clara comes by and whispers: 'The woman you have chosen, Gonçalinho, is a slut with hordes of lovers!' This woman certainly did not love him with a noble, firm love! But he had decided to place his uncertain fate in her beautiful hands quite comfortably—and then once more, with brutal regularity, comes the usual humiliation. Really Destiny was chastising him with excessive rancour!

'Why?' murmured Gonçalo, miserably removing his coat. 'So much deception in such a short life . . . Why? Poor me!'

He fell upon his vast bed as if into a tomb, and hid his face in the pillow with a sigh, a sigh full of pity for so frustrated and helpless a fate. He remembered Videirinha's proud verse sung to the guitar that very evening:

> 'Ancient house of Ramires
> Honour and flower of Portugal!'

How the flower had faded! What a paltry honour! What a contrast was the last Gonçalo, stuck in his little hole in Santa Ireneia, to those great ancestors extolled by Videirinha—all of them, if History and Legend did not lie, enjoying such glorious and triumphant lives! No! He had not even inherited the quality possessed by all of them throughout the centuries—natural courage. His father had still been a fearless Ramires, who, in the famous pilgrimage of Riosa, had advanced with a sunshade against three cocked rifles. But he . . . There, in the privacy of the darkened room, he could give vent freely to this bitter thought—he had been born with a flaw, the most discreditable flaw—this irremediable weakness of his which, in the face of any danger, any threat, any shadow, forced him to retreat, to flee . . . Flee from Casco. Flee from a rascal with fair side-whiskers who had insulted him first on the road and then in a tavern, and for no reason at all, merely through arrogance and to show off. Ah, base flesh, so easily frightened!

And his soul . . . In the silent murkiness of his room he could face the painful fact: the same weakness constrained his soul! It was this weakness that abandoned him to any influence, that whipped him up like a dry leaf, the plaything of any little breeze. Because one afternoon Cousin Maria's sharp eyes melt and she advises him from behind her fan to take an interest in Dona Ana, he, immediately, panting with expectation, builds on Dona Ana's fortune and beauty a lofty tower of happiness and luxury. And the election? This wretched election? Who had pushed him towards it and towards the indecent reconciliation with Cavaleiro, and the resulting troubles? Gouveia, with a few shrewd remarks murmured over his muffler as they walked from Ramos's shop to the corner where the Post Office was! But worse! Even in the Tower, he was automatically ruled by Bento, who imposed his tastes upon him, his diets and walks and opinions and ties! A man with such a character, however intelligent he might be, is an inert lump which the world is for ever moulding into various and contrary forms. João Gouveia had made a servile candidate of him. Manuel Duarte could make a vile drunkard of him. Bento could easily persuade him to tie round his neck, not a silk tie, but a leather horse-collar! How wretched! Yet it was Man's will that counted—only in the exercise of the will does enjoyment in life reside. Because, if a carefully applied will encounters submission, there is the pleasure of serene domination;

if it encounters resistance, there is the greater pleasure of an interesting battle. The only state which provides no strong, virile pleasure is that inertia which lets itself be dragged mutely along in wax-like silence and passivity. But he, descended from so many men famous for their strong will, had he not buried somewhere in his Being, warm and dormant like a hot coal beneath dead ashes, some spark of this hereditary energy?... Perhaps! But never in all his stupid and thwarted life in Santa Ireneia had the spark burst into life, into an intense and useful flame. No! Poor Gonçalo! Even in the movements of his soul, where most men achieve pure liberty, he always suffered the oppression of hostile Fate!

With another sigh, he snuggled further into the bedclothes. He could not sleep, night was ending and the lacquered clock in the corridor struck a hollow four o'clock. Then, through closed lids, in the confused exhaustion of so many tangled sorrows, Gonçalo saw, in the murkiness of the room, standing out palely in the darkness, faces passing slowly by ...

They were very old faces, with very old beards no longer in fashion, with scars made by ferocious weapons, some still flushed, as if in the fury of battle, others smiling majestically, as if participating in the pomp of some celebration—all of them magnified by the sublime habit of commanding and conquering. Gonçalo, peering above the edge of the sheet, recognized in these faces the real features of ancient members of the Ramires family, either actually seen by him in dim portraits, or imagined by him, as he had imagined Tructesindo, in accordance with the severity and splendour of his deeds.

Leisurely, more alive, they grew out of the shadows that pulsated thickly, as if peopled. Now their bodies emerged too, great robust bodies covered with rusty coats-of-mail; enclosed in armour of flashing steel; enveloped in dark mantles with unruly folds; clothed in magnificent doublets on which shone the precious stones of necklaces and belts—and all armed, with every arm mentioned in History, from the spiked Gothic club made from the root of an oak-tree to the ceremonial sword with its gold and silk ribbons.

Unafraid, propped on his bolster, Gonçalo had no doubt of the marvellous reality before him! Yes—these were his Ramires ancestors, his formidable, historic ancestors, who had hastened from their scattered tombs to gather in the ancient house of Santa Ireneia, nine centuries old, and to collect round his bed, round the bed in which he had been born, like some majestic Assembly of his resurrected race. He even recognized some of the most valiant ones who now, with his constant reading of Uncle Duarte's poem, and Videirinha's faithful rendering of the fado, were constantly in his mind's eye.

That one over there, with the white tunic, the whole breast of which was filled by a red cross, was surely Gutierres Ramires, the Overseas Ramires, as when he ran from his tent to storm the walls of Jerusalem. Another, a very old and very handsome man stretching out his arm, he guessed was Egas Ramires, refusing to welcome to his pure home the King, Don Fernando, and the adulterous Leonor! That one, with the fair, curly beard, who sang as he waved the royal banner of Castile, who but Diogo Ramires, the Minstrel, still jubilant from that radiant morning at Aljubarrota? Before the uncertain pallor of the mirror trembled the light scarlet plumes of the morion of Paio Ramires, who had armed himself to save St Louis, King of France. Swaying slightly, as if on the docile waves of a conquered sea, Rui Ramires smiled at the English men-of-war which, before the prow of his flagship, were submissively striking flag to Portugal. And leaning on the bed-post, stood Paulo Ramires, standard-bearer of the King on the fatal fields of Alcacer, his helmet gone, his cuirass broken, bending over Gonçalo his fair young face which had the sweet, grave look of a fond grandfather.

Gonçalo understood by that look of solicitous tenderness from the most poetic of the Ramires that all his forebears loved him—and that they had come from the darkness of their various tombs to watch over him and help him in his weakness. With a long groan, he pushed back the bed-clothes and unburdened himself, painfully explained to his resurrected ancestors the cursed Fate which oppressed him and which relentlessly piled upon his weary shoulders sorrow, humiliation and defeat! Suddenly a weapon flashed in the gloom, and a muffled voice cried, 'Grandson, dear grandson, take my never-broken lance! . . .' Then the handle of a bright sword touched his breast, while another grave voice encouraged him, 'Grandson, dear grandson, take this purest sword that fought in Ourique!' Then a battle-axe with a glittering blade fell upon the bolster, offered with words of reassurance: 'This axe, which destroyed the gates of Arzila, will never be destroyed! . . .'

Like shadows blown by a supernatural wind, all his formidable ancestors passed by, and proffered their weapons passionately—strong arms, all of them, well proven throughout History, ennobled in assaults against the Moors, in elaborate sieges of castles and towns, in splendid battles with the arrogant Castilians . . . All round the bed was a heroic glitter and a jangle of weapons. And all of them proudly shouted, 'Oh, grandson, take our arms and defeat your hostile Fate!' But Gonçalo, glancing with sorrowful eyes at the flickering shadows, replied, 'Oh, my ancestors, what's the good of your weapons if I lack your soul?'

He awoke very early, with a confused memory of a nightmare in which he had spoken to dead men; free of the laziness which usually detained him sluggishly among the pillows, he slipped on a dressing-gown and pushed open the windows. What a magnificent morning! A late September morning, soft and lustrous; not a cloud marred the vast, immaculate blue; the sun had already risen above the trees on the distant hill tops, diffusing an autumnal sweetness over all. But in spite of slowly inhaling the purity and brilliance, Gonçalo remained overshadowed—by the shadows of the night before, remaining within his oppressed soul like mist in a deep valley. It was with a sigh, wretchedly tugging his slippers, that he pulled the bell-pull. Bento was not long bringing the jug of hot water for Gonçalo to shave. Accustomed to the Nobleman's usual happy awakening, he was so surprised to see him wandering shrunken and silent about the room that he inquired if his master had had a bad night.

'Terrible!'

Bento immediately declared, with alacrity and reproach, that it was surely the Muscatel brandy that had upset him. Very sweet brandy that, very stimulating . . . All right for Sr Don António, who was a big, heavy man. But the Nobleman had a more nervous constitution, he should never touch that type of brandy. Or if he did, no more than half a glass.

Gonçalo raised his head, surprised to find, so early in the day, so flagrant an example of that dominance over him that everyone arrogated—and of which he had so deeply complained throughout that bitter night! Here was Bento laying down the law, rationing his portion of brandy! In fact, just then, Bento was insisting,

'You had more than three glasses, you know, sir. That's no good for you . . . And I was to blame, too—I should have taken the bottle away . . .'

Furious at such a blatant piece of despotism, the Nobleman of the Tower rebelled,

'Don't lay down so many laws, man! I'll drink as much brandy as I want!'

At the same time he tried the water in the jug with his finger-tips.

'This water's lukewarm!' he cried. 'I'm sick of telling you! I need boiling water to shave.'

Bento gravely dipped his fingers in the water, too.

'This water's almost boiling . . . You don't need water hotter than that even for shaving.'

Gonçalo glared at Bento in fury. What! More objections! More laws!

'Go and get some more water immediately! When I ask for hot water I want it boiling. Confound it! "Don't do this and don't do that!" I don't want any moralizing, I want obedience!'

Bento looked at Gonçalo, amazement puffing up his face. Then, slowly, with offended dignity, he pushed open the door and took away the jug. Gonçalo was already regretting his violence. Poor fellow—it wasn't Bento's fault if his life was ruined and barren! In such an ancient house, the tradition of ancient valets did not come amiss. Bento was a scrupulous reproduction of them, with his testiness and loyalty! His influence and freedom of speech was fitting—he deserved such things for his long and well-tried devotion.

Bento, still pink and swollen, returned with the steaming jug. Gonçalo said gently, to pacify him,

'A lovely day, isn't it, Bento?'

The old man grunted, still sulky,

'Very nice.'

Gonçalo soaped his face quickly, impatient to re-establish the old relationship with Bento, resume the old affectionate authority. Finally, even gentler, almost humbly, he remarked,

'Well, if you think it's a good day, I'll have a ride before lunch. What do you think? Perhaps it will improve my nerves . . . You're right, you know, that brandy didn't do me any good . . . Bento, be good enough to shout down to Joaquim and have the mare saddled immediately. A good gallop will surely calm me down . . . And now some nice, really hot water for my bath. Hot water is good for calming me, too. That's why I always need really hot water, really boiling. You and your old-fashioned ideas . . . All the doctors say so, you know: hot water's the thing for your health, really hot—sixty degrees!'

After a quick bath, while he dressed, he opened his heart even more intimately to the old valet, and explained the source of his sorrows:

'Ah, Bento, Bento. What I really need to calm me isn't a horse-ride but a long journey . . . My soul is heavy, man! And I'm sick of this eternal Vila Clara, too, and this eternal Oliveira. A lot of scandalmongering and disloyalty. I need a bigger land, greater distractions.'

Bento, already reconciled, affectionately reminded his master that he would shortly be enjoying a delightful distraction in Lisbon, in the House . . .'

'Heaven knows if I'll be going to the House, man! I don't know anything about it, everything goes wrong . . . Lisbon indeed! What I need is a really long trip, to Hungary, to Russia, to countries where there are still adventures.'

Bento smiled with a superior air at his fancy. Handing the Nobleman his grey velveteen jacket, he remarked,

'Actually, it does seem there's no lack of adventure in Russia. The *Século* says the whip rules there. But adventures, sir, you'll meet with along any road . . . What about your father, sir, God preserve his soul? It was just down there in front of the gate that he had that row with Dr Avelino da Riosa, and he whipped him and got a dagger in his arm.'

Gonçalo put on his light skin gloves, looking at himself in the mirror.

'Poor papa—he hadn't much luck either . . . And talking of whips, Bento, give me that hippopotamus-hide whip that you cleaned yesterday. It seems a good weapon.'

*   *   *

At the gate, the Nobleman of the Tower set off aimlessly on his mare, at an indolent pace along the usual road to Bravais. But at Casal Novo, where two youngsters were playing ball under the oak-trees, he thought of visiting the Viscount of Rio Manso. The company of so serene and generous an old gentleman would surely calm his nerves. If he invited him to lunch, he would allay his sorrows by visiting the renowned *Varandinha Farm* and courting 'the Rosebud'.

Gonçalo could only vaguely remember that the terrace of *Varandinha* overlooked the road lined with poplars, somewhere between the hamlet of Cerda and the scattered village of Canta Pedra. He took the old path that leads down from the oaks of Casal Novo to the valley, between Avelã hill top and the ruins of the Ribadais Monastery, on the historic soil where Lopo de Baião defeated the vassals of Lourenço Ramires. The path wound along, sometimes concealed between hedges, sometimes between rough, loose, stone walls, devoid of beauty and wearisome; but the honeysuckle gave off a sweet fragrance in the hedges among the ripe blackberries; the cool silence gained added coolness and charm from the passing wings of birds; and the radiant blue of the tranquil sky was such that something of its radiance and tranquillity penetrated the soul. Gonçalo, already less gloomy, did not hurry; it was only striking nine o'clock on the Bravais Church when he had passed through Casal Novo; after skirting a meadow with poor grass, he stopped leisurely to light a cigar, near the old stone bridge which crosses the Donas Stream. Almost dry after the drought, the dark water trickled with effort beneath the large, flat leaves of the waterlilies, between the reeds which hindered its flow. Further on, at the edge of a meadow in the shelter of a little poplar grove, gleamed the white stones of a washing-place. On the other bank, inside an old boat which had run aground, a boy and a girl were deep in conversation, two bunches of lavender forgotten in their laps. Gonçalo smiled at the idyll; then he had a surprise, discovering, roughly carved on the corner of the bridge, his coat-of-arms—an enormous goshawk stretching its fierce claws. Perhaps these lands had once belonged to his Family; or one of his beneficent ancestors had built the bridge for the safety of men and cattle over a torrent that had then been deeper. Who knows? Perhaps it was Tructesindo, in pious memory of Lourenço Ramires, conquered and made captive on the banks of that very river!

After the bridge, the path rose between harvested fields. The stacks, full and heavy, gleamed yellow in that year of plenty. Further off, from the low roofs of a small village, wisps of smoke rose, to dissolve immediately in the radiant sky. Gradually, Gonçalo felt

242

that all his melancholy thoughts, like those distant wisps of smoke, were fleeing from his soul, to vanish in the lustrous blue . . . A flock of partidges took wing from the stubble. Gonçalo galloped towards them, shouting and waving his strong, hippopotamus-hide whip which hummed like a fine blade.

Soon a path wound, skirting a grove of cork-trees, then plunged down between clumps of blackberries and great stones cropping out of the dusty earth; at the end, the sun sparkled on a freshly whitewashed wall. It was a one-storey house, with a low door between two glass windows, recent repairs to the tiled roof, and a flower-bed shaded by an immense, dark fig-tree. At one corner it was joined by a low wall of loose stone, prolonged by a hedge where, further on, an old gate opened on to the shade of an arbour. In the large space in front lay pieces of masonry and a pile of timber; then there was a road, smooth-surfaced and well maintained, which seemed to Gonçalo like the Ramilde road. Then beyond that, as far as a distant pine wood, swept plains and meadows.

On a bench near the door, with a rifle leaning against the wall, a heavy-built lad in a green wool cap sat and pensively stroked the nose of a setter. Gonçalo stopped.

'Excuse me . . . Do you happen to know which is the best way to the Viscount of Rio Manso's farm, *Varandinha* ?'

The boy raised a tanned face with a thin moustache, and fumbled diffidently with his cap.

'To Rio Manso's farm . . . Go along the road till you get to the stone-quarry, then take the next turning left, keeping close to the lea . . .'

But at that moment a huge fellow with fair side-whiskers appeared at the door, in shirt-sleeves and with a silk cummerbund round his waist. Gonçalo recognized with a start the hunter who had insulted him on the road to Nacejas, and who had whistled at him in Pintainho's tavern. The man glanced arrogantly at the Nobleman. Then, leaning one hand against the doorpost, he scoffed at the boy.

'Oh, Manuel, what are you doing giving him these directions? This path's not for asses!'

Gonçalo felt the pallor which stole over him—and all the blood beating in his heart, in a tumultuous confusion of both fear and rage. Another insult, from the same man, and without any provocation! He pressed his knees against his mount in order to gallop away. Trembling, he cried out in an effort which nearly choked him:

'Your behaviour's outrageous! This is the third time! I'm not the sort of man to create a disturbance in the road . . . But remember I know you, and you won't get away without being taught a good lesson . . .'

The man swiftly picked up a short staff and jumped into the road, facing the mare, his whiskers bristling, with a laugh of pure challenge.

'Here I am then! Let's have the lesson . . . You're not passing here, you sh . . . Ramires! . . .'

A mist clouded the Nobleman's horrified eyes. Suddenly, in an instinctive impulse, as if driven by a gust of pride and force which issued wildly from the depths of his being, he urged his mare to leap madly forward. He didn't even understand! The staff was raised. The mare reared up, her head furiously erect. Gonçalo caught a glimpse of the man's hand, dark and huge, grabbing his bridle.

Then, standing up in his stirrups, above the huge hand, he lashed out with the whistling hippopotamus-hide whip, catching the big fellow on one side of his face with such a stinging blow from its sharp edge that his ear dangled loose amid spurting blood. The man staggered back with a roar. Gonçalo fell on him again with another assault and another terrible blow which caught him on the mouth and tore it open, surely breaking some teeth, and knocked him howling to the ground. The mare's hooves trampled the fat thighs which lay in its path—and leaning over from his saddle, Gonçalo continued to wield his whip, desperately cutting open both face and neck until the body lay slumped and as if lifeless, streams of dark blood soaking its shirt.

A shot echoed across the open space! Gonçalo, wheeling round in his saddle, saw the dark boy, his rifle still raised, and smoking, but already hesitating in terror.

'Cur!'

He urged the mare forward, his whip held high. The boy ran nimbly across the open space in alarm, so as to scramble over the hedge and escape across the fields of harvested corn.

'Cur! You cur!' yelled Gonçalo.

In his confusion the boy stumbled over a piece of timber. He was getting up when the Nobleman caught him a blow with his whip on his neck, which was instantly bathed in blood. Stumbling forward, his arms stretched uncertainly before him, he fell and crashed against the edge of a post, and more blood spurted from his head. Then Gonçalo, panting, reined in his mare. Both men lay motionless! Good Lord! Were they dead? Blood streamed from both of them over the dry ground. The Nobleman of the Tower felt a brutal joy. But a horrified cry came from the flower-bed.

'Ai! They've killed my boy!'

An old man was running from the gate, head low, keeping close to the hedge, in the direction of the door of the house. So skilfully did the Nobleman jockey his mare to stop him that the old man collided with the animal's chest which was heaving and covered with sweat and foam. In the face of the nervous animal pawing the ground, and Gonçalo standing in the stirrups, his face suffused, ready to bring down the whip—the old man fell on his knees in terror and cried in consternation:

'Oh, your Lordship, don't harm me, for the sake of your father Ramires' soul!'

Gonçalo held him there for a moment, trembling, in supplication beneath his inflexible, blazing eyes; he delighted in those tough-skinned hands which were raised to plead his mercy and invoked the name of Ramires, once again feared, once again endowed with its former, heroic prestige. Then restraining his mare, he answered,

'This wretched boy of yours fired his gun at me!... And you don't look too trustworthy, either! What were you running into the house for? To fetch another gun?'

The old man opened wide his arms in desperation, offering his chest as witness to his honesty.

'Oh, your Lordship! I haven't even a staff in the house! May God help me and save my boy!'

But Gonçalo was still suspicious. If he now set off down the Ramilde road, the old man could quite easily run into the cottage, pick up another gun and fire it treacherously. Then, his wits sharpened by the battle, he devised a stratagem which was proof against any of the old man's wiles. He even smiled to himself, remembering 'plans of war' made by Don Garcia Viegas, 'The Wise One'.

'Walk ahead of me, along the road, and keep to the right!'

The old man did not move, but remained where he knelt, terrified.

He beat his heavy hands against his thighs, in an anguish which stupefied him.

'Oh, your Lordship! Oh, your Lordship! Leave my boy here unconscious?'

'The boy's only stunned, he's already moving . . . And the other scoundrel, too . . . Start marching!'

At this incontestable order, the old man, after slowly dusting his knees, began to move along the road, stooping a little, in front of the mare, like a captive, his long arms swinging, and grumbling in a sort of hoarse whisper, 'Ai, how troubles start! Ai! Christ Almighty! What a catastrophe!' Every now and again he stopped, gazing at Gonçalo with a black look of fear and hatred. But immediately his guard urged him on with a 'Forward!' And on he marched. A little further on, where stood a cross in memory of the murdered Abbot Paguim, Gonçalo noticed a broad track called Miller's Lane which led to the Bravais road. It was down there that the old man turned, and, fearing the isolation of the track, and that Gonçalo was driving him away from trodden paths in order to kill him more easily he burst out: 'Ai, this is the end of my life! Ai, Holy Mother, this is the end of my life!' He did not stop wailing, staggering and stumbling, until they emerged on to the high road between its steep slopes covered with wild broom. Then suddenly, seized by another fear, the man turned abruptly round, clasping his hands to his cap.

'Oh sir, your Lordship isn't arresting me, is he?'

'Keep going! And now run! Because we're going to trot!'

The mare trotted, and the old man ran clumsily, slackly, puffing like a bellows in a smithy. After a mile of this, Gonçalo stopped, tired of his captive and the slow pace. Moreover, before the man could run back to the house, get hold of a weapon and return to take his revenge, he could have galloped back to the Tower! So he shouted, with a stern look,

'Halt! Now you can go back . . . But first, what's your place called?'

'Grainha, your Lordship.'

'And what's your name? And the boy's?'

The old man hesitated, his mouth agape.

'I'm João, and my boy's Manuel . . . Manuel Domingues, your Lordship.'

'You're lying, of course. And the other rascal, with the fair hair?'

This time the answer came quickly.

'That's Ernesto of Nacejas, the bully of Nacejas, known as the Kiss-catcher, who's led my boy astray . . .'

'Right! Well, tell the two scoundrels that they struck me and fired at me, and that thrashing's not all they'll be getting. They'll have to answer to the law now. And don't think it won't reach them: it will! Now clear off!'

From the middle of the road, Gonçalo watched the old man hurrying off, forcing his exhausted steps and wiping off the sweat pouring down his face. Then he galloped off along the customary road to the Tower.

He set off in ecstasy, galloping with a wild joy that plunged him into fancy and daydreams. He had the sublime feeling of galloping over heights, on a legendary charger, magnificently increased in stature, touching the shining clouds . . . Beneath him, in the cities, men recognized in him a real Ramires, a Ramires of History, one of those that destroyed towers, that changed the shape of kingdoms— and an astonished murmur arose, that it was the wake of his great ancestors passing by. And they were right! They were right! Because only that morning, when he left the Tower, he wouldn't have dared approach a ruffian brandishing a staff at him! . . . Then suddenly, in the solitude of that cottage, when the brute with the fair side-whiskers hurled his foul insults at him—something indefinable had been released within him and overflowed, had filled every vein with fiery blood, and had stiffened every nerve with force and dexterity, and every pore of his skin was instilled with contempt for pain, and indued his soul with indomitable courage . . . And now he was returning, like a new man, suddenly supremely virile, freed at last from the shadow that had so painfully darkened his life, the vile, sluggish shadow of fear! Because he felt that now, even if all the ruffians in Nacejas attacked him, brandishing their staffs—this indefinable thing inside him there, would again be released, and would spur him on, with every vein swollen, every nerve tense, to a delicious engagement in battle! At last he was a man! When, in Vila Clara, Manuel Duarte or Tító, his chest thrust out, recounted their exploits, he would no longer have to cower in his chair and roll his cigarette—cowered and silent, not merely because of the pitiful lack of exploits to recount, but still more of the humiliating memory of his failures. He galloped and galloped, furiously gripping the end of his whip as if for still more glorious assaults. After Bravais, he galloped even faster when he caught sight of the Tower. Strangely enough it suddenly seemed as if his Tower were more completely *his*, and some new affinity, founded in courage and glory, made him more completely master of his Tower!

*　　*　　*

As if to welcome Gonçalo the more worthily, the great gate, generally closed, presented a triumphal entrance with its two heavy doors wide open. He spurred forward his mare to the centre of the yard and shouted,

'Oh, Joaquim! Oh, Manuel! Hey there! One of you!'

Joaquim emerged from the stables, his sleeves rolled up, and a sponge in one hand.

'Oh, Joaquim, quick! Saddle Rocilho and go quickly to a place on the Ramilde road, called Grainha . . . I've had a terrible fight there! I fear I've finished off two men . . . I left them in a pool of blood! Don't tell anyone you come from the Tower, or they may attack you! But find out what happened, if they're dead or not! . . . And hurry, hurry!'

Joaquim, stunned, went back into the dark stables. From above, from one of the verandahs of the corridor, there came horrified exclamations.

'Oh, Gonçalo, what's happened? Heavens above! What's happened?'

It was Barrolo. Without dismounting, not even surprised to see Barrolo there, Gonçalo immediately shouted up, in agitation, to the verandah, the whole story of the fracas. A scoundrel had insulted him . . . Then another had fired at him . . . And both of them had been struck down under the mare's hooves, in a pool of blood . . .

Barrolo left the verandah—and in another moment made his way nervously down to the yard, his short arms swinging. But how had it happened? Gonçalo, dismounting, trembling now from weariness and emotion, gave further details . . . It was on the Ramilde road! A ruffian had insulted him! He had torn the mouth of one, and severed his ear . . . Then the other one, a boy, had fired a rifle. He had dashed over and caught him such a blow that it had laid him out as if dead over a lump of stone . . .

248

'A blow?'

'With this whip, Barrolo! A terrible weapon!... Titó was right! I'm lost if I don't carry this whip.'

Barrolo gazed in confusion at the whip. Yes, it was indeed stained with blood. Then Gonçalo looked at the whip, at the blood... Blood! Men's blood! Fresh blood, that he had drawn!... Then pity mingled with his pride and he grew pale.

'How terrible! How terrible!'

He peered at his suit, at his boots, aghast at the spots of blood which spattered him. Lord above, it was true! There was blood on his leggings!... He felt an immediate desire to undress and wash, and hurried up the stairs with Barrolo wiping away the sweat and stammering, 'Just imagine such a thing! And suddenly like that! Right in the road!' But in the corridor, rushing up from the kitchen, appeared Gracinha, very pale, followed by Rosa, who plunged her fingers in between her scarf and her hair in mute terror.

'What happened, Gonçalo? Jesus, what happened?'

Then, discovering Gracinha beside him, in the Tower, at this magnificent moment for his pride, after overcoming such a fearsome danger, Gonçalo forgot André, and the gazebo and his humiliations, and in the embrace in which he enfolded her, in the passionate kisses which he bestowed upon that dear face, all his ill-humour dissolved into tenderness. With her clasped to his breast, he sighed gently like a tired child. Then, holding tight the two trembling hands with a slow, affectionate smile, his eyes still moist with confused emotions, with confused joy, he murmured,

'It was hellish, dear! A horrible affair, and I'm so peace-loving! Just imagine...'

As they walked along the corridor, he recommenced, for Gracinha, whose breast was heaving, and for Rosa, who was horror-stricken, the story of the encounter, the foul insult, the shot that had missed, the scoundrels who had been stung by the whip, and the old man, who had been marched along like a captive, moaning on the Ramilde road. Clasping her breast, as if about to faint, Gracinha murmured,

'Ai, Gonçalo! Suppose one of these men is dead!'

Barrolo, redder than a peony, shouted that such scoundrels richly deserved death! Even wounded as they were, they still merited a really long spell in Africa! Gouveia was the man! They must send to Vila Clara and let Gouveia know! . . . But heavy steps sounded over the floor—and there was Bento, who emerged before Gonçalo waving his arms in his anxiety.

'What happened, sir? . . . There's been some awful row, hasn't there?'

At the door of the study, where they had stopped, attentive once again, the story was repeated, for Bento now especially, who drank it in, with a slow smile of pleasure, growing and swelling, his small, moist eyes shining, as if he had shared in the triumph. At last he did triumph forcibly.

'It was the whip, sir! What helped you, sir, was the whip I gave you!'

It was true. Gonçalo, moved, hugged the old valet, who cried out excitedly to Rosa, Gracinha and Barrolo,

'Master put paid to the pair of them! . . . That whip would kill a man! . . . The poor devils are dead! . . . And it was the whip did it! It was the whip I gave the master!'

But Gonçalo now called for hot water to wash, to clean himself of the dust and sweat and blood . . . Bento ran out, still shouting along the corridor, and then down the stairs of the kitchen, 'That it was the whip, the whip that he had given the Master!' Gonçalo went into his room, accompanied by Barrolo. He put his hat on the marble-topped chest-of-drawers with a huge sigh of relief! It was the immense relief of finding himself, after so violent a morning, among sweet, accustomed things, treading his old blue carpet, brushing against the mahogany bed in which he had been born, inhaling the fresh air at the open windows, where the familiar shapes of the beech-trees waved their branches at him in greeting. With deep satisfaction he approached the mirror with its gilt columns, looked at himself over and over again, as if it were a new Gonçalo there, and so much greater, that he could see the extra breadth in the shoulders, and even a more virile thrust to his moustache.

It was only as he moved away from the mirror, bumping into Barrolo, that he felt a sudden curiosity.

'But Barrolo, how is it I find both of you at the Tower this morning?'

They had made up their minds yesterday, over tea. Gonçalo never appeared, never wrote . . . Gracinha had been brooding, restless. He, too, had been astonished at that disappearance after the basket of peaches. So, over tea, deciding that his pair needed a trot, too, he suggested to Gracinha, 'Shall we go to the Tower tomorrow? In the phaeton?

'Apart from which I need to talk to you, Gonçalo . . . I've been a bit worried lately.'

The Nobleman placed two cushions together on the divan, and settled himself there.

'How do you mean, worried? Why worried?'

Barrolo, his hands in the pockets of his flannel jacket which enveloped his broad hips, studied the flowers on the carpet disconsolately.

'It's so annoying. You can't trust anyone . . . Can't have any friends! . . .'

In a flash, Gonçalo imagined Cavaleiro and Gracinha rashly disclosing at *Cunhais*, as they had once done in the groves of the Tower, the emotion that governed them. And he foresaw poor Barrolo, assailed by suspicions and perhaps by intimate scenes which he had witnessed, unburdening himself. But the sublime emotion of his battle relegated to an inferior plane the cares that had oppressed him the day before: all the difficulties of life now suddenly appeared, in the exuberance of his newly acquired courage, as easy to overcome as insults from ruffians; and he did not become alarmed at the thought of such confidences from his brother-in-law, confident as he was that he could reassure that meek simpleton's soul. He even smiled lazily and asked,

'What's the matter, Barrolo? Something happened?'

'I've received a letter.'

'Ah!'

Barrolo gravely unbuttoned his jacket and pulled out of an inside pocket a large, shiny green leather wallet with a gold monogram. It was the wallet that he showed Gonçalo with satisfaction.

'Nice, isn't it? Present from André, poor fellow . . . I believe he had it sent from Paris. The monogram's really elegant.'

Gonçalo waited, amazed. Finally the good Barrolo took from the wallet a letter, at one time screwed up, now flattened out again. It was lined paper covered with some small hand-writing that the Nobleman barely glanced at, declaring immediately,

'That's the Lousadas.'

He read, slowly and serenely, his elbow sunk in the cushion:

'Dear Sr José Barrolo,

You have, sir, in spite of the fact that all your friends call you Zé Simpleton, shown great intelligence in welcoming, to your house and to your worthy wife, the handsome André Cavaleiro, our Civil Governor. There's no doubt that your wife, the lovely Gracinha, who has been looking so off-colour recently—almost faded, one might say (a fact which worried us all), has immediately revived, and is blossoming afresh since she has the invaluable company of the first gentleman of the district. You behaved like a most affectionate husband, sir, desirous of the happiness and health of your charming wife. It hardly seems in character with one whom all Oliveira considers its most illustrious simpleton! Our most sincere congratulations!'

Gonçalo kept in his pocket very quietly the letter which had cast him into infinite bitterness and fury some days earlier.

'This is the Lousadas . . . Do you pay attention to such nonsense?'

Barrolo retorted, his cheeks aglow,

'What do you think? I've always loathed anonymous letters . . . And then this insolence about my friends calling me Simpleton . . . Infamous, isn't it? Do you believe it? . . . I don't believe it! But it foments discord between me and the boys . . . I've not been to the Club since . . . Simpleton, indeed? Why? Because I'm simple and always frank, ready to be friendly? No! If the boys at the Club call me Simpleton behind my back, by Jove! they're an ungrateful lot! But I don't believe it!'

He waddled round the room disconsolately, his hands clasped over his fat bottom. Then, coming to a stop in front of the divan, where Gonçalo sat contemplating him with pity, he went on,

'As for the rest of the letter, it's so stupid and so muddled that I didn't understand it at first. Now I see . . . They're saying Gracinha and Cavaleiro are having an affair . . . At least that's what it seems like. Just imagine such nonsense! Even Cavaleiro's being a close friend's a lie. Since that night he dined with us, the poor fellow has only appeared three or four times, at night for a game of *manilha* with Mendonça . . . And now he's gone off to Lisbon.'

The Nobleman sat up sharply in surprise.

'What? Cavaleiro's gone to Lisbon?'

'He went three days ago.'

'For long?'

'For a long time, yes . . . He'll only be returning in mid-October, for the elections.'

'Ah!'

But Bento burst into the room at this point, with the jug of hot water and two lace-trimmed towels, still flustered with excitement. Barrolo stood before the mirror and slowly buttoned up his jacket again.

'Right, see you later, Gonçalinho. I'll just go down to the stable to see how the pair are getting on. Just imagine! All the way from Oliveira without a halt, trotting beautifully. And they didn't sweat a bit! Are you keeping the letter?'

'Yes, I want to study the writing.'

As soon as Barrolo had closed the door, the Nobleman resumed the delightful story of his battle once again, with Bento this time, going over the surprises and the moments of danger, acting out the mare's leaps and bounds, and catching up the whip to illustrate the whistling of his weapon as it came down, shedding blood and flesh. Suddenly he cried out, in his pants,

'Oh, Bento! Bring me my hat . . . I believe the bullet went through my hat.'

They both studied it, scrutinized it. Bento, in his excitement over the event, thought the crown was a little squashed—even singed, it appeared.

'The bullet grazed it here, sir!'

The Nobleman denied it, however, with the grave modesty of a man of strength.

'No, didn't even graze it! When the rascal fired, his arm was already shaking. We must thank God, Bento. But I was not really in any great danger.'

After dressing, Gonçalo wandered round the room, re-reading the letter. Yes, it was surely from the Lousadas. But now their malice, blown with such evil design upon Barrolo's fat cheeks, would cause no harm—rather would it serve a useful purpose, like a hot iron working a cure. Poor Barrolo was only shocked by the revelation of his foolishness, of the unkind nickname which his friends had given him in spiteful jest at the Club and under the Arches. The other terrible insinuation, that of Gracinha blossoming again in Cavaleiro's amorous warmth, he had scarcely understood, had barely acknowledged, with distracted, ill-concealed contempt. But the letter which

253

had winged its way to the good Barrolo, like an errant arrow, would find its mark in Gracinha, would wound Gracinha in her pride, in her impressionable modesty, showing the poor, silly girl how her name, and even her heart, were being dragged down, dragged in the dirt, by the low-minded, scheming Lousadas! Such a humiliating fact would not eradicate a sentiment—which had not been eradicated by more intimate and far more painful humiliations. But it would act on her reserved nature and her diffident modesty; and now that André had gone away to Lisbon, it would act on her, silently, solitarily, without his tempting presence to mar the salutary, soothing influence. So the vile paper would be to Gracinha's benefit, like a terrible warning pinned to a wall. Spitefully designed by the two old women to unleash scandal and pain in *Cunhais*—perhaps it would re-establish tranquillity and gravity in the threatened home. Gonçalo rubbed his hands together, thinking that, on such a felicitous morning, perhaps this piece of evil would be transformed into a boon!

'Oh, Bento, where's Senhora Dona Graça?'

'The young lady went up to her room a few moments ago, sir.'

It was her old room, a bright, cool room overlooking the orchard, which still contained her handsome inlaid wooden bed, a famous dressing-table which had belonged to Queen Dona Maria Francisca of Savoy, and the sofa and chairs covered in pale cashmere where Gracinha had sat embroidering the black Ramires goshawk—an interminable work which had lasted for years. Whenever she visited the Tower, Gracinha liked to relive, in her room, her unmarried days, going through the drawers, thumbing old English novels in the little glass-fronted book-case or simply standing on the verandah contemplating the beloved grounds stretching as far as the hills of Valverde, the green land, so much a part of her life that every tree murmured to her, every green nook was like a secret thought.

Gonçalo went up and knocked at the closed door with the words he once used to say: 'May brother come in?' She hurried in from the verandah where she had been watering the plants affectionately replanted and tended by Rosa, in their glazed pots. She at once blurted out the thought that occupied her.

'Oh, Gonçalo! How marvellous that we came to the Tower today, just when such a thing happened to you!'

'Yes, Gracinha, it was very lucky! I was not at all surprised to see you . . . It was as if you were still living in the Tower and I met you in the corridor . . . What puzzled me was seeing Barrolo! As soon as I dismounted, I thought vaguely, "What the deuce is Barrolo doing here? How the deuce is Barrolo here?" Strange, eh? Perhaps it was that, after the fight, I felt myself rejuvenated, with fresh blood, and I thought I was back in those times when we wanted a war again in Portugal, ourselves besieged at the Tower, under our pennant, our regiment firing cannons at the Spaniards . . .'

She laughed, remembering those heroic fancies. And with her dress caught between her knees, she resumed the leisurely watering of her flowers—while Gonçalo, leaning against the verandah, contemplating the Tower, was possessed again by that feeling of a closer union which had been established that morning between him and the heroic remains of the Manor of Santa Ireneia, as if his strength, for so long broken, had finally become firmly welded to the centuries-old strength of his race. 'Oh, Gonçalo! You must be very tired! After a real battle like that . . .'

'No, not really tired . . . But hungry. Hungry and stupendously thirsty!'

She immediately put down her watering-can, and dried her hands gaily.

'Lunch won't be long! . . . I've already been at work in the kitchen with Rosa, preparing hake à l'espagnole . . . It's a new recipe of the Baron das Marges.'

'Insipid, then, like him.'

'No, on the contrary: quite pungent: it was the Vicar-General who taught it him.'

As she sat before the Queen Maria Francisca dressing-table, hurriedly arranging her hair, he decided to take advantage of their privacy, forcing himself to confide his secret.

'How's Oliveira? What's going on there?'

'Nothing at all . . . Terribly hot, that's all.'

Gonçalo ran his fingers slowly round the frame of the mirror, a delicate interlacing of lilies and laurels, and murmured,

'I only know about the Lousadas, your friends the Lousadas. They're still as busy as ever . . .'

Gracinha answered with a candid denial.

'The Lousadas? No, they haven't even visited us recently.'

'But they've been trouble-making!'

As Gracinha's green eyes widened uncomprehendingly, Gonçalo

swiftly took from his pocket the letter in it, which now felt as heavy as a sheet of lead.

'Here, Gracinha! We might as well have this out! This is what they wrote to your husband a few days ago.'

In a moment Gracinha had devoured the terrible lines. Waves of blood rushed to her cheeks as she clasped her hands in anguish, in despair, crumpling the paper.

'Oh, Gonçalo! Then . . .'

Gonçalo reassured her,

'No! Barrolo pays no attention to it! He even laughed! So did I, when he showed me the wretched note . . . And to prove we both consider it a malicious piece of nonsense, I'm showing it to you frankly.'

She crushed the letter between her trembling hands, pale now and speechless with shock, restraining the heavy tears which glistened in her eyes. Gonçalo, moved by her distress, spoke gravely and tenderly.

'But Gracinha, you know what small towns are. Especially Oliveira! You need to be very careful, very reserved . . . Heaven help me! It was my fault! I resumed a friendship that I should never have resumed. And I've certainly regretted it since! Believe me! Because of this false and dangerous situation, I created, frivolously, through foolish ambition, I have spent some bitter days in the Tower . . . I did not even dare return to Oliveira. Today, I don't know why, after this adventure, everything seems to have lost its importance, been submerged into a great shadow . . . My heart doesn't burn within me . . . That's why I can speak out calmly like this . . .'

She burst into uncontrolled, pitiful weeping as if her heart would break. With fond affection, Gonçalo clasped the poor bowed shoulders shaken by sobs. As she nestled against his breast, he continued to advise her gently.

'Gracinha, the past is dead, and we all of us, for our honour's sake, need it to remain dead. At least on the outside, in all your gestures, let it appear dead! It's I who am asking you this, for our name's sake!'

Clasped in her brother's arms, she sobbed with infinite humility.

'But he's gone away! . . . He didn't want to stay in Oliveira any longer!'

Gonçalo stroked her downcast head, which had once again hidden itself against his breast, was pressing against it as if searching for the new-born mercy she felt rising up inside it.

'I know. And this shows me you have been strong . . . But you need a great deal of reserve, a great deal of vigilance, Gracinha! Now calm yourself. We won't ever mention this incident again. Because it was only an incident. One that I encouraged, foolish that I am, out of thoughtlessness, through an illusion. But now it is past, forgotten. Calm yourself now and rest. And when you come down I want to see your eyes quite dry.'

He slowly released her from his arms, where she had nestled as if in the safest refuge and most sought-for comfort. He was leaving, choked with emotion, restraining his tears too, when a timid cry of entreaty stopped him.

'Gonçalo! But you think . . .'

He turned, embraced her again, and kissed her slowly on the forehead.

'I think that you, well warned and well advised, are going to show extreme dignity and firmness.'

He left hastily, shutting the door behind him. On the narrow stairs, dimly lit by a dull skylight, he was wiping his eyes when he met Barrolo who was looking for Gracinha, to speed up lunch.

'Gracinha's just coming down!' stammered the Nobleman. 'She's just washing her hands! She'll be right down. But before lunch, let's go to the stables. We must visit the mare, my beloved mare which saved me!'

'So we must, by Jove!' agreed Barrolo at once, turning back down the stairs, enthusiastically. 'We must visit the mare . . . Big and brave, eh? But I bet she sweated more than mine would . . . Just imagine! A trot like that, all the way from Oliveira, and not a bit damp! Magnificent pair! But think how I look after them, how I care for them!'

In the stables, the two of them stroked the mare. Barrolo suggested they gave her an extra ration of carrots as a reward. Then, so that Gracinha had time to calm down, the Nobleman dragged him round the orchard and the vegetable-garden . . .

'You haven't been to the Tower for six months, Barrolinho! You must see everything, admire the progress. We have Pereira da Riosa's able hand in charge of things round here now.'

'I can imagine! A great fellow, Pereira! But I'm starving, Gonçalinho!'

'Me, too!'

★   ★   ★

One o'clock was striking when they entered the verandah where the festive, flower-decorated table lay ready, and Gracinha sat on the edge of the divan, looking pensively through an old *Porto Gazette*. Although they had been bathed, her beautiful eyes were still a little red; to justify this, and her forlorn air, she immediately complained of migraine. It was all the excitement, Gonçalo being in danger . . .

'I've got a headache, too,' declared Barrolo, circling the table. 'But mine's from hunger. You know, I haven't eaten a thing since a cup of coffee and a boiled egg at seven o'clock this morning.'

Gonçalo rang the bell. But the person who burst through the glass door, panting for breath and with a broad grin on his face, was Joaquim, the stable-boy, who had returned from Grainha.

Gonçalo raised his arms, avid for news.

'So what? So what?'

'Well, I've been there, your Lordship!' exclaimed Joaquim, his chest burning with importance. 'And crowds of people are there, everyone knows about it! A girl from Bravais saw everything from inside the garden . . . Then she ran off and told everyone about it. But the old man, this Domingues that lives there, and his son, have both disappeared. The boy, it seems, is not seriously hurt. If he fell unconscious, it was through fright. Ernesto de Nacejas, he really did catch it, heaven help him! They've carried him to the house of a *compadre* of his near by, in Arribada. It seems he's lost an ear and his mouth! And he used to be the darling of all the girls around! In the afternoon they're taking him to Vila Clara Hospital because they can't cure him at his *compadre*'s. Crowds of people, and everyone's on your side, your Lordship. That Domingues was a scoundrel. And as for Ernesto, no one liked him. Everyone was scared stiff of him. Your Lordship's cleaned things up a bit!'

Gonçalo's face glowed. Ah, good! Nothing worse than that the Don Juan of Nacejas had lost his beauty!

'So there's a crowd there, is there? Talking and looking at the place?'

'Oh, the people won't leave! Pointing to the blood on the ground,

258

and the stones scattered by your mare, sir . . . And now they're saying it was an ambush, and they fired three shots at your Lordship, and then further on in the pine wood, three masked men jumped out at you, and you thrashed them.'

'So that's the story that's spreading!' exclaimed Gonçalo.

Bento appeared with a steaming dish. His Lordship patted Joaquim's shoulder with a smile. He was to tell Rosa below to open two bottles of old port for the family lunch. Then with his hand on the back of his chair, he murmured gravely,

'Let us think for a moment of God, who has saved me from great danger!'

Barrolo hung his head in reverence. Gracinha, after a light sigh, murmured a light prayer. They unfolded their napkins; Gonçalo was praising the dish of hake à l'espagnole when Crispola's little boy pushed open the glass door 'with a telegram that came from the town!' Uneasiness checked their forks. There had been so much excitement and alarm that morning. But a smile of pleasure, of triumph, spread over Gonçalo's delicate feaures.

'It's nothing . . . It's from Castanheiro, about the chapters of the novel I sent him . . . Poor fellow! He's a good chap!'

Leaning back in his chair, he slowly recited the telegram which his eyes were caressing. 'Chapters novel received. Read them to friends. All enthusiastic. Definitely masterpiece. Congratulations.'

Barrolo, his mouth full, clapped his hands. Gonçalo, unaware of the dish of hake which Bento was offering him, but filling his glass with green wine with slightly trembling hands, murmured, a permanent, happy smile bathing his face,

'A really good morning . . . An excellent morning!'

* * *

Gonçalo, in spite of Gracinha and Barrolo's insistence, would not accompany them to Oliveira—intending that week to complete the last chapter of his novel and also to finish his lazy round of visits to influential electors in the constituency. Thus would he accomplish the work of Art and the work of Politics—and fulfil, God be praised, the task of this fertile summer!

First thing that night he picked up the manuscript of his novel, and in the wide margin recorded with a flourish the date and a note: 'Today, in the parish of Grainha, I had a terrible fight with two men who attacked me with staffs and guns but whom I punished severely . . .' Then, effortlessly, he attacked the episode so medieval in flavour: the entrance of Tructesindo Ramires, as he pursued the Bastard, into the encampment of Don Pedro de Castro, amid the dispersed, smoky glow of torches.

With friendly gravity, the old warrior welcomed his Portuguese cousin, who had brought his troops from Santa Ireneia when the Castros had fought a great host of Moors in Enxarez de Sandornin. Then, in the vast tent, glittering with weapons and carpeted with bear and lion skins, Tructesindo recounted, still panting with suppressed pain, the death of his son Lourenço, wounded in the battle of Canta Pedra, and finished off with a dagger by the Bastard of Baião in front of the walls of Santa Ireneia, with the sun high in the sky to witness the treachery! Indignant, old Castro crashed his fist down upon the table, where a gold rosary lay among the heavy chessmen, and swore on the life of Christ that he had never, in sixty years of arms and surprises, heard of so vile a deed. Grasping the hand of the Lord of Santa Ireneia, he passionately offered him, to carry out his sacred revenge, his entire host—three hundred and thirty lances and a considerable body of stalwart foot-soldiers.

'Holy Mother! A magnificent expedition!' shouted Mendo de Briteiros, his red beard aflame with joy.

But Don Garcia Viegas, the Wise One, thought that, to catch the Bastard alive, which is what they wanted if they were to enjoy a lingering death, it would be better to have a lesser, silent troop of horsemen and a few foot-soldiers . . .

'Why, Don Garcia?'

'Because the Bastard, after disburdening himself of foot-soldiers and carriages, at the bank of the river, will make for Coimbra, to seek protection from the Royal host there. Tonight he will surely rest, along with his exhausted band of lances, in the Landim Manor. At dawn, to shorten their route, they will naturally gallop along the old road to Miradães, which goes round and over the hills of Caramulo. Now he, Garcia Viegas, knew of a spot, a little further on, beyond the Well of the Forgotten Girl, where a few horsemen and a few cross-bows, well placed in the wild land there, would catch Lopo de Baião like a wolf in a trap.'

Tructesindo, pensive and undecided, put his fingers to his long beard. Old Castro was doubtful, preferring to fight the Bastard in open battle on level ground where all these lances, ready to set off, would be to their advantage, and would then rush with wild joy upon the lands of Baião and devastate them. Then Garcia Viegas besought his Spanish and Portuguese cousins to come out to the square in front of the tent, with plenty of torches to light them. There, amid inquisitive knights, in the light of lowered torches, Don Garcia bent his knee and sketched upon the ground, with the point of his dagger, the route of his 'hunt' to prove its beauty . . . At dawn the Bastard would set forth from the Castle of Landim. But their pursuers, when the moon rose, would set out with twenty knights from the Ramires band and from the Castros, so that men of both parties should enjoy the battle. Further on, hidden in the thicket, cross-bows and archers would be posted. Behind, on this side, to cut off the Bastard's retreat, would be Senhor Don Pedro de Castro, if he would honour the Lord of Santa Ireneia with such aid. Then, ahead, over there, in order to catch the villain by the throat, would be Senhor Don Tructesindo Ramires, who was the father and whom God had ordained should be the avenger. There, in the narrow pass they would overthrow him and bleed him like a pig—and since the blood was vile, they would find, an arrow's flight away, plenty of water to wash their hands—the water of the Leeches' Pool!

'Excellent plan!' murmured Tructesindo, convinced.

Don Pedro de Castro shouted, darting a gleaming eye at the knights of Spain:

'By Christ, if my great-uncle Gutierres had had Senhor Don Garcia here as his captain, the men of Lara would not have escaped when they took the young King in their flight to Santo Estêvão de Gurivaz! . . . Right, then, cousin and friend, we agree! To horse, for the hunt, as soon as the moon appears!'

They returned to their tents, for the young goats roasting on the fires were golden and ready for supper and the stewards were approaching between carts of grapes, carrying the heavy wineskins from Tordesilhas.

With the supper at the encampment (grave and silent, since mourning veiled the hearts of the guests), Gonçalo ended Chapter IV that night, with another note in the margin: 'Midnight . . . A full day. I fought, I worked.' Then in his room, as he undressed, he planned the entire, short, hectic battle in which the Bastard, like a wolf in a trap, falls captive to the vindictive mercy of the Santa Ireneia host . . . But next morning, before lunch, as he was sitting down to his work with pleasure, he received two telegrams which triumphantly distracted his attention from the chase after the Bastard of Baião.

They were two telegrams from Oliveira, one from the Baron das Marges, another from Captain Mendonça—both congratulating the Nobleman 'on escaping from such a terrible ambush and destroying the ruffians of Nacejas'. The Baron das Marges added, 'Bravo! You're a hero!'

Gonçalo, moved, showed the telegrams to Bento. So the news of his exploit had got around, had impressed Oliveira.

'It was Senhor José Barrolo who told them!' put in Bento. 'And you'll see sir! You'll see . . . Even in Porto they'll marvel at it!'

As noon was striking, the vast Tító rushed noisily along the corridor, accompanied by João Gouveia who had arrived the night before from the coast, learnt of the adventure in the Club, and had hurried to the Tower to give him a friendly embrace, before appearing in his official capacity. Gonçalo, while still in Gouveia's arms, begged him most generously 'not to have a case opened against the wretches . . .' The Administrator refused, curtly and resolutely, upholding the principle of Order and the need for a strict example to others, so that Portugal should not revert to the barbarous times of João Brandão de Midões. He and Tító had lunch at the Tower, and Tító, over-dressed, jestingly suggested a toast would be fitting, and himself shouted the toast, comparing Gonçalo with the elephant: 'always good and peaceful, tolerating everything, and then suddenly, whoosh, he crushes the world!'

Then João Gouveia lit a fat cigar and asked for a precise account of the rumpus, with all the leaps and shouts, so that he could understand the whole situation as his position demanded. So using the verandah, he acted out the heroic story, flourishing the whip on the divan (which was eventually torn to shreds) to demonstrate the blows which he had dealt, imitating the semi-conscious falls by the ruffian of Nacejas, when he began to be bathed in blood. The Administrator and Tító visited the famous mare in the stable; and in the yard, Gonçalo showed them the two leather leggings drying in the sun after being cleaned of the blood that had spattered them.

At the gate, João Gouveia clapped the Nobleman gravely on the shoulder.

'Gonçalo, you ought to put in an appearance tonight at the Club...'

He did, and was welcomed as the victor of a glorious battle. In the billiard-room, at old Ribas' suggestion, a great bowl of punch was glowing away—and the honoured Barros, flushed with excitement, insisted they should celebrate a Te Deum thanksgiving in S Francisco Church, the expenses of which he would pay, and proudly, by Jove! As he left, accompanied by Titó and Gouveia and Manuel Duarte and other members, they met Videirinha—who did not belong to the Club, but was prowling round waiting for the the Nobleman in order to sing him two verses of his Fado, improvised that very afternoon, in which he acclaimed him above all the other Ramires of history and legend!

The group stopped at the Fountain. The guitar throbbed lovingly. Videirinha's singing, straight from the heart, penetrated the silent branches of the Judas trees:

> 'The Ramires of other eras
> Won their battles with great lances,
> This one conquers with a whip
> And the enemy has no chances!
>
> Those famous Ramires
> Of times long past
> Bore their strength in their weapons
> While this one's is in his heart!'

At such an ingenious conceit, the friends broke out in cheers for Gonçalo and for the House of Ramires. As the Nobleman made his way back to the Tower, moved, he thought, 'Strange! All these people seem fond of me!...'

But what were his feelings next morning when Bento woke him with a telegram from Lisbon! It was from Cavaleiro who 'had learnt of the attack through the papers, and sent him enthusiastic congratulations on his good fortune and courage'. Gonçalo sat up in bed and shouted,

'By Jove! Then it's in the Lisbon papers, Bento! The story's famous!'

It certainly was famous, because the whole of that delightful day, the telegraph-boy, puffing and limping, was pushing open the gate of the Tower with other telegrams, all of them from Lisbon—from the Countess de Chelas; from Duarte Lourençal; from the Marquis and Marchioness de Coja 'with congratulations'; from Aunt Louredo with 'congratulations to her fearless nephew'; from the Marchioness de Esposende, 'hoping her dear cousin had given thanks to God!' And the last one from Castanheiro, with exclamations: 'Magnificent! Worthy of Tructesindo!' Gonçalo stood in the library and raised his hands in confusion.

'But in heaven's name, what could the papers have said?'

As the telegrams arrived, so did visits from the influential gentlemen of the neighbourhood—Dr Alexandrino, who was aghast and foresaw a return to Cabralism;[1] old Pacheco Valadares de Sá, who was not surprised at the behaviour of his noble cousin, because a Ramires' blood, like a Sá's blood, is always at boiling-point; Father Vicente from *Finta* who offered, along with his congratulations, a basket containing bunches of their famous black Muscatel grapes; and finally the Viscount of Rio Manso, who clutched Gonçalo and sobbed, almost proud, as well as moved, that the fight should occur like that on the road when 'his dear friend, Rosa's dear friend', was on his way to *Varandinha*. Gonçalo, blushing, wreathed in smiles, embraced him and patiently recounted the exploit. As he accompanied those gentlemen to the gate, as they mounted their mares, or entered their calashes, they smiled in the direction of the old Tower which stood dark and erect in the soft light of that September afternoon, as if acknowledging, not only the hero, but the centuries-old foundation of his heroism.

The Nobleman, striding up the stairs to the library, once again murmured in astonishment,

'Whatever could the Lisbon papers have said?'

He could not sleep in his anxiety to devour them. When Bento burst excitedly into his room with the mail, Gonçalo sat up and thrust back the sheet as if it were smothering him. Instantly, in the hungrily devoured *Século*, he found the news from Oliveira describing the assault! the shots fired! the immense courage of the Nobleman of the Tower who, with a mere whip . . . Bento almost tore the *Século* out of his Lordship's tremulous hands, to race to the kitchen and shout the glorious news to Rosa!

[1] Cabralism: political party of Costa Cabral.

In the afternoon, Gonçalo hurried to Vila Clara, to the Club, to devour the other Lisbon papers and those from Porto. Everyone related it, everyone acclaimed him. The *Porto Gazette*, attributing the attack to a political cause, furiously condemned the Government! The *Porto Liberal*, however, connected, 'with a certain revenge by the Republicans of Oliveira, the fearful assault which nearly caused the death of one of the greatest noblemen in Portugal and Spain, and one of the most powerful talents of our younger generation!' The Lisbon papers praised above all 'the splendid courage of Sr Gonçalo Ramires'. The most enthusiastic of all was the *Morning Post*, in a wordy article (surely written by Castanheiro), recalling the heroic traditions of the illustrious House, sketching the beauties of the castle of Santa Ireneia, and finishing by affirming that 'now we await with redoubled expectation the appearance of the novel by Gonçalo Ramires, based upon an adventure of his ancestor Tructesindo in the twelfth century, and promised for the first number of *Annals of Literature and History*, the new review of our dear friend Lúcio Castanheiro, that worthy restorer of the heroic conscience of Portugal!' Gonçalo's hands trembled as he unfolded the newspapers. João Gouveia, just as excited, devouring the articles over the Nobleman's shoulder, murmured, impressed,

'Gonçalinho, you're going to get a tremendous number of votes!'

That night, when Gonçalo returned to the Tower, he found a letter which disturbed him. It was from Maria Mendonça, on a sheet of paper perfumed with the same fragrance that had emanated so becomingly from Dona Ana in the yard of Santa Maria de Craquede.

'Only this morning did we hear of the great danger you were in, and we were *both* extremely upset. But at the same time I (and not only I) am very proud of the magnificent courage of my dear cousin. You are a true Ramires! I won't come along personally to give you a kiss (for fear of losing my reputation and *making certain people jealous!*) because one of my little ones, Neco, has a bad cold. Fortunately it's nothing to worry about . . . But all of us here, even the children, are longing to see the hero, and I don't think there would be anything extraordinary, either on the one side or the other, if you called here, cousin, the day after tomorrow (Thursday), about three o'clock. We could have a walk in the grounds, and even have tea, in the good old manner of our ancestors. Is that all right? Regards, *lots of them*, from Anica, and from your cousin, etc. . . .'

Gonçalo smiled, pensively, considering the letter and inhaling the aroma. Never had Cousin Maria pushed Dona Ana so clearly into his arms . . . And how Dona Ana was letting herself be pushed, ready and willing, her eyes closed . . . Ah, if it was only to bed they were going! But no, it was to church, too! Once again he heard the booming voice of Titó, on the steps below the little green door, the full moon rising above the black elms: 'This creature's had a lover, and you know I never lie!'

He slowly took up his pen and replied to Maria Mendonça:

'Dear Cousin,

I was most moved by your preoccupation and enthusiasm. But let's not exaggerate! I did no more than whip a couple of rascals who fired at me. It's an easy thing for one who has, as I have, an excellent whip. Regarding the visit to *Feitosa*, it would be most pleasant for me, but I can manage, much to my regret, neither Thursday nor any time this month . . . I am extremely busy with my book and the election and my move to Lisbon. A period of serious work has opened for me, ending sweet days of walks and dreams. I beg you to give Senhora Dona Ana my deepest respects. With my kindest regards to you and best wishes for dear Neco's recovery, I am your devoted and grateful cousin, etc.'

He closed the letter slowly. Pressing his seal with its coat-of-arms on the green sealing-wax, he thought,

'And that's how that rascal Titó lost me two hundred *contos*!'

*   *   *

All that mild week at the end of September, Gonçalo worked on the final chapter of his novel.

At last he had arrived at the morning of vengeance, when the knights of Santa Ireneia, reinforced by the noblest of the Castros' host, surprised, in the wild pass proposed by Garcia Viegas, the Wise One, the Baião band in their speedy flight to Coimbra. A short, savage battle with no skilful and chivalrous crossing of swords, more like the hunting of a wolf than an attack on a nobleman. That was how Tructesindo wanted it, Don Pedro de Castro's vociferous approval, since they were not fighting an enemy but catching an assassin.

Before dawn, the Bastard had left the Castle of Landim in such haste and so careless of his safety that not even a scout went ahead to spy out the land. The skylarks were singing when, trotting fast, he entered, between some steep, rocky, heather-covered cliffs, the pass which they called the Moor's Crevice, since it was Mahomet who had cut it so that the Moorish alcalde of Coimbra and the nun whom he carried behind him on his back could escape the Christian daggers of King Fernando the Great. No sooner had the last lance of the party entered the narrow pass, than from the other opening appeared the tightly-packed body of knights from Santa Ireneia with Tructesindo at its head, his visor up, carrying no buckler, merely waving a hunting javelin as if he were disporting at a hunt. From the woodland above emerged the Castro band, lances at the ready, sealing off the exit more closely than the grating of a portcullis. From over the tops of the hills, like water from an open dam, rolls a black, brutish mass of foot-soldiers! The terrible Bastard was caught, lost! But nevertheless he furiously draws his sword which crowns him with flashing light as he whirls it round. Nevertheless, he rushes violently at Tructesindo. But abruptly, from a dense throng of slingsmen, uncoils a hempen cord, which catches him round the throat and jerks him out of his Moorish saddle on to some boulders against which his sword strikes and breaks near the golden handle. While the knights of Baião defend themselves in dismay against the dense circle of lances surrounding them, a mass of foot-soldiers, howling wildly, like mastiffs attacking a boar, drag the Bastard to the slope where they tear away his buckler and dagger, rip off his purple woollen tunic, and break the fasteners on his helmet so they can spit in his face, and on the golden-hued beard, his so beautiful and proud possession!

Then the same brutish mob lift him up, well secured, on to the back of a powerful pack-mule, and lay him between two narrow boxes of arrows, like a captive animal brought home after the hunt. Serfs looking after the baggage were left to guard the glorious knight, the Bright Sun which had illuminated the House of Baião, now stuck between two wooden boxes, cords binding his feet and cords binding his hands, and a thistle stuck in them to denote his treachery.

In the meantime, the fifteen knights were strewn over the ground, crushed beneath the furious onslaught of lances which had attacked them—some stiff as if sleeping within their black armour, others twisted, disfigured, their flesh slashed and dangling horribly between their torn coats-of-mail. The captured squires were prodded at spear-point to the edge of a precipice without pity or redemption, like a low gang of thieves caught robbing cattle, and were decapitated with axes by the bearded Leonese soldiers. The entire valley reeked of blood like a butcher's yard. A group of knights went round undoing the gorgets and visors of the dead men to find out who they were, slyly pulling off the silver medals, charms and little bags of relics which they all wore as God-fearing men. One face, with a fine dark beard, stained by a trickle of bloody spittle, Mendo de Briteiros recognized as his cousin Soeiro de Lugilde, with whom he had sported and danced so happily in the Castle of Unhelo before the bonfire on St John's Day. Bowing his head as he sat in his high saddle, he said a devout Ave Maria for the poor soul which had departed the body without confession. Heavy ochre clouds veiled the sky that August morning. In a little group apart, at the entrance to the valley, beneath the foliage of an old holm-oak, Tructesindo, Don Pedro de Castro and Garcia Viegas, the Wise One, were discussing what prolonged, painful and ignominious death they could devise for the Bastard, a villain guilty of so black a crime.

Thus describing the gloomy ambush with the groaning effort of one pushing a plough through stony ground—so Gonçalo spent this delightful week in September. Early on the Saturday, in the library, his hair still wet from his shower, he rubbed his hands as he stood before his work-desk, because before lunch, with two hours of hard work, he would surely finish his novel, his great work! Yet the end, vile and horrible as it was, almost repelled him. Uncle Duarte had merely sketched it in his poem, evading the details, as a noble lyric poet, before a vision of such brutal ferocity, lets forth a wail, puts away his lyre and makes for more cheerful paths. As he took up his pen, Gonçalo could not help lamenting the fact that Tructesindo had not killed the Bastard in the heat of battle with one of those marvellous blows, so delightful to recount, that cleave the knight and then cleave the jennet, and for ever reverberate through History.

But no! Under the boughs of the holm-oak, the three knights slowly planned a terrible vengeance. Tructesindo wanted to return immediately to Santa Ireneia, set up a scaffold before the barbican on the ground where his son had been slain, and there, after being well flogged hang him like a villain—the villain who had slain his son. Old Don Pedro de Castro, however, advised a quicker death, albeit an enjoyable one. Why go all the way back to Santa Ireneia, and waste this entire August day which could take them to Montemor, to the aid of the Princesses of Portugal? Let them put the Bastard, tied on to a beam like a pig at Christmas, before Don Tructesindo, and let a stable-boy singe his beard, and then another, with a kitchen-knife, bleed him slowly at the throat.

'What do you think, Don Garcia?'

The Wise One unbuckled his iron helmet, and wiped the sweat and dust of battle from his wrinkles.

'My lords and friends! We have a better method, one at hand, without delaying over journeys, just beyond these hills, in Leeches' Pool ... We won't even be going out of our way, for from there, through Tordezelo and Santa Maria de Varge, we shall go straight on to Montemor, as straight as the crow flies ... Trust in me, Tructesindo! Trust in me and I'll arrange so vile a death for the Bastard that there won't have been another to compare with it since Portugal became a province.'

'Lower than death on the gallows for a knight, my old Garcia?'

'You'll see, my lords and friends, you'll see!'

'So be it! Have the trumpets blown!'

At a command from the standard-bearer, Afonso Gomes, the trumpets sounded. A group of Leonese cross-bows and foot-soldiers surrounded the mule which held the Bastard bound and captive between two boxes. Led by Don Garcia, the small party set off toward Leeches' Pool, at ease, as if taking a ride for pleasure, all of them chatting gaily, recalling, amid boasting and laughter, the most exciting feats of the battle.

Two leagues from Tordezelo and its beautiful castle, Leeches' Pool lay hidden among the hills. It was a place of eternal silence and eternal sorrow. Uncle Duarte had described the harsh desolation in impeccable verses:

'Not the trill of a bird on a swaying bough!
Not a single fresh flower near the fresh-running stream!
Only rocks and scrub and overshadowing banks,
And the Pool in their midst, gloomy and dead! ...'

When the first knights caught sight of it as they reached the top of the hill, in the melancholy, misty morn, their chatter stopped, and they tightened the reins, awed by so desolate a place, so fitting

269

for witches and phantoms and souls in torment. Before the grooved ravine in which the jennets' hooves slipped, extended a broad slope pitted with muddy pools almost dried up after the drought, shining dully between the big rocks and trailing gorse. Beyond, half a crossbow-shot away, lay the black Pool, a narrow lake, smooth, without a ripple on its surface, quite black, with even blacker patches, like a sheet of tin which has grown rusty from weather and neglect. All round rose hills spiked with tall bushes, traversed by red gravel paths like streams of blood, their crests rent by lustrous crags, whiter than bones. So heavy was the silence, so heavy the isolation, that even old Don Pedro de Castro, who had travelled so far, was horrified.

'An evil place! And I swear to God, and to the Holy Virgin, that no man before us entered here who was redeemed by baptism.'

'No, Don Pedro de Castro,' answered the Wise One. 'Many a lance has passed through here, some splendid ones, and indeed in the time of the Count Don Soeiro and your King Don Fernando, a famous castle stood on the bank of that water! See over there!'

He pointed to the farther end of the Pool, facing the ravine, where two strong stone pillars, polished like fine marble by wind and rain, emerged from the black water. A gangway of wooden beams, on slimy, half-rotten posts, linked the thickest pillar with the bank. Half-way up this rough support hung an iron ring.

In the meantime the crowd of foot-soldiers spread out along the bank. Don Garcia Viegas dismounted and shouted for Pero Ermigues, the captain of the cross-bows of Santa Ireneia. Beside Tructesindo's jennet, smiling and enjoying their surprise, he told the captain to have six of his strong men remove the Bastard from the mule, lay him on the ground and undress him, naked as his whore of a mother brought him into this black life . . .

Tructesindo looked at the Wise One, frowning with his hairy eyebrows.

'God alive, Don Garcia! You're not simply going to drown the villain and foul this innocent water?'

Certain knights around also murmured against so quiet and mild a death. But Don Garcia's little eyes danced and glittered with triumph and pleasure.

'Calm! Calm! Old I most certainly am, but the Lord God has still left me a little cunning. No! Neither hanged, nor beheaded nor drowned . . . But sucked, my lords! Sucked to death, and slowly, by the great fat leeches which fill this black water!'

Don Pedro de Castro was astounded and clapped his gloves against his metal cuisse.

'Christ alive! Having Don Garcia in one's host is like having, for military and political advice, Hannibal and Aristotle rolled into one!'

A murmur of admiration ran through the host.

'An excellent idea! An excellent plan!'

Tructesindo shouted, radiant with the idea,

'To work, cross-bows, to work! And you, gentlemen, get back up to the top of the hill to view the spectacle, for this will be a grand sight!'

Six cross-bows had unloaded the Bastard from the mule. Others approached with coils of rope. Like butchers skinning an animal, the whole uncouth crowd fell on the ill-fated man, tearing off from beneath the cords his upper coat, his greaves, his iron shoes and then the thick, soiled linen beneath. Held by his long hair, his feet tied, the men, in their frenzy to grasp him, digging in their finger-nails, his arms crushed beneath the weight of other tense, solid arms, the powerful Bastard still twisted and turned, bellowing and spitting in the blurred faces of the rabble, bloody, frothy spittle!

Amidst the dark throng clustered round him, his body, quite naked, tied with thicker cords, gleamed white. Gradually his maddened bellowing died away and his voice became breathless and hoarse. The cross-bows, one after another, straightened up, ex-hausted, breathing hard, wiping away the sweat from their efforts.

Meanwhile the knights of Spain and Santa Ireneia dismounted, flinging down the butts of their lances amid the furze and stones. The hillsides, like a grandstand on an afternoon at a tournament, were covered with the scattered host. On a smoother rock, which two tall limes shaded with their sparse foliage, a page stretched out sheep-skins for Don Pedro de Castro and the lord of Santa Ireneia. But only the old Castilian seated himself, for a lengthy rest, after undoing his iron bodice inlaid with gold.

Tructesindo remained erect, silent, his gloves resting upon the handle of his long sword, his deep-set eyes eagerly fixed upon the tenebrous lake, which would avenge his son's murder by so vile and bestial a death. Along the edge of the lake, foot-soldiers and a few knights of Spain stirred the muddy water, with arrows and the butts of their javelins, curious to see the black creatures which were concealed there.

Suddenly, at a shout from Don Garcia, who was walking round supervising, the crowd of foot-soldiers clustered around the Bastard drew aside, and the powerful body appeared in all its whiteness and nakedness upon the black earth, a thick growth of fair hair upon his chest, his genitals lost in another clump of fair hair, all bound by hempen cords which drew him taut. Stiff as a package, not even his ribs heaved—only his eyes shone, bloodshot and horribly protruding with fear and rage. Some of the knights went over to see the naked degradation of the famous knight of Baião. The Lord of the Manor of Argelim jeered noisily:

'Well I knew it, by God! A maiden's body—not a scar upon it!'

Leonel de Samora brushed his iron shoe against the ill-fated man's shoulder.

'Just look at our Bright Sun, so white, and so soon to be put out in such black water!'

The Bastard closed his eyes ponderously, and from under the lids escaped two large tears, which rolled slowly down his face . . . But a sharp cry echoed across the hillside:

'Justice! Justice!'

It was the officer-in-command who was marching down, waving a lance and thundering across the hillside:

'Justice! Justice to be carried out by the Lord of Treixedo and Santa Ireneia, upon the cur of an assassin! Justice upon a cur, son of a bitch, who murdered most foully and so must die foully for it!'

Three times did he proclaim thus before the host crowding the hillside. Then he stopped and solemnly and humbly saluted Tructesindo Ramires and the old Castro—as if to judges on a judge's dais.

'On with it! On with it!' shouted the Lord of Santa Ireneia.

Immediately, at a signal from the Wise One, six cross-bows, their legs bound in horses' blankets, lifted up the Bastard as if they were raising a corpse bound in his winding-sheet and entered the water towards the taller granite pillar. Others, dragging lengths of cords, ran along the muddy wooden gangway. With cries of 'Hold it!' 'Straight! Straight!' 'Lift him up!' the powerful white body was plunged, with a good deal of effort, into the water as far as his groin, against the taller pillar to which he was tied with a long rope which ran through the iron ring and held him, without his being able to slip, as tight and safe as a furled sail to a mast. Swiftly the cross-bows hurried out of the water, immediately pulled off the bindings, felt their legs and scratched them, aghast at the thought of the blood-sucking creatures. The rest hustled each other along the gangway in their haste to leave the spot. In the Pool remained Lopo de Baião, neatly arranged for his slow and spectacular death. The water reached to the top of his legs and cords bound his neck, like a slave to a post; and a thick bunch of his fair hair was caught up in the iron ring, thrusting forward his pale face, so that all might enjoy to the utmost the humiliation and agony of the Bright Sun.

The anticipation of the host, waiting scattered over the hillside, increased the gloomy silence of the desolate spot. The water lay without a ripple, its darker patches as black as a sheet of rusty tin. Among the rocky crags, halberdiers posted by the Wise One, waited and watched over the barren land. High above, a crow flew by croaking raucously. Then a gentle breeze moved the pennants of the lances stuck in the dense gorse thickets.

To stir up the leeches, to make them move, some of the foot-soldiers threw stones into the muddy water. Certain of the Spanish knights were already grumbling impatiently about the delay in that stifling hole. Others crouched beside the lake to show that the famous leeches would not come, dipping their ungloved hands leisurely in the black water, and afterwards shaking them, laughing and mocking the Wise One . . . But suddenly a tremor passed through the Bastard's body, and his tense muscles, in a furious effort to free himself, swelled between the cords, like the coiling of cobras; and from his bared teeth came growls and grunts, insults and threats against that coward Tructesindo and all the house of Ramires, which he cursed to the flames of hell within a year! One of the knights of Santa Ireneia indignantly snatched a cross-bow and tightened the string.

But Don Garcia restrained his impulse.

'For God's sake, friend! Don't rob the leeches of a single drop of that fresh blood! . . . See how they come! See how they come!'

A shudder ran through the thick water, around the submerged thighs of the Bastard, fat bubbles swelled and from them first one leech sluggishly appeared and then another and another, shiny and black, undulating and clinging to the white flesh of the belly, from which they hung, sucking, immediately fatter and shinier with the blood that was slowly flowing. The Bastard fell silent—and his teeth rattled. Sickened by the sight, even coarse foot-soldiers turned away their faces and spat into the gorse. Others, however, jested and encouraged the leeches, crying, 'At him, girls! At him!' The gentle Samora de Cendufe laughingly protested against so insipid a death! God above! A dose of leeches, such as you'd give to a man suffering from haemorrhoids! It wasn't a sentence for a nobleman—but a prescription by a Moorish herbalist!

'Oh, come now, what more do you want, Leonel?' asked the Wise One with a laugh, his face beaming. 'This is a death to be related in books! You'll not find a session round the fire this winter in any of the manors from Minho to Douro at which they won't refer to this pool and this exploit! Look at our Cousin Tructesindo Ramires! He's seen beautiful tortures in his long experience as a warrior, for sure! Look how he's enjoying it! How attentive he is! How he marvels at it!'

On the slope, beside the standard, which his standard-bearer had stuck between two stones and which was as still as himself, Old Ramires did not take his eyes off the Bastard's body, in savage delight and with a sullen gleam in his eyes. Never had he expected so magnificent a revenge! The man who had tied up his son with cords, had dragged him along on a litter and stabbed him with his dagger in front of the barbican of his own estate—was now abjectly naked, tied like a hog, hung from a pillar, submerged in dirty water and being sucked by leeches before two of the finest armies in Spain, who were watching him and jeering! That blood, the blood of the detested race, would not be absorbed by earth churned up in an afternoon of battle, flowing from an honourable wound through sturdy armour, but was darkly and sluggishly oozing away, drip by drip, sucked up by filthy leeches which were emerging hungrily out of the mud and would return to the mud sated, and would belch up on the mud the proud blood with which they were sated. In a pool where he had put him, slimy leeches were serenely drinking up the Knight of Baião! Where could there exist a family feud founded upon so sweet a revenge?

The old man's savage soul accompanied the leeches with un-relenting glee, as they climbed up and spread over that well-bound body, like a flock of sheep safe on the hillside where they grazed. His stomach had already disappeared beneath a black, viscous mass which throbbed and gleamed in the moist softness of the blood. A row of them was sucking at the waist contracted with terror, dripping blood in a slow fringe, and winding their way up, leaving behind a trail of mud. A tangled mass sucked at an arm. Those which were glutted, the shiniest, fattest ones, dropped off and fell inertly; but others at once latched on. From the open wounds the blood flowed slowly out to stop at the cords, from which it dripped like fine rain. In the dark water floated fat clots of waste blood. Thus devoured and oozing blood, the ill-fated knight emitted, amid foul oaths, curses of death and fire against the whole race of Ramires! Then with a heave which almost burst his bonds, and his mouth wide open and gasping, he broke into raucous howls, imploring Water! Water! In his fury, his nails, which several cords bound to his solid thighs, ripped his flesh and thrust into the wound, soaked in blood.

His frenzy died away in a long weary sigh—until he seemed to have fallen asleep in the thick knots of the cords, his beard gleaming with the sweat which soaked it as if with a heavy dew, and from the beard came a ghastly, white, delirious grin.

Meanwhile, the host scattered about the hillside, were losing their interest in this novel torture. It was getting near the time for their midday rations. The officer-in-command of Santa Ireneia, then the captain of the Spanish host, bade the trumpets sound. Over the entire rugged, desolate spot, men began to stir. The food store of both parties had halted behind the hills, on a short strip of meadowland where a stream trickled over pebbles between the roots of alder-trees and weeping-willows. In a famished rush, leaping over the rocks, the foot-soldiers ran towards the line of pack-mules, and received from the store-keepers and attendants their slice of meat and thick chunk of half a black loaf; dispersed beneath the shadows of the trees, they ate slowly and silently, drinking water from the stream in wooden bowls. Then they stretched and spread themselves on the grass—or went up in a crowd to the other side of the hill, across the scrub, in the hopes of shooting a roving beast. On the hillside opposite the lake, the knights, seated on their thick blankets round their open saddle-bags, were eating, too, hacking off morsels of fat with their daggers from the hunks of pork they carried, and drinking down long draughts from their big-bellied wine-skins.

Invited by Don Pedro de Castro, the old Wise One sat himself down and ate from a wide earthen porringer full of Papal Cake—a cake made of honey and fine flour, in which both of them slowly dipped their fingers—and afterwards wiped them on the lining of their morions. Only Old Tructesindo did not eat, did not rest, stiff and silent before his standard, between his two mastiffs, in his savage duty of accompanying, without missing a shudder or a groan or a drop of blood, the Bastard's agony. In vain did the Castilian offer him a silver tankard, boasting about his Tordesilhas wine, fresher than any from Aquilat or Provence, to quench the thirst of so harsh an expedition. The old nobleman did not answer; and Don Pedro, after throwing two chunks of bread to his faithful dogs, began conversing again with Garcia Viegas about the Bastard's obdurate love for Violante Ramires which had impelled him to so many murders and rages.

'Happy are we, Senhor Don Garcia! We whom age and weakness and surfeit have weaned from such temptations! For woman, as a certain physician told me when I was with the Moors, is a breeze which consoles and smells good, but which contorts and destroys everything. See how my family suffered because of them! Look at my father, for instance, that mad jealousy of his, when he killed my sweet mother Estevaninha with a hatchet! And she so saintly, and the daughter of an Emperor! That foolish ardour leads to everything! Everything! Even to dying, as this one, sucked by leeches, before an eating, jeering host! By God, Senhor Don Garcia, how long he takes dying!'

'But dying he is, Senhor Don Pedro de Castro. And with the devil beside him to take him away!'

The Bastard was dying. Between the knots of the bloody cords, he was a horrifying sight, black and scarlet with the viscous mass of leeches which covered him pulsating in the slow streams of blood which ran from every wound, flowing more freely and faster than trickles of moisture down a blackened wall.

His desperate panting had stopped, and his straining against the cords, and all his frenzy. Inert and lifeless as a bundle, with only a terrible bulging every now and then of the eyes rolling with stupefied fear. Then his head lolled, livid and flaccid, and his lips fell open, revealing the black hollow of his mouth, from which trickled a

276

mixture of blood and dribble. From his closed, swollen eye-lids dripped some slimy matter, like tears thickened with blood.

The foot-soldiers had meanwhile returned from their meal, and crowding over the slope, stood staring and jeering at the ghastly body at which the leeches were still sucking. The pages were now collecting up mantles and saddle-packs. Don Pedro de Castro walked down from the hill top with the Wise One to the edge of the muddy water, so near that he almost wetted his iron shoes, to get a closer view of the man dying from so rare an agony! Some of the men, tired of so long delay, fastened their hauberks and muttered, 'He's dead! He's finished!'

Then Garcia Viegas shouted to the captain of cross-bows:

'Ermigues, go and see if there's any life left in that bloody mess!'

The captain ran along the wooden gangway, and shuddering with horror, felt the livid flesh and put to the wide-open mouth the shining blade of the dagger which he had unsheathed.

'Dead! Dead!' he cried.

He was dead. Within the cords that bruised the flesh, the body slipped, shrivelled, sucked, empty. The blood no longer flowed, it had congealed in dark layers, where a few leeches still obstinately sucked and gleamed. Others were still belatedly climbing up. Two enormous ones were crawling in an ear. Another had blocked out an eye. The Bright Sun was no more than a decomposing lump of filth. Only a lock of fair hair, pulled back into the ring, shone like the glare of a flame, like a trail left by the ardent soul which had fled.

Waving his still unsheathed dagger, the captain advanced towards the Lord of Santa Ireneia, crying,

'Justice has been done to the cur of an assassin we have slain!'

Then the old man shot out his arm, his hairy fist clenched and threatening, and cried, in a hoarse shout that echoed over the cliffs and hills,

'He's dead! So dies of an infamous death a man who treacherously insulted me and my race!'

Then cutting stiffly across the hillside, over the shrub, and waving to the standard-bearer, he cried,

'Afonso Gomes, bid the trumpets sound! And now to horse, if it pleases you, Senhor Don Pedro de Castro, cousin and friend, who has been loyal and good to me!'

The Castilian smiled and waved his gauntlet.

'To Santa Maria, cousin and friend! Pleasure and honour have we enjoyed from you. To horse then, if it pleases you! For Senhor Don Garcia here has promised us we shall see, while the sun is still high in the heavens, the walls of Montemor.'

The foot-soldiers closed their ranks and the pages pulled the rested jennets that had been frightened by the dark water up the hill. With the two banners unfurled—the black goshawk and the thirteen torteaux—the line of horsemen set off at a trot up the steep path, loose stones rolling from under their feet. At the top, some of the knights even turned round in their saddles to gaze again in silence at the man of Baião, who was left there, tied to the pillar, in the solitude of the pool, to rot. But when the line of cross-bows and slingsmen from Santa Ireneia filed past, there was a loud shout and jeers and foul insults at the 'cur of an assassin' left there. Half-way up the slope, an arbalester turned and furiously wound his cross-bow taut. The long bolt hit the water. Another was immediately fired, and a shot from a sling, and a barbed arrow—which struck in the Bastard's side, amidst a black mass of leeches. The captain shouted, 'Line up! March!' The train of pack-animals advanced, to the cracking of whips; the baggage-lads picked up heavy stones and hurled them at the dead man. Then the serfs driving the carts followed in their brief, raw leather skirts, holding short goads; and their leader picked and flung a lump of dung with which he spattered the Bastard's face, and his beautiful golden beard.

11

WHEN GONÇALO, EXHAUSTED, his ardour fading, completed the last detail of this final insult, the bell in the corridor sounded for lunch. At last! God be praised! The eternal Tower of Ramires was finished! Four months, four arduous months, ever since June, he had worked on this sombre revival of his barbarous ancestors. In slow, heavy letters he wrote at the bottom of the sheet: FINIS. He dated it and put the time, which was fourteen minutes past twelve.

But now, the writing-desk at which he had toiled abandoned, he did not feel the anticipated contentment. The Bastard's torture had even left him with an aversion for that remote Afonsine world, so bestial, so inhuman! If only he were consoled by the certainty that he had reconstructed, with brilliant truth, the moral being of his savage ancestors . . . But no. He feared that beneath their confused armour, lacking in archaeological accuracy, he had merely sketched in vague souls without historical reality! . . . He even doubted the ability of leeches to climb out of a pool and cover the body of a man and suck him alive from thighs to beard, while an army sat and watched and chewed their food! Still, Castanheiro had praised the opening chapters. The public loves reading about grand passions and dripping blood; soon the *Annals* would spread throughout Portugal the fame of that illustrious house, which had assembled armies, had destroyed castles and had lain waste vast areas for the honour of their standard, arrogantly defying Kings in the curia and on the battlefield. His summer had therefore been fruitful. And to crown this success the election was coming up, which would liberate him from the desolation of his country hole . . .

So as not to defer any longer the visits still to be made to influential electors, and to get out and enjoy himself a little, he set off on horseback immediately after lunch, in spite of the heat, which although mid-October, had borne down on the village since the previous day with the blazing weight of an August noon. Round the bend in the Bravais road, a fat man with grubby white trousers came hurrying along, puffing and blowing, under a red cloth sun-shade, and stopped the Nobleman with immense courtesy. It was

Godinho, a clerk from the Administrator's office. He had taken an urgent message to the officer of justice of Bravais and now he was on his way to the Tower from the Administrator.

Gonçalo pulled his mare into the shade of an oak-tree.

'What's up then, Godinho, old friend?'

The Administrator wished to inform his Lordship that that scoundrel Ernesto, the ruffian from Nacejas, had been undergoing treatment in Oliveira Hospital and had recovered considerably. His ear had been stitched back on and his mouth had healed . . . And as there was now this matter of a court-case the rascal would be sent from the hospital to prison.

Gonçalo protested with a slap on his saddle.

'No, sir! Please be so good as to tell Senhor João Gouveia that I don't want the man arrested! He was insolent and he got a good hiding: we're quits!'

'But Senhor Gonçalo Mendes . . .'

'For the love of God, old friend! I have said I don't want him arrested and I don't. Explain things to Senhor João Gouveia. I hate taking revenge. It's not one of my customs, nor the custom of my family. No Ramires ever sought revenge . . . What I mean is, there was, but, I mean . . . Anyway, tell Senhor João Gouveia. I'll be seeing him in the Club. Enough if the man's been made ugly. I won't have him any further distressed! . . . I hate ferocity.'

'But . . .'

'I've made up my mind, Godinho!'

'I'll pass on your message.'

'Thank you. And goodbye! . . . Awful heat, isn't it?'

'Sweltering, Senhor Gonçalo Mendes, sweltering!'

Gonçalo went on his way, revolted by the thought that the wretched ruffian from Nacejas, still battered from the struggle, his ear scarcely healed, should have to descend to the sordid gaol of Vila Clara, to sleep there on a board. He even thought of galloping to Vila Clara himself and restraining João Gouveia's judicial zeal. But nearby, just beyond the washing-place, was the house of a man of influence, João Firmino, a carpenter and a *compadre* of his. So off he trotted, and rang the bell at the gate. His *compadre* had set out early for Arribada, where he was working on the construction of a press for Senhor Esteves. It was his wife who hurried out of the kitchen, fat and shiny, with two small children as black as the ace of spades hanging on to her skirts. The Nobleman kissed the two little runny-eyed faces tenderly.

'What a delicious smell of fresh bread, *comadre*! You've been baking, have you? Give Firmino a hug from me. And tell him not to forget! The elections are next Sunday. I'm counting on his vote. It's not for the sake of the vote, mind, it's a question of friendship!'

His *comadre* showed her magnificent teeth in a broad, delighted grin. 'Your Lordship can rest assured! Firmino's already sworn, even to the local officer, that everyone round about will be voting for the Nobleman, and those that don't vote for love will vote by force!' The Nobleman clasped the hand of his *comadre* who, from the garden-step, her two babies entwined in her skirts and a still more enraptured smile on her face, followed the dust kicked up by the mare like the wake of a beneficent King.

In the other places he called at, in Cerejeira, in Ventura da Chiche, he found the same fervour, the same smiles glowing with pleasure. 'What? Vote for the Nobleman? But of course! Even if he were against the Government!' In Manuel da Adega's tavern, a crowd of labourers drank noisily, their jackets flung on the benches. The Nobleman drank with them, joking, frankly enjoying the drop of green wine and the noise. The oldest of them, a dark, ugly old man with no teeth in his head, his face more wrinkled than a dried prune, gave an enthusiastic thump on the counter with his fist: 'This, boys, is the Nobleman who lends his horse when a poor God-forsaken wretch hurts his leg, and walks a league beside him on foot, as he did with Solha! This is a Nobleman of the right sort, boys!' Cries of 'Good health!' rang through the tavern. When Gonçalo mounted, they all grouped round him like ardent vassals who, at a mere nod, would run off and vote—or kill!

In Tomás Pedra's house, Grandma Ana Pedra, an old invalid, very ancient and very quivery, burst into tears because her Tomás was in Olival when the Nobleman called. 'It's like a saint visiting the house!'

'Oh, come now, Aunt Pedra! I am a sinner, a great sinner!'

Doubled up in her low chair, white strands of hair slipping out of her kerchief down over her hairy, wrinkled face, Ana slapped her skinny knee.

'No, sir! No, sir! Anyone who showed such kindness to Casco's boy should be on an altar!'

The Nobleman laughed, kissed families of grimy children, clasped hands as rough and wrinkled as roots, lit his cigarette at open fires, and chatted familiarly about diseases and flirtations. Then, amid the heat and dust of the road again, he thought to himself, 'Strange, but these people seem quite friendly!'

At four o'clock, exhausted, he decided to end his round of visits and return to the Tower by the coolest route, by the Holy Spring. He had passed the little hamlet of Cerdal, when at a sharp bend in the road, beside the grove of holm-oaks, he almost collided with Dr Julio, also on horseback, also making his round of visits. He was wearing an alpaca jacket, and was bathed in sweat, beneath a green silk sunshade. Both of them reined in their mares and greeted each other amicably.

'Pleased to see you, Dr Julio!'

'And it's a great pleasure to see you, Sr Gonçalo Ramires . . .'

'You're out on business, too?'

Dr Julio shrugged his shoulders.

'What do you expect, sir? Since I've been landed with this! And do you know the upshot, sir? The upshot is I'll be going along, next Sunday, and voting for you, sir!'

The Nobleman laughed. They both leant over to shake hands, gay and mutually respectful.

'How dreadfully hot it is, Dr Julio!'

'Terrible, Senhor Gonçalo Ramires . . . And what a bore!'

Thus did the Nobleman spend his week, visiting his electors—'great and small'. Two days before the election, a Friday afternoon, when the weather was gentler and cooler, he left for Oliveira—where André Cavaleiro had arrived the day before, after his long, much-talked-of stay in Lisbon.

When he jumped out of the calash at *Cunhais*, he was infuriated to learn from the good doorman João that 'the Misses Lousada are upstairs, visiting Senhora Dona Graça . . .'

'Have they been here long?'

'They've been stuck there for a good half-hour, sir.'

Gonçalo slipped furtively into his room, thinking, 'Shameless hags! As soon as André arrives, they come snooping round here!' He had washed and changed his grey suit when Barrolo appeared, puffing and panting and unwontedly radiant, wearing a frock-coat and a top-hat, while his fat cheeks were on fire, flustered and brilliant.

'Eh, Barrolo, old chap, what a dandy you are!'

'But this is a fantastic coincidence!' shouted Barrolo, after a hug, which he repeated with unaccustomed fervour. 'I was on the point of going out and sending you a telegram to come . . .'

'Why?'

Barrolo stammered, a repressed smile lighting up his face and puffing him out.

'Why? For no reason . . . I mean, for the election, of course! The election's the day after tomorrow, you know, boy! Cavaleiro arrived yesterday. I've just come back from the Civil Governor's. I was in the Palace with the Lord Bishop, so I dropped in at the Civil Governor's. André's excellent! He's trimmed down his moustache, looks much younger. And he's got news! Great news!'

Barrolo rubbed his hands together in such excitement, with such humour shining in his eyes and face that the Nobleman looked at him with curiosity, impressed.

'Look here, Barrolinho! Have you got something to tell me?'

Barrolo drew back and denied it vehemently, like a man slamming a door. He? Good gracious, no! He didn't know anything! Only the election! There'd be a tremendous number of votes from Murtosa . . .

'Ah, I thought you had,' murmured Gonçalo. 'And how's Graça?'

'Gracinha doesn't, either!'

'Doesn't what either, man? How is she? I'm simply asking, how is she?'

'Ah, she's with the Lousadas. For over half an hour, the drunken old hags! . . . Naturally it's about the bazaar in aid of the Orphanage . . . These confounded bazaars . . . Listen, Gonçalinho! Are you staying till Sunday?'

'No, I'm going back to the Tower tomorrow.'

'Oh! . . .'

'On election day, man, I must be in my house, in my right place, in the midst of my parishioners . . .'

'A shame,' murmured Barrolo. 'Knowing that at the same time as the election results . . . I'd have given you a marvellous dinner . . .'

'Knowing what?'

Barrolo was silent, another smile lighting up his cheeks, which were like two bright coals. Then he again stammered, rolling from side to side,

'Knowing . . . Nothing! The result, the count. A fine old celebration, fireworks and all! I'm opening a barrel of wine in Murtosa.'

Then Gonçalo smiled and caught Barrolo by the shoulders.

'Come on, Barrolinho, tell me now. You've got something nice to tell your brother-in-law.'

Barrolo slipped away, protesting noisily: what a stubborn fellow Gonçalo was! What foolishness! He didn't know anything. André hadn't told him anything!

'Right,' answered the Nobleman, convinced of some pleasant mystery in the air. 'Then we'll go down. And if these blood-sucking old women are still there, have the footman go to the drawing-room and tell Gracinha loudly that I have arrived and I wish to talk to her immediately in my room; those monsters don't deserve any consideration.'

Barrolo hesitated and stammered,

'The Bishop likes them . . . He was very pleasant to me a little while ago, the Bishop.'

But as they descended the stairs, they could hear Gracinha at the piano, singing. She had got rid of the Lousadas. It was an ancient patriotic song from Vendeia, which she and Gonçalo had sung ardently together once, in the Tower, when they were inflamed by romantic and aristocratic love of the Bourbons and the Stuarts:

> 'Monsieur de Charette a dit à ceux d'Ancenes
> "Mes Amis! . . ."
> Monsieur de Charette a dit . . .'

Gonçalo thrust aside the curtain of the drawing-room, continuing the verse, his arm upraised like a banner:

> 'Mes Amis!
> Le Roy va rammener les Fleurs de Lys!'

Gracinha jumped up from her stool in surprise.

'We weren't expecting you! I imagined you'd be spending the election in the Tower . . . How are things there?'

'Everything's all right there, with the help of God . . . But I have had a tremendous amount of work to do. I finished my novel, and then there were visits to the electors.'

Barrolo, who was fidgeting around the room all the time, bounced up to them with the same suppressed smile.

'Do you know what, Gracinha? This fellow's been in such a state

284

of curiosity ever since he arrived. He imagines I've got some good news for him, some wonderful piece of news to give him . . . I don't know a thing, except about the election! Isn't that true, Gracinha?'

Gonçalo took hold of his sister's chin very seriously:

'You know. Now tell me.'

She laughed and blushed . . . No, she didn't know anything, only about the elections.

'Tell me!'

'I don't know . . . This is just José's nonsense.'

But then, before his self-betraying, helpless smile, Barrolo could not contain himself and blurted out like a cannon exploding: Well, then, he was right! There was news! But André, who had brought it from Lisbon, fresh and hot, wanted it to be himself, and himself alone, who passed on the surprise to Gonçalo!

'So you see I can't tell you! I swore to André. Gracinha knows, I told her yesterday . . . But she can't either, she swore, too. Only André. And it's stupendous! Fabulous!'

Gonçalo, eaten away with curiosity, murmured simply, with a shrug:

'I know what it is—it's an inheritance! You earn fifteen *tostões* as a harbinger of good news, Barrolo.'

But during dinner, and afterwards in the drawing-room having coffee, while Gracinha began singing her old patriotic songs again, the Jacobite ones this time, in praise of the Stuarts—Gonçalo was dying to see Cavaleiro. He did not fear that there would be any feelings of bitterness or suppressed contempt at this meeting. All his fury with Cavaleiro, afire that painful afternoon at the gazebo and reflected upon during those nerve-racking days at the Tower, had gradually dissolved after his touching conversation with his sister, on the historic morning of the Battle of Grainha. Gracinha had then sworn, with great tears of purity and truth, reserve and withdrawal. André, abandoning Oliveira, had also showed praiseworthy resistance to the emotion or vanity which had misguided him. Moreover, he could hardly break with Cavaleiro again, while Oliveira was still full of gossip and amazement over that astonishing reconciliation which had summoned Cavaleiro into the intimacy of *Cunhais*. And anyway what was the use of rages and sorrows? Neither roars nor groans from him would undo the evil that had taken place in the gazebo—if it had actually taken place. So all his anger against André had disappeared in that frail soul where emotions, especially darker ones, heavier ones, always fade easily away, like clouds in a summer sky . . .

But at nine o'clock, when Cavaleiro came into the room, slowly and magnificently, his moustache trimmed even curlier, and a scarlet tie puffed out gaudily on his wide chest that was puffed out, too, Gonçalo felt a renewed aversion for all that petulance brimming with falsity—and all he could do was tap his friend listlessly on the back, while André gave him a hug of pronounced tenderness. Then as André, playing with his white gloves, languidly ensconced in an armchair which Barrolo had affectionately pulled up for him, spoke of Lisbon and Cascais—so gay—and bridge-parties and the Parade and His Majesty—Gonçalo relived the afternoon at the gazebo, his poor heart beating against the ill-drawn blinds, the bestial supplication murmured through that devilish moustache, and he was silent, as if petrified, as he nervously chewed the end of his extinguished cigar. But Gracinha retained such an attentive serenity, without any of her deep blushes, any of her unfortunate confused behaviour or gestures—just a little dry, with a deliberate, contrived dryness. Then André alluded quite nonchalantly to his return to Lisbon after the elections, 'because Uncle Reis Gomes, José Ernesto, those cruel friends of mine, are dumping all the work of the New Administrative Reform on to my shoulders.'

There seemed to be, between him and Gracinha, separated by a short carpet, a deep, league-long ditch in which all that summer romance had fallen, had sunk, without a blushing trace of its ardour remaining in either face. Gonçalo, insensibly content at appearances, finished by abandoning the chair in which he had sunk benumbed, and lit his cigar at the candle on the piano and asked after his friends in Lisbon. All of them, according to Cavaleiro, were longing for Gonçalo's arrival.

'I met Castanheiro there, too . . . He's delighted with your novel. It seems there's nothing, not even in Herculano or Rebelo, that's so powerful a historical reconstruction. Castanheiro prefers your realism even to Flaubert's, in *Salammbô*. He's really delighted! And we, of course, are anxiously awaiting the appearance of the sublime work.'

The Nobleman blushed deeply, and murmured,

'What nonsense!' Then he brushed against the armchair where

André had settled himself, and gently patted his broad shoulder. 'I've missed you, old chap, there's no doubt about it. Only the other day I was passing by Corinde thinking about you . . .'

Then Barrolo, unable to keep still, bright pink and apparently about to explode, flapping about the room, peering first at Cavaleiro and then at Gonçalo, with a silent, eager smile, was unable to control himself any longer and blurted out,

'Come on, enough prologues . . . Let's get on to the big surprise, André! I've been nearly bursting all afternoon . . . Still, I promised, and I kept quiet! But I can't any longer . . . Come on now. And you, Gonçalinho, get your fifteen *tostões* ready.'

Gonçalo, his curiosity afire again, merely smiled nonchalantly.

'Yes, really. It seems you have some good news.'

Cavaleiro stretched out his arms, sunk deeply as he was in his armchair, in no hurry to divulge the news.

'Oh, it's quite a simple thing, a very natural thing . . . Senhora Dona Graça already knows, don't you? . . . There's no cause for surprise . . . So natural, so obvious.'

Gonçalo exclaimed with impatience,

'Come on now, tell me what it is.'

But Cavaleiro, indolent, insisted that the amazing thing was that it was only now that so normal, so legitimate a thing was being realized. 'Don't you agree, Senhora Dona Graça?'

Gonçalo blurted out in exasperation,

'But what the devil are you talking about?'

Cavaleiro, who had raised himself leisurely from his chair, pulled down his cuffs and standing in front of Gonçalo, in the attentive silence, began gravely, almost officially, puffing out his chest,

'My Uncle Reis Gomes, and José Ernesto, had a very natural idea, which they communicated to His Majesty, and His Majesty approved . . . He approved to the extent of adopting it, of taking possession of it, of wishing it were his own idea. So now it's His Majesty's idea. His Majesty then thought, as we thought, that one of the greatest noblemen in Portugal, surely the greatest, should have a title, which would consecrate the illustrious antiquity of the House, and consecrate, too, the due value of the person representing it . . . Therefore, my dear Gonçalo, I can announce to you, and almost in the name of His Majesty, that you are going to become the Marquis of Treixedo.'

287

'Bravo! Bravo!' shouted Barrolo, clapping wildly. 'Fling over those fifteen *tostões*, Senhor Marquis de Treixedo!'

A flush swept across Gonçalo's fine face. In a flash he realized that the title was a gift of Cavaleiro's, not to the head of the Ramires house but to the complaisant brother of Gracinha Ramires . . . More than anything else he felt the inappropriateness that, on him—head of a House ten centuries old, with more than thirty of its males killed in battle, Mother of dynasties and architect of the Kingdom—there should be flung a hollow title, communicated through the *Diário do Governo*, as if he were some rich shopkeeper who footed the bill at elections. However, he acknowledged Cavaleiro, who was expecting effusion, arms thrown round him. Oh! Marquis of Treixedo! Of course, most elegant, most agreeable! . . . Then, rubbing his hands with a charming, somewhat astonished smile . . . 'But, my dear André, on what authority is His Majesty making me Marquis of Treixedo?'

Cavaleiro lifted his head sharply with offended surprise:

'On what authority? Simply on the authority that he has over all of us, as King of Portugal, which he still is, thank God!'

Gonçalo, very simply, without pomp or presumption, but with the same smile of gentle humour,

'Forgive me, Andrèzinho. There were no kings of Portugal, nor even a Portugal, when my Ramires forebears had their Manor in Treixedo! I approve of noble gifts among noble aristocrats; but it is up to the most ancient of them to begin. His Majesty has an estate near Beja, I believe, the *Roncão*. Well, tell His Majesty then that I have immense pleasure in making him Marquis of Roncão.'

Barrolo stood dumbfounded, uncomprehending, his fat jowls wan and drooping. From the edge of the sofa, Gracinha flushed with pleasure at his delightful pride which was so in keeping with hers, which linked her soul more closely with the soul of her beloved brother. André Cavaleiro, furious, but bowing his shoulders in ironic submission, merely murmured, 'Certainly, certainly! . . . Everyone sees things in a different light . . .'

The footman entered with the tea-tray.

★   ★   ★

Sunday was election day.

Still mistrustful, still superstitiously shy, the Nobleman spent

288

the day on his own, almost in hiding, and on Saturday, while all his friends in Vila Clara, and even those in Oliveira, thought he was settled at *Cunhais*, in a flurry of communications with the Civil Government, he mounted his mare at nightfall and trotted furtively to Santa Ireneia.

But Barrolo (still astounded by 'Gonçalo's nonsense, that was an insult to Cavaleiro! even to His Majesty!') stayed there with the job of telegraphing to the Tower the successive results from the various polling-stations as soon as they notified the Civil Governor. With noisy zeal, immediately after mass, a relay of servants, running back and forth, was established between *Cunhais* and the old Convent of S Domingos. Gracinha, in the dining-room, aided by Father Soeiro, copied out lovingly, in very round letters, the telegrams sent by Cavaleiro, who had added a friendly note in pencil—'Everything excellent! Victory increases. Congratulations.'

The telegraph-boy hobbled incessantly on his lame leg along the road from Vila Clara to the Tower. Bento burst into the library shouting, 'Another telegram, sir!' Gonçalo sat nervously at his work-table, with an enormous tea-pot before him, and a tray already strewn with half-smoked cigarettes, and read the telegram to Bento. Bento, with shouts of 'Hurrah!' along the corridor, ran to blurt out the telegram to Rosa.

So when at nearly eight o'clock the Nobleman consented to dine, he already knew his splendid triumph. What impressed him, as he re-read the telegrams, was the affectionate enthusiasm of the men of influence in the district, people whose help he had scarcely asked, and who had transformed the act of election almost into an act of love. The entire parish of Bravais had marched to church, in close formation like an army, with José Casco in front holding aloft an enormous banner between two crashing drums. The Viscount of Rio Manso had entered the churchyard of Ramilde in his victoria, his granddaughter dressed all in white, followed by an imposing line of public carriages with electors piled inside under canopies of foliage. In Finta all the farms were empty, with the women wearing their entire collection of gold, and the boys with flowers tucked in their ears, hurrying to the election of the Nobleman to the twanging of guitars, as if they were on a pilgrimage to a saint. And outside Pintainho's tavern, opposite the church, the people of Veleda and Riosa and Cercal erected a boxwood arch with words in red

289

on a cloth sign: 'Long live our Ramires—the best man around!'

Then, while he dined, a farm-lad came back from Vila Clara bursting with excitement, with news of the enthusiasm there—bands in the streets, the Club with bunting out, and over the door in the Town Hall, a picture of Gonçalo which crowds were applauding.

Gonçalo hurried over coffee. Shy, apprehensive of the cheering, he did not dare go to Vila Clara to see how things were. But he lit his cigar and went out on to the verandah, to inhale the fragrance of this night of celebration, which was full of flashes and bangs in his honour. But as he opened the glass door, he almost drew back in alarm. The Tower was lit up! A glow shone from its deep loopholes from behind the black iron bars; and high above on the old battlements glowed a crown of flame! It was a surprise planned for him, with delightful secrecy, by Bento and Rosa and the farm-lads—who now, in the darkness beneath the verandah, stood contemplating their work which lit up the serene sky. Gonçalo sensed their muffled steps and Rosa clearing her throat. He shouted down gaily from the edge of the verandah:

'Oh, Bento! Oh, Rosa! . . . Is there anyone there?'

A laugh rang out. Bento's white jacket emerged from the shadows.

'Did you want something, sir?'

'No man! I just wanted to thank you . . . It was you and the lads, was it? The illumination's lovely! Really lovely! Thank you, Bento. Thank you, Rosa! Thank you, lads! It must look wonderful from a distance.'

But Bento was not satisfied with such feeble lights. To show up properly, what the Tower needed was some bright gas flames. His Lordship couldn't imagine how high it was, and how vast the terrace was up there.

Suddenly Gonçalo felt an immense desire to go up to this enormous terrace in the Tower. He hadn't entered the Tower since he was a student—and he had always disliked it inside, it was so dark, the granite was so hard and cold and bare and silent as the tomb. First of all, in the ground-floor entrance, were the black, iron-plated trap-doors, which led to the dungeons. But now the lights in the loopholes warmed and seemed to restore to life that last relic of the Manor of Ordonho Mendes. There on the battlements, higher than his verandah, it seemed it would be interesting to breathe that noisy, far-flung sympathy, which, all around him in the parishes below, stirred and moved towards him like incense through the night. He slipped on a jacket and went down to the kitchen. Bento and Joaquim the gardener laughingly picked up big lanterns. He crossed the orchard between them and entered the squat postern with its low doorway, and began to climb up the narrow stone stairway which many an iron boot had polished and worn.

The place which the Tower had originally occupied in the complicated fortifications of the Manor of Santa Ireneia had been unknown for centuries. It was definitely not, according to Father Soeiro, the noble barbican tower, nor the keep, where the treasure had been kept, with the archives and precious sacks of spices from the Orient, so perhaps, obscure and nameless tower, it had merely defended some corner of the curtain wall, over where the castle faced the cultivated lands and elm groves of the river bank. But surviving the other, loftier towers, and integrated with the buildings in the beautiful structure that had been erected over the gloomy Afonsine castle and had dominated Santa Ireneia during the Avis dynasty, it was still connected by white arches from a terrace to the Italianate palace into which Vicente Ramires had converted the Manueline palace after his campaign in Castile; neglected in the orchard, but looking down on the vast house which had been slowly erected after the former palace had been burnt down in the time of King Don José, and the last to hear the clank of weapons and the bustle of armed men within—it had linked the ages and maintained in its stones, as it were, the unity of its long lineage. That's why the people called it vaguely, 'The Tower of Don Ramires'. Gonçalo, still under the influence of his ancestors and the times which he had brought back to life in his novel, admired with new respect its vastness and its strength, its steep steps and its walls, so thick that the narrow window-slits in its density looked like corridors dimly lit by the little saucers of oil with which Bento had brought them to life. In each of the storeys he stopped, entering with curiosity, almost with intimacy, the bare, echoing rooms with their great flagstones, their dark vaulted roofs, stone seats, the odd hole in the middle, round like a well, and on its walls still streaked with smoke-stains the ringed holders for torches. Then, on top, in the vast terrace that the row of lamps, encircling the battlements, filled with light, Gonçalo, turning up the collar of his jacket as the breeze blew more sharply, had the sensation of dominating the whole province and of enjoying a paternal supremacy over it, merely by the superior height and antiquity of the Tower, older than the province and the kingdom. Slowly he walked round the battlements as far as the look-out place, whose feudal appearance was destroyed by a paraffin-lamp placed on a wicker-chair facing the loophole. Occasional stars shone faintly from the soft, slightly misty sky. Beneath him, the whole vast expanse of fields, and the black mass of woods dissolved into the darkness. But every now and again, in the shadows and silence, distant fireworks flashed over near Bravais. A yellowish, smoky glow, further off, moving in the direction of Finta, was surely a crowd of children with festive torches. From the tall church of Veleda a pale, vague light flickered. Other lights, uncertain through the trees, half-illuminated the old arch of the Convent of Santa Maria de Craquede. From the ground at times rose a wavering roll of drums. These lights, torches and muffled roll of drums were ten parishes fondly celebrating the victory of the Nobleman, who received their affection and homage from the terrace of his Tower, enveloped in silence and shadows.

Bento had gone down with Joaquim to turn up the lamps in the loopholes, where they were dying out in the density of the walls. Gonçalo, alone, finishing off his cigar, began his round of the battlements again, lost in the thought which had already strangely moved him that eventful Sunday. He was popular! All through these villages, strewn beneath the long shadow of the Tower, the Nobleman of the Tower was popular! This certainty did not fill him with joy, nor pride—now did it rather fill him, in the calmness of night, with confusion and regret! Ah, if only he had guessed, if only he had guessed! How he would have walked with his head up high! his arms outstretched, alone, in smiling confidence that all this affection was awaiting him, so certain, so willingly proffered. But no! He had always imagined that he was surrounded by indifference in those villages, where he, in spite of his ancient name, was merely the familiar shape of the boy who had come down from Coimbra and lived quietly on the income of his lands, and trotted round the neighbourhood on his mare. From these naturally indifferent souls, he had never imagined he would be able to wrest the handful of votes, the handful of little papers necessary for him

292

to enter into Politics, where he would conquer by skill what the Ramires of old had received through inheritance—fortune and power. That was why he had clutched Cavaleiro's hand so keenly, the Civil Governor's hand—so that the fine gentleman, the good friend, should indicate him, should push him forward as the right man, the man wanted by the Government, the best among the good, and the man whom the parishioners one Sunday would offer their handful of votes.

Impatient for this favour, he had overlooked the memory of bitter insults; before an astonished Oliveira, he had embraced the man whom he had detested for years, whom he had mocked and denigrated in public places and newspapers; he had facilitated the revival of old sentiments which should have been buried for ever; and he had thrown the person dearest to him, his poor, weak little sister, into confusion and moral distress . . . Damage and depravity —and all for what? To snatch a handful of votes that ten parishes would have come running with gratuitously, effusively, with hoorahs and fireworks, if he had asked them . . .

Ah! That was the crux of the matter . . . It was his lack of confidence, that timid lack of confidence in himself, that, ever since college, had ruined his life. It was that same miserable lack of confidence that only a few weeks before, in the face of a shadow, a raised stick, a mocking laugh from a tavern, had forced him to run away, to flee, trembling and cursing his weakness. Finally, one day, at a bend in the road, he advances, raises his whip—and discovers his strength! And now he goes among the people timidly clutching the powerful hand, imagining himself unpopular—and discovers his immense popularity. What a misguided life, and how it had soiled him—through his ignorance!

Bento did not appear, he was so busy illuminating the Tower suitably. Gonçalo threw away his cigar-butt, and with his hands in his jacket pockets, stopped beside the look-out place and glanced vaguely up at the stars. The mist had almost cleared—stronger lights flickered in the deeper sky. From stars and sky came this feeling of infinity, of eternity, which enters, like a surprise, souls unused to contemplating them. Gonçalo's soul was filled, very fleetingly, with awe at these vast eternities beneath which moves, so proud of its movement, gloomy, abject, human dust. Far off a last firework flashed—to be immediately extinguished in the serene night. The little lights over the Chapel of Veleda, over the arch of Santa Maria de Craquede, grew dim and faded away. All the remote sounds of music died away in the deep silence of the sleeping fields. The day of triumph was coming to an end, as brief as the illuminations and fireworks. Gonçalo, still, beside the look-out place, now contemplated the value of this triumph for which he had so longed, so fawned. Deputy! Deputy for Vila Clara, like Sanches Lucena. Before such an ambition, so lowly, so trivial, all his desperate, unscrupulous efforts seemed less immoral than derisive. Deputy! What for? To have lunch in the *Braganza*, go up the hill in a cab to S Bento, and inside the dirty convent scribble on the state desk to his tailor; yawn over the surrounding inanity of both men and ideas, and accompany absent-mindedly, in silence or in bleating, the flock of S Bento sheep, as he had deserted the identical flock of sheep of Brás Vitorino. Yes, perhaps one day, after base flattery and intrigue with the leader and the leader's wife, and smiles and promises in the newspaper offices, and some ardently shouted speech—he would become a minister. And then what? There would be the same cab outside S Bento, with the messenger-boy behind on his white jade, the ill-made uniform on afternoons in the theatre, the fawning smiles of the clerks through the dark corridors of the Department and muck spattering him from every opposition newspaper . . . Ah! What a stupid, uninteresting life, by comparison with others full of supreme vitality, which pulsated so magnificently beneath the flickering of these same stars! As he huddled in his jacket, deputy for Vila Clara, triumphant at this miserable success—thinkers completed their explanations of the Universe; artists achieved works of eternal beauty; reformers perfected social harmony; saints improved souls in saintly fashion; physiologists lessened human suffering; inventors increased the wealth of nations; magnificent explorers wrested worlds from sterility and silence . . . Ah, these really were men, improving and embellishing humanity with their tireless hands! If only he were like them, the superhuman! Did such a supreme action need Genius—the gift that, like the ancient flame, descended from God upon the elect? No! Merely a clear understanding of human realities—and then a strong enough desire.

The Nobleman of the Tower, motionless on the terrace of the Tower, between the star-filled sky and the dark earth, ruminated a superior life for a long while, until he was carried away, as if the energy of the long race that had passed through the Tower were flooding his heart, and he imagined his own progress towards a vast and fertile action in which he could enjoy supremely the happiness of really living, and around him life would be created and a new lustre would be added to the old lustre of his name—pure riches would adorn him and all his country would glorify him, because he had given all of himself and all his efforts to serve his country . . .

Bento emerged from the low door on to the terrace with a lantern in his hand.

'Will you be here long, sir ?'

'No. The party's over, Bento.'

★   ★   ★

At the beginning of December, *The Tower of Don Ramires* appeared in the first number of the *Annals*. All the newspapers, even the Opposition ones, praised 'this learned study (as the *Evening News* put it) which, revealing a scholar and an artist, perpetuated, with more colourful and modern art, the work of Herculano and Rebelo— the moral and social reconstitution of the old heroic Portugal'. After the Christmas festivities, which he spent gaily at *Cunhais*, helping Gracinha to cook cod pasties from a sublime recipe of Father José Vicente's from Finta, his friends from Oliveira, the boys from the Club and the Arcade, gave the deputy for Vila Clara a banquet in the Town Hall, which was adorned with box-trees and flags; Cavaleiro was there with his Grand Cross and the Baron of Marges (who presided) drank a toast to 'the outstanding young man who would shortly, seated in Power, raise this courageous little country out from its atrophy, with the vitality and courage proper to his most noble race !'

★   ★   ★

One bitter rainy night in mid-January, Gonçalo left for Lisbon, and that winter in Lisbon he constantly appeared in the *Carnet-Mondain* and *High-Society* section of the newspapers, in the descriptions of suppers and *raouts*, of pigeon-shooting and hunts with His Majesty, and the least movement in his elegant life was reported to such an extent that the Barrolos took out a subscription to the *Daily Illustrated* to find out when he was passing in the Avenue. In

Vila Clara, in the Club, João Gouveia was already shrugging his shoulders and snorting: 'He turned out a dandy after all!' But at the end of April, a piece of news suddenly shook Vila Clara, and astounded the boys of the Club and the Arcade in quiet Oliveira, upset Gracinha (then in Amarante with Barrolo) so much that they both left for Lisbon that very night—and, at the Tower, sent Rosa weeping to a stone bench in the kitchen, uncomprehending and sobbing,

'Ai, my poor dear boy, my poor dear boy! I'll never set eyes on you again!'

Gonçalo Mendes Ramires had silently and almost mysteriously managed to obtain the concession of a vast piece of land in Mancheque in Zambezia, had mortgaged his historic estate of Treixedo, and was embarking at the beginning of June in the steamship *Portugal*, with Bento, for Africa.

12

FOUR YEARS PASSED lightly and swiftly like a flight of birds over the ancient Tower.

One mild afternoon at the end of September, Gracinha, who had arrived the day before from Oliveira accompanied by the good Father Soeiro, was resting on the dining-room verandah, stretched out on a straw-bottomed sofa, still wearing a large white apron—an old apron of Bento's—covering her dress to the neck. All day, in her apron, she had been working hard in the great old house, aided by Rosa and Crispola's daughter, tidying up and cleaning, with so much fervour and pleasure in her work that she had dusted all the books in the library herself—the untouched dust of four years. Barrolo had been occupied, too, giving instructions for work in the stables, which the valiant mare of the Battle of Grainha would soon be sharing with an English mare—a cross-breed bought in London. Father Soeiro was busying himself in the Archives, enthusiastically wielding a duster. Even Pereira da Riosa, the good lessee, had been chivvying two farm-boys ever since dawn in their final tidying-up of the vegetable-garden, very well-tended these days, with its melon-patch and its strawberry-patch, and two paths, each bordered by rose-bushes and screened by trellis already covered with thick vine.

The fact was, the ancient Tower was being embellished, amid all this enthusiasm and gaiety, because on Sunday, after four years in Africa, Gonçalo was returning to the Tower.

Gracinha, stretched out on the sofa in the old white apron, smiling pensively at the silent grounds, at the blushing sky over Valverde, recalled those four years since the morning when, suffocated with tears and trembling, she had hugged Gonçalo, in the cabin of the *Portugal* . . . Four years! Four years had passed and nothing had changed in her world, in her small world between *Cunhais* and the Tower, and life had flowed by, as uneventful as a slow river flows in a solitary place: Gonçalo in Africa, in some vague Africa, sending rare but happy letters with the enthusiasm of an Empire-builder, she in *Cunhais*, and her Barrolo, leading such a placid and routine life that the suppers in which the Mendonças and Marges, the

Colonel commanding the 7th Regiment, and others of their friends got together and after which two tables covered with green baize were opened in the drawing-room to play ombre or Boston—were almost exciting by comparison.

During this serene passage of the years she had calmly, almost insensibly, recovered from her heart's bitter torment. She could herself no longer understand how an emotion, which, in her nervousness and anxiety, she had justified, even secretly sanctified, as her only love, her eternal love—could disappear like that, insensibly, without leaving any scars, but merely slight repentance, vague regret, and a strangeness and confusion, the remains of so much that had burnt—no more than fine, powdery ashes . . . A succession of things had swept by, like gusts of wind, and she had been lifted up, borne away with the inertia of a dry leaf.

Immediately after the last Christmas spent with Gonçalo, André, who had accompanied them to midnight mass and had had Christmas supper at *Cunhais*, had returned to Lisbon, to his 'Reform' which he was for ever complaining about. To the silence that then increased between them was added the coldness of desertion . . . When André returned to Oliveira, to his Civil Governorship, she had left for Amarante, where Barrolo's saintly mother lay ill with a lingering sickness which was a combination of anaemia and old age and which in May carried her off to her Maker.

In June there had been Gonçalo's moving departure to Africa—and on the deck of the steamship, among the bustle and baggage, a meeting with André, who had arrived from Oliveira a few days earlier and gaily recounted details of the marriage of Mariquinhas Marges. They had spent that summer, since Barrolo had decided to have a considerable amount of work done to the old mansion in King's Square, on their *Murtosa* estate, which she had chosen because of the beautiful woods there and the high convent walls. Barrolo attributed her melancholy and her thinness, the weary gaze of one no longer interested in life, as she rested on the mossy benches of the woods, a novel forgotten in her lap—to the solitude of the place. To amuse her a little and to restore her health with sea-bathing, for September he rented the striking chalet on the coast belonging to the honoured Barros. She never went bathing, nor appeared on the beach at the cooler time of day when everyone came down to their beach-huts, and the ladies sat on their low chairs; only in the evenings she used to go for a walk across the long stretch of sand, close to the water, accompanied by two big greyhounds which Manuel Duarte had given her. One morning at lunch, Barrolo opened his *News* and leapt up with a cry of alarm. S Fulgêncio's government had unexpectedly fallen! André Cavaleiro had immediately telegraphed his resignation. There on the coast they also learnt from the *News* that this gentleman had set off on a 'long and picturesque journey'—the journey to Constantinople, to Asia Minor, that he had mentioned over dinner at *Cunhais*. She had opened an atlas: with a slow finger she traced his journey from Oliveira to Syria, across frontiers and mountains; André already seemed less distinct to her, away on those more luminous horizons; she shut the atlas, thinking merely, 'How people change!'

In November, they returned to Oliveira one wet Saturday, and as she sat in the carriage she felt all the melancholy and cold of the sky enter her heart. But on Sunday she awoke with a beautiful sun shining through the windows. For eleven o'clock mass in the Cathedral she wore a new hat for the first time; then, on her way to Aunt Arminda's house, she looked up at the great building of the Civil Government: another Civil Governor lived there now, Senhor Santos Maldonado, a fair young man who played the piano.

The next spring, Barrolo, who had been carried away by a passion for redecorating, suggested knocking down the gazebo to build another greenhouse in its place, a larger one, with a fountain set amid palm-trees, which would make 'a darling little winter-garden'. The workers began by removing from the gazebo the old furniture which had adorned it since the time of Uncle Melchior; the immense divan lay for two days in the garden against a box-wood hedge, and Barrolo, impatient with this old piece of lumber and its broken springs, would not allow it in the attic but had it burnt, along with other broken chairs, in a bonfire on the night of Gracinha's birthday. She walked around the bonfire. The threadbare material flared up, then more slowly, with a little smoke, the heavy mahogany, until only a single ember flickered, and finally died away into ash.

That same week, the Lousadas, sharper and darker than ever, invaded *Cunhais* one afternoon—and no sooner had they perched on the sofa than they immediately told her, with a malicious smile in their beady little eyes, of the great scandal involving Cavaleiro! In Lisbon! Quite shamelessly! With the wife of the Count of S Romão! A landowner in Cape Verde!

That night she wrote a long letter to Gonçalo which began, 'We're all well, with the same old routine as ever . . .' Life had indeed begun again, with its same routine, simple, continual, uneventful, like a clear river flowing in some lonely place.

At the glass doors of the verandah, Crispola's son peered in— Crispola's son who had stayed on at the Tower as a messenger-lad, but had grown far out of his old jacket with its yellow buttons, and now used old jackets which had once belonged to the master, and had a growth of down on his chin.

'Sr António Vilalobos is down at the gate, with Sr Gouveia and another gentleman, Videirinha, and they asked if they could speak to you, Madam . . .'

'Senhor Vilalobos! Certainly! Tell them to come up, and come through the verandah here!'

As they crossed the drawing-room, where two mat-makers from Oliveira were nailing down a new straw mat, Titó's voice echoed like thunder through the room, commenting on the 'preparations for the celebration . . .' When he came on to the verandah, his face, more tanned now and with a fuller beard, glowed with delight at finding the Tower at last awakening from that lethargy in which everything had seemed sunk and gloomily extinguished, even the kitchen fires.

'Please forgive our intrusion, Cousin Graça. But we were passing on our way back from a ride to Bravais, and learnt you had arrived with Barrolo . . .'

'Oh, it's a pleasure, Cousin António. I'm the one who must apologize for my appearance, all uncombed like this, and this huge apron on . . . But I've been tidying up the house all day, getting things ready. And how are you, Senhor Gouveia? I haven't seen you since Easter.'

The Administrator, who had not changed these last four years, dark and dry, wood-like, ever stiff in his black frock-coat, thanked Senhora Dona Graça. He had not been too bad since Easter—except for his wretched throat . . .

'And what about the great man, then? When's he coming? When's he coming?'

'On Sunday. We're all so excited! Won't you take a seat, Senhor Videira? Pull up that wicker-chair. The verandah has not been tidied yet.'

Videirinha, immediately after the elections, had received the promised post from Gonçalo, a simple one with plenty of free time so he should not forget his guitar. He was a clerk in the District Administrator's offices in Vila Clara. But he was still on familiar terms with his Chief, who used him for all sorts of jobs, even as a nurse, and sent him about his business with dry authority—even when they were dining together at Gago's.

Diffidently he pulled up the wicker-chair, and placed it respectfully just behind his Chief's. After removing his black gloves, which he now wore to emphasize his position, he ventured to mention that the train stopped at Craquede Halt at 10.40 a.m., if it were not late. But perhaps Sr Ramires would get out at Corinde, because of the luggage . . .

'I doubt it,' murmured Gracinha. 'Anyway José intends to leave at dawn and meet him at the cross-roads in Lamelo.'

'Not us!' said Titó, who had sat down familiarly on the wall of the verandah. 'Our crowd's only going as far as Craquede. It's land belonging to the family and a quieter place for the cheers . . . Our man didn't stay in Lisbon long, then, Cousin Graça?'

'Only since Sunday, Cousin António. He arrived on Sunday by the Sud-Express from Paris. He had a wonderful welcome! Really wonderful! I had a letter from Maria Mendonça yesterday, a long letter where she tells me . . .'

'What? Is Cousin Maria Mendonça in Lisbon, then?'

'Yes, she's been there since the end of August, visiting Dona Ana Lucena . . .'

João Gouveia pulled up his chair, showing a curiosity that had obviously been gnawing at him.

'Tell me, Senhora Dona Graça. I hear Dona Ana Lucena's bought a house in Lisbon, and is furnishing it. Have you heard anything about it, Senhora Dona Graça?'

No, Gracinha knew nothing about it. But it was very likely, since she spent so long in Lisbon now and came to Feitosa so seldom—and it was such a pretty estate . . .

'Then she's getting married!' exclaimed Gouveia, with conviction. 'If she's getting a house ready, she's marrying. It's natural—

she wants a position. It's four years now since she was widowed and...'

Gracinha smiled. But Titó, who was slowly scratching his chin, returned to the letter from Cousin Maria Mendonça, which described Gonçalo's arrival.

'Ah yes!' went on Gracinha. 'She tells me she was at the station in the Rossio. It seems Gonçalo's looking excellent, a bit fuller . . . Here, Cousin António, read the letter. Read it out loud! There are no secrets. It's all about Gonçalo.'

She took a thick envelope bearing a seal out of her pocket. But Cousin Maria always wrote so quickly, in such a scribble, with the lines running into each other. Perhaps Cousin António would not understand it. Indeed, before those four sheets of paper, densely covered with black writing and looking like a prickly hedge, Titó recoiled in alarm. But João Gouveia immediately offered his services—he was an expert at deciphering reports from village authorities . . . If there wasn't anything private in it, of course.

'No, nothing private,' Gracinha assured him with a laugh. 'It's only about Gonçalo, like a newspaper article.'

The Administrator glanced through the immense letter, stroked his moustache and began with a certain solemnity,

'My dear Graça,

. . . Silva's dressmaker tells me the dress . . .'

'No!' interrupted Gracinha. 'It's on the next page, on top. Turn over the page.'

But the administrator laughed and joked boisterously. Oh! This was definitely a lady's letter, all right, clothes talk straight away. And Sra Dona Graça pretending it was all about Gonçalo. Half-way through and they'd still be talking about dresses . . . Ah, these ladies and their clothes! Then he began again, on the next page, slowly and gravely:

'. . . You must be anxious to know all about Cousin Gonçalo's arrival. It was a really wonderful welcome, and seemed more like a reception for some member of royalty. There were over thirty of his friends there. Naturally everyone of the family was there; and if a revolution had suddenly broken out that morning, the Republicans would have captured all the flower of Portugal there in Rossio Station, all together, the old, the real nobility. Among the ladies there was Cousin Chelas, Aunt Louredo, the two Esposendes (with Uncle Esposende, who came in spite of his rheumatism and the grape-harvest, all the way from his estate in Torres) and myself. As for men, everyone. And since the Count of Arega was there, who is His Majesty's Secretary, and Cousin Olhavo, who is his chamberlain, and the Minister of the Navy and the Minister of Public Works, both of them fellow-students and intimate friends of Gonçalo, the people in the station must have imagined His Majesty was arriving. The Sud-Express was forty minutes late. It seemed like a reception-room, with all those people of high society, all very gay, and Cousin Arega, always so amusing and friendly, inviting people to a dinner (which he afterwards gave) to Gonçalo. I wore my new green dress to this dinner and it looked very well . . .'

Gouveia shouted triumphantly,

'There! What did I tell you! Clothes already. Her green dress!'

'Read on, man!' shouted Titó.

The Administrator, really interested, resumed with feeling,

'. . . which looked very well, except the skirt, which was rather heavy. I think I was the first one to notice Cousin Gonçalo on the platform of the Sud-Express. You can't imagine how he looks—magnificent! Even handsomer, and more virile. Africa hasn't tanned his face a bit. The same white skin. And so elegant, so refined! It proves how civilized things are getting in Africa! Cousin Arega said this was the latest style of loincloth in Macheque! . . . As you can imagine, there were plenty of hugs and kisses. Aunt Louredo wept a bit. Ah, I was forgetting! The Viscount of Rio Manso was there, too, with his daughter, Rosinha. She was looking very pretty, in a Redfern dress—she made quite a sensation. Everyone was asking me who she was, and the Count of Arega, of course, all eager to be introduced. Rio Manso was a bit tearful, too, when he embraced Gonçalo. Then we all trooped out of the station, a noble retinue, before the astonished populace. But instantly there was a scene. Suddenly, in the midst of all that cream of aristocracy, Cousin Gonçalo breaks away and falls into the arms of the little man in the braided cap who was collecting the tickets at the gate. The same old Gonçalo! It seems he knew him when he arrived at Lourenço Marques, where the fellow was trying to set himself up as a photographer. But I've forgotten the best bit—Bento! You can't imagine what Bento looks like! Magnificent! He's let his hair grow a little, with side-whiskers. He's really a model of a man, dressed in London, with a long, light-coloured travelling coat reaching down to his knees, yellowish gloves, and profound gravity. He was pleased to see me at the station—and asked after Senhora Dona Graça immediately, and Rosa, his eyes moist. In the evening, José and I had a little family dinner with Cousin Gonçalo in the *Braganza* to talk about the Tower and *Cunhais*. He told us a lot of interesting things about Africa. He's brought back notes for a book and it seems the land concession is prospering. He's planted two thousand coconut-trees during these few years. He's got a lot of cocoa, too, and rubber. And thousands of chickens. It's true a fat chicken in Macheque is only worth a *pataco*.[1] How I envy them there! Here in Lisbon one that's only skin and bone costs six *tostões*—and if it's got a bit of flesh on its breast it's ten *tostões* and you're lucky! He's built a big house on his piece of land near the river, with twenty windows, all painted blue. Cousin Gonçalo says he wouldn't sell the concession for eighty *contos*. And to complete his good fortune he's found an excellent administrator. But I doubt if he'll go back to Africa. I've got my own idea about Cousin Gonçalo's future. Perhaps you'll laugh. You won't guess . . . actually, it was only that night we had dinner together in the *Braganza* that it suddenly occurred to me. Rio Manso's also staying at the *Braganza*. When we went down into a private room for dinner we met the old man with the girl. The old man hugged Gonçalo again with *a father's tenderness*. And Rosinha went so pink that even Gonçalo, excited and oblivious as he was, noticed and blushed slightly. It seems they met years ago, through a basket of roses, and for years now fate has been secretly drawing them closer. She really is a beauty. And so sweet and well-educated! . . . Only eleven years' difference between them and an enormous dowry. The sum of five hundred *contos* has been mentioned. There is only the question of blood, and hers, poor thing . . . Still, as heraldry has it, a King makes a Queen of a shepherdess. And the Ramires not only come from Kings, but Kings come from Ramires. Now to go on to another less interesting subject . . .'

João Gouveia discreetly folded the letter which he handed back to Gracinha, judging Senhora Dona Maria an excellent reporter. Then, with a congratulatory bow, he added,

'And madam, if her previsions are correct . . .'

But no! Gracinha didn't believe it! This was just Maria Mendonça's imagination.

[1] *Pataco*: an ancient coin of little value.

'Cousin António knows her well, he knows what a match-maker she is . . .'

'She even wanted to marry me off,' thundered Titó, leaping up off the edge of the verandah. 'Just imagine, cousin: even me! With Widow Pinho, of the draper's.'

'God forbid!'

But Gouveia insisted with an air of superiority, with an air of knowing the realities of life,

'But Senhora Dona Graça, it would be a better arrangement than his returning to Africa . . . I don't believe in these land concessions. Not in Africa. Africa gives me the horrors. Only serves to vex us. Selling's the best thing to do there! Africa's like those little farms, half-wild, which you inherit from some old aunt on a bit of waste land miles away from anywhere, where you don't know anyone, where there's not even a tobacconist, the only people living there are goatherds, and you have fever all year round. Selling's the best thing to do there.'

Gracinha twined her fingers in her apron-strings.

'What! Sell something that's cost so much to get, so much effort at sea, so much loss of life and resources?'

The Administrator protested at once, with fervour, ready for an argument.

'What effort at sea, madam? All they had to do was disembark there on the sand, plant a few wooden crosses and aim a few blows at the Negroes. All this talk of glory in Africa is a lot of lies. You talk like an aristocrat, madam, obviously, a descendant of aristocrats. But I'm an economist. And I'll tell you something else . . .'

A finger pointed in the air threatened some pointed arguments, but Titó broke in to save Gracinha.

'Oh, Gouveia, we're taking up Cousin Grace's time and she's busy with her tidying-up. These questions of Africa are for later on, with Gonçalo, over coffee . . . So, my dear cousin, we'll see you on Sunday at Craquede. All the crowd will be there. I'm the one who's going to let the fireworks off!'

But Gouveia, stroking his bowler-hat on his sleeve, still hoped to convert Sra Dona Graça to healthy ideas about Colonial Politics.

'Selling's the best thing, madam, selling!'

She smiled in agreement, and offered her hand to Videirinha, who hesitated, his fingers rigid.

'Have you any new verses for our Fado, Senhor Videira?'

Videirinha blushed and stammered that he had 'arranged a little thing, another fado, for Sr Ramires' return'. Gracinha promised to learn it so she could sing it at the piano.

'Thank you very much, madam . . . At your service, madam. . . '

'See you on Sunday then, Cousin António . . . It's a lovely afternoon.'

'Until Sunday, cousin, at Craquede.'

But at the glass door, João Gouveia stopped, stiffened, and clutched his head.

'I nearly forgot, madam, forgive me! I received a letter from André Cavaleiro, from Figueira da Foz. He sends his regards to Barrolo. And he wants to know if Barrolo could let him have some of that green wine of his from Vidainhos. It's for another Africanist—the Count of S Ramão. It seems the Countess is mad about green wine!'

The three friends filed out across the drawing-room, Titó's voice still booming out, praising the new coloured matting. In the corridor, Videirinha peered into the library and noted the bunch of duck-quill pens standing in the old brass ink-stand, waiting in shining isolation upon the table bare of any papers or books. Then Rosa appeared at the door of Gonçalo's room weighed down with linen, a smile in very wrinkle of her round, brick-red face, which her full, brilliantly white cambric kerchief ringed like a halo. Titó patted the good cook's shoulder affectionately.

'So, Aunt Rosa, you'll be starting to cook your specialities again soon, eh?'

'God be praised, Senhor Don António! I thought I'd never be seeing my dear master again. But I was sure about one thing: if they'd buried me here in Santa Ireneia before I'd seen my boy, my soul would surely have gone to Africa to pay him a visit.'

Her little eyes blinked, tearful with pleasure—and she went on her way down the corridor, stiff and resolute with her bundle which smelt of preserved apples. Gouveia made a grimace and murmured, 'God forbid such a thing!' The three friends made their way to the yard where Titó's curiosity impelled them to see the changes in the stables.

'See!' he cried to Gouveia, who was lighting a cigar. 'You're denying there's any profit . . . Furniture, new buildings, an English mare . . . All of it paid for with money from Africa.'

The Administrator shrugged his shoulders.

'We'll see later on what his liver's like . . .'

At the gate, Tító stopped once again to pick a bud from the usual rose-bush to adorn his velveteen jacket. Just at that moment, Father Soeiro approached, returning from a ride to Bravais, with his enormous cotton sunshade and his breviary. They all welcomed the saintly, learned old man who so rarely put in an appearance at the Tower these days, with affection.

'So we've got our man back here on Sunday, Father Soeiro!'

The chaplain laid his plump hand upon his breast, with reverence, with gratitude . . .

'God has been kind enough to grant me this great favour in my old age . . . I little imagined it. Such wild land there, and he so delicate . . .'

In order to talk a little more about Gonçalo, about the welcome in Craquede, he accompanied the gentlemen to Portela Bridge. João Gouveia limped, tormented by some wretched new boots which he was wearing for the first time. They rested a moment on the beautiful stone bench which Gonçalo's father had had put there when he was Civil Governor of Oliveira. From this pleasant spot one could see Vila Clara, so neat and although usually white, at that hour all rosy, from the vast convent of Santa Teresa to the new wall of the cemetery above, with its elegant cypresses.

Beyond the hills of Valverde, far away, above the coast, the sun was sinking, as red as a piece of glowing metal between red clouds, turning the windows of the town to sparkling gold.

At the bottom of the valley, a pallor surrounded the tall ruins of Santa Maria de Craquede, set amid dense woods. Under its arch, the full river flowed without a sound, already dormant in the shade of the stately poplars, in which birds still sang. At the bend in the road, above the poplars concealing the house, the old Tower rose, older than the town and the convent ruins and all the farm-houses scattered about, its tall look-out place circled by the blind flight of bats, and gazing silently at the land around and at the sun over the sea, as it had every afternoon these last thousand years, since the time of Count Ordonho Mendes.

A little boy with a long goad passed by, rounding up two slow cows. Father José Vicente from Finta came trotting down from the town on his white mare, greeted the Administrator and his friend

Soeiro, and gave blessings for the arrival of the Nobleman, for whom he had already prepared a beautiful basket of muscatel grapes. Three foresters, with a pack of rabbiters, crossed the road and went down to the lane which ran round the Mirandas' farm.

A still, clear silence, extremely restful, and as serene as if it had descended from Heaven, lay over all the populated stretch of countryside, where not a leaf stirred in the soft, translucid September air. The smoke of fires was drifting in slow, thin wisps from the sparse tiles. At João's smithy, just beyond Portela, the glare of the forge grew brighter, redder. Drums throbbed gaily from the region of Bravais, increased in volume, and marching quickly, reached the hill-top, then slowly grew fainter and died away to vanish among the trees or in the deeper valley.

João Gouveia, who was leaning back on one end of the wide stone bench, his bowler-hat on his knees, gestured towards Bravais.

'I was thinking of that passage in Gonçalo's novel when the Ramires are preparing to go to the aid of the Princesses, and getting their army ready. It's like this, at this time of the evening, with drums sounding, and somewhere near here: "In the coolness of the valley . . ." No! "In the valley of Craquede . . ." No, that's not it, either. Wait a minute, I've got a good memory . . . Ah! "And through the cool valley to Santa Maria de Craquede, the Moorish drums sounded a muffled ta-rum! ta-rum! among the trees, or a sharper rat-a-boom! rat-a-boom! on the hills, summoning the men of Ramires in the softness of the afternoon . . ." It's lovely!'

Videirinha leaned across the broad back of Titó, who was sitting pensively scratching at the dust with his cane, and smiled intelligently at his chief.

'Oh, sir, do you know, I think an even more beautiful passage is the one in which the Ramires set out in pursuit of the Bastard! To me, it's more poetic. When the old man swears on his sword, and then back in the Tower the funeral knell slowly begins to toll . . . That's wonderful!'

On the edge of the seat, close against Titó so that the Administrator could stretch out comfortably, Father Soeiro sat with his hands on the handle of his sunshade and murmured agreement.

'Definitely! They are most interesting passages . . . Definitely!

There's a wealth of imagination in that novel, a wealth of imagination, and there's learning and truth.'

Titó, who, after reading *Simão de Nantua* as a little boy, had never opened another book, and had not read *The Tower of Don Ramires*, muttered, with a broad sweep of his cane in the dust,

'Extraordinary, our Gonçalo!'

Videirinha still wore his ecstatic smile.

'He has enormous talent . . . Ah, Senhor Ramires definitely has enormous talent!'

'And a lot of charm!' cried Titó, lifting up his head. 'That's what preserves him from his flaws. I'm a friend of Gonçalo's, and one of the most loyal. But I don't hide it, not even from him . . . Particularly from him. He's very frivolous, very inconsistent . . . But his charm's his saving grace!'

'And his goodness, Senhor António Vilalobos!' gently added Father Soeiro. 'Goodness, especially goodness like Sr Gonçalo's, is also a saving grace . . . You know, sometimes you have a very serious man, a very pure man, very austere, who never did anything except what duty and the law decreed . . . Yet no one likes him, no one seeks his company. Why? Because he never gave anything, never forgave, never caressed, never served. And alongside him there's a frivolous, careless man who has flaws, has sinned, has even forgotten what duty is, and has broken the law . . . And yet? He's agreeable, generous, devoted, helpful, always has a pleasant word, always a kind gesture . . . Because of this everyone loves him, and I don't know, God forgive me, if God Himself doesn't prefer him, too . . .'

The plump hand that was raised to Heaven returned to the bone handle of the sunshade. Then, blushing at the temerity of such a spiritual thought, he went on cautiously,

'This is not officially the doctrine of the Church! . . . But it's an idea accepted by many, accepted by very many indeed.'

Then João Gouveia, abandoning the stone bench and standing upright in the road, his bowler-hat askew, buttoning up his frock-coat, with the air that he always adopted when summing up, said,

'Well, I've studied our friend Gonçalo Mendes very carefully. And do you know, my friends, do you know, Father Soeiro, who he reminds me of?'

'Who?'

'Perhaps you'll laugh. But I declare there's a resemblance. All

Gonçalo's different qualities, his weaknesses, his kindness, his goodness, his exceptional goodness which Father Soeiro pointed out ... His crazes and enthusiasm, which peter out almost immediately, but at the same time his persistence and tenacity when he really latches on to an idea ... His generosity, his carelessness, his invariable chaos in business matters, his sentiments of honour, certain scruples, almost puerile, don't you agree? ... His imagination, which leads him always to exaggerate to the point of lying, and at the same time a practical spirit, always aware of the utility of a thing. His liveliness, his facility in understanding, in picking things up ... His constant expectation of some miracle occurring, the old miracle of Ourique[1] which will prove the answer to all his difficulties ... His vanity, the pleasure he takes in dressing-up, in shining, and his simplicity, which impels him to give his arm to a beggar in the street ... A streak of melancholy, in spite of his talkativeness and sociability. His terrible lack of confidence in himself which intimidates and restrains him, until one day he makes a decision and turns out to be a hero, destroying everything ... Even the antiquity of his family, stuck in their old Tower here for a thousand years ... Even that sudden departure to Africa ... Just as he is, good mixed with bad, do you know whom he reminds me of?'

'Who?'

'Portugal.'

The three friends continued on their way to Vila Clara. In the pale sky a star flickered over Santa Maria de Craquede. Father Soeiro, his sunshade under his arm, made his way slowly back to the Tower, in the silence and softness of the evening, reciting his Hail Maries and praying for the peace of God for Gonçalo, for all men, for the fields and the sleeping farms, and for the beautiful land of Portugal, so full of endearing charm, that it might be for ever blessed among lands.

---

[1] Battle between the Moors and the Portuguese, in 1139, at which Christ was supposed to have appeared to the first King of Portugal, Afonso Henriques.

E32.50
10/04
with

Printed in the United States
2207

9 780856 359682